Rosie Wallace was brought up in Milngavie, near Glasgow but has lived on Orkney since her marriage to Jim Wallace, MP for Orkney and Shetland, bringing up their two daughters. She is a speech and language therapist, and since 2003 has been working free-lance, specialising in dyslexia. In 2007, her husband stood down from the Scottish Parliament and was appointed to the House of Lords, so she acquired a title which is only used occasionally!

A Small Town Affair

ROSIE WALLACE

hachette
SCOTLAND

First published in 2010 by
HACHETTE SCOTLAND,
an imprint of HACHETTE UK

First published in paperback in 2011 by
HACHETTE SCOTLAND

Cataloguing in Publication Data is available from the British Library

978 0 7553 1934 3

Typeset in Bembo by Palimpsest Book Production Limited,
Falkirk, Stirlingshire

Printed and bound in Great Britain by
CPI Mackays, Chatham ME5 8TD

HEADLINE PUBLISHING GROUP
A division of Hachette Livre UK Ltd
338 Euston Road
London NW1 3BH

www.headline.co.uk

To all who feel they are a POW

ACKNOWLEDGEMENTS

Thanks must go to:

Ron Ferguson who gave me practical help and loads of encouragement.

Lindsey Fraser of Fraser Ross who not only agreed to be my agent, but helped me to turn a first draft into a manuscript fit for submission.

Wendy McCance for being such a tactful editor.

All family and friends who gave me constructive criticism along the way.

Chapter One

JESUS LOVES CHILDREN EVERYWHERE.

So announced the sign above the wax-crayon artwork. Gill thought that Jesus would make an exception of this venue if He had to come here every week. This was the third dreadful Tuesday afternoon she had spent in the echoing church hall. The decibel level was well above acceptable environmental limits and she had a headache.

She was sitting on an uncomfortable chair at the side of the hall watching her two-year-old son, Ian, drive a yellow plastic tricycle in an ever-decreasing circle. He was followed by a small boy on a red tractor. They were both making noises reminiscent of kamikaze pilots on a glorious mission to destroy the American Fleet. On a mat marked out with roads and pavements, several other boys were playing with a garage and a selection of toy cars. 'Playing' was, in fact, a euphemism for 'bickering interspersed with more kamikaze noises'. In the far corner, in the playhouse, a precocious three-year-old housewife was instructing a troop of two-year-olds in the domestic chores she expected of them. One of them had been silly enough to disagree with Mrs Homemaker and was now screaming loudly.

Mother-and-toddler groups are supposed to have a dual role:

the socialisation of toddlers and a support group for the mothers. Ian was socialising in a limited sort of masculine fashion, but no one in the room seemed to be offering Gill much support. They had not been exactly unfriendly, but no one had gone out of their way to talk to her. They all knew who she was, although she couldn't remember who they were because she was awful at names, and as usual, she hadn't actually listened when she had been introduced because she had been concentrating on being bright and smiley.

Four-month-old Kate stirred and began first to grizzle, then to cry. Gill undid the sling, took the baby out, lifted her faded sweatshirt and realised that she had forgotten to change it after it had been puked on that morning. She hoped the smell was not too pervasive. Allowing the cuckoo mouth to latch on, she glanced across the room and realised she was not the only lactating mother. A tall, elegant African woman was sitting in the far corner feeding a baby, while her daughter was establishing herself in the playhouse pecking order. Ethnic diversity had not yet arrived in this country town, where the only other non-white faces ran the Indian and the Chinese restaurants respectively, so Gill imagined that this family, notable for being different, would have caused more than a few stares when they had arrived last year. Gill smiled at the woman and decided she would go and speak to her after Kate had finished feeding. She was wondering what had brought the family here rather than to a city when her thoughts were interrupted by a very pregnant girl who came and sat down. She had been introduced the first week Gill had attended, but Gill had no idea what her name was now. Perhaps the girl would reintroduce herself. She didn't.

'Hello, Mrs Andrews.'

Gill would have to ask her name. 'Hello. Please call me Gill. I'm sorry I can't remember your name.'

2

'Angela.'

Kate momentarily became detached and a spray of milk jetted in an arc across the room. Angela's gaze followed the projectile.

'I tried feeding Allan but it didn't work. Has its advantages and disadvantages, doesn't it?' Her expression conveyed that she thought that the disadvantages far outweighed the advantages.

'That your wee boy on the yellow trike?'

'Yes, that's Ian.'

'That's my Allan on the tractor. What age is Ian?'

'He was two in June, so he's –' she did a quick calculation – 'twenty-eight months.'

'Same age as Allan. Is he potty-trained?'

The challenge has been issued. To compete or not compete, that was the question.

'Not really.'

'Allan is. Dry through the night too.'

What does one say? Gill wondered. Oh, good? Well done, Allan? Well done, Angela? Or does one compete on other motor milestones? He can feed himself. He can post the various shapes into the postbox. He can also say 'bugger' when you'd rather he didn't.

She opted for tact. 'Lucky you – you'll be saving a fortune on nappies.'

'Not for much longer.' She patted her bump. 'Didn't intend to fall so soon, but these things happen.'

For Gill, the term 'falling pregnant' had always conjured up an image of tripping up and falling on to some handy erect phallus. She tried to put this from her mind.

'Have you got long to go?' she inquired dutifully.

'Three weeks. Mum hopes it'll come on her birthday. She'll be thirty-seven.'

Good God, thought Gill. I'm thirty-two; no wonder she calls me 'Mrs Andrews'.

'You must have your children young in your family.'

'Mum was eighteen when she had me, and I was sixteen when I fell with Allan.'

Gill had to banish the unwanted image again.

'Snack time!' called another woman, who had a weeping child attached to her leg, like a terrier in search of sexual gratification. She hobbled towards the table in the corner with a large jug of sugar-free blackcurrant juice, her progress hampered by the snivelling child, who was hiding his face in her saggy tracksuit bottoms.

'Children, come to the table and sit down. Coffee for mums in the kitchen.'

Angela heaved herself off the chair and went to pluck the dry-bottomed Allan from the tractor to take him to the table. Now his partner on the Grand Prix circuit had gone, Ian looked towards his mother. Immobilised by the sucking Kate, Gill waved a hand in the direction of the Ribena and the plate of fruit segments. Angela tried to take Ian's hand to lead him to the table, but he was not going to let his mother off so easily. She was giving full attention to his sister and not attending to his needs. He jerked his hand out of Angela's.

'Doan wan duice,' he whined.

'It's lovely juice, and there's some apple too,' cajoled Angela.

'Mummy! Not you. Mummy!' Ian glanced over at his mother to see if this order was having the required effect. It didn't seem to be, so his sense of injustice increased and his anger level rose. 'Mummy do it! Mummy do it!' he screamed.

Gill realised that this was going to be one of the more spectacular of Ian's tantrums. With one hand clutching the still sucking baby to her semi-exposed breast, she got to her feet and walked across the floor to the screaming, stamping toddler. She was conscious that all consumption of coffee and custard creams had ceased as the other mothers waited to see if she

4

was a Smacker, an Ignorer or an Appeaser. In order to avoid being a Smacker, she was at home an Ignorer, but this was an occasion for Appeasement. Ian was enough of a spectacle already.

'Come on now, Ian,' she said. 'I'll come to the table with you.'

'No duice! No duice!' he screamed. Kate, who had been joggled off the nipple by this unexpected trip across the room, also started to scream.

Be firm, thought Gill.

'Ian! Behave yourself and come to the table!'

'BUGGER OFF.'

If there had been a silence before, it was nothing to this frozen moment. She took in the looks on the faces of the assembled adults. Some were shocked, but worse were those who realised that they were now in possession of a prime bit of gossip: *MP's two-year-old is not only foul-tempered but foul-mouthed as well.*

How should she play this? It would be a long time till Mike was up for re-election, but this was not a vote-winner. There was no childminder, no older siblings or resident demented grandfather to blame for being a bad influence. This phrase had to have been learned from her or Mike. In fact, it had probably been learned from both of them, as it was the constant rebuke given to Penny, their 'in-your-face' collie. From a politically face-saving point of view, Gill knew she had to be the culprit.

'Ian!' she said feebly. 'Don't say things like that. It's what I say to the dog when she jumps up.' She turned to the onlookers. 'They always pick up the wrong words, don't they? They never say, "Thank you very much, Granny, for my lovely birthday present," or, "Please may I play with my toys?"' Gill, you're prattling. Shut up, she thought.

Ian had stopped to draw breath. He didn't know why that

5

phrase had attracted everyone's attention, but it was certainly effective, and being bright enough to learn by experience, he decided to repeat himself.

'Bugger off. Bugger off. Bugger off,' he said with a smile of satisfaction.

Very gradually, the silence melted as people began to murmur to each other and children started to whine for more juice. The woman who had served juice had finally managed to get her son, Matthew, to let go of her leg on the understanding that he could stay with her in the kitchen and not join the melee in the hall. She was starting to wash up the coffee cups. Through the open serving hatch, she watched Gill put the baby over her shoulder to wind her. Gill took the now compliant Ian by the hand, led him to the table, sat him down and gave him a cup of juice and a piece of apple. Holding her head high, Gill made for the kitchen and picked up a cup of coffee.

'I'm sorry about that,' she said.

'Don't worry,' the woman said. 'It's made my afternoon. Anything to cheer up Black Tuesdays! I hate them! I loathe and detest mother-and-toddler group, but it is marginally better than having to be president of the Guild and spend Monday evenings being enthusiastic over yet another set of slides from someone's holiday to New Zealand. If I see another picture of boiling mud and Maoris with their tongues out, I'll scream. Let me introduce myself – I'm Ali Graham and I'm the minister's wife. I live next door. Sorry I wasn't here when the sessions started but I was away visiting my mother. And by the way, the baby has just sicked up down your back.'

'Oh, yuck. I'll sort that in a minute.' She pointed to the stain on her chest. 'It will match this morning's offering. I'm Gill Andrews. We've just moved here. My husband is the—'

'The MP. Yes, we all know who you are. The town grapevine has been working overtime about you and your husband. Let's see . . . what do I know? You lived in Edinburgh before you came here, you were the head of a primary school before you had your children, and you live in the McPhersons' house on Strathperry Road. You put in an offer for three other houses before you got that one. You drive a silver Golf, and your husband is away all week. You've got a dog, and you are looking for a cleaner and occasional babysitter according to the card on the notice board at Tesco. You hired John Johnstone to do your painting before you moved in, and you removed all the flock wallpaper and patterned carpets and replaced them with plain. You drink wine and gin – Mrs Caldwell saw you at the bottle bank – and either your parents or your husband's have just been to stay. Odds on they were your parents, as the granny looks a bit like you. You don't hang nappies out to dry, so it's either disposables or you use the tumble-drier.'

Gill was horrified. She knew that they were of local interest, but this woman seemed to know everything about her, including things that were a complete fabrication: she had only ever been a class teacher, and the McPhersons' house was the first they had offered on. She realised whatever happened at toddler group was not going to stay within the walls of the church hall.

'Everyone will hear about Ian, won't they?' she said.

'Probably, but it won't last long. They'll soon find something else to talk about. It's not malicious. Well, most of it isn't. It's a small town and everyone knows everyone else's business. Most of it is genuine interest, but beware of Chinese whispers and don't believe everything you hear.'

'Chinese whispers?'

'Yes, Chinese whispers, or one person's conjecture is their neighbour's fact.'

Gill looked puzzled, so Ali continued. 'Let's imagine Mrs A sees you walking along with your children. She thinks you look tired. She says to her friend Mrs B that she saw you and you

7

looked tired. She wonders if the baby is not sleeping. Mrs B meets Mrs C and says that the MP's wife is very tired because the baby is not sleeping. She wonders if the baby is unwell. Mrs C meets Mrs D and says that the MP's wife is very tired because the baby is ill and not sleeping and she wonders if it's serious. Mrs D meets Mrs E, who says that the MP's baby is seriously ill and wonders if she'll have to go to hospital, et cetera. On that premise, I'm afraid Ian will have used the F-word and probably the C-word, but it will only last a couple of days and then there will be someone or something else to talk about.'

Mothers began to put dirty cups and half-chewed pieces of fruit through the hatch, while their children returned to play-houses and pedal toys.

'Look,' said Ali cheerfully, 'come for a coffee after this and we'll have a proper chat. I've got to go and organise the craft session now. I'm afraid it involves gluing together used cereal packets, glitter and tissue paper, all of which will become unglued in the car on the way home. If you would like to be helpful, you could finish washing the cups and keep an eye on Matt. He hates this as much as I do. He's far happier in here.'

Gill looked at the child in the corner, who had taken all the pans out of the cupboard and was arranging them neatly in diminishing order of size.

'I'll just get the buggy to put Kate in. Thanks, I think I'd like to hide in here for a while.'

Gill was on her way back into the hall with the buggy when she heard Ian screaming, 'Shit! Shit!' He had fallen off the tricycle and wanted his comfort blanket, a bit of flannelette sheet.

Gill grabbed it from the buggy and waved it flamboyantly. 'It's OK. Here it is! Here's your *sheet*!' She put particular emphasis on the word 'sheet'.

Ian took the piece of material and held it next to his face while inserting his thumb in his mouth. His sobs subsided. Gill glanced around the room. All the eyes were suddenly averted and conversations restarted. She could hear them thinking, Nice try, dear, but not quite good enough.

She retrieved the buggy. Ali was organising children to come and sit round the table for the stimulation of the creative areas of their little brains. As she scuttled back to the kitchen, Gill noted with satisfaction the creeping dark stain on Allan's jeans.

Chapter Two

M ike Andrews opened his eyes. The luminous numbers on the radio alarm showed six forty-five and he fumbled with the switch to turn on Radio Four. Five more minutes, he decided, then he would get up. He missed Gill and his two children so much when he was away but it was good to have an uninterrupted night's sleep. Monday had been non-stop – meetings with constituents, then travelling south to London and sorting things in his office. It had been after eleven when he had got back to the small flat in Dolphin Square and realised he had not phoned Gill. It had been too late to risk it then, as she did not appreciate being woken up. He would call her in a while. He knew she would be awake by now: small children are no respecters of parental need to sleep.

When he had showered and dressed, he made himself a cup of tea and lit a cigarette. Another advantage of being away from home: he didn't have to stand out in the cold to have a smoke in case he polluted his children's lungs. He picked up his mobile and dialled home. It rang six times before Gill answered.

'Yes!' she said in a Basil Fawlty tone of voice. Mike could hear the dog barking, Kate crying and what sounded like Ian building up to a tantrum over the fact that he didn't like Weetabix any more.

'You OK?' Mike asked.

'Fine! And you?' She didn't sound fine.

'I'm all right, I suppose. Tired still, and I've got a hectic day ahead.'

'Me too! I've got housework, a trip to the supermarket and mother-and-toddlers. Bet your day isn't going to be as busy or exciting as that.'

She was obviously stressed. He would have to tread carefully. 'There's the committee at ten o'clock. Then I've to sit in on the Transport debate. Then there's the parliamentary party meeting later on, followed by dinner with Network Rail tonight.'

'In the interesting-day stakes, I think you win. Do you want to speak to Ian? It might take his mind off Weetabix.' She laid down the phone and Mike could hear her cajoling Ian to come and speak to him.

''Allo.'

'Hello. How are you today?'

'Me no like Weetbix. Me want Totopops.'

'Well, ask Mummy nicely and see if she'll give you some. What are you going to do today?'

'Doddlers.' There was a long pause. 'Daddy in TV?' he asked.

This notion had started when Mike had made a speech at the party conference about integrated transport links in rural areas. Gill had settled Ian in front of the TV and told him to watch for Daddy and now Ian thought that his father lived inside the TV when he was not at home.

'No, I'm not in the TV. I'm in London – at Big Ben.'

'Daddy's cock.'

'Clock, Ian, clock. There's an "l" in there!'

'Bye-bye.'

'Bye. Blow you a—'

Before he could say 'kiss' he heard the receiver clatter to the ground and the demands for Cocopops restart. He did feel guilty that Gill was left on her own to cope with the children for most of the week, the more so because since Kate was born, Ian had changed from an endearing cherub into something far less appealing. He could hear the sounds of family life going on and Ian being told that Cocopops were not an option. The screams began.

'Daddy div me Totopops. Wan Daddy.'

The phone was picked up abruptly. 'Did you give him Cocopops when you gave him his breakfast yesterday?'

'Yes. He was being good, so I thought he deserved a treat.'

'Great! I try to get him to eat a healthy diet and you fill him full of chocolate-coated rubbish.'

'I'm sorry, but I was eating them and it was a bit difficult to refuse him.'

The screams were getting louder.

'Anyway, I have to go. Speak to you later.'

The line went dead. Mike heaved a sigh. Whenever he tried to help with the children it wasn't right. When Ian was a baby, Gill had never been this stressed. The dog was another thing he had got wrong. An elderly constituent had been moving into sheltered housing and for some unknown reason had come to him to see what could be done with his dog. Gill had always been complaining she was lonely, so it had seemed a perfect solution all round. But she appeared to regard the dog not as a solution but an extra problem. He would have to phone her later, when she had calmed down a bit. He helped himself to a bowl of unhealthy cereal and lit another cigarette.

The four months since the general election seemed to have passed so quickly. Kate had been born a week early, ten days after the election. He had missed the birth, as he had been in

London, but felt he had managed to redeem himself by staying at home for a week when Gill came out of hospital. Admittedly, he was glad to escape back to London, where, although he was very busy, he was not expected to spend the day trying to negotiate with a toddler who was beyond reason because his place at the centre of the universe had been usurped.

Six weeks after the election, they had moved to Corrachan, a market town some fifty miles from Edinburgh. It had all gone remarkably smoothly, and despite occasions such as this morning, he thought Gill seemed to be settling into small-town life.

Starting a new job is always stressful, but Mike knew what he was now doing was interesting and challenging. Some of the traditions of the House of Commons seemed outmoded and unnecessary, but the political process fascinated him. He had fought council and parliamentary elections without any hope of being elected until a Liberal Democrat MP in that most unusual of things, a safe seat, announced his retirement. Mike had gone for the nomination and now here he was, Member of Parliament for Corrachan, Invercraig and Strathperry.

The nearest thing there had been to a holiday was the party conference in September, but what had, in years past, been an outing to indulge his hobby was now hard work. Suddenly he was in demand to speak at fringe meetings, and his opinions were constantly sought by those for whom politics was always likely to remain a hobby. And now he was back in London for the new session.

Mike glanced at his watch. He was running late. He gathered up his belongings and walked briskly up the Embankment, reaching his office by eight fifteen.

Just after nine, Janice arrived with the day's mail. She was a lady of middle years who had worked for several MPs. Mike had inherited her from an English Tory who had lost his seat at the last election. Janice had been unacquainted with Scotland

13

and with Liberal Democrats, so it was a learning experience on both sides.

'What's in there today?' Mike inquired.

'Much the same as usual. There are two green-ink ones with multiple underlinings, but only one is a constituent. It's Mr Peterkin again. I'll bin the other.'

'What is it today? It was flogging shoplifters and hanging everyone else last week.'

'He doesn't like immigrants and wants them sent back to wherever they came from. "Too many darkies here already." Signs it "Yours in Christ".'

'Send him the standard "immigration and asylum-seekers" letter.'

'You just encourage him by sending him a long, detailed letter. Give him the "Thanks for your letter, the contents of which have been noted."'

'No, he deserves a detailed reply as much as anyone else. I represent everyone. I can't ignore those I disagree with. What else?'

Janice looked at him and thought he could be really pompous sometimes. 'There is another one from Mr Hall, the Nazi, about the satanic plot hatched by the Jewish state to promote homosexual practice among schoolchildren. He's used his Letraset again. Must have taken him hours.'

'I take back what I said before. He can have the "contents have been noted" letter. Perhaps I should draft a "just to let you know a lunatic is using your name and address to write to Members of Parliament" letter.'

'There are two about benefit claims – I can sort them – and there are a couple of others: one from a Mr Lyle, who thinks that because he was injured on the Normandy beaches he ought to be exempt from paying income tax on his sixty-thousand-pound share income, and one from a Mrs Caldwell about the lack of litterbins in the town centre and how the bin men were very rude to her. I'll send that to the councillor.'

'No, don't. I think the woman is our next-door neighbour. I'll have to be seen to do something. She's probably written to poor Peter Graham already. Write a letter to the council, inquiring after their litter policy. Send her a copy and one to Peter, so he knows what we are up to. And tell the war veteran that we are all very grateful for what he did for us and suggest that he contact his accountant to see if he is using his allowances appropriately. Anything else?'

'Mr Taha, whom you saw at the surgery, has sent all his details and those of his mother and his aunt for their visas. I assume you know what this is about?'

'Yes. This is a guy who came from Sudan to university here. He's a permanent resident, works as a scientist in the biotech factory in Strathperry, and he wants his mother and his aunt to come for a three-week holiday to see his children, whom they have never seen. Not unreasonable, you would think, but the powers that be are refusing to grant them a visa because they can't prove that they are only going to be here for a holiday and not become illegal over-stayers. It's ridiculous. If they were white and came from Australia, no one would question their motives. I said I would try to speak to the embassy in Khartoum and see if I can put a word in.'

Janice handed him the letter. 'The others are all quite straight-forward, so I'll draft replies. There's an email from Rachel from the constituency office. Annie wants to move the time of the next surgery to the afternoon.'

'That's fine.'

Annie Cochrane was the local Member of the Scottish Parliament. They held their surgeries together as people were still confused about who did what and it saved time in the long run for them to see people together.

'And Minty Oliver left a message on the answer machine to say that she will come to discuss the new leaflet with you on Friday evening. She didn't sound like the sort of lady you argued with.'

'Minty's OK. She was my election agent and now sees it as her duty to be my local eyes and ears. But you're right, it's easier just to agree with her. Thanks for all that, Janice. I'll try to have a word with you later, after I've been in the chamber for question time.'

At about seven fifteen, just before he went to the Network Rail dinner, Mike tried to phone Gill. He hoped an afternoon socialising at mother-and-toddler might have improved her humour. There was no reply. He dialled her mobile, which rang out but was not answered, so he left a message asking if she had had a good day and saying he would phone later. Where the hell was she? If she had gone out, someone would be babysitting. But Gill didn't go out. She hadn't got any close friends in the town yet, and she didn't go to evening classes or anything like that. He hoped something awful hadn't happened to one of the children, but she would have phoned him if that was the case. Perhaps she was bathing the children. He would try to phone later.

Chapter Three

At the time of Mike's call, Gill was not bathing the children, she was out. And she was still out. She was now pleasantly, mellowly drunk. She lay back on Ali's battered sofa and realised that she was actually enjoying herself. In fact, she felt human for the first time since Kate was born. A cup of coffee had turned into a glass of white wine, which had turned into at least a bottle.

'Tom's in Edinburgh for some Church meeting. Then he's taking Lizzie – that's our eighteen-year-old – out for a meal, so why don't you stay and keep me company?' Ali had inquired.

A takeaway had miraculously appeared at the door and Gill had not had to organise any of it.

Kate was asleep in the buggy, and Ian, who had been playing in the next room with Ali's sixteen-year-old daughter, Ruth, was now asleep on a large beanbag in the corner. It was the best evening Gill had spent since leaving Edinburgh. She was not at anyone's beck and call or under scrutiny as the MP's wife.

At four o'clock, when drinking her mug of coffee, Gill had been cautious as usual, keeping her opinions to herself until she sussed out whether this woman was a serial gossip or a born-again Christian, or both. Then the wine had appeared and the wall of enforced politeness that Gill had built round herself since the election began to crumble. Ali was a kindred spirit.

Ali, too, had been cautious, aware that the contact could just be limited to a cup of coffee and a 'See you next week' if she thought they had nothing in common. Gill was having to learn the hard way all the things Ali had learned when Tom had been appointed minister to St Andrew's Church. She'd had Tom to confide in and they had been able to support each other. He had been brought up in a small village nearby and had gone to school in the town, so they had known a few people when they arrived. This woman had two small children and an absent husband, and her only contacts seemed to be the Liberal Democrat Committee, the majority of whom, with a few exceptions (such as Ali's brother-in-law, Peter), were entitled to their bus pass.

As the wine flowed, conversation had ranged from moving house to new people and new babies. By the time the Chinese takeaway had been eaten, Gill had learned that Ali had been a legal secretary and worked at the local solicitor's office for a while after her older children had gone to school, but that she had been a full-time mother since Matt was born. Ali learned that Gill had taught Primary Three in a large school in a socially deprived area of Edinburgh.

The diminishing contents of the second bottle of wine allowed Gill to let her nosiness get the better of her.

'Can I ask you a personal question?'

'Depends what it is.'

'What made you have another child after such a big gap?'

'God's punishment for an irresponsible Presbyterian!'

'Sorry?'

'Whenever I got broody, I used to think back to mother-and-toddler group and that scared me into being very careful.

18

The thought of another stint of Black Tuesdays struck terror into the soul, and anyway, two girls were enough to repopulate the world. You would have thought that God might let us off with a tiny lapse in responsibility, but no. His sense of rhythm was not, unfortunately, quite the same as mine and there I was, nearly forty, with two adolescent daughters and pregnant again. I was horrified! Tom was horrified . . . but not as horrified as Lizzie and Ruth. They couldn't bring themselves to look at me properly until after Matt was born.'

'What age is Matthew now?'

'He's just four, but you wouldn't think it. He's so different from the girls. They were outgoing and chatty. He hardly speaks and is quite happy with his own company. I'm going to have to try to take him to nursery again next week. We tried last year and he just screamed all the time, but he's due to go to school next year so he's going to have to get used to it.'

Gill looked at Matthew, who was sitting in the corner with a box of plastic dinosaurs, arranging them in order of size, as he rocked gently back and forth. She'd been a primary teacher long enough to have an idea of what might be Matthew's difficulty, but she was too drunk to pursue it further at the moment.

'What age is your elder girl?'

'Lizzie is eighteen. She's just gone to Edinburgh to do medicine. Oh, by the way, Ruth will babysit for you if you want, and Lizzie, when she's home. They're both good with babies and toddlers. They've had the chance to practise on Matt.'

As if on cue, Ruth appeared. She took in the empty wine bottles and looked with disdain on her slightly inebriated mother and her new friend.

'I'm just going upstairs. I'll put Matt to bed if you like.'

'Thank you. I've just said to Gill you are a good babysitter.'

Ruth said she would be glad to help and fled the room, trailing Matt and his dinosaurs. Ali poured the remainder of the wine into their glasses, then put the bottle up to her eye and peered into it.

'Wine bottles used to hold much more than they do now. They used to last several days sometimes. I can even remember putting the cork back in and putting the bottle in the fridge.' She placed the wine bottle on the floor and sat down again.

'My turn for personal questions now. Are you active in politics too?'

'If you mean do I have the sad little political gene that makes me want to become a public hate figure, spend my days sorting out other people's problems for half the money I used to earn, and talk to other people with the same sad gene about ways of convincing the apathetic public to vote me into office, then no, I'm not. On the other hand, if you mean do I have to attend Liberal whist drives where the leftover sandwiches are raffled afterwards, organise fundraising coffee mornings and raffle everyone's out-of-date packets and tins in the "Grocery Box", and spend my time making sure I don't offend anyone so they will vote for Mike next time, then yes, I am.'

'You sound a bit disillusioned, not to mention pissed off.'

'I am! I'm a Pissed-Off Wife. A POW. Yes, that just about sums it up. Imprisoned in an existence with small children! Sometimes I feel as if I have not a ball and chain round my ankle, but a ball and elastic. I can occasionally escape my child-minding role by going somewhere exciting like to Tesco on my own, but when the elastic gets to full stretch, it hurtles me back to where I belong.'

'POW. That's me too, you know. I'm sick to death of being Tom's answering service, being nice to the bereaved, the halt, the lame, the completely insane and the majority of the members of this congregation.' She tucked her legs underneath her and sighed. 'Do you know, they phone, they knock at the door, they accost me in the street and I have to be *nice* and *understanding* and *godly* and I can't say, "Actually, I'm not really interested, and actually, I'm having a bad day myself, and actually, looking after your spiritual needs or your gripe about Church politics is *his* job, not mine, so would you kindly take your problem, whatever it is, and as your son would say, bugger off." She peered into her empty wineglass in the forlorn hope that there might be another mouthful there.

'That's us. Pissed off and pissed!' opined Gill.

Deciding that her glass was indeed empty, Ali placed it carefully on the floor. 'Take today: I've been very nice and understanding to a man I met in the town whose wife died three months ago; I've been ecstatic about someone's daughter who wants to get married in two years' time; I have cooed over someone's granddaughter who is to be baptised the Sunday after next; and I've spent the afternoon being enthusiastic and organising at mother-and-toddler. Did I feel fulfilled while carrying out these activities? Did I hell? And where has Tom been while I have been holding the parish together? Enjoying an interesting and fulfilling day in Edinburgh. He won't be home till late and I'm "not to wait up". He should be so lucky! My days of waiting up clad in nothing but some perfume are long since past. I learned my lesson with Matt. Nowadays I'm sound asleep in a man-frightener nightie and a pair of harvest knickers as extra protection.'

Gill giggled. 'What the hell are harvest knickers?'

'All is safely gathered in!'

The two women dissolved into giggles. Every time they tried to stop laughing they made eye contact and were off again.

Eventually, Gill managed to control herself and shook her head mournfully. 'I'm so tired I don't care what Mike does to me as long as he doesn't wake me up. If it's a choice between sex and half an hour's sleep, then it's no contest. Sleep wins. I yearn for the day when I can sleep for longer than four hours at a time. In fact, if my fairy godmother was to appear, do you know what my pathetic little wish would be? It would be to have twenty-four hours all on my own. Imagine the bliss of going to the loo without company, of having a bath without an ear listening, of sleeping for hours and hours knowing that you don't have to get up. I could do what *I* wanted to do.' She thought for a moment. 'Like reading a book. In fact, the crux of the matter is, I would be responsible only for myself, not two small beings with no sense of danger and no ability to fend for themselves. Mike thinks he's hard-worked, and he is, but his job is intellectually challenging and more to the point he only has himself to consider. Please, please, please, can I have a day off? Surely no one should have a job where they are expected to work twenty-four hours a day, seven days a week. It's not fair.'

''Course it's not fair. You get days off for paid work, but child-rearing is not subject to employment legislation. We need to cheer ourselves up. Let's open another bottle!'

Ali weaved her way unsteadily to the kitchen and was to be heard scrabbling about in cupboards. The phone rang. She tottered across the kitchen and picked up the receiver. 'St Andrew'sh Mansh,' she said with some degree of difficulty. There was a pause. 'Oh, I am sorry. She was such a lovely lady.' The tone was solicitous and sober. Another pause. 'No. I'm afraid he's been in Edinburgh for the day and I'm not expecting him back till late . . . Yes, I'll tell him and he'll get in touch first thing in the morning. Is there someone with you? . . . That's good. I'll make sure he phones you first thing. Goodbye.' She replaced the receiver and continued to scrabble in the cupboard. 'Sorry – no wine left. Gin or sherry?'

Gill looked at her watch. It was nine thirty. 'No. I've had an ample suffishienshy. I sound like Tony Benn.' She giggled. 'Got to go home now.'

Ali watched Gill make her way along the street and hoped she wouldn't be picked up for being drunk in charge of a buggy. She closed the front door, locked it and made her way to the kitchen, where she tried to tidy up. Tom would be back from Edinburgh in an hour or so. She checked that the back door was open to allow him in from the garage. She paused at the door to what had once been a maid's bedroom, and had been occupied by Lizzie until a month ago, when she had left to go to Edinburgh. It was strange not to have her around the house. She had worked so hard to get five As, and Ali hoped that she had now loosened up a bit and was having a social life as well.

Unbeknown to her parents, Lizzie Graham had loosened up at the age of fourteen, since when she had been living a very effective double life. She was a bright girl and had realised that in order to survive at school, she had to shake off the image of goody-goody minister's daughter and that in order to survive at home, she had to appear to be conscientious and hardworking. She would come home from school, do her homework dutifully, watch TV with the family, then retire to her room at the back of the house by ten o'clock. By eleven, when her parents had gone to bed, she was either to be found sitting on a bench in the town centre with a selection of friends who were unknown to Ali and Tom or engaged in sexual congress with Darren Connerty, who had been admitted to her room through the well-oiled sash window.

She had chosen the then sixteen-year-old Darren to be her boyfriend for what she thought would be his total unsuitability in her parents' eyes and his ability to improve her credibility in certain factions within the school. He was the third son of a family of six, well known to the police and the local social workers. His father was a small-time criminal, regularly arrested for breach of the peace when he had a drink in him. He was a frequent visitor to the Sheriff Court and went for periodic holidays at Her Majesty's Pleasure. Darren was showing promising signs of following in his father's footsteps. His first appearance before the juvenile justice system had been at the age of ten for truancy. Further appearances for shoplifting, being drunk and incapable, being in possession of cannabis and joyriding had followed. He had narrowly escaped a period in a young offenders' institution because he was good at convincing his social worker and the Children's Panel that he was about to go to college to get some qualifications, but Darren's regular schooling had stopped in Primary Four, so any form of further academic achievement seemed unlikely.

Lizzie had started to go out with him shortly after her fourteenth birthday and had lost her virginity two weeks later in Darren's cramped bedroom, which he shared with two of his brothers, who had been given four cans of Carlsberg Special and told not to come back for at least an hour. Lizzie was streetwise enough to know that it was her responsibility to make sure she didn't get pregnant, so she developed the knack of buying condoms in every public lavatory in which she managed to find herself alone. On her sixteenth birthday, she had made an appointment with the GP and requested to be put on the Pill. She assured the doctor that she knew what she was doing and it appeared she did as she never told Darren she was on the Pill and kept buying condoms. His lack of fidelity was well known but she was secure in the knowledge that the arrangement suited both of them. She was also clever enough not to be around when the police might pick him up for something illegal. She didn't drink when they were in the town centre, although she was happy enough to drink the vodka that Darren brought with him when he climbed through the window. She had tried cannabis, but reckoned, wrongly, that her parents, who were students of the eighties, probably knew what it smelled like, and she was not averse to a tab of E to liven up an evening.

Most of the town knew that Lizzie Graham was Darren's girlfriend, and everyone between the ages of twelve and twenty knew that he was a nocturnal visitor to the manse several times a week. There were a lot of people who had it on good authority that Lizzie had had two abortions and had been sent to a clinic to cure her heroin addiction. Lizzie knew how to steer clear of anything that was going to blight her life, and her supposed stay in a clinic was just a six-week visit to her aunt, who lived near Avignon. She was always worried that someone would tell her parents about her double life, but being the minister sets one apart slightly from the rest of the town and it takes a brave friend to tell. One of the parishioners, Joyce Macdonald, had remarked to Ali in a 'just-thought-I-should-let-you-know' tone of voice that she had seen Lizzie with some friends 'sitting at the war memorial about midnight', which was town-speak for mixing with extremely bad company. When questioned, Lizzie had denied being there and said people often got her muddled up with Leanne McCafferty, who was always hanging around the town centre. The judicious purchase of a hoodie helped Lizzie to maintain her anonymity, and Ali fended off other comments with the assertion that it must have been Leanne. Ruth knew what Lizzie was up to, but she also knew her sister, so she opted for an easy life and kept her mouth shut.

Lizzie's eighteenth birthday fell the week before she left for Edinburgh. She sat with Darren in the bar at the Corrachan Hotel. She told him that as she was going away it was over. He said that suited him fine as he was moving in with Sharlene McPhee, who was six months pregnant.

★   ★   ★

Gill had managed to weave her way home with two sleeping children in the double buggy. The world had taken on a dream-like quality.

Phyllis Caldwell watched from next door as Gill fumbled for her key. Phyllis had been quite concerned that there had been no lights on in Gill's house. She liked to keep an eye on that poor woman all on her own next door. Where could she have been?

Gill eventually found her key and opened the front door. The dog shot past her and squatted on the front lawn. The dog! She had completely forgotten about Penny, who would now have to be fed. Somehow she had to get the children up the steps and inside. If she bumped the buggy up the three steps, she would wake them and the peace was too precious to lose. If she didn't feed the dog, who was jumping up and down on the spot, they were going to be woken anyway. So dog first.

She very carefully put on the brake, made sure the sleeping bodies were well wrapped up and lurched in the door in search of dog food. There wasn't any. It dimly impinged on her brain that she had intended to go to Tesco after mother-and-toddlers. She peered into the fridge. There was a box of eggs, a carton of milk, a tub of marge, some child-sized yoghurts and various jars and bottles containing things that would not impress a dog. No good. On her way to the cupboard, she heard her mobile, which she had left to charge, beeping at her from the work surface. Four missed calls . . . Too difficult to deal with at the moment. She opened the cupboard and looked in. Eventually, she unearthed a tin of tuna and sweetcorn in mayonnaise. After emptying the utensil drawer, she finally found the tin-opener on the work surface, scooped the contents of the tin into the dog's bowl with some milk and a slice of bread and dumped it on the floor. Penny sniffed at it, then looked at her in a hurt, bewildered fashion.

'That's all there is. Take it or leave it,' said Gill.

The dog made a second approach to the dish and delicately picked up a morsel of dolphin-friendly tuna and chewed it warily. Penny sorted . . . children next.

Phyllis Caldwell was relieved to see Gill come outside again. She had been concerned that the children seemed to have been abandoned in the front garden and she watched as Gill unfastened the restraint, lifted Ian out and stumbled in the door. He was, miraculously, still asleep. Gill puffed up the stairs and laid him on her bed. She peeled off his trousers, removed a very soggy nappy and put on a fresh one. He could sleep in his T-shirt. She paused and smiled at him. He looked so cute when he was asleep. Cuteness was a description that could rarely be ascribed to him nowadays when he was awake. She picked him up, carried him to his room and put him into his bed. One done.

Now for Kate. Gill reckoned she could lift the buggy up the steps, now it only had one occupant. She took hold of the frame and managed to negotiate the three steps into the porch. Unfortunately, the doormat was lying in wait for her and she spectacularly tripped, hurling the buggy into the hall ahead of her. Luckily, Phyllis missed this drama, having been told by her husband, Jack, to sit down and mind her own business. Gill picked herself up to see the buggy lying on its back at the foot of the stairs and a surprised Kate blinking at her.

'Sorry, darling, sorry,' whispered Gill, as she undid the clips and picked up the baby.

She shut the front door and negotiated the stairs once again. Kate was hungry now and wailing. Feed her, then I can go to sleep, Gill thought. No, pee first. She laid the screaming baby on the landing and rushed to the loo. Relief! The bathroom seemed to be moving slightly, but if she concentrated very hard, it was controllable. She made her way back to Kate, picked her up and set a course for her bed, stepping out of her shoes on the way. She lay back against the pillows, lifted her sweatshirt, opened her bra and let the baby start to feed.

Gill was having a dream about trying to find a ringing phone in a room full of cushions. Gradually, the insistent ringing dragged her into consciousness and she fumbled for the receiver beside the bed. It was Mike.

'Thank God you're there. Where on earth have you been? I tried phoning at seven, and then I phoned at half past nine between courses! Did you not get the messages on your mobile?'

Gill peered at the bedside clock. It was only eleven. She hadn't been asleep long. Kate was sound asleep beside her.

'We were out.'

'Out where?'

How dare he be so aggressive? She didn't check up on him all the time.

'At a friend's house.'

'What friend? You don't have any close friends there.'

'I do now.'

'For God's sake, Gill, don't be obtuse. I was worried something had happened to you.'

'Your son told everyone at mother-and-toddler to bugger off today, and Ali Graham took pity on me and asked me back to her house. We had a meal, the children fell asleep, and I had an evening of adult conversation. A pleasant change from talking about Thomas the Tank Engine and Bob the sodding Builder.'

'What are you on about? What did Ian do . . . ? Are you pissed?'

'Ian had a tantrum and told everyone to bugger off. Don't worry – I took the blame. We all know words like that don't pass your lips. In response to your other question, the answer is "Perhaps." I have had a very pleasant evening and it involved some wine. I am now very tired and I wish to go to sleep.

We are all home where we should be and I'll speak to you in the morning.' She replaced the receiver.

Mike did not think it was worth trying to phone again. He had obviously encroached on her sleeping time and perhaps she would be in a better humour in the morning. He wondered if his parents would take the children for a weekend and they could go to a nice hotel for a couple of nights. Then he remembered Kate wasn't weaned yet. It would have to wait until after Christmas.

Gill was woken by Ian just before six. She had a thumping headache and a churning stomach – drink and Chinese takeaways don't mix. She willed herself out of bed and went downstairs to make breakfast. She skirted round the buggy, which was still on its side, and opened the kitchen door. The stench hit her before she saw the floor. Tuna mayonnaise had evidently not agreed with the dog. Her stomach heaved and she ran for the downstairs cloakroom.

Chapter Four

The following Sunday, Gill and Mike stood on the doorstep of Kilmartin, a large, square red sandstone villa with its name in gold writing on a glass panel above the front door. Situated next door to their own house on the edge of the town, it had been built in the 1890s to satisfy the bourgeois ambitions of a local wool trader. Now it was the home of Jack and Phyllis Caldwell.

Jack was in his mid-sixties and a large fish in the small pond that was this Scottish market town. He had numerous business interests, including a Volvo dealership, an agricultural supply warehouse and various shops in the High Street, and he owned some 'residential property'. This was a euphemism for some rather down-at-heel flats that the council used for emergency housing and therefore guaranteed a good rent from housing benefit. Jack was the immediate past president of the Rotary Club, an elder of the church at which Tom Graham was minister and a member of both the Masonic Lodge and the more prestigious of the local golf clubs.

Phyllis, an inveterate curtain-twitcher, was also a doer of good works. She was on the committee of the local branch of Save the Children, she collected for the Lifeboats, she spent one afternoon a week helping in a charity shop, and she had enjoyed being part of the Inner Wheel at Rotary until all the younger members had indicated that they had better things to do than to produce forty-eight cocktail savouries for the Wine and Cheese evening and the Inner Wheel had ceased to revolve. Phyllis's hobbies were collecting commemorative china, playing bridge and writing to the local paper and local elected representatives bemoaning the falling standards of society.

It was Mike's prompt reply to her litter letter that had taken her to the Andrewses' front door on Saturday afternoon just as Mike had thought he was finally off duty. She had thanked him for his reply, and as he did not seem to be going to invite her in, she had, as a seeming afterthought, invited Mike and Gill to join her Sunday-lunch party the next day. In order to effect a rapid return to his snooze on the sofa, Mike had thanked her very much and said they would be delighted to come.

'Does the invitation include the children?' Gill had asked.

'Oh, I don't know. She didn't say.'

'Didn't it occur to you to ask?'

'Well, she said "you and your wife", so it probably doesn't. Can't you find a babysitter?'

'Can't you? You accepted the invitation.'

'I don't know who babysits, do I?'

'Well, with one exception, neither do I. I'll try Ruth Graham, but if she can't do it, you'll have to phone up and say we can't go – and don't think you'll just go on your own to chat up the great and the good and leave me here.'

Gill had phoned the manse and got Ali.

'Sorry, there's a congregational lunch for Christian Aid tomorrow and Ruth is involved in the serving-up, and I have to be there too. You could try Angela or her mother, Moira.'

'I think Ian would send Angela into labour. What's her mother like? Do you think she would do it?'

'She might. She's very capable and seems to manage her own children with no obvious man on the horizon. And she works full-time at Jack Caldwell's car dealership. You could ask her. No, wait a minute, despite being due to drop any moment, I think Angela is still doing her Sunday stint at the Corrachan Hotel, so Moira will already be childminding.'

'Never mind, it was a nice thought. I'll just get Mike to tell Phyllis we can't come. I think he was quite looking forward to roast beef and two veg, but he'll have to do without.'

Mike had gone to phone the Caldwells and had come back looking pleased with himself. 'Phyllis just said, "Bring them along," so I said that would be fine.'

'Is this a family-friendly occasion, or is it a collection of sixty-somethings having a grown-up lunch with grown-up conversations?'

'Don't worry, I'm sure the Caldwells have boxes of toys for their numerous grandchildren. You'll find Kate will be dandled on knees and Ian will be amused by granny types reading him stories.'

Gill, long-starved of any sort of social life, had been desperate enough to believe him, but now, standing on the doorstep holding Ian firmly by the hand, she was beginning to harbour serious doubts. As Phyllis opened the door and ushered them in, Gill's fears were confirmed.

The hall was deeply carpeted in a green, brown and yellow patterned Axminster. There was a small antique sofa table on which rested a table lamp in the form of a china doll dressed in peach satin holding a parasol above its head. It appeared that a hidden switch located in the satin folds caused the parasol to become illuminated. Ian was transfixed and his sticky hand stretched out to caress this effigy of doubtful taste.

Gill swept him past temptation and into the sitting room, where one glance confirmed that she had left the frying pan and was now definitely in the fire. There were numerous small piecrust occasional tables, each of which had a Dresden shepherdess or similar placed tastefully upon it. On the coffee table and various other low shelves there were Minton bowls filled with pot-pourri, various commemorative plates and other china items celebrating royal events and a whole shelf of china dolls with real hair and elaborate costumes – all within easy reach of little fingers.

Her second glance took in the assembled company. There were two couples sitting on the olive-green brocade suite making conversation with Jack Caldwell, who stood up and moved forward to shake hands. He was a tall, heavy-set, balding man with a red face and a loud voice, and after shaking hands with Mike and Gill, he addressed Ian in booming tones.

'Hello! You must be Ian. I'm Uncle Jack.' He thrust his large red hand with fingers resembling raw beef sausages under Ian's nose, causing him to turn away in terror and bury his face in the folds of Gill's skirt.

'He's a bit shy, I'm afraid. Best just to ignore him for a while.'

'And this must be the baby.'

He bent down and tickled the sleeping Kate under her chin. She woke up and began to grizzle. Why couldn't he have left her alone? Gill had been careful to feed both Ian and Kate before they left home in the hope that Kate would sleep for the duration and Ian would play quietly in the corner with the toys that Mike had assured her would be there by the boxful.

'Isn't she sweet!' said Phyllis. 'It's always been a great sadness that Jack and I were not blessed with children.'

So no boxes of toys, then. Good thing she had brought some with her. The other two couples were introduced as Joyce and Bill Macdonald and Mary and George Franklyn-Hayes. The Macdonalds lived in Corrachan, Joyce being Phyllis's friend and bridge partner, and Bill the senior partner in one of the local firms of solicitors. Mary Franklyn-Hayes was Bill's sister and had completely shed any Scottish accent she may once have had. She now lived in a Queen Anne manor house within striking distance of Cheltenham. Her husband, George, had worked in the City and retired on the profits to live the life of a country gentleman. Having spent several days shooting in Aberdeenshire, he was allowing Mary a weekend with her brother on the way home.

'The MP!' beamed George. 'I'm glad you're at Westminster. Don't need all this devolution nonsense. Just all the socialists trying to create jobs for themselves and their cronies. I said to my friend Henry that we ought to get Central Office to be a bit more forceful on the matter. Scotland getting all this money and then they waste it on students and new parliament buildings. Perhaps you could put a word in. Do you have any influence with Central Office?'

'Very little. I'm a Liberal Democrat.'

'A Liberal! Good God, you don't look like a Liberal. Thought they all wore corduroy trousers and sandals, and ate lentils and got very heated about dog shit on the pavements.' He laughed heartily. 'Always thought this was a Tory seat.'

'It used to be, about twenty years ago,' said Mike. If you are going to be patronising, then so can I, he thought.

He moved past George and shook hands with Mary and the Macdonalds and settled himself in an armchair. Phyllis appeared at his elbow holding a silver salver with two schooners of sherry. Mike took one and engaged Joyce Macdonald in polite conversation about the changeability of the weather. Gill took the other sherry and perched on the edge of the sofa, Ian still hanging on to her. She tried to rock the baby seat to coax Kate back to sleep. Mary, who was next to her, launched into small talk.

'You'll just be up from London for the weekend, then.'

'No. We live here. Mike has a flat in London and comes home at the weekend.'

'How unusual,' gushed Mary. She glanced at the children. 'Is it your nanny's day off, then?'

'We don't have a nanny. I look after the children and we couldn't get a babysitter, so Phyllis said we could bring them.'

'My dear, I am impressed. I don't know how you manage it. What happens when you go to London, then? When George was in the City, I couldn't have managed without the nannies we had, especially before the boys went away to school.'

'I haven't actually been to London yet. Mike was just elected in June and I've been having a baby and moving house since then.'

'My friend's daughter is married to an MP – Conservative, of course – and she has such a busy time hosting dinner parties and just being there for her husband. MPs lead such a stressful life, you know.' She paused, lowered her voice and whispered, 'So many temptations, if you know what I mean.'

Gill chose to ignore the last remark and to lie blatantly about her entertaining capacity. 'We do most of our entertaining here. It's important to keep a high profile in the constituency.' God strike her down! The only people they had entertained were their parents, and Mike's mother had resorted to doing the cooking herself in order to eat before bedtime.

Gill took another sip of her sherry and watched Phyllis make for the kitchen for a final check on the lunch, which had been safely tucked into the hostess trolley half an hour before. She glanced down at Kate in the hope that she had gone back to sleep. Kate had ceased grizzling but was engaged in other things. Her face had taken on a faraway look of intense concentration. She turned puce and a loud eruption was heard such that it distracted the others in the room from their conversations.

Gill picked up the nappy bag. 'I'm afraid I'll have to go and change her.'

'Luncheon is served,' said Phyllis, appearing in the doorway.

'I'll be as quick as I can. Please just start. Ian, you wait here with Daddy.'

Ian looked at Mike, who was in deep conversation with 'Uncle Jack' about the one-way system in the town.

'Go with Mummy,' he pleaded.

'I won't be long. Just stay here with Daddy, please.'

'Go with Mummy. Go with Mummy,' he wailed desperately.

Mike looked up and it impinged upon him that paternal duties were still expected of him while he was in the role of local MP and, worse still, that Ian was about to make a scene. 'He'd be happier with you. Just take him.'

Clutching the nappy bag, baby seat and Ian, Gill made for the door.

'Upstairs, straight ahead. We'll just wait for you, dear,' said Phyllis.

The bathroom was pink, frilly and fluffy. It was a large room with a suite in a delicate shade of pink that was popular when installed in the sixties, and the cream shag-pile carpet was obviously a touch of luxury from the seventies. The window was of frosted glass to make sure that no one could peek at Jack and Phyllis performing their ablutions and was framed by what looked like an enormous pair of pink nylon bloomers. The bath was set into a recess with a shower curtain that resembled another pair of even bigger pink bloomers. The lavatory had been re-equipped with a grey marbellised seat and contained the only piece of non-colour coordination, blue water. The lid was covered in pink fur, part of a set that included the bathmat and the mat to catch mis-shots made by gentlemen. On the windowsill, ladies, when seated, were faced with a framed witticism that instructed them, 'If you sprinkle when you tinkle, be a sweetie, wipe the seatie.'

Phyllis clearly believed a naked toilet roll to be an abomination because although the bathroom was equipped with enough rolls to deal with a mass outbreak of dysentery, or even a thunder shower of sprinkling tinkles, not one was visible. The one in use was covered by a pink floral china cover, and the spare was encased in a pink knitted poodle begging on the cistern. There was an interesting accessory next to the toilet that resembled the pink and white lacy tissue box beside the basin, but this was about two feet high and sat on its end. Inside were a dozen more double-quilted pink rolls.

Ian went over to the loo and stroked the cover. 'Furry potty,' he said in wonder.

Gill undid the nappy bag to make a mat and spread it on the shag pile. Then she took Kate out of the baby seat and laid her down.

'Wash hands,' said Ian, looking at the basin, which was set into a pink Formica vanity unit. Thinking it would keep him occupied, Gill lined up a small white stool with a pink quilted top in front of the basin, put the plug in and ran a little water. There was some soap resting in a pink plastic swan beside a pink nailbrush. She lifted the soap out of the swan and put both the swan and the nailbrush into the water.

'You play boats while I change Kate.'

She knelt down and removed the well-filled nappy and cleaned up with baby wipes. Kate grinned at her and Gill tickled the baby's tummy as she fastened the clean nappy. She was about to seal up the dirty wipes into the nappy when she glanced up at Ian and watched with horror as he lifted up a large glass jar filled with pink and white cotton-wool balls and tipped the contents into the basin. She leaped to her feet to see the swan and the nailbrush perched on top of a soggy pink and white mess. She lifted Ian off the stool and started to squeeze the water out of the cotton wool. She grabbed a nappy-disposal bag and scooped the cotton wool into it. She would have to grovel and buy Phyllis some more tomorrow. Turning back to put the dirty nappy into another bag, she looked in disbelief at the cream shag pile. It was covered in small shitty footprints! With dawning horror, she realised that she had lifted Ian off the stool and deposited his left foot into the very dirty nappy. Ian had then made several circuits of the room, investigating what might next take his interest.

Gill grabbed him, pulled off his shoe and put it in the basin. She would have to clean the carpet somehow and keep Ian out of the mess. She removed his other shoe, lifted him into the bath, pulled the ties on the pink bloomers, causing them to descend until they merely resembled a shower curtain, and said, 'There! You have got a little house to play in.' She put Kate into the baby seat, where she started to howl. How was she going to clean this? She couldn't go downstairs and tell Phyllis in the middle of her lunch party that her bathroom carpet was covered in excrement. She took a wad of toilet paper and tried to remove some of the bits but with little success. She tried baby wipes, but they just seemed to smear it further. Perhaps there was cleaning stuff under the basin. She opened the door, but there was nothing useful, just more rolls of pink paper stacked neatly on the shelf.

There was a knock at the door.

'Are you all right in there?' inquired Phyllis. 'Your husband is quite worried about you. I said I would come and see if you were OK.'

Not worried enough to come and see for himself, thought Gill.

'Just having to feed the baby to get her settled. Won't be long. Do just start without me,' she shouted over the noise of crying.

'All right, if you're sure, dear.'

'Quite sure!'

The pink shower curtains parted and Ian's head appeared.

'Boo!' he said. Then he looked at the carpet and pointed to the mess. 'Poo!'

'Yes, Ian, lots of poo!'

Perhaps wet toilet paper was the answer. She took a large wad and ran it under the tap, then got down on her hands and knees and scrubbed. It seemed to be helping a bit, so she scrubbed some more. Double quilted had obviously been specially designed to biodegrade thirty seconds after becoming saturated and biodegrade it did into small pink shreds, which became embedded in the shag pile so that it looked like coffee icing with a sprinkling of pink vermicelli. It was much worse now. She pulled a small embroidered hand towel off the towel rail, ran it under the tap, squeezed it out and began to rub at another footprint. This was a bit better. It hadn't removed it but it was paler. Kate continued to howl. She really would have to feed her to shut her up.

She picked her up and sat down on the loo. As Kate fed, Gill surveyed the damage. It was horrendous, but perhaps with careful scrubbing with the towel she could get rid of it. Ian was pottering away happily behind the shower curtain and she could hear him talking to himself. She would have to clean the bath too when she was finished. Eventually, Kate drifted off to sleep again and Gill laid her carefully in the baby seat, before returning to her scrubbing.

She had almost managed to remove three footprints when she heard what sounded like hail coming from behind the shower curtain and the smell of old English roses began to waft in her direction. She pulled the curtains apart to view Ian wearing a pink frilly bath cap and standing in a heap of pink gravel. Phyllis kept her various bath salts on the shelf at the end of the bath and Ian had evidently upended a tub of the expensive granules.

'Like the hat, Ian, but you mustn't touch the jars. OK?' She scooped up the granules and decanted them back into the jar, screwed on the lid and then returned to the carpet.

She reckoned she was making some progress but it was far from its state prior to Ian's walkabout. She would have to go and own up and face condescension from superior Mary. A glance at her watch indicated that she had been in the bathroom for forty minutes. Surely Mike would come and see what was keeping her. Then he could explain to Phyllis and sort everything out. God, this was awful!

Suddenly, there was an outbreak of coughing and retching from behind the curtain. She pulled it aside. Ian stuck his head out and vomited prodigiously over the carpet. Gill tried to deflect his head so that the second emission landed in the bath, but she was only partially successful.

Ian stood in the bath and roared, 'Horrid weetie! Horrid weetie!'

In his hands were a red ball and a green ball. Various other coloured globes lay in the mess in the bottom of the bath. He had evidently thought that the brightly coloured marble-sized bath balls were sweets and had bitten into one.

She held him in the bath until he had finished retching, then lifted him out, remembering to take off his socks. She sat on the stool, put him on her knee and gave him a drink of water, then squeezed some toothpaste on to her finger and rubbed it round his mouth to take the taste away. Placing him on the stool at the basin in case he was sick again, she turned round to survey the carpet. Ian was a picky eater but he did like pieces of bread and grated cheese in Heinz tomato soup and they, along with a strawberry yoghurt, were now splattered in a semi-digested form all over the carpet. Defeated, she sank down on the remaining piece of clean floor and began to weep.

There was no option but to go downstairs and own up.

Where was Mike? It had been three-quarters of an hour now. Surely he must have realised there was something wrong. Just then there was a tap on the door behind her, and assuming it was Mike, she drew back the snib and opened the door. It wasn't Mike. It was Joyce Macdonald.

'Are you all right, dear? You've been up here a long time.' She looked at Gill's tearstained face. 'You are obviously not. What's happened?'

Gill opened the door properly and Joyce surveyed the devastation.

'Ian walked in a nappy and I've been trying to clean it up, and then he ate a bath-ball thing and he was sick and I can't clean that. Where's Mike? He should be helping.'

'He's defending devolution to an unimpressed audience.' Joyce looked at the room again and said, 'Nothing here that some antibacterial cleaner, carpet shampoo and a scrubbing brush won't sort. Phyllis has all of these in abundance in the utility room. I'll go and get them, and if I'm asked, I'll say Ian wasn't feeling well and has been sick. In the meantime, rinse his socks, wash his shoe and turn on the taps in the bath.'

Joyce returned with a bucket, scrubbing brush, old towels and a varied selection of cleaning products. She rolled up the sleeves of her Jaeger knitted suit and got to work, directing Gill as her assistant.

'Let me do this, please,' said Gill. 'You shouldn't have to clear this up.'

'Many hands, dear, many hands . . . I was a nurse before I was married, so I've seen worse than this.'

Ten minutes later, they vacated a pristine bathroom with only slight damp marks remaining on the carpet. Gill took the children downstairs to the sitting room and Mike looked up from his coffee.

'All right?' he inquired.

'Ian was a bit sick, but he's OK now,' she said stiffly. 'Can he sit on your knee while I have my lunch?'

Mike looked alarmed. 'He's not going to be sick again, is he? Perhaps you had better take him home.'

'If you're worried, you take him home, otherwise I'll take him after I've had my lunch.'

She lifted Ian on to Mike's knee, placed the baby seat beside him and made her way to the dining room, where a solitary place remained at the polished table. She had worked her way through the melon cocktail and was just starting on the roast beef when Mike walked past the door with Ian held firmly by the hand.

'Where are you going?' she asked. 'Is he feeling sick again?'

'He keeps saying "shit", so I'm taking him to the loo, before all those who are slightly deaf realise what he is saying. I thought he used the word "poo". Where on earth did he learn "shit"?'

'I think you'll find he wants his piece of sheet. It's in the nappy bag.'

'Ah, I see.' Mike hesitated, unsure whether to return to the lounge or continue. He reckoned that any extra chance to perfect the potty-training should not be passed by. 'Perhaps we'll just go to the downstairs cloakroom and then we'll find his sheet on the way back.'

Gill continued with her lunch, while Phyllis, who was refilling the cafetiere in the kitchen, kept popping her head through the hatch to ask if she needed anything. What else could she need? She was having a whole child-free fifteen minutes while Mike would be trying to stop Ian fingering dolls and smashing shepherdesses. Serve him right.

Lunch over, she returned to the sitting room. Ian was nestled in the crook of Mike's arm, sound asleep, and Kate was sleeping in the baby seat at his feet, making him look like an advert for the new man.

★   ★   ★

'God, that was hard work,' said Mike, as they walked up their garden path. 'Remind me never to accept an invitation from that woman again. That had to be the last bastion of Toryism. I am shattered. I spent the whole meal under political attack. The worst of the lot wasn't that Franklyn-Hayes man, it was Joyce Macdonald. She was so far to the right she must be Attila the Hun's mother. She's chair of local Tory Ladies' Group, you know.'

'I thought she was all right,' said Gill.

'You didn't have to listen to her. You spent the whole of lunch upstairs in the bathroom. It was very embarrassing. I kept having to apologise for your absence. Why didn't you come down and let us know that Ian wasn't well?'

In words of one syllable, Gill told him.

Chapter Five

Earlier that Sunday morning, Tom Graham had stood at the lectern and surveyed his congregation. To one side, in the choir area, were three elderly men and six middle-aged to elderly women. They had turned to face the rest of the congregation and were singing the opening hymn as if they were being filmed for *Songs of Praise*. Joyce Macdonald was 'Beholding the Mountain of the Lord' in a loud, slightly warbling soprano, while Mr Templeton, who had, with the exception of military service, been in the choir since 1939, was 'Rising in Latter Days' in a cracked bass. Phyllis Caldwell, who usually tried to out-sing Joyce, seemed to be absent. Tom assumed it must be one of her Sunday-lunch parties today. The majority of the congregation was over sixty and sitting in the pew they had inhabited for the past forty years. There were a few below pensionable age: several young families; Alistair Hamilton-Sinclair, who still looked like the army officer he used to be; and in the manse pew were Ali, Ruth and Matt, and a box of dinosaurs. Tom's brother, Peter, was there too, sitting at the far end of a side pew well away from everyone else. Bill Macdonald seemed to have guests with him, but otherwise the congregation was much as it was every Sunday.

After this hymn, Bill, session clerk and chief elder, would

come forward and read the intimations about the Guild meeting, about the stewardship campaign and the Christian Aid Feast or Famine lunch, and then he would issue an invitation to any visitors to join the congregation in the hall afterwards.

Tom had been in this charge for ten years and ordained for nearly ten years before that. Conducting a service was a straightforward exercise and he was on autopilot. He even failed to notice that, yet again, the choir had chosen an anthem that was beyond them.

Those who sat there believed him to be their weekly source of wisdom from the Almighty, the pillar of faith who married them, baptised their babies and buried their dead with appropriate words of hope, joy or comfort. He knew now that he was lacking in both wisdom and faith. As a small child and son of the manse, he had known that God was all around him, and he was only twelve when he had known that he wanted to be a minister. He had been so sure of his vocation and his faith, but now God was absent, a parting that had been so gradual Tom had hardly noticed it at first. He had been sure everyone had doubts sometimes and his faith would return, but it hadn't. He should have sought counselling for this spiritual crisis, but it was easier now to avoid the issue than to have to admit that he should have shouted, 'Help' earlier. He had preached many times that Hell was the absence of God, and that was where he was now – adrift in a sea of nothingness with no prospect of rescue.

He conducted services, he visited the sick and the housebound, he presided over weddings and funerals as he had done for years, yet no one, except perhaps Ali, had noticed any difference. He had withdrawn from his marriage too, allowing him to avoid talking about his spiritual problems or about the marriage itself. It wasn't as if they fought, they just were mentally separate, more like flatmates than a couple. He wanted to wake up one morning and find that he believed again in God, the

Resurrection and the power of the Holy Spirit, and find that he desired his wife, but he knew it wouldn't happen. His whole life was a lie now. Public admission of his lack of faith would mean the loss of a job, a house and the only way of life he had known. To be honest about everything, including some things he couldn't fully admit to himself, would result in a drastic upheaval for his family, but trying to pretend everything was fine was becoming more and more difficult.

Ali sat in the pew and looked at this person who was the spiritual leader of his flock. It was difficult to reconcile this image with the man who left his wet towel on the bathroom floor and had a habit of walking around the bedroom wearing nothing but his socks. The public face and the private face seemed to belong to two different people, but she hadn't really seen the private face recently. He had been so busy, especially since he had been appointed to the Church and Society Council in Edinburgh, and he always seemed to be away at meetings or closeted in his study writing sermons, preparing for a funeral or doing God only knew what. He was unwilling to discuss the fact that Matt might have some sort of difficulty and whenever possible avoided the minutiae of family and parish life.

As she listened to him expound on the duty of the Christian to feed the hungry, she reflected that it was she who had spent a large proportion of this week organising today's Feast or Famine lunch, bullying certain ladies into producing pots of soup and quantities of mince and potatoes, not to mention trifles for the feast, and she herself had boiled the rice and coloured the 'dirty' drinking water with a teabag for the famine. As usual, Tom had managed to delegate and she, as usual, had been landed with the task.

At the end of the service, the congregation filed into the church hall, each person paying their five pounds for the Feast and Famine lunch and drawing a ticket from the bag. A red ticket entitled the bearer to a three-course lunch and a glass of wine. A blue ticket meant only a small bowl of rice and a glass of dirty water.

Tom drew a red ticket, Ali a blue one. What a surprise, she thought. Bill Macdonald had sidled up to her at the end of the service and pressed an envelope into her hand with apologies that he and Joyce were going out to lunch but he would like this small donation to be added to the proceeds. A glance in the envelope had revealed a twenty-pound note. She wished she could buy off her responsibilities so easily.

After supervising the distribution of the food, she sat down at the famine table and began to eat her rice. She looked around at the other unlucky diners and her eyes fell on Alistair Hamilton-Sinclair. He had been brought up in the Episcopal Church, where his parents, Brigadier Sir Charles and Primmy Hamilton-Sinclair, still worshipped, but Alistair could not bear to pass Sunday morning under his mother's disappointed and his father's disgusted gazes, so he had started to attend St Andrew's and was there most Sundays, despite some mutterings from the less tolerant members of the congregation.

Alistair was an army child, who had been sent first to prep school at the age of seven and then to public school. It had always been anticipated that the next step would be Sandhurst. Alistair loved the army and was thought to be an officer with a promising future until he could no longer deny his sexuality. Ten years earlier, he had been caught by his commanding officer in a more than compromising position with a squaddie and two army careers had been terminated forthwith. His father's disgust was twofold. That his son should be what he called a 'shirt-lifter' was hard enough to take, but that he should have been lifting the shirt of one of the squaddies showed a distinct lowering of social standards.

Publicly Sir Charles chose to deal with the situation by pretending that it hadn't happened – Alistair had left the army of his own volition and was running a restaurant until he took over the estate. Lady Hamilton-Sinclair was wont to tell friends that Alistair was an 'unclaimed treasure' and it was such a shame he was so busy with his restaurant that he didn't have time to find a nice wife. Everyone knew wife-hunting did not figure on Alistair's list of hobbies. He and his partner, Frank Callaghan, the aforementioned squaddie, ran an award-winning restaurant in an old house on the edge of the town centre – a house that Alistair had inherited from his grandmother. Frank was the chef, while Alistair ran the front of house in Chez Marguerite – named after Margaret, his grandmother, thereby further angering the brigadier.

In fact, the use of his grandmother's name was more than appropriate. Before matrimony and respectability claimed her, the old lady had been a society flapper and was what her more timid friends had classed as 'fast'. She had passed several summers at house parties in the south of France, where all forms of sexual practice were not just tolerated but encouraged. When Alistair was twenty, she had asked him if he preferred men, and when he admitted that he did, she advised him to be true to himself and altered her will to leave him her house.

Alistair and Frank's relationship had survived and their business was thriving. They served coffee and lunch for the likes of Phyllis Caldwell and her friends, and in the evenings it was a popular place to dine.

'This lunch is a jolly good way of showing the difference between the rich and the poor,' said Alistair.

'Just a shame we're the poor ones,' said Ali. 'Tom, as usual, seems to have got the better deal.'

'He's just had to take the service, so he deserves a good lunch,' said Peter, for ever loyal to his brother.

Ali glanced at Peter and looked away again. She knew it wasn't worth making a flippant remark to him about the fact that she had organised all this. It would pass straight over his head. Peter took everything very literally and organised his life to a strict timetable. He lived in the small bungalow to which his late parents had retired and kept all the fixtures and fittings as they had always been. An IT consultant, he had no room in his life for anything as unpredictable as a wife. In fact, the socialisation involved in finding one was too stressful to contemplate, though he did have an email relationship with a lady in Eureka, California. She, too, worked in the world of computers and they had 'met' in an Internet chatroom specialising in combating computer viruses.

For Peter, this lunch was just tolerable. He knew everyone and all he had to do was eat and go home. Besides his computer, his other abiding interest was politics. Like Mike Andrews, he was a Liberal, but closer to the sort that George Franklyn-Hayes would have recognised. He was a local councillor, particularly concerned about dog mess on the pavements. He was usually to be found clad in old corduroy trousers, a well-worn checked shirt and a green jersey that had seen better days. But Ali had to admit that Peter got on well with his nephew. Perhaps he saw in Matt the echoes of the small boy he once was, and he would talk to him at great length about species of dinosaur and the comfort of having everything in the correct order. Matt seemed to recognise someone who saw the world in the same way he did and always responded well to Peter.

Ali watched them arranging dinosaurs together on the trestle table. It was a small comfort to know that they probably had a common gene and she was grateful for Peter's help on this occasion, as Matt was not clinging on to her as he usually did.

At the table of plenty, Tom was tucking into his trifle and teasing the elderly McKenzie sisters, who sat beside him giggling in a girlish fashion. It was all so familiar and predictable after ten years. Perhaps they needed a new challenge. Perhaps it was time to move on, but Tom had been brusque to say the least when she had raised the matter, and Ruth had her exams this school year, so an immediate move was impossible – next year, perhaps. If they went to another church, she certainly wasn't going to be as involved in church activities. She would attend on a Sunday and go to things that interested her, but she would flush duty down the pan.

Chapter Six

From the depths of a dream, Gill heard Ian stirring in his room. She registered the warmth in the bed with her and remembered it was Saturday. Mike was home, so she did not have to pull her exhausted form from under the duvet and make breakfast. Mike always did early mornings on a Saturday – he had to get up anyway because he usually had a surgery – and she did Sundays. She opened an eye. The clock indicated it was five twenty-five. She wouldn't have to get up till at least eight thirty, so she could sleep for another three hours knowing that someone else was in charge. She was going to spend the afternoon at the hairdresser having a cut and colour. So much freedom from small children in one day was almost too delicious to contemplate.

Ali had persuaded her she needed to be pampered following the bathroom disaster of the previous weekend. Gill had confessed the whole incident, including her return to Phyllis's house on Monday morning with a bunch of freesias and a bag of pink cotton-wool balls. Ali had told her she had already heard that Ian had poohed on Phyllis's sitting-room carpet, before being sick into a bowl of pot-pourri. They decided that Joyce must have talked, as Phyllis, being rather prim concerning bodily functions, was unlikely to have told anyone. In fact, Joyce Macdonald had only told Helen Cooper and she had only told two other people, but as gossip spreads in an exponential fashion, most of the town was now of the impression that as well as having a vocabulary comprising only swear words, the little Andrews boy had a weak stomach to the extent that Phyllis had had to get a cleaning firm in.

'But it's not true! It's not fair.'

'Don't worry – most people think Phyllis is a snob, so you and Ian will have gone up in everybody's estimation. Cheer up! You need to do something just for you that makes you feel better.' She had looked at Gill's hair. It was touching her shoulders and more than a little untidy. 'When did you last have your hair cut?'

'Oh, ages ago. Before the election, before Kate was born . . .'

'Definitely time for a makeover, then. Can you find three hours to spare?'

'Mike's home on Saturday afternoon. Don't suppose I'll get an appointment, though.'

'Leave it to me. I know Vicki who owns the salon.' So Ali had phoned and booked an appointment for a cut and colour at two thirty.

Ian was moving around his room now. Gill dug Mike in the ribs.

'Mmm? Swap you. I'll do tomorrow. I'm knackered.'

'Oh, no! You've got to get up anyway.'

'Don't have to get up – surgery's this afternoon instead. Please? I'll do tomorrow.'

Gill sat bolt upright. 'What do you mean, your surgery's this afternoon?'

'The morning didn't suit Annie, so we changed it to the afternoon.'

'Well, the afternoon doesn't suit me. I'm getting my hair cut! When did you change it and why didn't you tell me?'

'About two weeks ago. Thought I'd told you. Anyway, you never told me you were going to the hairdresser.' He turned over and pulled the duvet round his shoulders. 'Can't you get an appointment for this morning instead?'

'No! I can't! I only got this one as a favour. You'll have to spend the morning finding me a babysitter or you can take the children with you to the surgery. I'll do breakfast now I'm awake, but I mean it, you'd better not lie there all morning because you have got to organise some sort of childcare from quarter past two till quarter to six because I AM GOING OUT . . . ON MY OWN!'

She swore at the dog, which got under her feet, and noisily put the clean contents of the dishwasher into the cupboards, taking the opportunity to drop a pan on to the draining board in the hope that the noise would carry up the stairs. Mike's new job and a new baby had completely changed the family dynamic. After Ian was born, Gill had gone back to work as a teacher and she and Mike had shared the childcare duties fairly equally. Now, Mike was away all week and there were two children rather than one, but he seemed to assume that, because she wasn't working, childcare was her sole responsibility. Gill felt he thought he was doing her a huge favour if he agreed to let her go to Tesco on her own on a Saturday. Spending time with his children now seemed to be something he did if his constituents or the party didn't need him. Even when he did spend time with them, she got the impression he would rather be asleep or watching the football on TV. He seemed to think he had come home to rest, not to do what he considered to be her job. If a child-free zone was what he wanted, he could rent a room from Phyllis next door. She felt left behind, both physically and metaphorically.

By nine forty-five, she had fed the children, put two loads of washing through the machine, hoovered the sitting-room floor, made a toy fort out of Duplo, watched a banal TV programme designed for the under-fives and read two Thomas the Tank Engine stories. There were no sounds from upstairs to indicate that Mike was stirring. She put a slice of bread in the toaster and turned on the kettle in certain knowledge that he would sleep till at least eleven if not woken and that finding a babysitter was obviously not a priority. She buttered the slice of toast and told Ian to take it to Daddy. Ian was difficult to ignore. When she heard voices, she took the tea upstairs.

'Don't forget about the babysitter,' she said, as she laid the tea on the bedside table. The tone was only mildly reproachful.

'It's OK, I'm remembering. I'll sort it after I've had a shower.'

After his shower, Mike shaved and dressed. Then he went to the study armed with the Grahams' phone number. He didn't like phoning people to ask favours. He would check his emails first. There was one from a constituent wanting his views on Third World debt, so he decided to deal with it immediately in case he forgot later. By the time he had done that and two others, emailed copies to his office and played several games of Minesweeper, it was nearly midday. He heard Gill coming upstairs, so he picked up the phone and dialled the number. It rang for a long time and then the answer phone kicked in. He left a message and replaced the receiver.

There had been no reply to the message by the time Mike had finished lunch.

'Look, I can't take them with me. People are coming to see me about things that are important to them. I can't be a child-minder at the same time. I'm sorry I didn't tell you I'd changed the surgery time, but you never told me you had a hair appointment. You can make another one for next Saturday and I promise I'll be home to look after them.'

He put on his coat, gathered up his briefcase and car keys and went out through the door. Gill looked at the clock. It was one fifteen. Her appointment wasn't for another hour and a quarter. She would try phoning the manse again before she cancelled. She plonked a plate of fish fingers and beans in front of Ian and picked up the phone and dialled. It rang and rang. One more ring and she would get the answering machine again, so she hung up, resigned to an afternoon at the play park with an exciting detour to feed the ducks on the pond on the way home. Half an hour later, she reached for the phonebook and started to look for the number of Vicki's salon.

Then the phone rang. It was Ruth Graham.

'I got Mike's message about babysitting. Sorry it's taken so long to get back to you but we've been to Edinburgh. Lizzie wanted to come home for the weekend and Mum had to get something from John Lewis. I can babysit till half past four if that's any good.'

'Wonderful. Mike's surgery is due to finish by half past three and he should be home by a quarter past four at the latest. You are a star, Ruth.'

It was nearly a quarter to six when a sleekly coiffured Gill opened her front door. Her long hair had been cut into a bob and dyed a rich golden brown. She had had her head massaged, read magazines, drunk two cups of coffee, had her nails done and been responsible only for herself. Life now seemed tolerable.

The opening of the front door caused the kitchen door to bang shut. She opened it to see Mike and an attractive young dark-haired woman sitting on the back steps. They each had a cigarette and a bottle of beer and were laughing about something. They looked up as she came into the kitchen.

'Ooh, like the hair, very smart,' said Mike. 'This is Lizzie.

The surgery was very busy today and I wasn't home till five. Ruth got Lizzie to take over when she had to go.'

Anything less like the studious daughter of the manse Gill would have found hard to imagine. Lizzie stood up and came to shake hands. Gill took in the long, shiny dark hair, top revealing a slash of midriff, tight jeans and spiky-heeled boots, all of which was combined with an air of supreme confidence. All the beneficial effects of an afternoon of self-indulgence vanished and she felt middle-aged and dowdy once again.

'Good to meet you,' she said in an 'I'm a friend of your mother's' tone of voice, 'I've heard a lot about you from your mum. Are you enjoying life in Edinburgh?'

'Yes. It's cool, but it's good to come home occasionally.'

'Sorry you had to come and take over. Mike's nearly always home within an hour of the surgery finishing. I hope the children were good.'

'Yes, they were. Ruth took them to the park. All I did was read Ian a story, change Kate's nappy, then just play with them till Mike got home.'

Gill looked around the child-free kitchen. 'And where are they now?' she inquired.

'They're in the other room watching a DVD,' said Mike. 'We've not heard a cheep for the past twenty minutes or so.'

'Haven't you been to check what they are doing?'

She went into the sitting room expecting to find some sort of mayhem. Except for the TV, the room was in darkness. Thomas, Gordon and Clarabelle were continuing their adventures on the screen, but neither child was watching. They were both fast asleep, guaranteeing that they would be wide awake all evening.

She returned to the kitchen. Mike seemed to be making no move to find his wallet, so Gill opened her bag and looked at Lizzie inquiringly. 'What's the hourly rate here?'

Lizzie told her.

'When did you get back, Mike?' She was damned if she was going to pay for the beer and fag interlude.

'About quarter past five, I think.'

'There you are. Can you give Ruth her share, please?'

'Lizzie isn't going back to Edinburgh till Monday morning, so I said I'd give her a lift to the airport, where she can get the bus into town.'

'That's good,' said Gill absently. She was already deciding whether she should make Ian's tea then wake him or wake him now and suffer twenty minutes of crying and whining in the knowledge that by the time his food was ready he would actually eat something. Mike and Lizzie had finished their cigarettes and closed the back door, and were sitting at the kitchen table discussing aspects of student funding.

What the hell, thought Gill. I'm tired of being responsible and tending to other people's needs all the time. She went to the fridge, took out a bottle of white wine, poured herself a large glass and sat down, remembering as she did so that she was due a lie-in in the morning. Her eyes fell on a heap of orange and blue beads sitting in some wrapping paper.

'What's this?'

'It's a present from Mrs Taha from Sudan. You know the one I got the visa for – to come and see her grandchildren. You said her daughter-in-law took the children to toddlers. She and her sister called in at the surgery to say thank you for all I'd done. They'd had a wonderful trip and were on their way to the airport.'

Gill picked it up. 'What on earth is it?'

'It's a beaded wall hanging.'

'Ah! It's a bit of an "Oh my gosh" present, isn't it? What do you think, Lizzie? You like it?'

'It's gross. I certainly wouldn't have it on my wall.'

Mike was more positive. 'I think it's quite fun. It's colourful!'

'Well, I wouldn't disagree with you there. You can hang it in your study. I'm not sure I want to look at it all the time.'

'I might just do that. It's a nice gesture. It's not often anyone bothers to say thank you for what I've done.'

Chapter Seven

Gill was late arriving at mother-and-toddler group the following Tuesday. As she came into the church hall, the children were playing as usual, but all the mothers were gathered in the kitchen talking. Perhaps there was some sort of meeting that she had forgotten about, so she directed Ian to his usual tricycle and made for the kitchen. Marie, who worked part-time as an auxiliary nurse at Strathperry Infirmary, was holding forth.

'. . . She's on the danger list and they've transferred her to Edinburgh. It's touch and go.'

'It's absolutely gross,' said Angela. 'Do you really mean they've cut off all her bits?'

'Yeah, I do. It looked as if it had been done with something like scissors and then stitched up, and nothing had been sterile. It had all got infected. She was screaming in agony, the poor little thing!'

Gill looked round. 'Sorry, I've missed the beginning of this. What are we talking about?'

'It's dreadful!' said Ali. 'You know Settina and her daughter, Poni? Well, they had relatives from Sudan staying and while Settina and her husband were out, the granny and the aunt circumcised Poni. She's now got septicaemia and she's in intensive care.'

Gill thought of the orange and blue beaded wall hanging now prominently displayed in Mike's study. A horrible cold, sick feeling was creeping through her. Mike had been so pleased he had scored a point over the visa issuers in Khartoum. She had not been a political wife long, but she knew this had huge and unpleasant ramifications.

'Have the police lifted the old witches?' asked Angela.

'They've gone home evidently. Did this just before they left,' said Marie.

'Excuse me a moment, I've just remembered I need to make a phone call. Could you hold Kate a minute?' Gill thrust the baby at Ali and made for the car park.

Mike's mobile rang and went to the answering service. She tried Janice, who told her he was in a committee. She dialled the paging service and left a message asking him to phone her mobile urgently. She walked round the car park taking in the enormity of what had happened – known and unknown. Were the parents complicit in this, or were they as appalled as everyone else? Mike had acted in good faith but that doesn't always save you in the political world. Naïve can equate with stupid, and the racial, religious and ethical issues were huge.

Her mobile rang.

'What's the matter? Is it one of the children?'

'Not one of ours! You obviously haven't heard, then?'

'Heard what? What do you mean?'

'You know those friendly Sudanese women who gave you that lovely wall hanging?'

'Yes, what about them?'

'They circumcised the three-year-old and now she's in intensive care in Edinburgh with septicaemia.'

There was a silence.

'Mike, are you there?'

'I'm here. Oh Jesus . . . What have I done?'

'Yeah.'

'What should I do?'

'I don't know. Can you ask someone? Perhaps you should contact the police. They're bound to be involved now.'

'I'll go and speak to some people here. See if they have any suggestions. Then I think I'll come home. I'll speak to you later when I've sorted my flight.'

Pocketing his phone, Mike left the committee corridor and made for the chief whip's office, which was located at the side of the Members' Lobby. He walked past those in the outer office and knocked on the door of the inner sanctum. After being invited to enter, he opened the door and went in.

'Can I have a word? I've got a bit of a problem.'

It was nine thirty when Mike arrived home. He put his overnight bag and briefcase on the hall chair and came into the sitting room, where Gill, now the children were asleep, had been watching mindless TV. He looked, she thought, absolutely awful. He was a sort of grey colour and he seemed to have shrunk within his suit.

'How's you?' she inquired.

'Shit!' He slumped down on the sofa and took off his tie.

She went and sat beside him, took his hand and gave it a squeeze. 'Anyone tell you what you should do?'

'No. Oh, they were sympathetic, but no one had any useful suggestions. They all had stories about dreadful things they had done, but I don't think accidentally attaching a file note saying, "This woman is off her trolley," to a letter is quite the same as helping two women to gain entry to this country in order to commit grievous bodily harm. The chief whip suggested I went to the police before they came to me, so I've made an appointment for tomorrow morning, but I don't know what to do about the parents. Should I go and see them?'

'God, I don't know. Perhaps you need to find out if they were in on this. See what the police say. They might advise you.'

'I don't know how much they'll tell me if it's an ongoing inquiry.' He sounded doubtful. 'Have you heard how Poni is?'

'Ali phoned earlier. She'd heard that there was no change. They should know by tomorrow morning if the antibiotics have done their job.'

'Poor kid. If she survives, she's permanently maimed. If I hadn't been so pushy with the embassy, the women wouldn't have got a visa. I said the Tahas were a hardworking, law-abiding – huh – family and it was a breach of human rights to deny the grandmother access to her grandchildren. I laid it on thick. It worked! They were here in Corrachan within a week of my intervention.'

'It is not your fault. You didn't know what they were going to do.'

'Gill, what's going to happen if she dies?'

'I don't know.'

'I don't know either.' His face crumpled and he started to weep.

Neither Mike nor Gill had a good night. Gill had dozed while Mike tossed and turned. Eventually, Mike had fallen asleep and consequently so had Gill . . . for about fifteen minutes, until Ian had woken with a temperature and she had spent the rest of the night with Calpol and cold flannels, thoughts of meningitis adding to her fears.

In the morning, Mike had taken himself to the police station and made a statement but had not taken much comfort from the chief inspector's comment that he could not have foreseen what would happen and that he shouldn't blame himself. He came home with the news that the press had got hold of this. This was not, of course, a surprise, but it required defensive action. He spent the rest of the day on the phone to the party press office drafting statements that said little more than 'No comment' and declining offers to appear on TV news bulletins.

The following morning, Mike left early for the constituency office for further damage limitation. Another bad night with Ian meant that Gill had not slept at all. Now, with Ian finally asleep upstairs and Kate safely contained in the high chair, Gill closed her eyes. Still in her dressing gown, she was asleep with her head on the kitchen table when the doorbell rang ten minutes later. She found Phyllis on the doorstep.

'Oh! Sorry to disturb you. I didn't realise you were unwell.'

'I'm not ill, but Ian is. I had a disturbed night. Come in. Excuse the mess.'

Phyllis picked her way over the abandoned toys in the hall, followed Gill into the kitchen and stood while the pile of laundry was removed from a chair and the discarded Sunday papers cleared in order to grant Phyllis a seat and a portion of table on which to place a cup if necessary.

'Have a seat. Can I get you a tea or coffee?'

'No, no, I'm fine. I can see you're busy. I just brought you my paper in case you don't know what's going on. It's all about that poor little coloured girl and what they did to her. They're suggesting that your husband might have something to do with it. I just thought I should come by in case and let you know.'

She pushed the tabloid newspaper in Gill's direction. There was a grainy picture of Poni under the headline 'Tot on Danger List: Grandma Performs Ritual Maiming.' The article said MP Mike Andrews had been instrumental in getting visas, which was of course true, but the tone suggested that in the absence of the perpetrators they were intent on scapegoating Mike.

'Thanks for bringing it round, Phyllis. We did know about it, but not what was in the paper.'

'So the grandmother had trouble getting a visa to visit in the first place?' inquired Phyllis. 'It said in the paper that Mike had endorsed their application.'

Through the fog of her exhaustion, Gill realised that Phyllis was on a fishing expedition for her circle of retired ladies.

'I don't know all the details, Phyllis. Mike doesn't talk to me about his dealings with constituents. It's all confidential . . . a bit like going to the doctor.'

'Oh, I quite understand.' The tone was disappointed. Sympathy might produce a response. 'Must be very trying when the press get hold of something and you can't say anything in your defence.'

'Yes, it is difficult, but as I said, it's all confidential, so Mike can't give out any details.'

Gill was about to reissue the invitation for a cup of coffee in the hope that Phyllis would again refuse and take her leave when she heard Ian crying upstairs.

'Excuse me a moment, Phyllis. I'll just check what's the matter. He's been quite poorly.'

While Gill was upstairs, Phyllis sat and looked around the kitchen. She glanced at Kate in the high chair. The baby stared back at her. She found small children quite unnerving sometimes, especially when they stared. Apart from the piles of what could only be described as 'stuff' on the kitchen table, the sink was full of dirty dishes and the floor was littered with a mixture of toys and dog hairs. Kitty McPherson would be appalled to see the present state of her once-immaculate house. Phyllis felt a tickle in her nose. Dust always did this to her. She reached out and took a tissue from the box on the table just in time to catch the sneeze. She wiped her nose and flipped open the pedal bin, dropping the tissue on top of a heap of blue and orange beads. She wondered what it was and if Ian had put them in the bin by mistake. She had better point out they were there. When Gill returned a few minutes later carrying Ian, who was wearing nothing but a nappy, it wasn't his lack of clothes that caught Phyllis's attention. It was the red spots. They were all over him – his face, his toes and all parts in between.

'Now I know why he's been so unhappy. It's chickenpox!' said a cheered Gill, relieved to jettison the fear of meningitis.

'Poor wee soul. I hope he's better soon.'

Phyllis, who was of the mistaken belief that any contact with chickenpox resulted in shingles, focused her attention on leaving as quickly as possible. She gathered up her handbag and the paper and was out through the door in thirty seconds with no mention of coloured beads in the bin, never realising how near she had been to a gem of gossip for the coffee morning she was about to attend.

Ian was hot and very itchy. He had spots on every part of his body, including the inside of his mouth, and was most unhappy for several days. Consequently, Gill's mind was not totally on the circumcision issue, especially when, after two days, Poni was pronounced out of danger. Mike, however, was totally consumed with what he ought to do next. He kept asking Gill for advice. Should he go and see the parents? Should he write to the parents? Should he issue another press statement? Why hadn't he realised the reason the women wanted to come to the UK?

'I don't know,' was her reply to everything. She wished he would stop going on about it and give her a break from the childcare instead. Mike wished she would stop being so wrapped up with Ian and his spots and give him some support in this awful situation. The final straw for Mike came when he was running a possible damage-limitation strategy past her during a small oasis of peace when both children were asleep at the same time.

'D'you think that would be worth doing, then?' There was

no reply. He turned to look at her and she was sound asleep. 'Fine! I'll go and speak to someone who's interested.' He picked up his car keys and left. It was time to go and see Minty.

Minty Oliver may have sounded like a peppermint biscuit but she was a Liberal of impeccable pedigree. Born the Honourable Araminta Barswick, her great-grandfather had been a manufacturer of nuts and bolts in Yorkshire in the mid-nineteenth century and had amassed a large fortune. His son, Minty's paternal grandfather, had become a Liberal MP and, later, a minister in Gladstone's government and had been given a peerage. The income from the nuts and bolts continued to be considerable and had paid for a large Gothic mansion in rural Yorkshire and a country estate, Corrachan House, in Scotland. Minty's father had been further gentrified by his years at Eton and, following service in the Boer War, had been a Liberal peer and country gentleman.

Unlike many of his generation, Minty's father had not thought educating girls a waste of money and she had been sent to Roedean. Had it not been for the war, she would have gone to Oxford, but when she left school in 1941, she enrolled in the Wrens, where she had met Christopher Oliver, a naval officer who commanded a motor torpedo boat. Two months after they had married, in 1943, he was killed on operations in the North Sea. Three weeks after that, a devastated Minty had the consolation of discovering she was pregnant. She was discharged from the Wrens and made her way to Corrachan to await her baby's arrival far from the bombs that were raining on London. When she was seven months pregnant, she went into premature labour and gave birth to a daughter, who survived only a few hours. Grieving her double loss, she decided to remain at Corrachan until the war ended.

Now, more than sixty years later, she was still living in Corrachan, not in the big house, which was sold to Sir Charles

Hamilton-Sinclair's father in 1950, but in what had been the factor's house, now called Nethercorrachan – a three-bedroomed eighteenth-century farmhouse near the loch.

Minty was known by everyone. She was exceedingly wealthy, as the income from the nuts and bolts had been wisely invested, but she lived frugally. She was now eighty-six but looked as if she was in her early seventies. She was tall and angular, and dressed either in clothes she had worn since the fifties or in offerings from Liberal jumble sales. She drove a B-registration Metro the colour of tomato soup on the bits that weren't rusty. How it passed an MOT each year was a topic of local discussion and it had been suggested that the local mechanic, who was the son of the former Corrachan House chauffeur, still knew his place and produced an annual test certificate for her.

She took up numerous good causes, organised candlelight vigils for Amnesty International and wrote letters to presidents and prime ministers pointing out the error of their ways regarding human rights. She saved whales, trees from being felled, old buildings from being demolished and, in years past, milk-bottle tops to pay for guide dogs. At least once a year, she would disappear off in the aforementioned Metro for two or three weeks, and many people used to believe that she had a lover somewhere. Only the local Liberal Committee knew that was not quite the case. Minty just adored by-elections and whenever and wherever there was a Liberal and latterly a Liberal Democrat seeking election, Minty would be there indefatigably delivering leaflets and engaging a disinterested electorate in conversation on the doorstep, totally oblivious that she was calling in the middle of *Coronation Street* or *EastEnders*. In her younger days, these visits had allowed for several sexual encounters with itinerant leaflet deliverers if they were intellectually interesting enough, but more often with visiting party grandees. She had never brought them home.

In the dark days of the fifties and sixties, her Banda machine had churned out leaflets, the purple inking process giving her a temporary high, an early version of glue-sniffing. These she had hand-delivered, much to the amusement of the local Tories. In the early eighties, there had been a by-election in the Corrachan constituency and she had called in all her favours among both by-election workers and the party hierarchy; a team descended to cover the constituency with leaflets, posters and canvassers. She phoned and wrote and cajoled wives and secretaries, and managed to secure visits from David Steel, and a now slightly deaf but still charismatic Jo Grimond, her hero since she was seven, when she had known him as her brother's school friend. All this effort had resulted in Basil Young winning the seat with a majority of two thousand from a surprised and very disgruntled Tory candidate, Charles Hamilton-Sinclair. Since that time she had acted as unpaid election agent and the organising force for the local Liberal Democrats.

When Mike arrived at her house, Minty was sitting at her kitchen table enjoying a cup of tea and reading the *Guardian*. She took one look at him, lifted a rather fine Minton cup from the cupboard, dropped a teabag into it and topped it up with water from the kettle sitting on the Aga.

'Milk?'

Mike nodded and sat down at the table. Minty fished out the teabag and dropped it into a large china chamberpot, which served as a compost bin, then added some milk and handed him the cup.

'What's the problem, then? Much as you and I like each other's company, you are not in the habit of dropping in at this time for a cup of tea.'

'I need your help, Minty. I don't know what to do about the Taha family. I don't know how to play it, and no one seems to be much help, certainly not Gill. Ian's got chickenpox and that's all she can think about, and none of my colleagues have any constructive advice. They're just glad it wasn't them who got the visas. God, I wish I'd never bothered!'

'Well, when I saw the Tahas yesterday, they were holding it together quite well, and now Poni's out of danger, they're thinking constructively about their future.'

'You saw them yesterday? I didn't know you knew them!'

'Oh, yes, I've been teaching Settina English for several months now. I was behind her in the queue in the post office and I could see she didn't understand what the girl was saying to her, so I did a bit of translating. I learned some Arabic a few years ago before I went to visit my godson. He was ambassador in Cairo, you know. It was extremely useful in the souk. I managed to do some very successful haggling. Got that rug the dog's lying on for a song.' She waved her hand in the direction of an elderly spaniel, which was sound asleep on a small Persian prayer mat. 'Anyway, we managed with the post-office lady in a mixture of English and Arabic. I offered Settina a lift home and then I started visiting once a week to give her English lessons. I got her to go to mother-and-toddler group. If anyone is to blame for the visas it's me, because I advised her husband, Jafar, to come and get your help. But if you do things in good faith, there is no point in torturing yourself.'

Mike didn't know what to say and before he could formulate a reply, Minty was off again. 'I just thought yesterday that I should go to Edinburgh to the hospital and see if I could be of any support to Settina. Some of these nurses just don't seem to realise that English might be a problem for some people. So I went over to the hospital. Turns out they were fine as there was a Sudanese nurse on the ward, so it was I who had the language problem. Anyway, you can console yourself that they weren't part of this and are very upset at what has been done. One reason they came here was to escape things like that.

But they don't blame you, so don't blame yourself.' She paused in her narrative to take a mouthful of tea and then continued, 'They're moving, though. They won't be back to live in Corrachan. Jafar's got a transfer to his company's factory in Leicester. Best that way – some anonymity for Poni.'

Mike stared in disbelief. All the time he had been worrying about the family and the political fallout and Minty had been sorting it out.

'What should I do? Should I write or go and see them?'

'They will be back here at the weekend to pack up. I'm sure they would be happy to see you. I think you need to talk to them to understand this. It's part of their culture, and although they don't like it and didn't wish it for their daughter, they don't view it in quite the same way as you do.'

'Minty, you have no idea how wonderful you are. I just wish you had told me all this days ago.'

'I told you on the night you were elected I was here for advice if you wanted it, but you are the MP, not me, and I am not going to become an interfering old woman. I do have one further idea to put to you, however. Then I will shut up and leave you to get on with things.' Before she could tell him, the dog stood up with some difficulty and walked to the back door, where it barked and looked at Minty.

'All right, then, just a minute. I'm coming.' She got up, opened the door and then returned to her seat. 'Where was I? That's the terrible thing about getting old: something distracts you and you forget what you were doing and saying.'

'You had an idea?'

'Oh, yes! That's right! Why don't you make female circumcision a speciality? Find out about it. Make yourself an expert because it's an important issue within the ethnic-diversity debate. When does one person's acceptable custom become someone else's grievous bodily harm? If we are going to have an inclusive society that recognises diversity, then it's issues like this that will be the stumbling blocks. We are going to need politicians who understand the complexity of the situation. What do you think?'

Mike looked at her in amazement. He was actually speechless. This old woman seemed to have sorted the situation, absolved him from blame and seen the way forward.

'Well, Mike, don't you think that would be a useful thing to do? You look doubtful?'

'I'm just stunned that what has been consuming my thoughts for days seems now to be all sorted. You appear to have found solutions for everything.'

'Not quite everything, but I can't be doing with sitting around saying, "Isn't this dreadful?" If there is a problem, there is a solution and there is no point wasting time feeling sorry for yourself. Just get on and sort it. I can give you a whole lot of literature on the subject that I got off the Internet, and there is a seminar in Edinburgh soon about this. Book yourself on. Go and see the Tahas at the weekend, then file it in your "I'll know next time" folder and get on with other things.'

'Thanks, Minty. Don't know how we would all manage without you.'

'The churchyard is full of indispensable people. You'd manage. Now, a small malt for the road?'

'That would be very welcome, Minty. Thank you.'

Chapter Eight

Phyllis sat in Chez Marguerite toying with a goat's cheese and spinach tartlet, while Joyce Macdonald tucked into lasagne and held forth about the chairwoman of the Save the Children committee and her inability to chair a meeting. They had spent the morning at the planning meeting for the Christmas Fayre and various old grievances about who was to be responsible for what had been taken out and aired. Joyce had lost control of the baking stall to Helen Cooper and had been given *Christmas decorations* instead. She was not pleased.

'Helen had obviously been on the phone before the meeting to half the committee to lobby support. It's so underhand, you know.'

Phyllis was not really paying attention. She had said 'Yes', 'No' and 'Oh dear', as was expected of her, but her mind was on Jack and his recent out-of-character behaviour. He seemed to be forgetful, snappy and was of the belief that Her Majesty's Revenue had a vendetta against him. At a recent visit to the hairdresser, she had read an article about the early symptoms of Alzheimer's disease, many of which Jack seemed to be displaying. His behaviour at breakfast this morning had further fuelled her fears of a future caring for a husband with dementia.

It was the Caldwells' custom to spend part of February in Madeira. Two weeks of comfort, bridge and sunshine at Reid's Hotel was the perfect antidote to a Scottish winter and Phyllis had remarked at breakfast that she intended to go to the travel agent that afternoon to book the holiday. She had been totally unprepared for Jack's reaction. Instead of the expected grunt of agreement, he had announced he wasn't going to Madeira. They should wait and go away later in the year, a Caribbean cruise next autumn perhaps.

'That's nearly a year away,' Phyllis had protested. 'We'll need to see the sun before that or we'll fade away. We usually go to Cyprus in September, anyway. I thought we could go to that new place with the five-star hotel and the golf course near Paphos. Kyrenia was pretty this year, but I prefer the Greek part. And you spent all your time with the people you met at the Kyrenia Rotary Club and I hardly saw you. Why not Madeira? We've been going for years.'

'Time we had a change, then.'

'But, Jack, why this sudden change of mind? Why didn't you tell me?'

'Phyllis, we are not going. That's my final word on the matter.'

With that he had left the house. No proper explanation at all. They had been going to Madeira for years and they had always agreed that without a fortnight in the sun, the long winter would be unbearable. Regular holidays in prestige hotels were part of their lifestyle and Jack had never been one to allow business to get in the way of his recreational activities. When he used that tone of voice, however, she knew better than to argue with him.

'Don't you think I'm right, Phyllis?' barked Joyce.

'Sorry, Joyce, what were you saying?'

'I said that the takings will be down if the baking stall is not run properly, and Helen Cooper doesn't have any idea who usually bakes for us. She also under-prices things. The Lifeboat coffee morning was a case in point.'

'Mmm. I'm sure you're right.'

'Whatever is the matter with you, Phyllis? You've not been on form all day.'

Phyllis told her about Jack and Madeira.

'Hmph. That's men for you. Just assume that you'll do whatever they suggest. If he won't go away in February, go by yourself.'

Phyllis was appalled. You would have thought that Joyce had suggested that she run naked through the town. 'Oh, I couldn't do that! I couldn't go to a hotel by myself! I would hate it. Jack always sees to the currency and the tips and deals with everything. I wouldn't know where to begin.'

Joyce looked at her in exasperation. 'Well, go away and stay with a friend or something. You need to make a stand. Don't be the compliant little woman.' She picked up the menu and began to consider the desserts. 'Do you want pudding? I think I'll treat myself to the pecan and maple pie.'

'No, just coffee.'

Phyllis prided herself on still being a size twelve, unlike Joyce, whose ample bosom and well-upholstered rear could not be squeezed into anything smaller than an eighteen. Joyce's response made Phyllis feel like a silly girl, but at least she, Phyllis, watched her weight and took care of her appearance. She had an elaborate daily cleansing and toning routine, and she had her hair and nails done each week, while Joyce just rubbed in some moisturiser when she remembered. Joyce didn't see the point in being smartly turned out whatever the occasion, but Phyllis felt that she was a commercial for all Jack's business interests and if she wasn't looking her best, then it would reflect on him. Accordingly, she had an extensive wardrobe, courtesy of regular shopping trips to Edinburgh. Passing pedestrians would see her weeding the garden wearing an immaculate cashmere cardigan and a pair of tailored tweed trousers. That was how Phyllis liked it.

'Perhaps I could go to London to stay with Evelyn, my school friend. She never married, but she's got a very good job in the House of Commons library. I must ask her if she knows Mike Andrews. She's always asking me to come down. They should have all the spring ranges in the shops by February.'

'There you are, then. Don't you feel better already? Alistair! Could we have one pecan pie and two cappuccinos, please?'

'I'll have my coffee black, please,' said Phyllis.

She wasn't going to let Joyce boss her about. The thought of a London shopping trip was cheering her up. She would phone Evelyn when she got home.

By the time Joyce had had her pecan pie, they were the only customers in the restaurant. Alistair brought them their coffees and inquired if they had enjoyed their lunch. Then Frank emerged from the kitchen to say hello. Frank and Alistair were, on the surface, an unlikely couple – Alistair from the privileged world of public school and the country estate, and Frank from the less privileged world of Catholic secondary school and Glasgow council estate – but they had both been misfits in the world they had been expected to inhabit. Alistair suffered his parents' mixture of disappointment and denial, but Frank had not even told his family. In his part of Glasgow, no one admitted that the closet existed, let alone emerged from it.

The couple were well accepted in the town, even by those who could not be said to approve, although whenever one or other of them was seen coming out of the health centre, the rumours of an HIV-positive diagnosis or full-blown AIDS did the rounds. Phyllis did not like to think what went on in the flat above the restaurant, but Joyce was more tolerant, and as someone who hated hypocrisy, she did not approve of the attitude of Alistair's parents. While she was paying the bill, she thought she had better tell Alistair that his mother had plans.

'Your mother was telling me that she is having a little party just before Christmas with several suitable unmarried "gels" for your perusal.'

'Oh God, she's not, is she? She just doesn't give up. She knows I'm not interested and she also knows that we are so busy here at Christmas that I don't have any time off. How do I make her realise it's a waste of time?'

'I don't know. Explain your orientation in words of one syllable?'

'Done that! The only two-syllable word I used was "mother". The other words were "I AM GAY". You don't think she still believes the word means "happy", do you?'

'Your mother can be a little unworldly, but she's not totally detached from reality.'

'Joyce, you could adopt me. Life would be much easier if you were my mother. And Phyllis could adopt Frank. He hasn't seen his mother for years. You could both come on the next Gay Pride march with us.'

'That sounds good, Phyllis. Are you up for that?' laughed Frank.

Phyllis looked uncomfortable. She had a lot of sympathy for Alistair's mother. Imagine even suggesting that she adopt a gay Glaswegian chef. It wasn't something to joke about.

'Alistair! You shouldn't say things like that. Your poor mother.'

'Phyllis, I love her dearly, but she and Pa have to accept me for what I am, not what they want me to be. I suppose I'd better go and see her tomorrow and sort this nonsense out. Thanks, Joyce. Don't know what I would do without my spies.'

Joyce and Phyllis strolled down the road and into the town centre. It was the end of November and all the shops were bedecked with fake snow, tinsel and fairy lights.

'They are so early with their decorations nowadays. We never put ours up till a couple of days before Christmas,' mused Joyce.

'What are you doing at Christmas?' Phyllis inquired.

'Louise, David and the family are coming to stay. Christmas is much more fun when there are small children about, isn't it? What about you?'

Phyllis had no idea whether or not Christmas was more fun with small children. She thought Joyce could have been more tactful about mentioning children. She had been Phyllis's friend since their twenties, when they had both been newly married. Joyce had quickly become pregnant with Douglas – in fact, he was a honeymoon baby – and then three years later, Louise had arrived. At first, Phyllis built her hopes up each month but then had come to expect disappointment. At Joyce's insistence, she had gone to see her GP, an elderly man nearing retirement, who had advised her to stop thinking about it and nature would take its course. It hadn't. The next step was 'investigations'. Phyllis had endured the embarrassment and indignity of that, but there had been no obvious cause and adoption had been suggested. Jack would not countenance it. He said that he wasn't going to bring up someone else's mistakes, so there were no babies in the house. She had come to terms with her child-lessness eventually, keeping herself busy running her house and her charities and being the perfect hostess. For several years, when her friends' children had left home, she had not felt the aching inadequacy, but now, when all her circle were glorying in being grandparents, she felt the emptiness once again – especially when photos were passed round and the achievements of the next generation boasted about. Joyce had been so understanding in the past, but she did not realise that chatter about grandchildren reopened old wounds.

Phyllis and Jack used to spend what they called a 'quiet family Christmas', which included only Jack's elderly, religious and disagreeable mother for turkey and all the trimmings. Jack was an only child and Phyllis had been very good to his mother. Every day she would visit the sheltered flat with containers of soup and casseroles ready to deal with the dirty laundry. For this she received no thanks from the woman who considered that her son had married beneath himself and whose only wish was to be 'called to her higher reward'. Finally, last February, after many years of prayer, God granted her request. So this year it was just the two of them.

'Oh, I'm not sure what we shall be doing. Jack and I might go out for Christmas dinner or even go away to a hotel for a few days now that we don't have his mother to consider.'

The fact that she would not cook Christmas dinner had just occurred to Phyllis and the more she thought about it, the more she liked the idea. Three nights in a decent hotel would be nice, especially if they weren't going to Madeira. Gleneagles, perhaps, or one of these luxury country-house hotels. One with a spa would be a treat. She would sort it out when she got home.

She glanced across the street and saw Gill trying to steer the double buggy along the pavement. She could hear that little boy screaming from here. He certainly seemed to be very angry about something. Christmas in luxurious surroundings without little children suddenly seemed much more appealing.

Chapter Nine

Gill had decided that a walk to the town centre with the children in the buggy might send both of them to sleep. She would have to turn her mind to Christmas soon, so it would be useful to see what was in the shops. The dog looked at her inquiringly, as outings with the buggy usually meant a walk.

'Not today, Penny, but I'll put you in the back garden till we get back.' She opened the back door and shooed the slightly huffy dog into the enclosed garden.

Despite the walk, Ian was still awake when she entered the Emporium. Following the demise of Woolworths, Jack Caldwell had bought the premises and was attempting to run the shop as a cross between its predecessor and a pound shop. It was at its Christmas best with decorations, cards, sweets, toys and selected tat of all descriptions. She balanced a wire basket on top of the buggy and filled it with chocolate decorations for the tree, a set of fairy lights and several strands of tinsel. Ian was being surprisingly biddable, so she thought she would stroll down the toy aisle with a view to returning on her own at the weekend. She stopped to examine a box of Duplo. She took it off the shelf to have a closer look. On the shelf below, there were large plastic trucks. Ian leaned out of the buggy and managed to get hold of one. Gill removed it from his hands, replaced it on the shelf and moved on. Ian's speech was quite good but he did still have problems with two consonants together, like 'tr'.

'Wan big vuck!' he whined. 'Wan vuck!'

Why couldn't it have been a car? 'Truck' was a word they tried to avoid in public places.

'Well, you can ask Santa to bring it for Christmas.'

'No Santa. Wan vuck now!'

'Well, you can't have it now. We'll go and look and see if there's a book for you along here.'

Ian was cross now. He raised his voice. 'Vuck, vuck, vuck!'

Various shoppers positively identified them as the MP's wife and her out-of-control, abusive toddler. Working on the distraction theory, Gill made for the shelf of children's books in the hope that if she moved very quickly, no one would be able to make out what Ian was saying. She saw a plastic-covered bath book about trains for £1.99. That would do.

'Here's a book with lots of engines. Let's get that.'

'Wan big vuck,' he yelled.

'Ssshhhh, Ian. Here, look at this book. It'll float in your bath.'

She handed him the book, but he started to cry, getting louder and louder as she made her way towards the checkout near the exit.

'WAN VUCK! WAN VUCK! VUCK NOW!' screamed Ian. He hurled the book sideways, hitting an elderly lady on the shins as she was considering whether to top off her pick-and-mix selection with three raspberry creams or just toffees as usual.

Gill bent to pick up the book and to check that the pensioner was not seriously injured. 'I'm so sorry. Are you all right? He's just at the terrible twos at the moment.'

'Aye, I'm fine. It missed my varicose ulcer. I always found a good skelp on the backside worked wonders when mine were wee.'

'Thank you. I think we are fast approaching that point.'

'Vuck. Wan vuck!' screamed Ian.

The pensioner, who up to this point had been quite sympathetic, now adopted a different attitude. 'He needs his mouth washed out with soapy water! It's disgusting a child of two knowing words like that.' She glared fiercely at Gill. 'You ought to be ashamed of yourself.'

All the Christmas shoppers now stopped what they were doing and turned to look. Some of them had even heard about the mother-and-toddler incident and were enthralled to be present at another outburst from the MP's foul-mouthed child. Gill decided that standing in a checkout queue was out of the question, immediate flight being her only option. While she was bending down to 'hide' her basket under a rack of pink lurex party dresses for the under-fives, Ian threw his piece of flannelette sheet out of the buggy. As Gill moved towards the door, the assembled audience at the checkout were treated to Ian's wails of 'SHIT! SHIT! SHIT, MUMMY! SHIT!'

Gill didn't pause as she swept through the automatic doors and out on to the High Street. There were plenty of other pieces of sheet at home. As the door closed behind her, the checkout operator, Mrs Low, who had recently seen a documentary on Channel Four about Tourette's syndrome, remarked to Mrs McNeill, whom she was serving, that perhaps that was the little boy's problem, and a rumour was born.

Gill walked home. Zipping up the plastic cover to muffle Ian's shouts, she could feel the flush on her cheeks and cringed as she relived the outburst. This would be all over town now. She couldn't have chosen a better place for the jungle drums to work to maximum effect. She saw Phyllis and Joyce watching her from the other side of the road. How she wished Ian would stop making that awful noise. She pushed the buggy briskly in the direction of home and as she passed the health centre saw Ali coming out of the door, trailing Matt behind her. She waved and waited for Ali to catch up so she could tell her of her latest humiliation. As Ali approached, Gill saw that she was wiping away the tears. She looked dreadful. Crushed was the best way to describe it. Something awful must have happened.

'Ali, what's the matter? What's happened?'

'It's Matt. I've just seen the paediatrician and the psychologist.' She burst into fresh sobs.

'Have you got the car? No? Right, come on, up the road and you can tell me what's the matter.'

Gill shepherded the weeping Ali into her house and sat her at the kitchen table. Something more medicinal than tea was in order, so she made a very large gin and tonic and went to check on the three children. Kate and Ian were now both asleep in the buggy, and she put Matt in the corner of the kitchen and opened the door of her pot cupboard. The dog was barking, so she went to let her in and noticed that the horrible Rottweiler from down the road was in the garden again. It was always getting through the hedge to play. Penny shot between Gill's legs into the kitchen. She closed the door and sat down.

'Right, then, Ali, tell me what this is all about.'

'Well, you know that Matt wouldn't settle at nursery and I had to take him to the speech and language therapist and then they wanted me to see the community paediatrician and the psychologist. I've been trailing back and forth all over the place for weeks while people looked at him and asked me questions. Today was a meeting with all of them to "discuss their findings". Tom was supposed to come with me, but he had to take

Mr Bruce's funeral at the crematorium. He thought he might get back in time, but he never showed up.'

'Couldn't he have arranged the funeral for another time? They can't do it without him.'

'One thirty was the only time available, and Mr Bruce's daughter, who lives in Canada, flies back tomorrow.'

'It's nearly half three now. Do you want to phone and see if he's home?'

'No. He can stew.'

'OK. Tell me what happened.'

'Well, they talked round in circles for a while, but they finally got to what they wanted to say. He's autistic. Well, "on the autistic spectrum" was what they said.'

'Ah!'

'You knew!'

'I had a suspicion.'

'You might have told me!'

'I might have been wrong.'

'I don't know anything about it. I've not had anything to do with autism.'

'Well, it tends to run in families, so perhaps you need look no further than your brother-in-law.'

'Peter?'

'My guess is that if Peter was at school now, he would be labelled as autistic.'

'I'm very fond of him, but he seems such a lonely man. I want Matt to grow up and marry and have a family – not have a solitary, regimented existence.'

'Perhaps "self-contained" is a better word than "lonely". I don't think Peter's unhappy.'

Ali swallowed half her gin in a gulp. 'Mmm. Perhaps.'

'Are you going to get any help?'

'Yes, he'll get a sort of chart at nursery so he knows what's going to happen next and we're going to see the speech and language therapist. They also said that he could have another year at nursery. It's one thing suspecting something is wrong, it's another knowing that it is. You always imagine that your children are going to be successful and popular.' Ali started to cry again.

Gill topped up the gin and tonic and poured herself one too. She thought she deserved it.

'Well, my afternoon hasn't been as traumatic as yours, but it has certainly been embarrassing! Ian has been throwing books at old ladies and shouting "fuck" and "shit" at the top of his voice in the Emporium.'

'He what?'

Gill explained. Ali managed a laugh through her tears.

'Perhaps they couldn't hear properly what he was shouting.'

'By the looks on their faces, I think they could.'

'Your son has got a knack of making life as difficult as possible for you, hasn't he?'

'Yes, he certainly has.' Gill paused and looked at Ali. 'And your son isn't going to make your life impossible. Teachers are much more clued up about learning difficulties.'

This was not the best choice of words. Ali bristled. 'He's not got learning difficulties! He's very intelligent sometimes. He might not be a conversationalist, but he knows all the names of his dinosaurs. I couldn't remember all that!'

'OK, OK, calm down. Learning difficulties doesn't necessarily mean he's unintelligent. But enough of the lecture. Come on, drink up, then you had better go home . . . and tell Tom.'

'I suppose I can't put it off, so I should get on with it.' Ali stood up and sat down again. 'God, that was a strong gin, especially on an empty stomach. I've been so nervous about the meeting I haven't eaten all day.'

'Stay there,' said Gill. 'I'll make you a coffee and a sandwich.

If you have to explain it all to Tom, you'll need to be coherent at least.'

As Gill was making a bacon sandwich, Ali glanced at a pile of papers on the kitchen table. She picked up several sheets, which were stapled together, and held them at arm's length between two fingers.

'What is this about? It's revolting!'

'Sorry, I hadn't realised Mike had left it lying around. It's his new hobby.'

'Hobby? Female circumcision is his new hobby?'

'Don't speak! Minty told Mike to make it his special interest and there are printouts and diagrams all over the place. He could score twenty points at least on *Mastermind*. "Name?" "Mike Andrews." "Occupation?" "Member of Parliament." "Specialist subject?" "Female genital mutilation in sub-Saharan Africa." When I've eventually settled Kate and come to bed, he's reading all this stuff and showing me the diagrams and photographs. If I wasn't already this asexual automaton craving nothing but sleep, it would put me right off.'

Ali turned over the page and looked at the photographs. 'Ugh. I'm not surprised! Reading this would put you off for ever.' She shifted in her seat. 'It certainly makes it difficult to sit comfortably.'

After half an hour, Ali felt a bit better and was fit to leave. She was going to have to be the positive one when she got home. Tom spent so long propping up the emotionally needy he seemed to be unable to deal with similar situations at home. He had become even more withdrawn recently – a vortex of negative energy that sucked the joy from everyone else in the house – but he refused to talk about it.

Matt had taken all the pots and pans out of the cupboard and had arranged them in a long line in diminishing order of size. He was midway through doing the same thing with the lids. Ali took hold of his hand to pull him to his feet.

'Come on, Matt, time to go home now.'

He resisted her pull, yanked his hand out of hers with a shriek and sat down again to select the next lid for his sequence.

'Let him finish, Ali. He won't take long.'

When the line of lids was complete, Matt picked up his dinosaur and stood passively regarding the pans while his mother put his arms into his fleece and took him by the hand. Gill walked with her to the front door and put a hand on her shoulder.

'Hope the conversation with Tom goes OK. If you want me to explain about autism, I will. Phone me?'

Ali gave her a semblance of a smile. 'Thanks, but I don't expect it will make much difference.'

As Ali walked down the path, Phyllis was standing at her lounge window ostensibly dusting her ornaments. They were not in need of cleaning and she had been flicking a duster over them since she had returned home after walking up the road behind Gill and the weeping Ali. She was having trouble deciding what was wrong. She had considered bereavement . . . Ali's mother, perhaps? She was quite frail – she had seen her in church when she came to visit. Or another relative? Or was it to do with Tom? Had they had a fight? Perhaps that trollop of a daughter of theirs had got into trouble again. That was the most likely answer – she had discovered that her oh-so-perfect medical-student daughter wasn't the paragon of virtue she thought she was. Phyllis watched Ali and Matt disappear along the road and wondered how she could find out. It was such a pity that Gill was not the chatty sort of neighbour Kitty McPherson had been. She wondered if Joyce had heard anything. It would be useful to know, otherwise it was so easy to put one's foot in it . . . to say the wrong thing, to offend someone. Definitely much better to be in possession of the facts and it made her feel uncomfortable that, in this case, she wasn't. She reached for the phone and dialled Joyce's number.

Chapter Ten

Gill was 'on duty' on the day of the mother-and-toddler Christmas party. This meant she was responsible for Santa's sack in the corner of the church-hall kitchen where mothers had to put a small wrapped gift with their child's name on it. Later in the proceedings, Tom was due to appear in the Santa outfit that lived in a cupboard in the vestry and hand out the largesse to the delight of the assembled tots.

Angela arrived without the required gifts for Allan and three-week-old Kieran. She was at the stage where she was doing well if she had managed to get dressed before lunchtime.

'I've not got any money with me. I can't go and buy anything,' she had wailed.

Ali gestured towards the carrier bag in the corner. 'There are some books that I wrapped in there and some blank gift tags. I thought someone might forget.'

'Didn't forget,' said a sulky Angela. 'No one told me.'

Phyllis Caldwell had been imported for the occasion to play the piano and she was thumping her way through 'The Farmer's in His Den' in the main hall. This was not the best musical game for young children as it involved one child choosing another. The most popular were chosen to be the farmer and his family, the less popular were not picked at all, and the most unpopular was chosen to be the bone and was battered by all the others. As Phyllis finished the end of the 'We all pat the bone' line, half the children were in tears from pain or a dawning realisation that their peers disliked them.

Phyllis launched into 'In and Out the Dusty Bluebells' and drummed up business for the local chiropractor as adults bent double to get under the 'arches' created by two-year-olds. This was followed by Pass the Parcel. Ali went and stood beside Phyllis and told her when to stop playing in order to make sure that every child had the chance to remove a wrapper and that Chantelle, a permanently snotty child with a squint, who was not usually one of life's winners, was the one who removed the last sheet of wrapping paper.

After Musical Bumps, the children repaired to the table, where the usual fruit and Ribena had been replaced by crisps, pizza fingers, Rice Krispie squares and Coke. While they were eating and spreading sticky bits all over the floor, which would later hamper the players in the Badminton League, Gill went to the vestry to check that Tom had managed to transform himself from minister to Santa and to take him the sack of presents. Opting for the jolly approach, she knocked on the door and shouted, 'Ho! Ho! Ho!'

There was no reply. She opened the door and saw the Santa outfit and beard on the chair but no Tom. She checked her watch. They were into the last twenty minutes of the party and it would take at least fifteen minutes to hand out the presents and sing 'Jingle Bells'. She opened the door into the church, but it was dark and silent, so she stuck her head round the door of the Gents' and called his name. Silence. Had he forgotten the time? She went outside and walked the short distance to the manse, but there was no one there. Where on earth was he? Back in the vestry, there was still no sign of him and she could hear Phyllis playing 'Away in a Manger', accompanied by various tuneless voices. This was obviously the build-up to Santa's arrival.

Gill considered dressing up herself, but at five foot three and a generous thirty-four D cup, she was not really the correct build. In desperation, she went out to check the car park. There was no sign of the man of the cloth, but there was a man of commerce sitting in his top-of-the-range Volvo smoking a cigar and reading the *Daily Mail*.

Jack Caldwell had arrived a little early to pick up Phyllis. He was doing his best to be nice to her as she was still sulking about Madeira, even though he had agreed to three nights at Gleneagles over Christmas. He would at least have good food and wine and a game of golf if the weather was reasonable, while Phyllis pampered herself. He needed to win his way back into her favour, and if he saved her a walk in the rain, he thought she might thaw out a little.

'Jack!' said Gill, opening the car door and grasping hold of his hand. 'I need you now!'

Jack, who had been reading an article about Kylie Minogue and having a pleasant little fantasy about Kylie saying much the same thing to him, couldn't believe his ears. Gill Andrews was a pleasant enough little thing, but he had never considered her in that way and he had never been propositioned in the church car park before. (Well, not since 1958, when Joyce Wilson, later Macdonald, had taken him outside at a Youth Fellowship dance.)

'Sorry! What did you say?'

'I need you to be Santa. Tom Graham has disappeared and the children are waiting for their presents. Phyllis is running out of tunes to play. Come on! Please!'

Jack found himself dragged into the vestry and hurried into the Santa outfit.

'There should be a present for every child with their name on it. Just go in, sit on the chair and hand out the presents. When you've finished, they will sing "Jingle Bells" and you can leave.' She thrust the sack into his hand. 'Count to twenty and follow me.'

Gill entered the hall and gave the thumbs-up to Ali, who said, 'Children, I think I can hear sleigh bells,' in a Joyce Grenfell tone of voice.

Phyllis launched into 'Jingle Bells' and Jack made his entrance. Ali looked at this corpulent six-foot-two Santa who certainly wasn't Tom. She looked at Gill, who raised her eyebrows.

Jack sat himself down on the chair, opened the sack and pulled out a present. Now he was dressed up, he was throwing himself into the role.

'Hello, boys and girls. How are you today? I have a present here for someone called Ryan. Is Ryan here? Come and get your present, Ryan.'

Ryan sidled up and was about to take his present and run when Jack took hold of his hand and asked, 'And what do you want me to bring you for Christmas?'

Ryan averted his gaze and muttered, 'PlayStation.'

'That's for your toy train, is it? I'll see what I can do.'

Jack passed Ryan his present, then delved into the sack again. 'Allan!' he said.

Allan ran up and grabbed his present, dodged sideways and fled before Jack had a chance to quiz him on his requirements.

'Kerry-Ann?'

A child with ringlets wearing one of the lurex dresses from the Emporium skipped up.

'And what do you want, then?'

'A Wii.'

Jack assumed she was on the point of wetting her pants. 'Well, take your present quick and go and ask your mummy to take you.'

'Chantelle?'

The unfortunate Chantelle walked up to Jack with her mouth wide open on account of her catarrhal problem and gazed at him through her thick glasses.

'And what do you want for Christmas, young lady?'

Chantelle continued to gaze at Jack in silence. The extent of her squint was slightly disconcerting and Jack found himself turning round to see what she was looking at. 'Would you like me to bring you some toys?'

Chantelle silently nodded her head, took her present and returned to her place.

'Ian,' called Santa.

Over the past weeks, Ian had been getting excited about Santa and now he had a chance to get a close look at him. He had been holding Gill's hand and giggling as each name was read out. Now he heard his name and he ran up to get his present, which was being held in the large red hand with the fingers that resembled beef sausages.

'And what do you want me to put in your stocking?' said Jack, bending down to get close to Ian.

Something stirred in Ian's memory about loud voices and large red hands with sausage fingers and his face crumpled. He looked round in rising panic and wailed, 'Mummy!' He fled back to Gill.

Jack got up and walked towards Ian with the present, saying, 'Here's your present, young man. No need to be frightened of Santa. Santa likes little boys.'

Ian looked as if Santa liked little boys for breakfast and buried his face in Gill's chest, howling, 'Go away, Santa, go away!'

Gill stretched out her hand, took the present and Jack returned to his sack.

'Shit! Shit!' shouted Ian, knowing that the comforting piece of flannelette sheet was in the nappy bag. Tourette's syndrome was now confirmed.

The children were beginning to wonder if Santa was in fact a child-eating giant in disguise. Luckily, the next few presents were for babies and collected by the mothers. When Angela, in her postnatal haze, went up to get Kieran's present, she suddenly woke up to the fact that Santa was not Tom. She looked at the towering figure in red and started to giggle. It was the best thing she could have done, as the tense atmosphere melted away and the remaining gifts were given without too much fear and alarm.

After he had handed out the final present in the sack, Jack noticed Matt in the corner, holding on to Ali, and realised that he had not given him a present. Like many autistic children, Matt found Christmas very stressful. The routine was different, there were all sorts of bright lights and tinsel, and a strange man with a beard and red suit was going to come into your house in the middle of the night. Ali had told Matt that Santa would leave a present for him at the door as he left; in fact, she had already put it there.

Had Tom been Santa, the problem would not have arisen, but Jack thought that he had missed one child out and decided to make amends. He walked towards Matt and tried to take his hand. Physical contact with those Matt knew well was bad enough, but he could not cope with being touched by those he didn't know. Matt's anxiety level went through the roof and he started to scream. Jack backed off and looked at Ali.

'Just leave it on the shelf by the door and we'll get it later, Santa,' said Ali over the screams of terror.

The teacher in Gill took over. 'Right, children, Santa's got to go now as he has lots of toys still to make before Christmas. So wave bye-bye and we'll sing "Jingle Bells" as Santa goes back to his sleigh.' She nodded at Phyllis, who had been more than a little surprised to see her husband dressed up.

'Phyllis! "Jingle Bells"? Please?'

Santa departed to the vestry and thence to his turbo-charged, Swedish-engineered, tinted-window sleigh in the car park. Children were bundled into coats and then into buggies or cars and taken home. Ali had managed to calm Matt by finding the wrapped parcel that contained a new dinosaur, so Santa was forgiven. She was now trying to sweep up the sticky bits of Rice Krispie squares, while Gill mopped up spilt juice with a rather insanitary squeezy mop.

'Well, thank God that's over,' said Gill, as she leaned on her mop. 'I think we ought to video the next party and send it round the secondary schools to go with the contraceptive lecture. Much cheaper than giving everyone a crying, peeing doll.'

'Jack was quite a good Santa . . . until he got chatty. Then they all thought he was going to eat them. I wish I knew where the hell Tom is. I reminded him about the party at lunchtime. He could at least have come and told me if there was a problem. It's not as if it was far from the house. Surely it would have occurred to him that there would be a sackful of toys and no one to give them out.'

'Perhaps he left a note on the kitchen table or somewhere. I didn't look for notes when I went to see if he was there.'

'We're more or less finished here. Let's go and see and have a glass of something medicinal.'

When they got back to the manse, there was no Tom and no note. His mobile seemed to be switched off, so perhaps there had been some sort of emergency and he was at the hospital. Ali opened a bottle of wine and filled two generous glasses.

'Compliments of the season! Well, that's the first of several stress-inducing activities. Next is the nativity play. I refused to be involved in casting this year, as most of the parents are still not speaking to me after last year. All the Heavenly Host thought they ought to have been Mary, all the shepherds thought they should have been Joseph, and all the animals in the stable thought they ought to have been shepherds. Immediately after saying, "Behold! I bring you glad tidings of great joy," the Angel Gabriel vomited all over the shepherds, so by the time we got to the end everyone was in tears. I think they're doing a non-speaking tableau this year, with all parts drawn out of a hat.'

'Sometimes I miss teaching, but when it comes to Christmas performances, I'll be a brain-dead bottom-wiper any day.'

Ali looked at her watch. 'It's quarter to five. Where the hell is he?' She tried Tom's mobile again but still no reply. 'He could at least find a payphone and let me know where he is.'

Tom was in the car, sitting in the pitch dark in the car park beside Loch Corrachan, some five miles from home. At two o'clock, he had decided to go for a drive to try to clear his head. He knew he needed to think things through properly and he couldn't do it in the manse with all the comings and goings. He had an hour and a half before the party and he had to get away from everyone. Things were getting worse and now he had a child with special needs to consider. In his unwillingness to confront small problems, they had grown into something too large to contemplate, let alone solve. He wasn't sleeping well. He wasn't eating properly. He was constantly tired and seemed to have a semi-permanent headache. He felt as if he was clinging on to a rock while the waves were breaking over him and there was no one to pull him up, just lots of people trying to pull him under. It wouldn't have to be a big wave to wash him out to sea.

Sitting in the car, he closed his eyes, letting his thoughts drift. When he woke up, it was dark. He turned on the ignition and the dashboard clock showed four fifteen. He had missed the party. Ali would be so cross. It seemed easier just to sit here a while longer – to hide from everyone in the darkness. He turned on the engine to heat up the car and closed his eyes again.

Chapter Eleven

Christmas in Corrachan had come and gone in its usual fashion. People had met the same people in various houses, over the same smoked-salmon canapés and mulled wine until they longed for an alcohol-free evening at home with a boiled egg.

Mike and Gill had both sets of parents to stay. Mike's parents were there for Christmas and Gill's for New Year. Ian was in a permanent state of over-indulgence and over-excitement. By 3 January, when everyone had gone, Gill and Mike were in a state of collapse.

Ali had believed Tom's story about the car breaking down and his long wait for the AA on the day of the mother-and-toddler party. He had only been berated for not letting her know where he was. This had further fuelled his self-loathing. He knew he told lies more often than the truth these days and that in itself was exhausting, without coming on top of a hectic schedule of carol services and Christmas events where he had to appear cheery and in control. On Boxing Day, Ali had suggested they take down the decorations and tree because Matt was getting so upset. Despite the girls' complaints, it was decreed that peace with Matt was more important than tinsel and twinkling lights.

Ali and Tom retired to their own areas in the house – Tom to his study to brood and Ali to the kitchen – and life returned more or less to normal.

Phyllis and Jack had three nights at Gleneagles Hotel. Unfortunately, it was sleeting most of the time, so Jack didn't get any golf, but he found a congenial self-made businessman like himself who was happy to keep him company at the bar all day, while their wives enjoyed the facilities at the leisure centre. Phyllis did not get on quite so well with the wife of Jack's drinking partner, whom she considered to be over-familiar, over-made up and over-adorned with large diamonds. She was disappointed to find out at the gala dinner that they were sitting next to them rather than the retired surgeon and his wife from Aberdeen with whom Phyllis had had coffee and an interesting chat between her massage and swim. She had decided there was definitely something about wearing dressing gowns that broke the ice and encouraged conversation, although there were some conversational topics she could have done without, including the self-made lady's menstrual problems, her resulting hysterectomy and its effect on her love life, which had never been the same. Although Phyllis was glad to get home, she felt she had to embellish the stay when she saw Joyce, who was full of the wonderful time she had had, showing off pictures of small children opening stockings.

Alistair and Frank were permanently busy from the beginning of December with work nights out and Christmas lunches, as well as people like the Andrews who were entertaining visiting relatives. Alistair had staved off his mother's matchmaking attempts, but the situation with his parents had not been resolved. When the restaurant closed its doors for a week after serving thirty people with lunch on New Year's Day, Alistair and Frank retired to their flat with a large plate of smoked-salmon sandwiches, cracked open a bottle of champagne and settled down to watch *Brief Encounter* on DVD.

At the end of the film, just as the train was pulling out of the station for the final time, the phone rang. It was Alistair's mother inviting him to lunch the following day. Perhaps it was the result of watching a film full of lost opportunities or perhaps it was just an issue that had been unspoken long enough, but Alistair decided he was going to be compliant no longer. He inquired as to whether Frank was included in the invitation.

'I don't think that would be wise, dear. It would be extremely awkward with your father. You know what he's like; it would be very difficult. And Lucinda and the children will be there. Perhaps you could come round for coffee with Frank on Tuesday. Your father is out shooting all day.'

Alistair paused, then chose his words carefully. 'I'm sorry, I'm not putting up with this any more. Either Frank is included or I won't be coming.'

'Alistair, please don't make trouble.'

'Ma, I am not making trouble and I'm not going to come visiting behind Pa's back. I'm asking again. Is Frank included in the invitation to lunch?'

'I wouldn't mind if he was there, but your father . . .'

'Well, then, I won't be there. Come round and see us whenever you want, but I won't be coming to Corrachan House again until Frank is included.'

Alistair replaced the receiver and sat down. 'Well, I've said it. Can't go back now.'

'Thank you.' Frank paused and turned to look at Alistair. 'Took you a while, but better late than never.'

'You know I've been wanting to say that for ages. The moment was never right.'

'So why now?'

'Because I've realised it's not my being gay that upsets him, it's the fact that I'm a disappointment and always have been.'

Frank moved and sat on the arm of the sofa and put his hand on Alistair's shoulder. 'I hate the old bastard, but I think that might be a bit of an exaggeration.'

'You think so? I was seven when he abandoned me at prep school. He patted me on the head and said, "Make me proud of you, Alistair." Then he and Ma drove away. I worked so hard that term and on the first day of the Christmas holidays, I handed him the sealed envelope containing my report. He skimmed over all the positive comments, then found what he was looking for – something to criticise. "You don't know your times tables properly," he says, so every mealtime for three weeks he fired multiplication and division sums at me and I knew my tables by the time I went back to school. That next term, I was top in every subject except history, in which I was beaten by one mark. He asked who had beaten me. I told him it was Kingston, a son of someone who had been at school with him. "You were beaten by a Kingston. They are as thick as pig shit," was all he said. And that was the pattern from then on.'

'Come on, Al, he must have praised you occasionally.'

'Not that I can remember. Whatever I achieved, I should have achieved more. He has never once said, "Well done," to me.'

'What about Lucinda? Was he the same with her?'

'No, Daddy's little girl could do no wrong.'

'So why was he like that with you?'

'Learned behaviour, I expect. I can only vaguely remember my grandfather, but he was fierce. Always telling me to stand up straight and speak up. He never managed to subdue Granny, though. She was wonderful.'

'Margaret?'

'Yes. She was the only person who really understood me. I do miss her.'

Frank ruffled Alistair's hair. 'I know you do. Perhaps she's keeping an eye on you. But getting back to the bastard, you think he would never be happy whatever you did?'

'If I was married to royalty and commanding a regiment, he would be inquiring why I wasn't chief of staff. He's a bully. My mother is now a timid creature who opts for a quiet life by appeasing him. All my life I have been trying desperately to win his approval and it's not going to happen. So I've decided my New Year's resolution is to stop trying. I think the best way to do that is to be upfront.' He got up from the sofa and topped up Frank's glass of champagne and filled his own.

Frank looked at him doubtfully. 'What d'you mean?'

'We'll let everyone know that we are a couple – we'll have a civil-partnership ceremony with a big party, a proper reception. That way, he can't go on pretending I'm straight.'

'A proposal at last! What if I said I wanted to think about it?'

'I'd be very offended.'

'Oh well, all right, then. You'd better buy me a nice ring.' Frank could be quite camp if he wanted to be.

'Of course. Nothing but the best! You shall have as many diamonds as you wish.'

They began to discuss the logistics. Frank wanted to have it on Valentine's Day and Alistair considered that might be naff enough to cause further offence at the big house. They then moved on to the reception.

'I'm not catering for my own wedding!' Frank declared.

'Well, we could have it here but get the Golden Slipper in to cater. He may have three AA rosettes, but Will Farquharson owes me a favour.'

'Ooh, you've got me intrigued now.'

'A good relationship has some secrets!'

'Suit yourself. Come here, fiancé. Fiancé, I like that. Perhaps we should put a notice in the paper: "Both families are horrified to hear of the engagement of Alistair and Frank . . ."'

'What about your parents, Frank?'

'What about them?'

'Are you going to tell them?'

'No. You know they think I'm in Australia married to a Ukrainian with fertility problems, which is the reason why there are no grandchildren. A little email from my Hotmail address lets them know I'm still alive, but there are too many layers of lies to unwrap that parcel now. My father would be worse than yours. Let's just leave it be, shall we?'

'Sure?'

'Definitely sure. If I was living down the street from them, it might be different, but I'm not. I want to enjoy this occasion, not live in fear that my father would start a fight.'

By mid-January, everything was arranged. The civil ceremony suite was booked for a Friday afternoon at the end of February: all the Valentine's Day slots had gone long since. They had decided on a guest list of about eighty. Alistair sent an invitation to his parents and to his sister and family, and waited to see what would happen.

His sister and her husband had accepted the invitation but declined on behalf of their children, saying they did not consider it a suitable event for them to attend. This had annoyed Alistair, but Frank had told him that he should take any attendance at all as a generous gesture. Sir Charles had opened the invitation, immediately ripped it up and then thrown it in the bin. He was so incensed that he did not even tell his wife he had received it, so she was rather puzzled as to what Minty Oliver was talking about when they met coming out of the library.

'I was so touched yesterday to get an invitation from Alistair and Frank,' Minty said in a rush. 'It was so unexpected – and so exciting! It's the first one I've been asked to, but hopefully not the last. So good to see that we as a society are moving on and accepting change.'

Primmy looked at her blankly. 'What are you talking about?'

'Alistair and Frank's reception . . . after the civil-partnership ceremony!'

'The civil-partnership ceremony?'

'Yes. Oh dear, have I put my foot in it? You don't know, do you? He said Lucinda and her husband were coming, so I thought . . . I assumed . . . you and Charles would be there too.'

'Oh, yes, we were asked, but we are going to be away, I'm afraid. It's something difficult to cancel. Now, if you'll excuse me, I have to rush or my time will be up in the car park. I don't want to get another fine!'

Primmy bustled off down the street, leaving a slightly bemused Minty staring after her. Primmy was very cross. That explained why she was suddenly included in Charles's trip to London for his regimental dinner. He thought she would like to catch up with some friends! Huh! He was not going to let her anywhere near this event! Never the best of drivers, her journey home was more dangerous than usual and she was oblivious to the fact that she had backed into the car opposite as she left the car park and had nearly killed a lady cyclist on the outskirts of town. Primmy was not a brave woman and knew life was easier if she did not cross her husband, but very cautiously, over lunch, she decided to broach the subject.

'I don't think I'll come with you to London after all at the end of February.'

Sir Charles laid down his soup spoon and glowered at her. 'Why ever not?'

'I suspect you know why not. Were we not asked to Alistair and Frank's wedding?'

'It's not a bloody wedding! If it was, one of them would be wearing a white dress, though if that was the case, it wouldn't

103

surprise me. It's just a government sop to all their homo friends in the media.'

'I think it's quite romantic.'

'Romantic! Don't be stupid. This is not Alistair's sort of thing; it will be that money-grabbing Glaswegian's idea. You'll see, in two years' time he'll be off with half of Alistair's assets. And to answer the rest of your question, yes, we were asked and I binned the invitation. We're not even replying, and neither you nor I are going anywhere near the occasion. How did you find out about it, anyway?'

'I met Minty Oliver. She's been asked.'

'That woman! If they are spreading the net that wide, then the whole county knows. He's just doing this to rub my nose in it. Make me look a fool.'

Aren't you one already? Primmy thought. She let the moment pass but decided a severe stomach upset on the morning of their departure to London might be her answer. Now a change of subject was in order.

'Can I pass you the salt?' she inquired.

While his parents were discussing things over lunch, Alistair was entertaining Tom at the restaurant. When the waitress had placed their food in front of them, Alistair got round to the reason for this conversation. He wanted a church blessing following the ceremony. Tom, who had been enjoying his beef and ale pie, felt his appetite leave him abruptly. This was not what he needed at the moment. As if his life was not stressful enough without adding something that would cause offence to someone whatever he decided. He tried to look enthusiastic.

'Tell me why you want a blessing.'

'Because I do not consider homosexuality to be wrong, and because I wish my relationship with Frank to be recognised in the eyes of God. I know that sounds pompous, but I can't think of any other way to put it.'

'And Frank?'

'There's enough of a legacy from his Catholic upbringing to make him want God's approval and he's never going to get it from Father McIver, is he?'

'Probably not.'

'Well?'

'Eh . . . a bit of a difficult one that. Not on my part, you understand, but there are complications.'

'Why? I thought it was a matter of conscience.'

Tom hesitated. What Alistair said was true, but Tom knew that if he performed a blessing, there would be complaints and disapproval from both his congregation and most of his fellow ministers in the area. Personally he had no problem in blessing such a union, but his ability to cope with any kind of adversity was at an all-time low. He stalled and embroidered the truth just a little bit.

'Theoretically it is a matter of conscience, but the whole thing's so uncertain at the moment. I'm not sure if I'd be disciplined if I did it. Look, I'll take some soundings and get back to you in a day or two.'

Tom walked home slowly. He had a sermon to write and no idea what he was going to say. The blessing was the final straw. He should just have told Alistair what his decision was, but then he would have felt bad for not standing up for what he knew to be a reasonable request. He was no use at anything. Useless husband, useless father, useless minister!

When he got home, Ali was in the kitchen doing the ironing.

'Nice lunch with Alistair? What did he want?'

'He wants a church blessing for himself and Frank.'

'Ooh, that's good. That will upset the likes of Donald Cumming on the presbytery. I take it you said yes?'

105

'I said I'd think about it.'

'What is there to think about?'

The façade of pastoral concern he had maintained throughout lunch had gone and the trapped animal was back. He snapped at Ali, 'Can't you see the problems? Surely I don't have to explain them to you? You always think things are so clear cut. You just don't see the pressures I'm under.'

'Sorry I spoke!'

'I have a sermon to write. Please don't disturb me, and keep Matt out of the way.' He turned on his heel, went to the study and closed the door.

Ali clattered the iron into the holder and waved two fingers at the closed door. 'Fine, then. You just stay in there till you think you can be civil to the rest of us. I wish to God you would tell me what's the matter!'

Chapter Twelve

Mike was not at home over the second weekend in February. Both children were running temperatures and Gill would have welcomed some help, but Mike said he had no option but to attend the MPs' teambuilding weekend of seminars as he was presenting one of them on his new specialist subject. He promised to get up early and do the children's breakfast on both Saturday and Sunday the following weekend. The extent of Gill's sleep deprivation made this seem an attractive option, but she might have thought differently had she known the truth.

That Saturday evening, Mike was not teambuilding. He was seated next to Lizzie Graham in an Italian trattoria in Pimlico, the remains of two spaghetti marinaras in front of them. Lizzie was nibbling Mike's index finger, while her toe was running up and down the back of his leg. Hunger had driven them from the flat, and safe in the anonymity of London, they were enjoying the luxury of being out together. Mike would have shunned dessert and coffee in favour of a return to the flat had he been able to stand up in a public place.

Their affair had started in November, not long after Lizzie had done her babysitting stint. That Monday, Mike had given her a lift as far as Edinburgh Airport. Wanting some music, Lizzie had rummaged in the glove compartment looking for CDs that took her fancy and, finding nothing to her taste, had to settle for *50 Greatest Country Hits*. They had spent the journey smoking and singing along to the banal lyrics. Mike parked the car and they walked to the door of the terminal building.

Lizzie had put her bag on the ground and stood on tiptoe to give him a peck on the cheek. 'Thanks so much for the lift. Much better than the bus all the way.'

'No problem. It was a pleasure. It's good to have company, and you must have a future as a country singer if you decide against medicine.'

'I'll remember that. Perhaps I'll see you next time I'm home.'

Lizzie had picked up her bag and gone to buy her bus ticket into town from the kiosk. Mike had watched her get on to the bus and had then turned and walked towards the door of the terminal building. Before he went inside, he paused and looked back. Lizzie was watching him from the top deck. He raised his hand and waved.

Four days later, on the Friday evening, Mike was sitting at the bar in a pub in Edinburgh waiting for his friend Gavin, who, as usual, was late. The seminar on ethnic diversity had taken up Mike's afternoon, and as he had party meetings on the Saturday morning, he was staying in Annie Cochrane's flat, up a tortuous winding staircase off the Royal Mile. His mobile rang.

'Hi, Gavin. What's keeping you this time?'

'Sorry, Mike, something's come up at work. I can't make it.'

'On a Friday night at six o'clock? What's her name?'

'Kelly. She's on secondment from the Manchester office. She doesn't know anyone here.'

'Except you, of course.'

'I knew you wouldn't deny me my social life. Let me know next time you're at a loose end and we'll meet. Cheers, mate.'

'Cheers, mate.' Mike put his phone in his pocket with a sigh. He'd been looking forward to an evening when he didn't have to be on his guard. Newly divorced Gavin might be having a social life, but he certainly wasn't. He felt a hand on his shoulder.

'What's a country singer like you doing here all on his own?'

'Lizzie! Hello! Nice to see you. I've been stood up by my friend Gavin, so I'm having a pint before I go and get myself a takeaway.'

'That sounds a bit sad. Come and join us?' She pointed to a group of students at a table in the corner.

'Don't think so. Thanks all the same, but I'm not up to being quizzed on the military presence in Afghanistan. It's been a long week.'

'Well, I'll join you, then.' She sat down on the stool next to him and held up her empty glass. 'Vodka and Coke, please!'

He bought her a double and another pint for himself.

She sipped her drink, then looked at him. 'Not a good week, then?'

'Not really. Four different constituents with urgent problems that took up a lot of time. How about you?'

'Lots of assessments coming up, but I'm having a night off. What are you doing here?'

'Meetings tomorrow morning, so I'm staying in a friend's flat nearby.'

They sat in silence for a moment or two. Then Lizzie half turned on the bar stool towards him. 'Tell me something, did you always want to be an MP, or did it just sort of happen?'

'I've wanted to be an MP since I was about sixteen, but there are not too many openings for Liberals, so I never really thought it would happen. I suppose you could say I've been a sad anorak since an early age.'

'I was sixteen when I decided to do medicine.'

'That's not anoraky, though.'

'You're right, it's not. Do you enjoy your job?'

'Most of the time. It's exciting because it's never the same from one day to the next, but it can also be frustrating and it's definitely bloody hard work.' He paused. 'Gill thinks I spend my time going to receptions and eating out. Would that I did. Whatever you do, the press is always ready to pounce. The trouble with the Taha family was a case in point. I'm crucified for trying to sort something for a constituent.'

He was sounding so morose Lizzie thought she would try a different tack. 'Have you met the prime minister? What's he like?'

'Once, but I don't know him. People are always asking me that, or bending my ear about what they think should be done with asylum-seekers, income tax, the health service, education . . . You name it it's my fault and I ought to be doing something about it. No offence, Lizzie, but I do not want to spend my limited social life talking about politics.'

'Ooh. Has been a bad week, hasn't it? Well, then, what will we talk about? I don't do rugby or Premier League and you're not into student gossip. Your children, then? Do you miss them when you're away?'

''Course I do. I miss the things they say and do. I miss just seeing them every day. The weekends are so busy with other things I hardly have any time with them.' He stared into his pint. 'Gill thinks I'm not interested in the family any more. She feels I should be spending all weekend babysitting so she can go out. I know looking after small children is exhausting, but surely I'm entitled to some time off. Gill's not that hard done to. She's got two healthy children, a dog to keep her company, a good friend in your mother and other friends too. She's in her world and I'm in mine. Do you realise she hasn't even been to London yet?' He drained his glass and signalled to the barman for refills.

110

'You sound lonely.' She reached over, placed her hand briefly on top of his and then withdrew it.

'I suppose I am. I'm certainly an occasional visitor in my own house.'

He bought her another drink, and another. She was funny, flirtatious and interested in what he was doing. By ten he was in need of food, but he didn't want this conversation to end.

'Come and have something to eat with me.'

'Sounds good. Where?'

'Anything you like. Italian? Chinese? Indian?'

'Indian, I think.'

'Indian it is, then. I know the very place. Come on.'

The next morning, Mike opened his eyes and saw the trail of clothes from the front door to the bedside. As the intake of alcohol had increased, so Mike's awareness of the inherent dangers of the situation had decreased, and as their meal had progressed, it had become clear to both of them how the evening would end. It had been exciting, new, uninhibited and, most of all, fun. He looked at her lying sleeping with one arm behind her head and her hair spread across the pillow. With sobriety had come his conscience. He had cheated with the daughter of his wife's best friend. He was thirty-six and a public figure, albeit a minor one, and she was eighteen. This was tabloid fodder. Pleasurable though the interlude had been, he now had to extricate himself.

He was tentatively trying to get out of bed when she woke. 'Conscience' was not a word in Lizzie's vocabulary. She lived life to the full, sampling experiences that presented themselves. If she enjoyed them, she would repeat them, and if she didn't, then she moved on to something or someone else. Mike being married was not her problem, and the fact that he was married to her mother's best friend was just an interesting addendum. She grabbed his arm and pulled him towards her.

'Not getting up yet, are you? Come back and wake me up properly.'

Mike sat on the edge of the bed and tried to explain. Lizzie wasn't impressed.

'But you told me last night that Gill's so involved in looking after the children she doesn't have anything left for you. Mike, I don't want an emotional involvement. Sex, that's all. We meet occasionally for sex. You feel better. I feel better.' She reached out and took hold of him, all the while giving him a Diana look through her lashes.

'Come back to bed. Pleeease. You look really ridiculous perched there on the end of the bed with nothing on but an enormous erection.'

Mike hesitated. He was certainly not going to get himself in this situation again, but as he was in it at the moment, he might as well make the most of it. He managed to rebury his conscience, which surfaced again later as he got dressed. He told her firmly this wasn't going to happen again.

'That's it, Lizzie. In the words of Kenny Rogers "Know when to walk away."'

'Not even occasionally?'

'Not even occasionally.'

The following weekend, Mike's conscience was still bothering him, so he had taken the children out for the whole of Sunday afternoon to allow Gill time to herself. Later that evening, they were sitting together on the sofa enjoying a glass of wine and watching a DVD when the phone rang. Recognising the exhaustion that follows childminding, Gill got to her feet and went to answer it. She came back, sat down and told him that Lizzie wanted a lift to Edinburgh in the morning. She would be round at half past seven.

As Mike and Lizzie got into the car the following morning,

Gill put in a plea. 'Do you think you could try and phone this week when the children are awake? Ian needs to talk to you and eleven at night is no good.'

'Fine, I'll try, but it's not always that easy.' He closed the car door, started the engine and reversed out of the driveway. Yet another area in which he had fallen short and now he was stuck in the car for at least an hour with last week's major error of judgement.

Mike discouraged conversation at the start of the journey by appearing engrossed in the *Today* programme. After about ten minutes, Lizzie located the *Country Hits* CD.

'Can we have this instead? This programme's boring. It's all politics.'

Mike looked at her and sighed. 'That's my job, in case you've forgotten. OK, I've heard all I need to at the moment.'

They passed another ten minutes in silence listening to Tammy Wynette and Dolly Parton and watching the windscreen wipers going back and forth.

Mike pulled out to pass a lorry and was attempting to see through the wall of water being thrown out when Lizzie announced, 'I've been thinking about you, all the time. You certainly know how to fuck.'

'Jesus, Lizzie, you pick your moments!' Mike concentrated on driving through the deluge and moved back to the correct side of the road. 'I told you, Lizzie. It's not going to happen again.'

'Didn't you enjoy it? I did.'

'That's not the point.'

'You must have enjoyed it. You stayed for some more.'

''Course I enjoyed it, but it's still not going to happen again.'

'It makes me aroused just thinking about it.' She squirmed in her seat. 'My nipples have gone really hard.'

He glanced over at her and, sure enough, they had. Then he felt her hand on his thigh.

'Remove your hand, Lizzie.'

She did as she was told, but she proceeded to describe in graphic detail what she had enjoyed during their last encounter and what she would like to try if there were to be another. Then she put her hand back on his thigh and he felt her fingers inching upwards.

'For God's sake, Lizzie, stop it. We'll have an accident.'

She continued to move her hand up his thigh until she found what she was looking for. Then she moved her hand back and forwards.

'Still want me to stop?'

'Yes . . . No . . . God, Lizzie, I can't stand this.'

Being in a confined space with a very attractive young woman who was not only talking dirty but was doing something wonderful with her hand was more than he could bear. He turned up the next side road and drove at some speed till he reached the forestry tracks. Fifty metres into the trees, he parked the car.

In the weeks following, lust triumphed over common sense. They had managed to meet several times when Mike could invent a reason for an overnight stay in Edinburgh. Annie's flat was usually vacant on a Friday and Lizzie had managed a couple of mid-week trips to London courtesy of easyJet. A night of energetic sex was not conducive to efficient working the next day and Janice was not convinced when he pleaded a hangover as the excuse for falling asleep at his desk.

'He forgets I've been working here for years,' she told the other secretaries during her lunch break. 'I would bet it's that researcher who works in the whip's office. She's supposed to like them married.'

Mike's conscience troubled him occasionally, but he justified his actions by telling himself this relationship was purely sexual and free from emotional strings. This weekend was a rare treat, two whole days and three nights together.

He was surprised by his stamina and couldn't get enough of her. She was surprised to find that, despite what she considered to be his advancing years, he was more sexually sophisticated than Darren Connerty or any of the medical students she had bedded since leaving home.

While nibbling Mike's finger and telling him what she was going to do to him when they got back to his flat, Lizzie glanced towards the door.

'Fuck!'

'Well, I was hoping so,' said Mike.

'No! Fuck as in "Oh fuck, Phyllis Caldwell and another old biddy have just walked in." Don't turn round! Argh! She's coming over.'

'Elizabeth! Fancy meeting you here.' Phyllis drew level with the table. 'This is my friend Evelyn Lipton. Evelyn, this is Elizabeth Graham, our minister's daughter.'

Mike was seated with his back to the door and it was only when Phyllis turned in expectation of an introduction to Lizzie's escort that she realised it was him. 'Oh! Oh! And . . . er . . . this is our MP and my next-door neighbour, Mike Andrews.' Phyllis's eyebrows had disappeared into her hairline.

Mike stood up. His previous perceived difficulty with this action had disappeared. He shook hands with the ladies. 'Evelyn, nice to meet you. Are you down on holiday, Phyllis?'

'Just a shopping trip and catching up with Evelyn. She lives round the corner. Not home this weekend, Mike?'

'No. I've been at a teambuilding weekend in Oxford. Just got back, in fact. Lizzie's been down for an interview for a summer job at St Thomas's, so I suggested she stay at my flat.

No point in paying for accommodation. As she was in when I got back, we decided to pop out for something to eat.'

'Did you get your job, Elizabeth?'

'What? Er . . . I don't know yet. They'll let me know.'

'Ladies, this way, please.' The hovering waiter ushered them to the next table but one.

'Let's get the bill and go,' hissed Mike.

'Sit still, have your coffee and talk to me in a paternal fashion.' Lizzie smiled across at Phyllis.

Unfazed, she described various lecturers and talked loudly about Chris, who had taken her to the Medics' Ball. Small talk had deserted Mike, so Lizzie kept going. She managed to drop Gill's name into the conversation twice and mentioned her mother once. After what seemed to Mike like an eternity, he asked for the bill, and with Lizzie giving a cheery wave to the ladies, they made for the street.

'God, that was funny!' shrieked Lizzie. 'Phyllis Caldwell, of all people.'

'It wasn't funny in the slightest! What if she mentions it to Gill or your mother? Do you think she saw what you were doing to my finger?'

'Phyllis is so prim and proper it wouldn't occur to her. Why did you have to make up the job at St Thomas's? Now I'll have to tell Mum I've been down for a mythical interview.' She paused. 'Perhaps I should apply for a job there. You are here most of July, aren't you? We could have two months together.' She took the door key from him, entered the building and pulled him into the lift. As it rose, she started to unbutton his shirt.

'For God's sake, can't you wait?'

'Don't you like sex in interesting places?'

'Not with all the CCTV around. I don't intend to find myself on YouTube.'

'Boring!'

Opening the door to the flat, she started to peel off her clothes.

'I suppose you can tell Gill that I was staying in the flat 'cos I had an interview and then we're in the clear.' Lizzie was by this stage wearing only a thong. 'Stop worrying about it and take your clothes off. I've got an anatomy exam next week. I need to do some revision.'

Phyllis lay awake in the narrow bed in Evelyn's spare room. Her first impression on seeing Lizzie was that the girl was involved in a very intimate conversation with what Phyllis assumed to be a new boyfriend who had to be an improvement on Darren Connerty. But it was Mike Andrews with her. Surely he wouldn't get involved with an eighteen-year-old whose mother was his wife's best friend? She knew that most men had an eye for an attractive young woman. Jack's eye, and she hoped it was just his eye, had wandered several times in their forty-year marriage. Their conversation as they had their coffee had been innocent enough. On the other hand, Lizzie Graham was a minx . . . and she was being very familiar!

Phyllis, for all she enjoyed gossip, was not, at heart, a malicious woman. By the time she heard the clock strike two, she was sure of what she had seen, but an hour later, she was still undecided as to what she should do about it. Speak to Gill . . . or Mike? They had a plausible explanation. She would look like an interfering busybody. She couldn't discuss it with Jack either, as he would tell her to mind her own business. She would say nothing, just wait and watch. She allowed her thoughts to turn to her shopping itinerary and she finally drifted off to sleep.

Evelyn was sitting at the kitchen table with a cup of Earl Grey and a slice of toast and marmalade reading the *Sunday Telegraph* when a bleary-eyed Phyllis appeared in her dressing gown.

'Bad night? Too much garlic after eight o'clock can play havoc with the digestive system, you know. By the way, that neighbour of yours, the MP, was being rather economical with the truth.'

'Oh?'

'Well, I had to find some information for that Liberal MPs' gathering in Oxford and their researcher told me it started on Thursday and finished Friday lunchtime, so he must have been back long before yesterday evening.' Evelyn turned another page in the paper. 'There's some tea in the pot, dear, and if we want to get to St Columba's on time, we'll have to be away from here by ten fifteen.'

Phyllis poured herself a cup of tea, reassured that she was right, but disappointed that she wasn't going to say anything to anyone.

Chapter Thirteen

Mike and Gill's party was the following weekend, on Valentine's Day. They had run out of excuses such as a new baby or moving house and now they had to entertain those who had entertained them, as well as those who had helped at the election.

They had assumed, mistakenly, that not everyone asked would come. The kudos of being asked to a party at the MP's house, combined with the nosiness of those who wanted to inspect their interior decoration, had guaranteed almost a 100 per cent acceptance – a guest list of forty-two. Gill was horrified.

'I cannot cater for that number with two children clinging to my legs.'

'How about a caterer?' was Mike's reply.

Outside caterers were not easy to find. Careful inquiry revealed that such a service was available from Chez Marguerite or the Corrachan Hotel. The former was a good deal more expensive but an improvement on the cold ham and coleslaw offered by the hotel.

With a buffet ordered from Alistair and Frank, and Ruth employed for the evening to mind the children, Gill was confident that, with Mike's help, the house could be made presentable.

Not only was there hoovering to be done but someone had to collect up pieces of Lego and things that squeaked when stepped on, check the chairs for elderly half-eaten biscuits, wipe clean the door handles and clear the bathroom of assorted detritus.

After breakfast, just as Gill was about to give him a list of chores, Mike left to attend a meeting arranged by Minty about the proposed boundary changes on council wards. Gill had inquired why he had allowed Minty to organise a meeting on such an inconvenient day and he replied that where Minty was concerned, it was easier to go along with things rather than try to alter them. He assured her he would only be an hour or so.

Deprived of assistance, Gill tried to tidy as best she could, but as she cleared one room Ian was making a mess in another. The post arrived and she could see the Valentine's Day card she had sent Mike in the pile of mail (they had played the game of posting anonymous cards to each other for years) but there was no card for her. Lunchtime came with a text from Mike saying the discussion was still going on, so she decided she needed a childminder. Ruth was out, but Lizzie was home and agreed to come and remove the children for the afternoon.

Mike arrived back at two thirty, following his pub lunch, and had the hoover thrust into his hand by an angry and hurt Gill.

'You've got some time to make up, boy!'

'I know. I'm sorry. Things sort of ran on a bit. Then I had to go shopping.' He took a red rose from behind his back and presented it to her along with a card. 'Happy Valentine's Day, my love.'

'Oh, thank you. I thought you'd forgotten! There appears to be a card for you in the pile.' She gave him a kiss.

Mike took in the child-free environment. 'Children having a nap? Perhaps we could manage a lie-down for half an hour or so. A Valentine's Day treat?' He grabbed Gill round the waist and nibbled her ear.

'We have got forty-two people coming to this house for dinner and you want to go to bed? That's male priorities for you. Just because you gave me a card and a red rose you think you'll get immediate access to my knickers?' She giggled. 'Hey, stop doing that to my ear – you know it turns me on.'

Mike continued nibbling. She began to see the advantages. As a result of weaning Kate, Gill's oestrogen levels were rising. That, combined with the ear nibbling, made the frivolity of sex in the afternoon begin to look like an acceptable alternative to housework.

'Hoover the carpets, then . . . just perhaps, we might manage half an hour before the children come back at four.'

'The children are out?'

'Yes. Surprise, surprise, it was impossible to tidy up when they were about, so I phoned the manse and arranged for them to be removed.' Gill disentangled herself and handed him the hoover and pouted. 'I'm going upstairs. Finish your chores and I'll be waiting!'

Stuff the chores, thought Mike. He couldn't work out why she suddenly wanted sex now when she never seemed to want it at any other more conventional time, but if it was on offer, he wasn't going to complain. He grabbed a bottle of wine and two glasses and followed her up the stairs two at a time. Gill was sitting provocatively on the bed wearing only a pair of black lace knickers. Mike peeled off his clothes, remembering to take his socks off before his trousers, and poured two glasses of wine. He buried his face in her ample chest and stroked her nipples, albeit with a degree of care. He wasn't convinced the weaning process was complete.

'Careful,' said Gill. 'You'll spill the wine.'

'That sounds like a good idea.' He poured some into the hollow of her navel and began to lick it up.

'Hey! Don't! That tickles. Drink the stuff. Don't pour it over the bed. We don't have time to change sheets.' She drained her glass and then ran her tongue up his inner thigh.

Some twenty minutes later, Mike climaxed with his usual sound accompaniments and rolled on to his back. Orgasm has been described as 'the little death', but he sounded as if he was being murdered.

As he was kissing Gill on the cheek, a voice came from downstairs. 'Hello! Gill! Mike!'

'That's Lizzie! There must be a problem with the children.' Gill leaped from the bed into her tatty towelling robe encrusted with bits of Weetabix.

'Lizzie? Lizzie's got the children?'

'Yes, I told you.'

No, you didn't, he thought.

Gill shot out of the room and went downstairs. Ian, wrapped in Lizzie's coat, was looking very subdued. Lizzie removed the coat to reveal a shivering, wet and muddy child.

'Mummy, I fell in.' He held up his brown slimy hands for Gill to inspect. 'Duck poo!'

'Lovely,' said Gill. She looked questioningly at Lizzie.

'We were feeding the ducks. He leaned over a bit far and fell in the pond.'

'How did that happen? Weren't you watching him?'

'I was sorting the clips on the buggy, and as I turned round, he slipped and sat down in the water . . . and the duck poo. I think he needs a bath.'

No apology, no offer to help clean him up, thought Gill.

Lizzie looked pointedly at Gill's dressing gown.

'We decided we would have showers before we tidied the bathroom. Right, Ian, it's a good job we haven't cleaned the bath yet. Come on, we'll get you warm and clean.' She took him by the hand and went upstairs, passing Mike on the way down. He was dressed.

'Hi, Lizzie. Sorry we didn't hear you come in. Gill was trying on outfits for tonight.'

The bathroom door closed and the sound of taps could be heard.

'That's a new way of describing it! You were at it. You may not have heard us coming, but I certainly heard you. In fact, the whole street must have heard you. You must have made Phyllis Caldwell's day.' She paused and the tone changed from angry to injured. 'You told me that you and Gill don't have sex any more.'

'We don't. Well, we didn't, but she grabbed me and dragged me upstairs. It must be because the children were out of the way. She is usually so paranoid about waking them up or Ian coming into the room.'

'The noise you make, I'm not surprised she thinks you'll wake them. Here! Take your daughter! I've just remembered I have to be somewhere else.' She thrust the buggy in his direction and left in a cloud of indignation.

'Not that it's any of your business!' he said to her departing back.

The dog looked up at him, hopeful that she might be taken for a walk.

'Tomorrow, Penny, I'll take you out tomorrow. You need more walks. You are getting very fat.'

The more Mike thought about Lizzie's attitude, the angrier he became. How dare she come into his house and dictate what he did with his wife? This was outwith the terms of their agreement. She had been getting more possessive recently, phoning him up at inconvenient times to chat and sending explicit texts. Then there was the meeting with Phyllis. Every time Gill had opened her mouth to say something he expected to be interrogated about Lizzie's visit to London, but as yet nothing had happened. Perhaps Phyllis had accepted the story and had seen nothing untoward. Lizzie was turned on by the illicit nature of the relationship, but to him it was becoming debilitating. The lust had been exhausted the previous weekend, and a guilty conscience and the fear of discovery had taken over. He made a decision. This had gone far enough. He found his mobile and texted her to say it was finished and that she should find someone her own age. Immediately, he felt better, liberated from this duplicity.

It was a sense of freedom that lasted till seven o'clock, when the doorbell rang and Gill opened the door to Ruth, who had arrived to put the children to bed. Lizzie was with her.

'Hi, Ruth. Kate's in her cot and Ian is waiting for you to read him a story. Oh, hello, Lizzie. What are you doing here? I thought you had other things to do.'

'I thought you might like a waitress to pour the wine and clear up.' She took off her coat to reveal an outfit that although not quite 'French maid', was not far away. A stretchy white top with a deep V-neck and a black skirt just covering her backside was completed by sheer black tights and black strappy stilettos.

'That was a kind thought, Lizzie, but I think we'll manage fine.'

'It's OK, you don't have to pay me. I'm happy to help you after letting you down this afternoon by rushing off to visit my friend in hospital. I completely forgot that I'd arranged to go. She's got cancer, you know. Terminal.' That was a good touch, Lizzie thought. Dare you to tell me to go now, Mummy Gill.

Mike appeared at the kitchen door with a bottle of red wine in each hand.

'Gill, where's the corkscrew? Lizzie!' He took in the outfit and the atmosphere and realised that she wasn't going to go quietly.

'Lizzie is offering to be our waitress. She says she'll pour wine and clear up the dishes. It would be quite useful. It would mean we could talk to people.'

Lizzie turned her back on Mike and bent down to adjust the strap on her shoe, displaying her bottom and the tantalising suggestion that she just might be knickerless under her tights. Then she stood up and turned to face him.

'It would free you up to talk to all your friends and . . . neighbours. I'm sure they would appreciate your full attention.'

'Fine, fine! Whatever you think. I'm just going to open the red wine to let it breathe. Gill will tell you what to do.'

'That's good,' Lizzie continued. 'I need something to distract me this evening. My boyfriend texted me this afternoon to tell me we're finished. Couldn't even tell me to my face. It was completely out of the blue. He'd sent me a Valentine's card and a red rose too. I slept with him because I thought he loved me and all the time he was sleeping with someone else.' She began to sniff loudly.

'Poor you,' said Gill. 'He sounds a real shit. Perhaps you're better off without him.' I'm sure it will take you about half an hour to find a replacement when you get back to Edinburgh, she thought.

'Yeah, he is a shit, isn't he? Don't you think he's a shit, Mike?'

Mike placed the red wine on the table. 'I really wouldn't know, Lizzie. Come and I'll show you where we keep the white wine. It's in the fridge in the utility room.

'What the hell are you playing at?' hissed Mike a few moments later, as he opened the fridge door to display the chilled bottles of wine. 'The white wine is all in here,' he said loudly. Then he dropped his voice. 'This is totally out of order. It's over! Go and play with someone your own age. It was good fun, but I am married and intend to remain so. Just serve the wine, clear the dishes and clear out.'

'And where do I put the empty bottles?' Lizzie asked loudly.

'Over there in the box.'

Confident that they were out of both sight and earshot, Lizzie put one hand on Mike's crotch and caressed gently, while she put her other hand behind his head. 'See, whatever you say you still want me.' She pulled his face towards her and kissed him. 'You can't do without me.'

'Yes, I can! Stop it, Lizzie! I told you, it's over. It was fun, but it's over.'

'You reckon? We'll have to see, won't we?'

Later in the evening, Phyllis, whose hip was troubling her, decided she would use the downstairs facilities rather than climb the stairs. As she passed the door to the kitchen, she glanced in. Mike had his back to her. He had his hands on Lizzie's shoulders and seemed to be talking earnestly to her. She couldn't quite see where Lizzie's hands were, but they certainly weren't by her sides. Poor Gill, she thought, and the Grahams have no idea what a tart that girl is.

Ali was enjoying herself. It was so long since she had been to any sort of party – Tom always seemed to find a reason not to socialise nowadays. She looked at him in conversation with Alistair, who had arrived to collect the remains of the buffet. At least he was talking. He had become increasingly silent and morose and wouldn't tell her what was wrong. Whenever she asked, she was told she didn't understand. Stuff him, she thought. I intend to enjoy myself.

She had lost track of the amount of red wine she had poured down her throat and was talking animatedly to all and sundry. Lizzie, who had refused to refill Ali's glass the last time she had passed, had been told by her mother that it wasn't just students who knew how to enjoy themselves. An interesting conversation with Minty Oliver about rainforests and why they were disappearing had been followed by a discussion about asylum-seekers who were trained as brain surgeons and Ali had agreed it was a huge waste of talent.

While they had been talking, Minty watched Tom finish his conversation with Alistair and sit down in a chair in the corner with his head in his hands. She excused herself and went over and sat beside him. Sensing company, Tom looked up.

Minty raised an eyebrow. 'All right?'

'I suppose so. Just had to sort a complicated bit of parish business.'

Minty raised the eyebrow again and inquired if it was confidential.

'Confidential? In this town? That will be right. I probably shouldn't tell you, but as you'll find out about it one way or another, I can't see it makes a difference. Alistair wanted me to perform a blessing after their ceremony and I said no. He was trying to get me to change my mind.'

'Your prerogative to say no, surely?'

'Yeah, perhaps.'

'A matter of conscience is just that . . . what you feel you have to do. It may not be what Alistair and Frank wanted to hear, but they can't blame you. If they really want a blessing, they will find someone to perform one. It may be on another day in another place, but if it's important to them, they'll have one. If it's not that important, they'll manage without, so it's not something for you to feel bad about.'

'I expect you're right, Mrs Oliver.'

'I'm really looking forward to the occasion, but I can understand why it causes problems for some people. Personally, it doesn't bother me what people's sexual preferences are, as long as they don't harm others, but that's just me.' She patted him on the arm and stood up. 'Getting a bit late for an old bird like me, so I'm going to make tracks in a minute. You've made a decision – that was the difficult bit – so be good to yourself and don't keep turning it over in your mind.' Minty made purposefully for the door but only got as far as Peter Graham and Jack Caldwell before she got embroiled in another conversation. Tom watched her get sidetracked and wished it was as easy as Minty had made out.

Ali had looked around for someone else to talk to and spied Phyllis sitting on her own. She lurched across the room and put her hand on Phyllis's shoulder.

'Phyllis! How you doing, then?'

'Fine, thank you,' said Phyllis, clutching her glass of orange juice. She looked at Ali and concluded that the woman was very drunk. Joyce Macdonald's cleaning lady, Mrs McCafferty, must be correct. Her daughter worked in Tesco and every time Ali had been through the checkout recently she had been buying wine. Twice within the last fortnight Mrs McCafferty herself had seen Ali coming out of the wine shop in the High Street with a carrier bag. It had been concluded that Ali had a 'problem'. It was so disloyal to Tom and his position to overindulge like this in public.

'Not off to Madeira this year? You usually go about now, don't you?'

'Not this year, no. Jack's very busy at the moment. We'll probably go on a cruise later on.'

Ali glanced over at Jack, who was having his glass refilled by Lizzie while he was ogling her cleavage and resting his large red hand in the small of her back. Poor Phyllis, she thought. You have no idea what a lecher your husband is.

Phyllis had followed Ali's glance but had interpreted the scene differently. Shameless trollop, cosying up to a man old enough to be her grandfather, she thought. She said, 'Lizzie enjoying life in Edinburgh?'

'Oh, yes, she seems to be having a good social life but is managing to work hard as well. She's getting good grades for her assignments.'

For all her previous good intentions, Phyllis couldn't resist asking the question. 'Did she get that job in London?'

'London? A job in London?'

'Oh, have I spoken out of turn? I met her when I was there last week. A summer job at St Thomas's Hospital. She was down for an interview.'

Lizzie heard the words 'St Thomas's' and 'interview' and appeared at her mother's elbow to refill her glass.

'Phyllis says you were in London last week . . . for an interview?'

'That's right. There are some summer student placements. Thought I would try for one. Didn't think I would tell you unless I got one. I knew you'd just worry about me going south.'

'It was so good of Mike to put you up,' smiled Phyllis sweetly.

'Wasn't it,' said Lizzie, and moved on with her bottles.

Ali's ability for joined-up thinking was, by this stage in the evening, severely impaired. There seemed to be some sort of subplot here that she couldn't quite get a handle on.

Tom appeared beside her. 'It's eleven thirty. I think it's time we went home. I've got the service in the morning.'

This was not Ali's opinion. ''S early yet. Don't be boring. The party's hardly started.'

'I really think it would be better if we went now.' Tom's tone was controlled but definitely assertive.

Ali glanced at him and her irritation with him over the past weeks boiled over. 'You go if you must. I'll find my way home later. I'm having a good time here . . . for once!'

'I think you should come now, before you make a complete fool of yourself.' He put his hand under her elbow.

She shrugged him off. 'I'm not making a fool of myself. I'm just having some fun for a change, which is more than can be said of you. You are so boring these days.' She turned towards Phyllis. 'Isn't he boring, Phyllis?' She raised her voice. 'Listen, everyone, my husband is all duty and no fun. Then he expects me to be boring too, but actually . . . I am someone who enjoys a few glasses of wine and some social interaction.'

Phyllis was very embarrassed. That poor man was just trying to maintain his position and her dignity, not that she deserved to be helped. The fact that she enjoys a few glasses of wine was very obvious.

'Perhaps you should go, so you are fresh for church in the morning. I think we're going soon. I always find my voice is affected after a late night and we're singing that Rutter anthem tomorrow, so I must be on top form.'

'Sorry, Phyllis, much as I enjoy your singing, I think I might just have to give that a miss. I have an appointment with my bed and a racy novel. The third Sunday in February is designated "Lie-in-Bed Sunday".'

'Home! Now!' Tom hissed at her, 'I can assure you, you are making a complete arse of yourself.'

Phyllis excused herself and went over to Jack. He did not look too pleased at being told it was time to go home. Phyllis decided that if she collected their coats from upstairs and then presented Jack with his, they would soon be wending their way home. All these Liberals were far too left wing – too much toleration of gay rights, rehabilitating prisoners and the like. Jack would start to get argumentative soon. He had already persuaded Lizzie to find him some whisky and was warming himself up for a political discussion with Tom Graham's strange brother, Peter, and that eccentric woman Minty Oliver, who really ought to have known better than to be a Liberal. After all, she had been to Roedean.

As she climbed the stairs, Phyllis noticed that Gill and Mike had removed the lovely flock wallpaper. White walls were so stark, especially with a beige carpet. She was quite disappointed to discover that the doors were all shut, save the spare room, which housed the coats. She wondered if they had changed the décor in the master bedroom. She went into the spare room and leaned over to pick up her coat. Unfortunately, her immaculate Aquascutum three-quarter-length coat, purchased last week in London, had become the chosen whelping bed for Penny, who seemed to be on the point of delivering her fifth puppy into the luxurious cream cashmere folds.

Chapter Fourteen

'The coat is quite ruined now. They've offered to pay for specialist dry-cleaning, but I wouldn't be able to wear it again. You know I hate dogs. They claimed they had no idea the dog was pregnant and thought it was shut up in the back bedroom. Then they had a public spat, with Gill declaring she never wanted a dog in the first place. You would have thought they could have had their disagreements in private. It's so embarrassing for everyone else.'

'Poor you,' said Joyce, as she bit into her carrot cake. 'You will have to persuade Jack to let you go to Edinburgh to look for a replacement. Anybody or anything else of interest at the party? What was the food like? Good wine?'

'Food was fine. It came from here, so that wasn't a problem, although I'm surprised Gill didn't manage to do it herself. It's all shortcuts these days. Wine was mediocre – some Australian stuff that was on special offer in Tesco – but that didn't seem to stop Ali Graham drinking too much of it.' She took a small sip of her coffee. 'You know, I think you're right. I think she does have a problem. She made a complete fool of herself, and Tom was trying to take her home when I found the puppies. Ugh! Horrid things. It still makes me feel sick to think about it.'

'Here, drink your coffee and you'll feel better.'

'And that trollop of a daughter of hers was there helping to serve out the wine. Looked as if she should have been on a street corner. I don't know how Tom Graham copes with it all. Poor man – a drunk wife and a tart of a daughter.'

'That's a bit harsh, isn't it, Phyllis?' Joyce turned to look at the display of cakes, wondering if she might have room for a bit of millionaire's shortbread.

'Not if you'd seen what I saw in London last week.'

'What did you see?' Joyce stopped eyeing the shortbread and gave Phyllis her full attention.

'Nothing, nothing. It doesn't matter.'

'Phyllis, you can't tell me half a story and then say it doesn't matter.'

Phyllis looked around Chez Marguerite. It was Monday morning and they were the only customers.

'Well, you mustn't tell anyone else.'

'Promise I won't.'

'Well, I was in this Italian restaurant with Evelyn and you'll never guess . . .'

Ali was sitting at her kitchen table with a mug of coffee and a Twix bar. It was Monday afternoon and this was the first food she had felt able to eat since the party. The special-offer wine had given her a headache and gastrointestinal disturbance unlike anything she had known before. She had spent most of Sunday in bed, not fit even to read her novel. She cringed to think how drunk she had been and how the assembled company would enjoy regaling their friends with her behaviour, along with the details of the Andrewses' interior decorations. At least the discovery of the puppies had stopped her domestic discussion with Tom, but in retrospect she thought it had not been a good idea to laugh uproariously at the state of Phyllis's cashmere coat.

133

She also had several blanks when she tried to recall the events of the evening. She had a hazy recollection of Phyllis saying she had met Lizzie in London, or had she dreamed that?

Matt was arranging his saucepans in the corner and she thought she would have to make something to eat soon. Lizzie had gone back to Edinburgh, and Ruth and Tom had both been distinctly cool with her yesterday. She had decided she would never drink again. After she had put a casserole in the oven, she would go round and see Gill. Matt might like to see the puppies.

It was six o'clock when they got home. Gill seemed to be coping well with the six new arrivals, despite wondering how she had not noticed that the dog was pregnant – one mistaken assumption that the dog had been spayed had led to another that not enough exercise and too much food were the cause of the expanding waistline. Matt had shown interest in the puppies, which was a promising sign. Perhaps she could persuade Tom to let him have one. There was no one about when they got home, only a note from Ruth to say she had gone to Sacha's house.

It was after seven when Tom rang. He told her he didn't know when he would be back. He was with Frank Callaghan at the Edinburgh Royal because Alistair had been involved in a road accident and was now in intensive care. He said the Hamilton-Sinclairs would not allow Frank to see Alistair.

'They can't do that, can they?' asked Ali.

'They can if they want to. They are next of kin. I have to go now. I'll tell you about it when I get back, but I have no idea when that'll be.'

It was after two when Tom got into bed beside her. He lay on his back staring at the ceiling.

'Alistair died at ten o'clock. He never regained consciousness.'

'Oh, no! How awful! What happened?' Ali asked.

'He was on his way to see his lawyer in Edinburgh. There was black ice and a multiple pile-up and Alistair was in the middle of it. He never had a chance.'

'How come you ended up at the hospital?'

'Frank phoned me in a terrible state about five. He'd been out and came home to a message on the answering machine from Alistair's sister. The police contacted Corrachan House in the first instance because that was the address on Alistair's licence. The message only said that Alistair had had an accident and was in hospital. Poor Frank had to phone round all the hospitals to find out where he was. The Royal Infirmary wouldn't give him any more information as he wasn't family. He had no car, so that was why he phoned me. It was all unbelievably awful.' He paused and Ali took his hand and squeezed it. 'Sir Charles refused to let Frank see Alistair. Said it was Frank's fault that Alistair had left the army, that Frank had ruined his son's life. Primmy and Lucinda just sat there and said nothing. I tried speaking to each of them and asking that Frank be allowed in for just a few moments, but it was no good. It was only after he died and the Hamilton-Sinclairs were closeted with the charge nurse dealing with formalities that I persuaded a sympathetic staff nurse to let Frank into the room for a few minutes.'

'How is Frank now?'

'Poor man is distraught. I tried to get him to come and stay here tonight, but he wanted to go home. God, Ali, it was awful and unfair and uncaring. How could they be like that? Alistair and Frank have been together for ten years. Their civil partnership was going to be next Friday.'

He turned on the light and sat up. 'Why am I castigating his parents? I'm as bad. I told Alistair on Saturday night that I definitely wouldn't do a blessing in the church, said it would upset too many people! Why don't I face up to things? I'm just useless!'

Ali sat up and put her arm round his shoulders. 'You are not useless. Listen to me. Whether you did or did not agree to give Alistair and Frank a blessing has nothing to do with what happened today. I'm sure he understood your reasons.'

He closed his eyes and shook his head. 'It's not quite as simple as that.'

'Why?'

'It's too complicated to explain.'

'You could try?'

'I can't. Not at the moment.'

'What is the matter with you these days? Come here, love.'

He turned towards her and they lay down. She switched off the light and put her arms properly round him and stroked his hair till he fell asleep.

The next morning, Ali felt more secure than she had in ages. Tom had slept in her arms all night. Perhaps in the midst of this tragedy, she was getting her husband back. They were dealing with parish life as a team again. Tom had gone to see Frank and brought him back for some breakfast, but he sat grey-faced at their table and ate nothing. After half an hour, Tom had taken him back to the flat to help deal with the inevitable phone calls and sympathy visits.

When they arrived, there was an elderly Rover saloon in the car park in which Primmy was sitting staring straight ahead. Tom went to offer his condolences and she thanked him politely. When they got into the flat, they found Sir Charles sitting at Alistair's desk going through his papers.

'What are you doing, and how did you get in here?' asked Frank quietly.

'I got in by using Alistair's key. I take it you have no objection. I am looking for his will and the details of his bank accounts.

We have to get his affairs in order. I've found his bank statements and a will from before he went into the army, so that's all I need just now.' Despite his words, he continued to rifle through the papers in the desk drawers. 'By the way, Mr Callaghan, I shall want you out of these premises, both the flat and the restaurant, one calendar month from today. Lucinda wishes to turn this house into a family home again. It belongs to her now, you know. I have asked my lawyer to arrange for the business to be valued the day after the funeral and we will discuss whether you buy our share or the business is wound up.'

Frank walked over to the desk and stood beside Sir Charles. He had the benefit of standing, while his adversary was still sitting down, and the sense of injustice from the previous day boiled over. He leaned down and put his face close to that of Sir Charles.

'Alistair has made a new will! He was signing it yesterday. He has left the house and his share of the business to me, and actually, I do object to you coming into my house without an invitation and I am asking you to leave now.'

Sir Charles stood up abruptly, forcing Frank to take a step backwards. They were now glaring at each other. Tom thought Frank was about to swing a punch.

'Alistair was involved in the accident on his way to Edinburgh, Mr Callaghan. He never signed the new will, so this is the only one we have.' He brandished the will in Frank's direction. 'And, as I said before, this is not your house! It is Lucinda's! I am, on her behalf, giving you four weeks' notice! Is that clear enough for you?' He turned his back on Frank and addressed Tom as if he were a junior subaltern.

'Mr Graham, we will need the use of your church for the funeral as St Mary's is very small and we expect a large number to attend. My son was well liked in this community. I've instructed the rector to get in touch with you.'

The brigadier marched downstairs and into his car, where his wife was waiting. He had made a list of what needed to be done and had begun delegating tasks. Richard Cooper was organising the funeral. He, personally, was sorting Alistair's affairs and making sure that that odious little man understood that he had no claims on the house. He was determined that the funeral would be dignified and fitting, not a nancy boys' outing.

As they drove home, the brigadier told his wife that he had put Frank straight about a few things. Primmy said nothing. She hated herself. She had said nothing when Alistair was sent away to school aged seven. She had said nothing as he grew up into a polite young man whom she didn't know. She had said nothing when he had told her he was gay, and she had gone along with the pretence that he was an eligible bachelor. She had said next to nothing when she had been forbidden to attend the partnership celebrations. Everyone had told her for years what a kind man Alistair was and she had agreed with them, but she didn't really know him at all. And now it was too late. She had failed him as a mother. She had allowed him to become estranged instead of accepting him and saying it didn't matter. And it didn't matter now.

After Sir Charles had gone, Tom had turned to Frank, who was sitting at the desk in a state of disbelief.

'Even if the will hadn't been signed, they might have taken account of what were clearly Alistair's wishes. How can he do that? As to the other bit, Alistair was a member of my congregation anyway, so I'm pleased the funeral will be in St Andrew's, but I need to have some control over the proceedings if it's in my church. I'll speak to the rector and discuss the form of the service. Do you know if Alistair had any wishes regarding his funeral?'

'No. We never talked about things like that. What is it going to be like if that man is organising it? It will be a sham, and if I venture an opinion, he's bound to do the opposite. Al just wanted that old bastard's approval; that's why he never said anything for years. But he did tell them, on New Year's Day. He told his mother either I was recognised as part of his life or he wouldn't go there any more.' At the word 'life' Frank's eyes filled with tears and he reached for the whisky bottle. 'I need a drink. Want one?'

'Not just now, thanks. I'll come back and see you later, when I know what is happening about the funeral. I'll try and not let it be too awful.'

But Tom found he was fighting a losing battle. He tried to engage the help of the rector of St Mary's regarding Frank, but Richard Cooper was of the firm belief that homosexuality was a sin and that the funeral should concentrate on the 'positive aspects' of Alistair's life.

'I don't doubt that Frank loved Alistair and that he is very upset, but he has committed a sin and there is no way that I will condone that by mentioning anything to do with their relationship during the service. I shall pray privately that God will comfort Frank in his distress.'

Eventually, all Tom was allowed to do was to choose the final hymn and pronounce the benediction.

The funeral was held the following Tuesday afternoon. The church was packed. The front four pews were reserved for family and close friends. Frank was not included in this group. He arrived early, dressed in a pale linen suit with the rainbow tie that he had intended to wear on Friday for the civil partnership. He was accompanied by a group of friends, all of whom were dressed more for a wedding than a funeral.

The service started with the rector thanking everyone on the family's behalf for attending the funeral and thanking the minister of St Andrew's for allowing the service to be held in this church. He then announced that there would be refreshments at Corrachan House after the committal. The first hymn was 'Soldiers of Christ, Arise and Put Your Armour On'. All the ex-army types sang lustily. Then Alistair's godfather, General Sir William Campbell-Drummond, stood up to give what was termed 'An Appreciation of Alistair's Life' in the order of service.

The congregation listened to him describing Alistair's happy childhood at school and on the grouse moor, his distinguished career at Sandhurst and his father's pride when he had followed him into his old regiment. Here, Sir William had experienced some difficulty in knowing what to say next. He had eventually settled for saying that Alistair's love of good food and fine wine, as well as a yearning to be nearer home, had brought him back to Corrachan to start his award-winning restaurant. He had been a good businessman and an understanding employer. Sir William continued that he understood that the same chef had worked in the restaurant since it started, and he concluded by saying it was a great shame that Alistair had never married, as he would have been a loving husband and a wonderful father.

The intake of breath was palpable. There was a shifting in seats and glances exchanged. Was this man uninformed or being deliberately obtuse?

The rector then stood up and delivered a prayer that informed God about the accident and the distress it had caused Alistair's parents and proceeded for five minutes with a lot of 'beseeching' and 'pleas for mercy on miserable sinners'. That was as near as he got to mentioning Frank.

Tom's anger grew as the service progressed. As he rose and walked to the lectern, he intended to give an alternative address about the real Alistair before he announced the last hymn. No one would be able to stop him. He opened his mouth to begin. Then he looked at Alistair's mother seated with her husband on one side and his sister, Lucinda, and her husband, Torquil, on the other. Primmy oozed misery. She didn't deserve a scene at her son's funeral. He wavered for a couple of seconds, then reverted to the agreed order of service.

'Before we sing the closing hymn, I would like to say two things. Firstly, Alistair has been a member of this church for five years, so it was fitting that his funeral service be held here. We all feel that we have lost a good friend. Secondly, I have to tell you that Alistair's partner, Frank, wishes to issue an invitation to all to come to Chez Marguerite. It will be open house. Now we shall conclude the service by singing the final hymn in your Order of Service, "Just As I Am, Without One Plea", which Alistair felt summed up his life and the inclusive nature of God's love. I would draw your attention to the words of the third and fourth verses:

> *Just as I am, you will receive*
> *Will welcome, pardon, cleanse, relieve;*
> *Because your promise I believe,*
> *Oh lamb of God, I come.*

> *Just as I am, Your love unknown*
> *Has broken every barrier down;*
> *Now, to be yours, and yours alone,*
> *Oh lamb of God, I come.'*

Tom, in fact, had no idea whether or not this was a favourite hymn of Alistair's, but he felt the words were appropriate. The singing of this hymn was lustier in an attempt to redress the balance resulting from the earlier call to arms.

Some felt they should go to Corrachan House and partake of afternoon tea and a dram, but after a polite interlude many made their way to Chez Marguerite, where the contents of the extensive wine cellar were lined up awaiting consumption, along with numerous bottles of spirits and mixers.

Tom had arrived at the restaurant and had taken Frank to one side, inquiring if it was wise to let the world drink his share of the business.

'What business is that, then? I have no premises and no capital to purchase any other premises. They are putting the valuers in tomorrow, so I intend that there won't be much left to value. There is no point in them chasing me for their share. I have no assets. Al is dead, Tom. I can't bring him back and his bastard family want me out of the way. So I thought I would just share out what's here. Nice gesture, eh? What do you fancy? There is a very pleasant vintage bottle of Burgundy, or there is a crate of Moët in the fridge.' He put his arm round Tom's shoulder. 'You deserve the best! You stood up for me. Have a drink on the brigadier, Tom. Drink with me to my Al, the best friend and lover I ever had. People thought I was his bit of rough, but it wasn't like that. Now it's all gone to fuck!'

Frank lifted a bottle of thirty-year-old malt to his lips and drank. Tom left him alone. He hated Frank's gratitude. He hadn't stood up for either of them. Frank had been sidelined and Tom had let it pass. He recalled his conversation with Alistair about the blessing and he knew he had failed a good man in order to make life easier for himself.

The restaurant was full of people all evening, and in the early hours, as they left to go home, Frank was to be seen handing out bottles of expensive wine and vintage port like goodie bags after a children's party. He had also managed to give away all the tables and chairs, not to mention the cutlery, crockery and the kitchen equipment. Various white vans had appeared from as far away as Glasgow when word got out that the contents of a restaurant were going free.

When Frank vacated the premises early on Wednesday

morning, there was no drink or fixtures and fittings left. On the mirror behind the bar, which no one had been able to unscrew, was the lipsticked message 'FUCK YOU' and on the shelf below was an envelope containing a copy of Alistair's unsigned will. On the outside of the envelope, Frank had written, 'These were his last wishes. Hope he haunts you!' The door was left wide open and the small front garden was full of empty bottles and broken glass. The wheelie bin had been tipped over and the rancid remains of a salmon carcass and rotting vegetable peelings were scattered over the path.

Never had so many people walked along the road in front of the restaurant, hoping to witness Lucinda Gordon, née Hamilton-Sinclair, come to claim her inheritance. They were all unlucky. Lucinda's husband, Torquil, had arrived at nine o'clock to meet the valuers and had witnessed the devastation. He parked at the back of the restaurant and went inside. A quick call on his mobile had cancelled the valuation, and another two calls had arranged a cleaning firm to come in and a locksmith to install new locks.

A scandal in a small town focuses the collective attention and with every conversation the facts became slightly exaggerated, so by the end of the day the accepted version of events was a long way from the truth. The details, and subsequent embroidery, kept everyone enthralled till the end of the week. On Saturday, Joyce Macdonald was discussing the week's events with Helen Cooper in Tesco's car park. Helen was telling Joyce how her husband, Richard, had been annoyed with Tom's attempts to make him include Frank in the funeral service.

'What if he had acknowledged Frank and he goes and trashes the restaurant like that? Richard says they are all the same these people with liberal views. They think anything goes and all sorts of behaviour should be tolerated.'

The mention of liberals and tolerating bad behaviour reminded Joyce of what Phyllis had told her. As a secret is something told to just one person and as Helen Cooper was so easy to shock, Joyce couldn't resist passing on such a gem.

'By the way, you'll never guess who Phyllis saw together in London.'

Chapter Fifteen

The following Sunday morning, Ali sat at her kitchen table with her head in her hands. Tom walked past her towards the back door. He had his robes over his arm and his Bible and a folder of notes in one hand.

'Please, please don't do this! I beg you, don't do it this way,' said Ali.

He paused at the back door but didn't look at her. 'I'm sorry, but it's the only way.' He went out the door and down the path to the church.

Ali sat with tears streaming down her face. How could he think this would sort anything? He must be having some kind of breakdown, but that was no excuse for what he was about to do. At least Ruth was at Sacha's and had missed the last four and a half hours. Matt was watching his dinosaur DVD, oblivious to all around him. She reached for her phone to text Ruth, to tell her not to go to church and to come home immediately.

She could not believe what was happening. She had been unhappy about the state of her marriage for a long time, but over the last few days she had felt more hopeful. Tom had been so upset both by the events surrounding Alistair's death and about not giving the blessing and she felt that she had been a support to him. They seemed to be talking to each other and connecting much better.

This morning, she had woken at just after six and realised the other side of the bed was empty. She could hear Tom downstairs in his study. He often got up early on a Sunday to collect his thoughts before church, but never as early as this and he didn't sound as if he was in quiet contemplation. She got out of bed, put on her dressing gown and went downstairs. She opened the study door ready to ask him if he wanted a cup of tea and saw he was putting books into cardboard boxes.

'What on earth are you doing?'

'Sorting my books. These ones I want to keep. These you can send to a jumble sale.'

'Why are you doing this now, at this time in the morning?'

'Because it needs to be done today.'

'Why? What's the hurry?'

'Because I'm going away.'

Ali looked at him with incredulity. 'What are you on about? You're not going away.'

'I'm afraid I am. I was going to make you a cup of tea and come and talk to you.' He straightened up, looked at her and then looked away. 'I am going away today. I have to.' His tone of voice was flat and resigned.

'What are you talking about?'

'I can't take any more hypocrisy. I've come to the end.'

Ali looked at him with incomprehension. 'What do you mean?'

'I'm not going to pretend any more. I have no faith left. I don't believe in anything.'

Ali's relief was obvious. 'So this is what it's all been about! A loss of faith! Why on earth didn't you tell me?'

'Because it's got way beyond that, and there's an even bigger issue that I've never told you about.' He looked as if he were about to continue, but he stopped.

'Go on.'

He sighed and then said in the same quiet, flat voice, 'I'm gay. I've denied it for twenty-five years, but I'm not going to deny it any more. I am gay.'

Ali had stared at him. 'You're not! You're married! You've got children! You can't be gay. Oh, stop being silly. Is this some sort of wind-up?'

'No, it's not a wind-up. I am sexually attracted to men. I always have been, since my early teens.'

'I'd have known if you were.'

'Then I must have hidden it well.'

Ali had gaped at him. She had heard the words, but the enormity of what he was saying was just beginning to register. 'If you're gay, why did you marry me? I thought you loved me . . . fancied me.'

'I did in my own way.'

'What the hell do you mean by that?'

'I was brought up to believe that homosexuality was a sin, one that could be repented, and God knows I tried. It worked for a while too. It's much easier in life to be heterosexual. When I married you, I thought I was over my "sinful deviation", but I wasn't.'

'And for how long have you known that you were not "over it"?' asked Ali quietly. Her incredulity had turned to an awful realisation that he was serious. Nothing was ever going to be quite the same.

'Since Matt was born, but if I'm honest, there was something missing for longer than that.'

'That was four years ago! You have been pretending for four years. Or was it twenty?'

Tom was silent. Ali felt the shock turn to anger, which centred in a tight ball in her chest. 'It's all been a sham! You bastard! You let us live a happy little family life and you felt like that?'

'I love the children and I love you. You're kind and you're funny and supportive, but I am not sexually attracted to you.'

Ali had sat down. Her life had been based on a lie.

'I'm leaving today. After church.'

'Today? No, you can't just go like that. You can't just walk out – walk away as if you have no responsibilities. Look, we can sort this out. Lots of couples co-exist without sex. We could arrange separate rooms. Tell the girls I can't stand your snoring any longer.' Ali knew she was gabbling, but she was now fighting for her way of life.

'I told you, I've had enough of lies and hypocrisy. I am going.'

'If we are going to separate, we have other people to consider – the girls and Matt, not to mention the congregation. We have to think carefully about this and do things in the way that is least damaging. You can't just walk out on a whim.'

'It's not a whim. I can't go on being a minister. I have no faith left. I have not believed anything for ages. I've been pretending. That sham of a funeral was the last straw and I went along with it. I was going to stand up and tell them what Alistair was really like, but I copped out just as I copped out of giving a blessing. But not any more. I intend to stand up in church this morning to tell the congregation that I am leaving and I'm going to tell them why.'

He was still speaking in the same flat, expressionless tone, and the more Ali got upset, the less he seemed to be responsive to her comments.

'You're mad! You can't do that! Think about this, for God's sake. There will be an uproar. The press will be here by this afternoon. Tom, we live in a tied house! You will be making us all homeless. I know you've been a bit depressed, but you'll have to pretend for a bit longer. You could tell the presbytery you are demitting. We can then leave here, and if we haven't sorted this out, we can separate quietly.'

148

'You think I've been a "bit depressed"? There's an understatement!' There was now bitterness behind the quiet determination. 'When I am here in Corrachan, there is a huge black void inside me, and if I don't get out, it will overwhelm me. I have been thinking about this for a long time and I cannot go on any longer. I am sorting this today. I have to be honest with you and everyone else. I'm telling the congregation at the service and then I'll go. If you are worried about the press, I'll issue a press release. Everyone will be kind and understanding to you and the children. Anyway, you'll be much better off without me.'

'Please! Please! You can't do this. For all the reasons I've mentioned, you can't do this! You seem to think that you can just leave and it'll all be fine. Perhaps it will be for you, but it won't be for anyone you leave behind. Listen to me, you are having some kind of breakdown. You can get help. I promise you we'll sort this, but don't go and announce it from the pulpit.'

'I'm sorry, but that's what I am going to do,' said Tom. The flat determination was back again.

'Don't keep telling me you're sorry! If you were the slightest bit sorry, you wouldn't do it this way!'

He left the study and went upstairs to pack his clothes. Ali had followed him and watched him selecting clothes from the drawers as if he was going away to a conference for a week.

'I'll send for the rest of my things later.'

'Where do you intend to go?'

'Edinburgh.'

'Where in Edinburgh?'

'I'm going to stay with a friend. You will be able to contact me on my mobile.'

'A friend . . . or a lover?'

'His name is Mark. I think you'd like him.'

'Don't go there, please! How long has this relationship been going on?'

'About six months.'

'Six months! And have there been other lovers?'

'No. No relationships, just . . .'

'Just what?'

'Encounters.'

'What do you mean?'

'There are certain places where you can go.'

'And then you've come home and shared a bed with me. Oh Jesus.' She felt the anger being replaced with revulsion.

She ran for the bathroom and vomited till there was nothing left. She stood up, took off her robe, got into the shower and tried to scrub herself clean of the enormity of the situation and the catastrophic way in which Tom intended to deal with it. She felt angry, revolted, betrayed and afraid. She wrapped herself in a towel, went into the bedroom and begged him to sort his problems another way. She stormed, she swore, and she pleaded. She agreed that he could go and live his life as he pleased if they could leave this place with some dignity and deal with this problem in a measured and calm way.

Tom listened to her, unmoved. He was completely detached. He had reached the bottom, and now that he thought he had found a solution, he did not have the will or the energy to consider any other. He closed the suitcase, made himself some breakfast and got ready for church.

Ali sat down at the kitchen table, heard the back door close and knew that was the end of the life she had complained about, the life she wanted to alter. She would give anything to have things stay the way they were.

Chapter Sixteen

This was the second Sunday Gill had been to church. Her mother's insistent questioning about Kate's christening had finally forced her to act. She felt it would be cheeky to ask Tom Graham to perform the ceremony if she never attended, so she had told Mike he could have some quality time with his children on a Sunday morning while she went to church.

She hadn't listened to much of Tom's sermon the previous week, but it had been blissful not to be responsible for children or puppies for an hour. On returning home, she had noted with satisfaction that Mike was slightly fraught. He complained that he had got nothing done because the children were always crying, wanting him to do something or needing a nappy changed. Welcome to my world, she thought.

Ruth arrived in the manse pew with two minutes to spare. There was no sign of her mother or Matt. What was going on? Dad was distant, and Mum was angry and seemed to do nothing but snap. It had been a joy to stay the night somewhere where people behaved normally. She looked in her bag to turn off her mobile and realised she had left it at Sacha's. She glanced over and nodded to Gill.

The bells stopped ringing and the choir filed in and sat in

their places facing the congregation. Phyllis placed her music for the anthem under her seat. She had a short solo today and she was looking forward to it. Glancing up, she was glad to see that Jack was sitting in his usual pew seat. He had gone off to his office at the car showroom at half past eight this morning, saying he was behind with some work. That was unlike him. He was always so efficient. There were a great many things that were out of character recently. Glancing past Jack, she saw Gill and wondered if she had any idea what Mike was up to. A pretty woman, but she seemed to have let herself go. She looked a bit, well . . . ungroomed was probably the word. No sign of Ali Graham – more evidence that the drink had got hold of her, but she could at least come and support her husband.

Joyce was seated next to Phyllis and she surveyed the congregation also. She noted Gill was there again and remembered that stage in childrearing when doing nothing for an hour was the height of luxury. Perhaps the Church of Scotland should market itself as a child-free zone for stressed women. Such a pity if that husband of hers was carrying on with Lizzie Graham. There must be hundreds of secretaries and researchers in London if his mind turned to adultery without having to bring it so near home. Perhaps Phyllis had got this wrong, but Phyllis never saw a double-entendre or laughed at a doubtful joke, so if she had noticed, it must have been blatant. Her eye passed along the pews and she noted that Ali was again absent – two Sundays in succession was unusual. Perhaps the rumour about the drink problem was correct.

Tom stood at the lectern and announced the first hymn, 'Send Thy Light Forth and Thy Truth'. You'll get the truth soon, he thought. Having decided what he was going to do, he was perfectly calm, serene even. He couldn't consider doing it another way – wait for months to demit with numerous farewell events. That was just more hypocrisy. It was only fair to the congregation to tell them exactly what he was and why he was leaving. Ali and the children would be fine. Lizzie was leading her own life, Ruth was a quiet, sensible girl, and Matt was too young to understand. All he seemed to want was his dinosaurs. Another quarter of an hour and he would have told everyone. Another hour and Mark would be at the manse to collect him.

Bill Macdonald, who was Session Clerk, stood at the lectern to give the intimations: the Guild would meet on Monday evening at seven thirty in the hall, where Mrs Fraser would give a talk on her coach tour to Lake Garda; the mother-and-toddler committee would meet in the manse on Tuesday evening to discuss the forthcoming jumble sale; the Sunday Club wished everyone to know that they would be holding a fundraising coffee morning next Saturday in aid of the school in Kenya run by the missionary partners; and it was the eighty-fifth birthday of Mr Templeton, who had been in the choir for nearly seventy years. They all sang 'Happy Birthday'.

Next was the children's address. Tom asked the children to come to the front of the church. When they were seated at his feet, he began.

'Who knows what a fib is?'

Several children put up their hands. Tom pointed to a small boy with red hair.

'It's something that is not true.'

'That's right. And is it always wrong to tell fibs?'

'Yes,' they all chorused.

'What if your friend had a new dress that you thought was horrid and she asked you what you thought of it. What would you say? Would you tell the truth, or would you say it was lovely?'

'Horrid!' shouted a little boy.

'I'd tell her it was nice so not to hurt her feelings,' said a girl.

'Yes, Sarah. Sometimes people tell a little white lie to spare other people's feelings. Now tell me about secrets. Is it all right to have a secret?'

This was a harder one and the smaller children were nonplussed. However, Primary Six had recently had their 'what to do if someone wants to do unmentionable things to you' talk and one girl had obviously listened carefully.

'There are good secrets and bad secrets, and it's OK to have a good secret, but you must tell someone about a bad secret.'

'Exactly,' said Tom. 'Well done, Gina. Some secrets are good and others are bad. A bad secret can cause no end of trouble if you don't tell anyone. Now we will sing the children's hymn "Jesus Bids Us Shine With a Pure, Clear Light", and to do that we must have no bad secrets.'

As they opened their hymnbooks and searched for the hymn, Joyce hissed to Phyllis, 'Call that a children's address? No preparation involved there. So unlike him. I bet he's spending all his time dealing with Ali.'

All the adults, pleased that this hymn was not one of the new ones about people who lived in council flats but one they remembered from their Sunday-school days, sang enthusiastically. Then the children and the Sunday Club teachers, including Ruth, left the church for the hall. This departure was usually followed by the readings, but today Tom climbed up the steps to the pulpit and opened his folder. He paused just long enough to make sure everyone was looking at him.

'You may wonder why I am in the pulpit and not at the lectern. Well, I have something important I wish to say to you now that the children have left the church. During my discussion just now, Sarah told us that sometimes people tell a lie to spare people's feelings. Gina told us there are good secrets and bad secrets. Well, I have been telling lies to spare people's feelings and I have a bad secret. But before I tell you what the lies and the secret are, I want to say something about Alistair Hamilton-Sinclair. Alistair was a good man who had worshipped here with us for a long time. As you all know, he lived in a monogamous and loving relationship with Frank Callaghan for ten years.'

Phyllis closed her eyes. This was so unnecessary – everybody knew this. Why couldn't he just leave it unsaid?

Tom continued, 'Those of you who were at the funeral could not have failed to notice that this aspect of Alistair's life went unmentioned. Frank, who was about to become his civil partner, was referred to as his "employee". I would like to publicly acknowledge that relationship and ask you to remember Frank in your prayers. He has lost everything – his partner, his home and his livelihood – due to the small-mindedness and bigotry of others. And I am no better, as I refused to bless their relationship in this church, not because I thought it was wrong, but because I couldn't face the fallout that I knew would follow.'

Phyllis inhaled deeply. This was all too much. She was horrified to note that Joyce was nodding in agreement. Phyllis, who had failed to understand why Joyce, for all her right-wing views, was so tolerant on this matter, had also failed to understand why Joyce's forty-year-old son, Douglas, had remained unmarried.

Tom continued, 'Now I would like to turn to a more personal matter, to the lies and the secret that I referred to earlier.' He had total attention from the congregation – all fumbling for a handkerchief or searching for peppermints had ceased.

'For several years now, I have been living a lie. I am supposed to be your minister, to perform the sacraments, to preach the Gospel and to minister to you as a congregation. Well, I cannot do this any longer. I have no faith. You, as a believing congregation, deserve someone who can lead you in an honest and true manner. For that reason, I cannot continue to be your minister. I am leaving the Church as from today.'

There was a horrified stillness. Then the congregation began to exchange glances.

Oh my God, thought Phyllis.

That explains his behaviour, thought Gill.

Did Bill know about this? thought Joyce. A glance at Bill's stricken expression supplied the answer.

'That was the lie I have been living. But I have been keeping a secret for longer than that. Since I was a teenager, I have known that I was a homosexual. For years I pretended I wasn't. Recently, I stopped pretending to myself, but I have continued to pretend to my wife, my family and to you that I was a happily married heterosexual man. Well, I am not.'

Why couldn't he just have resigned because of his lack of faith? thought Phyllis.

Poor Ali, thought Gill. No wonder she's not here.

'I am leaving immediately after this service, but Ali and the children will be living in the manse for a while and I ask that you will be supportive to them in what is going to be a difficult period of adjustment. I have made many friends here and I hope you will not think too badly of me, but I cannot go on lying and pretending. I'm sure you will find a new minister who can lead this congregation as it ought to be led.'

Tom closed his folder, left the pulpit and made his way out of the church. The congregation watched him go in silence. The door to the vestry shut and the murmurs began. No one knew what to do next. The elderly McKenzie sisters began to weep noisily. Realising that as principal elder, it was his place to say something, Bill Macdonald stood up and went to the lectern.

'Er, I think perhaps we should close the service with the benediction.' He cleared his throat. 'Go in peace to love and serve the Lord, in the name of the Father, the Son and the Holy Spirit. Amen.' He paused and looked around for some sort of inspiration. Joyce caught his eye and gestured with her head to the exit. 'I suggest we all go home now,' he said.

The congregation, except for Peter Graham, got up and moved silently towards the door. Peter sat in a side pew staring straight ahead. He had heard his brother tell everyone he had no faith. Peter couldn't imagine being without his faith. It made him feel safe and gave him a structure on which to base his life. Coming to church was familiar and comforting. Then there was the other bit. He wasn't homophobic, and he had no objection to anyone who was gay, but this announcement was a huge Pandora's box of emotions, relationships and upsets. He couldn't lift the lid to consider the contents because that involved all the things he wasn't good at. Tom was going away and he was here. Would he be expected to do something about it, like speak to Ali? It meant everything was going to change. He hated change.

Ruth was discussing the parable of the Good Samaritan with her group of six-year-olds when she noticed Bill Macdonald come into the hall. He whispered to Mrs McCall, who gasped and put her hand across her mouth. Then they looked in her direction and continued whispering. Mrs McCall came over and took Ruth aside.

'I think you should go home. Your mother may need you.'

'What do you mean? What's the matter?'

'It's not my place to tell you. Just go home, dear.'

Ruth came out of the hall to see all the parents waiting. They were half an hour too early. Everyone avoided her gaze. What had happened? Was it her father, or Matt? She went up the path to the manse dreading what she might find. A man she had never seen before was standing in the kitchen.

'What's going on? Who are you?'

'I'm Mark — a friend of your father.'

'What's happened? Is Dad OK? Where's Mum?'

'They're both upstairs.'

Ruth ran upstairs and met her father on the landing carrying a suitcase. Ali was standing behind him.

'What's happening? Why has the service finished?' She looked at the suitcase. 'Where are you going?'

'Edinburgh.'

'Why? What for?'

'I'm sorry. I'm afraid I'm leaving. Your mother will explain.' He started down the stairs.

'Like hell I will,' said Ali. 'You can tell her. I'm not doing your dirty work.'

Ruth looked at Tom. 'Well, tell me, then.'

'Your mother and I are separating. I'm going to live in Edinburgh.'

'You can't. You work here.'

'I'm resigning because I don't believe any more. I can't go on being a minister.'

'You are not going to be a minister?' echoed Ruth.

Ali looked at Tom, who was still trying to get down the stairs. 'Go on, then. Tell her the rest.'

'It's a bit difficult to say this to your daughter . . .' He closed his eyes and took a deep breath. 'I'm gay. I can't go on living with your mother. I'm sorry. You will all be much better off without me.' He continued down the stairs and handed his case to Mark, who had come out of the kitchen.

'Could you take that to the car? I'll just get my laptop.'

He went into the study and came out with his computer bag. He glanced up at Ali and Ruth, who were both on the bend on the stairs. Ruth was devoid of colour.

'I'll be in touch soon. I'm sorry.'

'Stop saying you're fucking sorry!' screamed Ali.

Tom turned and walked out of the front door.

Ali heard the door shut with the finality of a coffin lid. Her life, based around the family and the Church, had seemed safe and secure, but had been an illusion. And now he had just walked away, leaving them to deal with the mess. She turned to Ruth and tried to put her arms round her.

'Are you all right? Come here and let me give you a hug. He's just told the congregation everything, so I think we might be the talk of Tesco.'

Chapter Seventeen

J ack and Phyllis Caldwell left the church and went to the
Corrachan Hotel. They had intended to go there after
the service for the carvery lunch, so they decided to sit in the
bar until the dining room opened. Jack ushered a shaken Phyllis
to a table at the window. Not only had it all been so uncomfortable and embarrassing, but she had been denied the
opportunity to sing her solo. Jack went up to the unmanned
bar and pressed the bell. Angela, who was doing her weekend
stint as barmaid and waitress, came through from the public bar.

'Morning, Angela. Your mother babysitting for you?'

'Yes, she always does it on a Sunday to let me go to work.'

'She's a good woman, Angela. She works for me all week, then
babysits for you all weekend. Could you fix us an amontillado
and a large Grouse, please?'

'You're early today,' said Angela.

'You're right, we are. It's been an exciting morning at the
kirk.'

'How d'you mean?'

'Tom Graham dropped two bombshells. Firstly, he tells us he
doesn't believe anything any more, and then – you're not going
to believe this – he tells us he's gay!'

'Jesus! You're joking?'

''Fraid not. Announced this from the pulpit and then walked out. Said he was leaving today.'

'Holy hell! I never thought he was gay! His brother perhaps, but not him. Where's he gone?'

'Who knows!'

'Frank from the restaurant went to Edinburgh. Perhaps he's gone to him. D'you think he's been carrying on with him?'

'I have no idea, although he did say that Frank had been badly done to.' He took out his wallet and produced a ten-pound note. 'What do I owe you?'

Jack took the drinks over to Phyllis. He had not even sat down before Angela was back in the public bar, where several local stalwarts were topping up their blood alcohol levels. By the time Phyllis had commented on Angela's coarse language, Angela had told the drouths, who included Gerry Martin, the reporter on the local paper. By the time Phyllis had told Jack that she had never known a morning like it, Gerry Martin, never one to miss the chance of making some money, was on the phone to his friend Colin at the *Daily Scot*, closely followed by his contacts at the *Sun* and the *Scotsman*. By the time Tom Graham was being driven out of town, the tabloid journalists were on their way, and by the time Jack and Phyllis entered the carvery for their roast-beef lunch, three-quarters of the town were of the impression that Tom Graham had run away to be with Frank Callaghan.

Gill came out of the church and saw a man putting a suitcase into the boot of a sports car parked in front of the manse. This was, perhaps, not the best moment to call. She would come back in half an hour or so. She was shaking as she walked along the street. Poor, poor Ali. Why did he have to humiliate her with a public announcement like that?

When she got home, Mike was sitting on the floor making a complicated building out of Duplo bricks to the accompaniment of *Bob the Builder*.

'You're back early.' He looked up from his engineering masterpiece. 'What's the matter? You look awful.'

As Gill was telling him, his mobile started to ring. He looked at the display and cancelled the call. 'I'll get that later.'

'I'm going to go round and see if there is anything I can do,' said Gill. 'You'll have to give the children lunch. There's some leftover mince and potatoes in the fridge.'

The mobile rang again and he again cancelled the call. 'It's Gavin. I'll call him back in a minute.'

'I'd better take something medicinal with me.' She opened the drinks cupboard and found a bottle of brandy.

The mobile signalled the receipt of a text.

'God, you're popular today.'

The child-free status of the room registered with Gill. 'Where are Ian and Kate?'

'They were here a minute or two ago. Ian was helping me with the Duplo, and Kate was crawling around.'

Gill put the brandy on the table and called for the children. Silence. She went into the front sitting room, which was supposed to be the child-free area, to find Ian creating a mural on the white wall with a red marker pen. Kate, the artist's assistant, was decorating herself and the beige carpet in blue. Gill confiscated the pens and gave Ian a telling-off. He started to cry.

'Mike, come here and look at this mess! You'll have to clean them and the carpet. I think we are going to have to paint the bloody wall again. They must have been in here for ages. You can't just forget about them, you know. You have to watch them all the time.'

'They weren't in here for long, honestly. Ian, you're a naughty boy. You know you're not supposed to do that.'

Ian's cries were not quite loud enough to drown the noise of another text delivery, which was followed by the phone ringing again.

'Why the hell don't you answer that?' said Gill.

'I'll sort the children first. Then I'll call Gavin back. Can't think what's so important.'

Gill collected the bottle of brandy, put it in a carrier bag and made her way along the road wondering how she was going to deal with this. What could she say? Anything was likely to be inadequate.

As Gill had closed the front door, the mobile had rung again. This time Mike answered it.

'Hello.' He listened. 'I know. Gill was in church.' He listened again. 'No. I can't see you today. Not on your own. Are you on the way home? I think your mother needs you.' He listened to her pleading. 'OK, OK. Look, I'll meet you off the bus and drive you home, but we are not going to spend time alone together. What time do you get here?'

Ali opened the door after inquiring through the letterbox who it was. Gill put her arms round her, but it was like hugging a stone pillar.

'He's gone.'

Gill pulled the brandy out of the bag. 'Come on, you need some of this.'

'Yes, I think I could cope with that. I've not had a thing to drink since your party. I swore I was going to be teetotal for evermore, but I think I've now changed my mind.'

They went into the kitchen and Gill poured out a large measure for Ali and a smaller one for herself.

'Did you know he was going to do this?'

'Only since six o'clock this morning. I tried everything I could think of to dissuade him from doing it this way, but he was adamant. Gill, it's as if he's had some sort of breakdown. He was so detached and matter of fact. He had decided what he was going to do and he wasn't open to reason. He just couldn't look at it from our perspective – how awful it will be for the girls and Matt and me. He had found a solution to his problems and I think he was quite surprised at how upset I was.'

'Perhaps he has the autistic gene, too?'

'Perhaps he has. He certainly seems to be lacking in the communication, interaction and imagination stakes. See! I've been doing my reading on the subject since we knew about Matt.'

'Did you . . . did you know he was gay?'

'You'll think I'm really dense, but I didn't. Oh, it all begins to make sense now . . . with the benefit of hindsight, but Tom was my first serious boyfriend. We met at a Scripture Union rally and, I know it's hard to believe, but I was a virgin when I got married, so there wasn't anyone to compare him with.' She began to cry. Tears poured down her face. Gill waited, then offered her a clean tissue and inquired where Ruth was.

'In her room. She won't come out. D'you know the bastard was going to make me tell her?'

'What about Lizzie?'

'I had to break it to her. She's coming home on the bus. She'll be here about three.'

'Matt OK?'

'He knows something is up, but he doesn't know what. I had to sit with him for a while, but he's watching his dinosaur DVD and he finds that more comforting than me. It seems no one wants me for anything any more.' She burst into tears again.

'Has Tom put out a statement, or is someone in Church headquarters going to say something? This is a gift to the press. You need to think damage limitation.'

'He said he would put out a press statement, but I expect he hasn't.'

Gill took a deep breath. 'I was at church today. Do you want to know what he said?'

'No. I think I heard it all from him.' She paused. 'How did everyone react?'

'Gobsmacked is probably the best word to describe it. The two old ladies – the McKenzies, is it? – they were weeping, and my friend and yours Mrs Caldwell looked as if a dog had just had puppies on her coat.'

'His congregational fan club must be so disillusioned.'

'Has anyone from Church phoned or been to see you?'

'No, not yet, but I expect someone will conquer their embarrassment and appear eventually.'

'Do you need to tell anyone else before the press get this?'

'I suppose I'd better call my sister . . . and my mother. That will be another disillusioned member of the fan club. I expect she'll think I drove him to it.' Ali got up from the table and went to the phone.

Gerry Martin was waiting at the bus stop on the High Street for Colin from the *Daily Scot*. Colin, who had never learned to drive, always seemed to be able to find someone to chauffeur him when he was on a story. Gerry sat in his car and smoked. The local paper didn't go to press till Wednesday, so he had days to follow up leads and talk to people. The important thing now was to maximise his takings from the national story. A silver Golf drove into the parking space in front of him. It had two small children strapped in the back and a slightly harassed-looking man driving. It was only when the driver got out, shut the door and leaned with his back against the car that Gerry recognised Mike Andrews. He could see flailing legs and hear muffled screams coming from the car. He tried to remember . . . there was something wrong with their little boy. What was it? That swearing thing . . . Tourette's syndrome, that was it.

Mike had had a stressful time since Gill had gone out. His attempts to clean the sitting room had not been wholly successful. Ian had tried to pat the puppies and been snapped at by Penny. He had heated the mince and potatoes in the microwave and had shovelled a spoonful into Kate's mouth without testing the temperature. She screamed and spat it out, but not soon enough to stop Ian loading his mouth with a large spoonful. He started screaming also. There were some ice lollies in the freezer, which had numbed the pain, but there was no way the children could be persuaded to sample the mince again. In the midst of this chaos, Lizzie had phoned again, begging that they have some time together. He repeated that he would meet her at the bus stop on the High Street. Now he was here, he wasn't sure it was a good idea. He needed to distance himself from her, but he wasn't so hard-hearted that he could ignore her when her family was falling to bits. He would play the friend-of-the-family role properly this time.

The bus from Edinburgh pulled in and Lizzie and Colin got off. Lizzie ran to Mike and threw her arms round him and burst into tears. Mike tried to detach himself, glancing around to see if anyone was watching them. There just seemed to be a couple of men. One of them looked a bit familiar, but he couldn't place him.

Gerry Martin greeted Colin and they glanced at Mike and Lizzie.

'That's the gay minister's daughter. No better than she ought to be so the story goes. And that's Mike Andrews, the MP, meeting her. Though she behaves as if she's known him a long time, she hasn't. The Andrews have only been here for about six months.'

'Well, she spent the bus journey on her mobile. I thought it was her boyfriend she was begging to meet her. Perhaps we should watch this space.' Colin took his small digital camera from his pocket and snapped the scene.

Mike got Lizzie into the car. Kate had fallen asleep, but Ian was still awake and grizzling. Lizzie was in full spate.

'What am I going to do? I can't deal with this! My father, gay? Denying all he has based his life on. How can he do this? Everyone will be laughing at us.'

'What you can do is go home and support your mother. You have a life in Edinburgh. Her life, and your brother's and sister's, is here and it has just fallen to bits. You are an adult now. It's time to act like one.'

'Please don't lecture me, not now. Oh, Mike, I need you. Can I meet you tonight? Make an excuse and we can go somewhere in the car. I love you, Mike.'

'No, we can't meet tonight. Look, I've told you it's over. Forget me and concentrate on your family. When everything's died down, you'll find someone else without any problem. What we had was fun, but that's all it was. Fun.'

It took about three minutes to drive from the bus stop to the manse, so any further discussion was curtailed. Mike switched off the engine and told her to get out and go inside and be helpful.

'The press will probably appear. Don't answer the phone and don't open the door. If anyone does get to you, just say, "No Comment."'

Gerry Martin took Colin to the public bar at the Corrachan Hotel. It seemed a good place to begin gathering information. He started by offering Angela a drink when he bought his rum and black.

'Thanks. I'll have one later.'

'You know the Grahams, do you?' he inquired.

'Well, I know her. She runs the mother-and-toddler group I go to. Bit bossy, and her little boy's mental.'

'How d'you mean?'

'There's something wrong with him. Not right, if you know what I mean. He should be going to school in August, but he isn't.'

'What about the other members of the family?'

'Lizzie was in my year at school. She's really clever, but she's a slag. I got pregnant when I was sixteen, but at least I kept it. She was shagging Darren Connerty for ages. He just thought she was an easy lay. When she was going with him, she had two abortions and she was on smack. They had to send her to some fancy clinic to come off it. She thought she was so cool, but we all hated her.'

'Isn't there another daughter?'

'Yeah, Ruth. She's the opposite of Lizzie. Mousy and quiet. Teaches in the Sunday school and things like that.'

'What about him, the minister?'

'Don't know really. He used to come into school and do boring assemblies. Never thought he was queer, though. He's been with that Frank from the restaurant since Alistair from the big house was killed. Now, they definitely were queer. Frank had a big party after the funeral and I know Tom Graham was at that. Frank told Alistair's parents to fuck off and he gave everything away. Then he trashed the restaurant. All his gay friends were here for the funeral and they had some sort of orgy in the place and wrote things all over the walls. It's true. Friend of my mum's works for the cleaning company that had to come and sort it. I reckon Tom's with Frank. If you can find Frank, I'll bet you'll find him.'

This story was getting better and better. A handicapped child, a slapper of a daughter and a gay orgy. Who said life in the country was dull?

'So how did you hear about what went on in church this morning?'

'Jack Caldwell. He came in here straight from the church.'

'Who's Jack Caldwell?'

'He owns most things in this town. As I said, he came in after church with his wife and told me all about it.'

'And where would I find him?' inquired Colin.

Chapter Eighteen

Bill Macdonald was not having a good day. The fact that Tom had not talked to him first before making his announcement had annoyed him and offended his lawyer's way of doing things. Following the bombshell, the realisation that he was temporarily in charge caused him more than a mild panic. He was used to being in control, and in this instance, he wasn't. After he had managed to get everyone to go home, he went into Tom's office and considered what to do next. It was impossible to locate anyone from the Church hierarchy at a quarter to twelve on a Sunday morning, when all good Presbyterians are at their devotions. Unable to think of anything else, he and Joyce drove to Invercraig and parked outside the church of Donald Cumming, the minister whose turn it was to be in charge of the local presbytery. They waited for a quarter of an hour, until he had finished shaking hands with his departing congregation, before getting out of the car and telling him the news.

The Reverend Donald Cumming was in his mid-forties and married with six children. He was on the evangelical wing of the Church of Scotland, basing his life and preaching on a fairly literal interpretation of the Bible. Life was a matter of faith based on the teachings of Jesus with some Old Testament prophecies thrown in. To him, things were black or white with no shades of grey, and sodomy was black. He had never had much in common with Tom Graham, whose liberal theology and inability to control his wayward daughter offended him. To Donald, homosexuality was an abomination and those who indulged in such practices were destined for a large shovel in Hell.

When Bill Macdonald, desperate to hand over responsibility for this crisis, told him of Tom's departure, Donald had felt a mixture of emotions. Although disgusted by the sin, he had felt vindicated in his thinking that Tom had never been a true Christian. Turning his thoughts to Ali, he realised now why she had that drink problem. Although he wasn't exactly sure what he was going to do next, he knew this was a God-given opportunity to decry the evils of sodomy.

Bill knew that someone had to go and visit Ali, but after hearing the Reverend Cumming's views, he wasn't sure Donald was the right person. After some discussion, it was agreed that they should both go.

'You know Mrs Graham well. I don't. We'll both go and see her this afternoon.'

At four thirty, the doorbell rang at the manse. It was unfortunate that Colin had rung the bell some ten minutes earlier and had been told through the letterbox that there would be 'no comment'. Lizzie heard the bell again, went to the door, which was on the chain, and opened it a crack.

'Look, I've told you already – no comment. Why don't you just eff off back to where you came from?' She was about to shut the door when she looked up and saw not Colin, but Bill Macdonald and another man, who was wearing a dog collar, standing on the doorstep.

Bill cleared his throat. 'Lizzie, er, do you think we could see your mother?'

'I'll go and find out if she wants to see you. She's very upset.' Lizzie closed the door and left them on the step for several minutes before she reopened the door, showed them into Tom's study and announced ungraciously, 'She'll be through in a minute.'

Left alone, Bill and Donald Cumming perched on the seats reserved for engaged couples come to discuss their wedding arrangements and waited in silence. Ali, not wanting to see them on her own, had asked Gill to come in with her. Gill declined, saying it was a family matter, and not knowing that Lizzie had already told them what they should do with themselves, suggested that her elder daughter should be present.

Ali shook hands with Donald, and Bill gave her a kiss. Both smelled the brandy fumes. She sat in Tom's chair and looked questioningly at them. Bill and Donald exchanged glances. Then Bill began.

'We have just come to see if you are all right and to work out how to handle this with regard to the press and things.'

'Well, I can't say I'm all right. My whole life has just fallen to bits. My husband has gone to live with his gay lover and left me here . . . to deal with everything!'

A muscle in Donald's cheek twitched at the mention of the gay lover.

Ali continued, 'As for the press, they have already been at the door and on the phone. Tom said he would put out a statement, but I expect he hasn't. Clear thinking is not his forte at the moment. You can contact him on his mobile, Donald, and suggest he does something about it. I don't intend to speak to him in the near future.' She had the small satisfaction of thinking that Tom's evening with his lover would be disturbed.

'Alison, we are all so sorry for what has happened.' Donald was holding his hands together as if in prayer. 'We are praying that you will have the strength to weather this storm, which has been sent to test you, and that Tom will repent his sin. With God's help, I'm sure he will be able to return to his family. Jesus forgives everyone who sincerely repents.'

'Well, I wouldn't hold your breath for the repentance, Donald.'

'And how are your other children taking it?' he inquired.

'Ruth has shut herself in her room, and Matt is in a world of his own.'

'Your little boy has problems, doesn't he?' asked Donald unctuously.

'He's autistic.'

'Ah,' said Donald.

Ali looked at him and thought he was going to say something about the sins of the fathers. You dare, she thought. Then she looked at them and, seeing how uncomfortable they were, realised that this was probably more difficult for them than it was for her.

'Would you like a cup of tea, or a drink? Bill, I'm sure you could do with a dram. Donald, what about you?'

'I am an abstainer. A cup of tea would suffice.'

Pompous git, thought Ali. She looked at Bill.

He really needed a drink, but he chickened out. 'Cup of tea would be fine.'

'Lizzie, could you go and ask Gill to put the kettle on?'

Ali looked at them. 'Well, what happens now? How long have we got in this house?'

'I don't think we need to discuss that yet – it will be a while before another minister is appointed. Someone from Church HQ in Edinburgh will contact you.'

'Donald, I have to think about it now. I have three dependent children, no income and I am about to become homeless.'

'Remember, my dear, that God will take care of you and help you in your time of trial. Our Lord told us to consider the lilies . . . I'm sure you're aware of the passage. Your husband has committed an unspeakable sin – for which he will answer when he comes before the heavenly throne – but we will pray constantly that he sees the error of his ways. You must be strong for your children. Do not allow yourself to take comfort in alcohol; it is a false crutch. Only God can keep you strong.'

She almost, but not quite, felt herself to be on Tom's side against this text-quoting dog collar. As for the alcohol reference, she had only had one brandy and surely that could be classed as medicinal under the circumstances. Lizzie had come back into the room while Donald was talking. Angry as she was with her father, she wasn't going to let Donald get away with this.

'My God, you are a sanctimonious fart. My father is evidently gay. I must say it was news to me, but if he's gay, he was born that way, like being left-handed. At least now he's being honest, even though he has abandoned us here, in a huge pile of shit. We don't need a sermon; we need some practical help regarding where we are going to live and how we are going to deal with the press. We need to know what support the congregation and the Church in general are going to give my mother, who has done as much work as my father over the years. And another thing, if my mother has a drink today to help her through this, then she doesn't need to be treated as if she is an alcoholic.'

Bill tried to intervene. 'Lizzie, I know you're upset, but it doesn't help to speak to Donald like that.'

Donald, convinced that on account of her past behaviour Lizzie was also going to roast in Hell, saw his opportunity to point out the error of her ways. 'And I shall pray for you, Elizabeth, that you might realise that fornication is a deadly sin and that no man wishes to marry a jezebel.'

Lizzie looked Donald up and down. 'I have no idea what you are talking about. I think I've told you already to fuck off back to where you came from. Do I have to repeat myself?'

174

She turned round and left the room just as Gill came in with a tray.

'Tea, anyone?'

They all heard the front door shut and turned towards the window to see Lizzie running down the front path.

She ran most of the way to the Andrewses' house. She hadn't meant to abandon her mother, but that man had really annoyed her. Now, she realised Mike would be on his own, except for the children of course. She walked up the Andrewses' front path, oblivious to the fact that Phyllis was watching from her garden. As Mike opened the door, she threw her arms round him and burst into tears. She was genuinely upset about a lot of things — Mike ditching her, her father, her mother's situation, not to mention the embarrassment. As someone for whom life until now had proceeded without a hitch, she was not good at coping with disappointment and situations outwith her control. Therefore she behaved as if she was eight years old. She wept, she complained that it wasn't fair, she pleaded with Mike to take her back — all this with her arms round his neck — while Ian looked on in fascination.

Mike managed to get her inside, took her into the sitting room and sat her on the sofa. He then sat beside her, put his arm round her shoulders and gave her a paper hankie. Eventually, the tears subsided and she laid her head on his chest. He stroked her hair and kissed the top of her head.

Gill's intense dislike of net curtains meant that it was easy for people to see into the sitting room when walking up the garden path. It was unfortunate that Colin chose this moment to call on Mike for a comment. He surveyed the scene inside and concluded that this was taking the role of 'friend of the family' to a new level. He rang the bell. Mike answered the door to provide only a 'no comment'. As Colin turned to go, he noticed that Lizzie was no longer in the sitting room. This was not today's story but had definite possibilities for later. As he walked down the path, he wondered why the Andrews had a large pink smudge all over their white wall.

Bill Macdonald returned home to find Joyce discussing the events of the day with Phyllis and Jack. He made himself a very large gin and tonic and wearily sat down. The assembled company looked at him expectantly.

'Oh, don't ask! It was dreadful.' He took a substantial gulp of his gin and closed his eyes.

'What happened? You'll have to tell us.' Joyce's curiosity was not to be thwarted.

Bill sighed. 'Suffice to say, Donald Cumming is a decent man, but his pastoral skills leave a little to be desired. Combine that with Ali smelling of drink and Lizzie behaving like a spitting cat, it was not a happy encounter.'

'So what actually happened? Details! Details! Come on, tell us!'

'Well, Donald gave Ali a lecture about sin and repentance. Lizzie called him a sanctimonious fart. Donald called her a jezebel and she told him to eff off. Then Gill Andrews came in with a tea tray and we all had to make polite conversation till we could get out of there. At least I got out of phoning Tom. Donald is going to do that. God, what a day it's been!'

'Ali was drunk again?' asked Phyllis, eager to have a theory confirmed.

'She smelled of drink, but she wasn't drunk,' said Bill wearily. 'If she's had a drink today, I don't think you can blame her. I'm sure it's not been the best day of her life. Oh dear, oh dear, what did Tom think this would achieve?'

'Has he gone off with Frank?' asked Joyce.

'I haven't a clue. Ali said he had gone off with his lover, but she didn't say who it was.'

176

'Has to be Frank,' said Phyllis. 'Who else could it be?'

'If the popular press is anything to go by, about ten per cent of the population,' said Jack.

'It's never that many, surely,' said Phyllis. 'You must be confusing it with something else. Are you sure you are not thinking of dyslexia?'

'Phyllis, I can assure you I know the difference between a bugger and an illiterate.'

'Jack! Language!' Phyllis remembered that the use of bad language in inappropriate situations was another symptom of early Alzheimer's.

The doorbell rang. Joyce made her way to the front door and found Colin, who had combed his hair and put on a tie, standing on the doorstep. He told her he was from Edinburgh, he was here about Tom Graham, and he wondered if he could speak to Bill. She invited him in and led the way to the sitting room, where she introduced Colin as someone from Church HQ. Colin had just come from the Caldwells' house, so to find them here and to be a lucky victim of mistaken identity was more than he could have hoped for. He was offered a drink and decided that a small sherry might be in character.

'What a shock you must have had this morning,' was his opening line.

'That's one way of putting it,' said Bill.

'It was absolutely dreadful,' said Phyllis. 'Couldn't he just have resigned over a loss of faith? We did not need to know his preferences in the bedroom department. It was very upsetting for the congregation. Edith and Cissie McKenzie were in tears.'

'You had no idea he was having problems?'

Bill replied before Phyllis could. 'No, I speak to him every week and he seemed just the same as ever.'

Phyllis thought it was important to give this man the full picture. 'I think he was having problems with his wife.' She

177

made a drinking motion with her hand. 'You know. And his older daughter is . . . free with her favours. Then the boy's got something wrong with him.' This time she tapped her index finger on her forehead.

No wonder the wife has taken to drink, thought Colin.

'Does the elder daughter still live at home?'

'She's a student in Edinburgh, so she's away most of the time. Have you been to visit Ali Graham yet?' asked Bill.

'No, not yet. I thought it would be helpful to speak to you first to try to get a picture of what has been happening.'

'We went to see her this afternoon. It was not a very happy encounter. I don't want to speak out of turn, but Donald was not particularly helpful in the way he handled it and Lizzie – that's the elder daughter – went off at the deep end and swore at him.'

'Donald? Who's Donald?' asked Colin.

'Donald Cumming, the presbytery moderator. He was the one who phoned you.'

'Oh, yes, yes, of course. Do you know where Tom is, Mr Macdonald?'

'Edinburgh somewhere. He evidently has a . . . partner, but we don't know where he is or with whom.'

Phyllis thought that she could be more helpful. 'It has to be Frank Callaghan from the restaurant. He's . . .' she paused before saying the distasteful word '. . . homosexual. His partner was killed recently and Tom had a lot to do with Frank at the time.'

'Well, we don't know that for certain. We just think it's a possibility,' said Joyce.

'Do you have Tom's mobile number? We will need to speak to him.'

'Yes, it's in our phonebook. Wait a minute.' Bill got up and went into the hall and returned with the number.

Luck had been with Colin so far, but he felt he should go

178

before he was discovered. 'Well, I'd better be getting along to see Mrs Graham now. You've all been so helpful. I'll be in touch.'

Bill showed him out. As he closed the door, the phone rang. It was a man from the Board of Ministry at Church HQ wishing to come and speak to him tomorrow. The person on the other end of the phone was adamant that no one from the Church of Scotland had come to Corrachan today and he had no idea who Colin was.

It was eight o'clock before Gill got home. She had dealt with numerous reporters, coaxed Ruth out of her room and made them all scrambled eggs and bacon. Matt, sensing something was wrong, had refused to eat and had had a screaming fit. This gave Ruth something to think about as she comforted him and put him to bed. Lizzie had not returned and her mobile was switched off. An exhausted Ali had gone to bed after railing at length about Donald Cumming and his remarks. Gill waited for a while, with rising irritation, to see if Lizzie came back. She was supposed to be here to support her mother, not flouncing off in a huff for hours. She decided she couldn't wait any longer and she had to get home.

There was no one in the kitchen when she returned. She took a bottle of white wine from the fridge, poured herself a large glass and made for the sitting room, where the television could be heard from behind the closed door. Expecting to find Mike snoozing after his afternoon with the children, she was surprised to find Lizzie sitting watching a film.

'So this is where you got to. Your mum's worried about you.'

'I had to come somewhere and I didn't want to go back till I knew that dreadful man had gone.'

'They went about ten minutes after you did. As it's now eight o'clock, I think it's safe to go home.'

Lizzie said nothing, picked up her coat and climbed halfway up the stairs. She shouted towards the bathroom, where Mike was dealing with the children, 'I'm going home now, Mike. Thanks for letting me be here.' She turned to Gill and said, 'Bye, then,' and walked to the front door.

When Mike had finished bathroom duties, Gill read Ian a story, then bent down and gave him a kiss. He put his arms round her and buried his face in her neck.

'Like kisses Mummy. Lizzie like kisses. Lizzie was sad. Daddy kissed her better.'

Chapter Nineteen

Tom had looked forward to this first evening of freedom for a long time. The secret he had lived with for what seemed like an eternity was a secret no longer and the deceit was over. He was euphoric and felt he knew for the first time what it was to be born again. The past was wiped out and a new future was there for the taking.

His visits to Edinburgh on Church business had initially allowed him to dabble on the fringes of the gay scene, then to use his time after meetings to maximum advantage. At first, he had been tentative. The Internet had provided the names of some venues and he had started with a New Town pub that was said to cater for the more mature gay clientele. He walked past the premises on several occasions before he ventured in one grey evening in November four years ago. After ordering a pint, he chatted to the barman, telling him he was killing time before he had to catch a train. It wasn't long before a small, dapper man in his fifties came and sat beside him and introduced himself as David. Tom said his name was Simon. It transpired David had a wife waiting for him in Morningside and he nodded at Tom's wedding ring, suggesting that perhaps they both ought to be getting home and could he give Tom a lift to the station? They went the long way to Waverley Station via Holyrood Park. In the darkness, in the back seat of a silver Jaguar, David confirmed him into his new orientation.

They drove in silence out of the park. At a red light, beside the Commonwealth Pool, David told him abruptly to get out of the car. Tom was left standing on the pavement in the rain as the Jag disappeared round the corner, taking David home to his wife and beef casserole.

Tom walked back towards Princes Street, his thoughts and his emotions racing. He was an ordained minister who was supposed to believe in heterosexual sex between married couples and he had just had a contrary experience with a complete stranger in the back of a car in an Edinburgh park. He had allowed himself to be picked up and he had knowingly accepted the lift. There was no denying what he was now. If he tried hard enough, he wondered if perhaps he could live his life as usual and keep his needs under control. Numerous gay Christians led a celibate life, if the various Church authorities were to be believed. By the time he reached his car in the St James Centre car park, he had decided that was what he would do.

He managed for several months. A guilty conscience, combined with the fact that Matt was a sleepless and difficult baby, made it reasonably easy to avoid both visits to the New Town pub and the duties of a husband. He went to several meetings in Edinburgh and came home immediately afterwards, but the niggling itch gradually increased until it caused him to take a walk up Calton Hill late one May evening after listening to a day of erudite discussion at the General Assembly of the Church of Scotland. He had removed his clerical collar, stuffed it in his pocket and opened the top buttons on his shirt. He found himself in the bushes with a young man. The anonymity was thrilling, but being relieved of his wallet at knifepoint was not. As he handed it over, the dog collar fell out of his pocket and was snatched up as a

182

souvenir. In a panic, he walked back the way he had come with beads of cold sweat running down his back. His attacker now had all the information he needed to blackmail him. His credit cards had to be stopped, so the theft would have to be reported. As he reached the end of Princes Street, still buzzing with tourists, an idea filtered through his layers of panic. Pickpockets! His wallet had been stolen from his pocket!

He walked slowly via the guesthouse he was staying in, where he collected another clerical collar, to Gayfield Police Station. An apt name, he thought, in the circumstances. He reported his wallet lost somewhere between the Mound and the guesthouse, surprising himself that this lie tripped so easily from his lips. He was given the sympathy and respect due to a man of the cloth and he left the police station feeling only relief. The guilty conscience came later, in the privacy of his small room, when he realised both the extent of his deception and that he could have been seriously injured, or worse. He spent the next few weeks dreading the arrival of the postman, making sure he collected the mail as soon as it came through the letterbox. But there was no anonymous letter and he came to realise that ready cash and the dog collar as a trophy were all his assailant had wanted.

His conscience, combined with the fear of discovery, again acted as a deterrent, but only for a short while. Soon he was delaying his return home after meetings, but this time he was more careful. He frequented gay bars and cafés, maintaining his alias as Simon, a social worker from Inverness, and made sure he had a chance to converse and make a character judgement before adjourning to his car or someone's flat. His confidence grew, and one evening he got into conversation with Mark – thirty-eight, tall, rich and good-looking. At first, Tom could not believe Mark, who had recently finished a long-term relationship, was interested in him, but there was an immediate intellectual connection as well as attraction. After their second meeting, Tom told Mark his real name and realised he was in love. Mark occupied his waking thoughts and his need to invent reasons to go to Edinburgh was all-consuming. Every time he drove out of Corrachan, his depression left him, only to return like a black cloak as he drove home.

Ali accepted the more frequent committee meetings without comment and looked forward to his absences as a day free from negativity, when she didn't feel as if she was being dragged into the abyss with him. Every lie took him further from his family and his congregation into a spiritual wilderness.

Alistair's funeral had been a catalyst, forcing him to act. By that time, he was incapable of logical, responsible thought, and in the days in which he planned his escape, he focused only on getting out – the need for self-preservation overriding any consideration of the possible consequences. Mark, who had been quite content with an occasional relationship, had agreed to help him with his escape and offer him a bolthole. Tom took this to be a sign of long-term commitment.

Many times he had imagined this first night of freedom, a quiet evening together in Mark's New Town flat. The evening had started well, with Tom relaxing on the sofa, glass of champagne in hand, while Mark had cooked dinner. He had done it! He had told everybody! There would be no more lies. No one could get to him because no one knew where he was. Unfortunately, he had forgotten to switch off his mobile, which rang halfway through the main course. He glanced at the number, recognised it as being from the Corrachan area and made the wrong guess that it was Bill Macdonald. Some lingering stab of conscience caused him to answer it. He heard the voice on the other end and realised with dismay that it was Donald Cumming. He listened in silence to an entreaty to return home, to see the error of his ways. He told Donald politely there was no going back. He listened while Donald inquired why Tom had not discussed his loss of faith with him.

Realising that he no longer had to be polite, Tom replied with great satisfaction, 'Because, Donald, I know you never thought I had a faith in the first place.' He cut the call off and tossed the phone on to the sofa with a suggestion as to what Donald could do with himself. He had just finished his steak when it rang again.

'Answer it, Mark, and tell them I'm not available.'

'Tom Graham is unavailable for comment.' He listened to the person on the other end, then handed the phone to Tom. 'It's someone from the Church of Scotland HQ. They say they really do need to speak to you.'

Tom took the phone. Colin put on his best Church of Scotland voice, saying he had got the number from Bill Macdonald and was sorry to bother him this evening but the Church required an address for him because there would be paperwork that needed to be attended to. Tom gave him Mark's address. Colin inquired solicitously as to why Tom had decided on such a sudden revelation.

'I couldn't go on lying to everyone. It's as simple as that. The situation was intolerable. It was that or a big dose of pills. I couldn't take any more. I'm sorry.'

He ended the call and this time switched off the phone.

Colin filed his story, as had all the other reporters, and by nine thirty the next morning the newsagent in Corrachan was sold out of tabloids and the Scottish broadsheets, as the town residents, hungry for details, bought everything available, leaving only a few sad copies of the *Daily Telegraph*. Colin's story was under the headline 'Gay Minister Shock: Congregation Hear Minister Tell Them He Is a Gay Unbeliever.'

Phyllis was pleased with the coverage. She had asked Joyce

185

and Helen Cooper round for coffee, but Joyce had initially declined, embarrassed that her false assumption about Colin's identity had greatly helped the compiling of these news stories. Phyllis insisted she would get Helen Cooper to pick her up and, against her better judgement, Joyce reluctantly agreed. Once her guests were seated with a cup of coffee and a selection of fancy biscuits, Phyllis could contain herself no longer.

'Well, have you seen the papers, then?'

Helen said she had seen *The Times* but there was no mention, and Joyce had seen the *Scotsman*, in which there had only been a small paragraph on the inside pages.

'Just listen to this, then! There's much more in here!' She picked up the *Daily Scot*, showed them the headline and started to read. '"The town of Corrachan was reeling yesterday as its minister of ten years, Tom Graham, forty-four, told the congregation he was really a gay unbeliever. He walked out of the church and left town, leaving his distraught wife, two teenage daughters and son, who has learning difficulties." What exactly is wrong with that child? He's a very peculiar little boy.'

'Richard says Tom told him he's autistic. They can be very clever actually, autistic children, especially at remembering lots of facts,' replied Helen.

'That's right,' said Joyce. 'Did you see that film *Rain Man* with Dustin Hoffman? He was autistic . . . not Dustin Hoffman, the man he played in the film. He was good on numbers, wasn't he?'

'Yes, I did see it. That was a while ago now. I remember I saw it on a plane. We went to Chicago for that Anglican conference. What year was that, now?'

Phyllis cleared her throat and rustled the paper. 'Ladies? We are digressing! Will I go on . . . ?'

The ladies exchanged glances and were silent.

Phyllis continued, '"Rev. Graham is holed up in a love nest

in Heriot Row, one of Edinburgh's most expensive streets. He told our reporter he had contemplated suicide. 'It was get out or take my own life,' he said." I never thought he was suicidal. Did you, Joyce?'

'Seemed his usual self to me.'

'Well, a crisis of faith is such a huge issue if you are an ordained minister.' Helen bit into a Viennese finger. 'Richard says that's what happens if you're too liberal. You pick and choose which bits you want to believe and eventually you realise what's left doesn't add up to anything. Then your whole life must seem a bit pointless!'

Phyllis continued with a smirk on her face, 'It mentions my name, listen. "Shocked Phyllis Caldwell, sixty-four—" They didn't need to put my age in. Wait a minute, I never told him my age. How did he find out?'

'I don't know, Phyllis. Perhaps he guessed,' said Joyce.

Phyllis picked up the paper again. '"Shocked Phyllis Caldwell, sixty-four, long-time member of his congregation, said, 'We didn't need to know his preferences in the bedroom department. It was very upsetting." That's fair. I did say that, didn't I, Joyce?'

'Can't remember,' said Joyce, who was now wishing she had trusted her earlier judgement and stayed at home.

Phyllis continued, 'Oh, now, there's a bit about Bill: "Session Clerk Bill Macdonald has been left to pick up the pieces and try to comfort Mrs Graham, forty-three, and children Lizzie, eighteen, Rosie, sixteen, and Michael, four." He's got their names wrong! That's just carelessness. Look, there's a bit more about Bill: "'It was very difficult. They told us to eff off. I know they were upset, but we were only trying to help,' he said." That's accurate, though. Bill did say that, didn't he, Joyce?'

'Mmm. Yes,' said Joyce, sinking further down her seat.

'Now there's a bit about Mike Andrews. Calls him a "friend

187

of the family". Then here is a bit about Donald Cumming. You would have thought he would have put a dog collar on for the photo. He looks so untidy.'

'Let's have a look,' said Helen. 'Oh, I see what you mean. Richard says it's important to maintain the dignity of the clergy. He's never without his clerical collar.'

'What? Even in bed?' asked Joyce.

'Oh, don't be silly, Joyce, of course not. Come on, Phyllis, what does it say?'

'"The Rev. Donald Cumming described Mr Graham as a sinner who would answer on the day of judgement."'

'Quite right too,' said Helen. 'Richard says that if God had wanted men to have sex with other men, He wouldn't have created women. It's unnatural and I don't think anyone can argue with that.'

'I quite agree,' said Phyllis. 'What do you think, Joyce?'

Joyce stood up. 'I think I ought to be going now. I have a lot to do today and I can't spend hours sitting about drinking coffee!'

'You've hardly arrived and I haven't finished reading this yet. This best bit is still to come. Sit down and listen to this.'

Joyce slowly sat down again but got no further than the edge of the sofa.

Phyllis continued, '"Another scandal hit this small town recently. Chef Frank Callaghan trashed a local restaurant, then disappeared following the horrific car crash that killed his gay lover, restaurant owner Alistair Hamilton-Sinclair. Frank is also believed to be in the Edinburgh area." That must mean they know he's with Frank!'

'Fancy Frank having a flat in Heriot Row! I didn't think he had that sort of money,' mused Joyce.

'Charles and Primmy must have paid him off,' said Phyllis, 'to go away and not make trouble. That'll be it!'

'Perhaps,' said Helen, 'but Richard says that Charles absolutely detested Frank. On the other hand, it could be worth their while to spend a little to get rid of him.' She looked at the article again. 'They'll be so annoyed that Frank has been called his "gay lover".'

'Well,' said Joyce, 'he was his lover. They were about to go through their civil partnership. It's like being married.'

'You really surprise me, Joyce, taking that attitude. It's unnatural,' said Helen.

Helen, like Phyllis, had not worked out why Douglas Macdonald was another unclaimed treasure.

Like his wife, Bill Macdonald was mortified. That he had given all sorts of confidential information and a phone number to someone without checking their credentials was not only embarrassing but a slur on his standing as a solicitor. He had bought the papers as he walked the dog before breakfast and found he had no appetite for his usual porridge and toast. At work, he closeted himself in his office, telling the front desk that he wasn't to be disturbed. He even broke the habit of thirty years and did not go to the lunchtime meeting of the Rotary Club, where Jack Caldwell's retelling of the previous day's events eclipsed the local doctor's talk on new trends in general practice. It was not only Bill who was absent: Tom was also a member, and although no one had ever been heard to question his sexuality before, several people claimed they had always suspected he was gay and there was a deal of speculation over coffee as to whether Tom had been involved in a threesome with Frank and Alistair.

At lunchtime, Gill had gone to visit Ali, who asked what was in the papers.

'It's all inaccurate. Perhaps you'd be better not seeing it.'

'Show me, please.'

Gill handed her the paper.

'They've got Ruth and Matt's names wrong.' She read on. 'Bill spoke to them. How could he? And Tom! And Phyllis! Well, that doesn't surprise me. She'll just love her ten minutes of fame. Why do they think he's run away with Frank? Oh, Gill, this is awful.' She handed the paper back and started to cry again.

Gill sat down beside her and took her hand. She looked at the paper with the picture of Mike and Lizzie at the bus stop. Last night, after Ian's remarks, she had asked Mike what he thought his son had meant. 'A hug because she was so upset,' was the reply, but looking at the photo in the paper, she had a niggle of doubt.

'Isn't that taking the comforting role a little too far?' she had asked him.

'I told you. She was very upset. She's not as tough and grown-up as she thinks. She just needed some reassurance.'

Gill had looked at him. 'You are obviously more naïve than I thought. Just watch yourself with that one.'

Mike had busied himself pouring more tea, relieved that he was off to London later in the morning.

Colin knew he needed more evidence to run the Mike and Lizzie story. He decided to enlist the help of Michelle, the most junior female reporter.

'Pretend to be a student and see what you can find out.'

Michelle, dressed in jeans and carrying a pad of paper and a couple of books in a shoulder bag, walked around the university. She waited for the first-year medical students to emerge from a lecture and followed a group into the union bar. One girl had a copy of the *Daily Scot* and they were discussing the scandal.

'That's Lizzie's dad! Look, there's a picture of her with some man.' The paper was spread on the table in front of them.

'Imagine your dad suddenly saying he's gay, especially if he's a minister.'

'No wonder she's not here today,' said one.

'Trust Lizzie to have an interesting family scandal,' said another.

Michelle waited a moment or two and then approached them. 'Hey, are you lot first-year medics?'

They stopped talking and looked up. A dark-haired girl answered, 'Yeah. Why?'

'I'm looking for Lizzie Graham. Do you know where she is?'

'She's had a bit of local difficulty,' said one of the boys, pointing to the paper.

'I know,' said Michelle. 'That's why I'm looking for her. I know her from school. I wanted to see if she was OK.'

'Someone said she went home yesterday.'

The dark-haired girl decided it was her chance to find out more about Lizzie.

'You're a friend from home?'

'Yeah.'

'What was she like at school? No one knows what to make of her here. One minute she's your best friend, or if you're male, all over you . . . Isn't she, Chris?' She looked at the boy reading the details in the paper. 'And the next minute she's with someone else or disappeared.'

'Disappeared?'

'Suddenly she's not about and then she's back again. Has she still got a boyfriend at home?'

'Er, don't think so, but she always was independent.' Michelle thought it was time to change the subject. 'Where is her flat? I might go round and see if she's there.'

'She's in the flats in the Cowgate. You could ask her flatmates. They'd know if she's gone home or when she's coming back.'

'Thanks. I'll do that.'

As she walked towards the student flats, Michelle had a quick change of faculty. Now a medical student, she knocked on the door of the first flat and after a while an unshaven hangover appeared.

'Is this the right flat for Lizzie Graham?' asked Michelle.

'Upstairs,' said the hangover, and shut the door.

Michelle climbed the stairs and knocked on the door. A girl opened it.

'Hi! Is this where Lizzie Graham lives?'

'Yeah, but she's not here. She's gone home.'

'I know. It's awful for her. I texted her. I'm a medic and she had my notes to copy for a lecture she's missed and I need them back. She said they were on her desk in her room. Can I go and see if they are there? I wish she would just go to the lectures – then she wouldn't be borrowing my notes all the time.'

The girl let her in. 'Her room's that one there. She never bothers to lock the door.' The girl returned to the kitchen.

Michelle went into the room and looked round. It was reasonably tidy, and furnished with the necessities: single bed, wardrobe, desk, chair, bookcase and a washbasin. There were some photos pinned to a notice board – family group shots and partying students in various stages of inebriation. Half a bottle of Bacardi and a bottle of Coke sat on the desk next to some folders that Michelle discovered contained only handouts from lectures and labs. She opened the desk drawers and found a couple of easyJet boarding passes for flights to London. This was more promising. Then she tried the drawer in the bedside cabinet . . . a large box of condoms, a packet of cigarettes, some cigarette papers, some cannabis and a strip of pictures taken in one of those booths – Mike Andrews and Lizzie making silly faces. Yes! She used her small digital camera to take several close-up photos before returning the evidence to the drawer. She made her way to the kitchen.

'Can't find them. Perhaps she's taken them with her by mistake. I know she's having a difficult time but she's always borrowing my notes and then I have to nag her to get them back. It pisses me off. How come she can't get up and go to lectures?'

'She's got a man, but she never brings him here. Disappears off for the night every so often, then comes back and sleeps for hours. Marathon shag if you ask me.'

'Don't you know who it is?'

'Nah. She won't say, but I think he works in London. She's always off to the airport. On the other hand, he is in Edinburgh sometimes. She has dirty stop-outs, usually on a Friday night.'

'Well, thanks, anyway . . . Sorry – I didn't catch your name,' said Michelle.

'Zoe, Zoe Parkin.'

'Well, thanks, Zoe. I'd better go and do some work if I want to go out tonight.'

By Tuesday, Ali found that the initial shock of Tom's departure had been replaced with seething anger. She had lain awake most of the night considering her years of marriage, in which she had focused on childrearing and being a supportive wife regarding the church and congregation. She felt used, belittled and abandoned to be the focus of local gossip. With the exception of Gill, no one seemed to be much help. Ruth had refused to go to school and only came out of her room for meals. She was supposed to be sitting her Higher prelim exams this week. The bastard had probably not even realised what an important year it was for her when he was hatching his escape plan. Lizzie was still at home, but spent most of the day saying how unfair life was and how she couldn't face the embarrassment.

There was an impending food crisis, so Ali asked Lizzie to go to Tesco. Not realising that people were more interested in the putative affair with Mike than with Tom's departure, Lizzie was initially unaware that her progress round the store was being watched by everyone, all of whom managed to become engrossed in choosing a brand of instant coffee or the like when she looked in their direction. As she moved from aisle to aisle, there was a buzz of conversation in her wake. On reaching the checkout, she realised she had forgotten to buy apples, so made her way back to the fruit, bringing conversations to an abrupt halt as she went.

Angela and her friend Leanne were standing beside the apples with their backs to Lizzie. Angela had both her children in the trolley, and Leanne was supposed to be stacking bags of potatoes on the display opposite.

'That photo of them at the bus stop just proves it. They must be at it. Mrs Caldwell saw her go into the house when Gill was out. They were doing it in the bathroom. Mrs Caldwell saw it all from her back garden,' said Angela.

'And you're surprised?' said Leanne. 'Once a slapper, always a slapper.'

Lizzie stretched between them. 'Angela, Leanne, excuse me, I need to get some apples.' She filled her bag with Granny Smiths and then turned to them and said with a charming smile, 'And, Leanne, once a poisonous cow, always a poisonous cow.'

As Lizzie swept off towards the checkout, Leanne shouted at her departing back, 'Takes one to know one!'

As she drove home, Lizzie decided being supportive to her mother was one thing, but remaining here if the world thought she was sleeping with Mike Andrews was another. She took the shopping into the house and told her mother she was going back to university on the six-o'clock bus.

On her arrival in Edinburgh, she had not made her way to her flat, but had walked to Waverley Bridge, boarded the airport bus and was just in time to catch the last plane to London. When Mike returned to his flat after midnight, following several relaxing drinks with colleagues, she stepped out of the shadows and burst into tears.

'Everyone in Corrachan is talking about us.'

Dolphin Square is the temporary home to many MPs and in an effort to avoid the whole House of Commons talking about them also, he took her inside.

Chapter Twenty

Colin almost had enough to run the Lizzie and Mike story, but he wanted corroboration from London. He had been caught out before when a politician sued and cost the paper a fortune in libel damages, so he had asked the *Daily Scot*'s political correspondent, Drew, if there was any gossip about Mike Andrews and a woman who was not his wife.

Drew had a wife and three small children who lived on a new estate near Falkirk. They had not wanted to move to London, so like most of the Scottish MPs he reported on, Drew commuted to London, leaving home on a Monday and returning on a Friday. While in London, he enjoyed the comforts of a hotel and other comforts provided by a twenty-three-year-old who was secretary to a Labour MP. She was a useful source of information for what was new within the Westminster village. He sent a text to her before the lunchtime gathering of secretaries and received her reply at two o'clock: *mikes secy thnks its researcher from libdem whips office.*

Drew passed this message on to Colin, who was now in a quandary. Was the original story wrong, or was the new story even better? He decided to leave it a little longer.

★　★　★

Mike came into his office at the House of Commons on the Wednesday morning looking more than a little tired and stressed. Janice glanced up from her computer and thought adultery didn't suit him. He was obviously not used to leading a double life and had trouble separating his women into appropriate compartments. Janice had been around Westminster long enough to know that this was not a promising trait. To be a successful adulterer, one had to be a bastard and Mike wasn't that. She felt she ought to warn him that various members of the press were showing an interest in his extramarital activities.

'Have you been doing things you shouldn't?'

'What do you mean?'

'I mean, the press are sniffing about trying to find out if you've been playing away.'

'Have you been speaking to them?'

'No! But I know they've been asking about.'

'There's nothing to tell them. I am not doing anything I shouldn't. I am a happily married man.'

'Well, in that case there's nothing to worry about.'

Mike went to his office and closed the door.

Guilty! That piece in the whip's office isn't worth ruining a marriage for, Janice thought, as she typed a letter informing a constituent there was no chance of Parliament putting forward a bill to allow medical experiments to be performed on those with an IQ below 85.

In the middle of the afternoon, the security officer at the main door phoned to say there was a constituent claiming to have an appointment. Janice checked the diary and there was nothing. Mike asked her to find out who it was and what they wanted. It transpired that a Miss Elizabeth Graham wished to talk to him on a confidential matter.

Mike was furious. She should be on a train to Edinburgh. Last night, they had discussed the situation and come to the conclusion the rumour would die away after a week or so, when everyone found something else to talk about. He had told Lizzie they were not to meet, except in Corrachan, and then always when someone else was present. Much to his surprise, Lizzie had meekly agreed and Mike had allowed her his bed and curled up on the inadequate two-seater sofa. At 3 a.m., he had been woken by Lizzie's exploring hand and her voice in his ear: 'Just once more. No strings. Please!'

'No, Lizzie. Get off me! I told you it was over and I meant it. Now go back to bed and leave me alone!'

In the morning, they had hardly spoken as he had made a pot of tea and some toast.

As he prepared to leave, he put his hand on her arm. 'I don't think it's wise to be seen leaving together. Just pull the door to when you leave. Goodbye, Lizzie. Good luck with your life. Go and get on with it!'

Mike asked Janice to go and collect his visitor.

'She's the daughter of the minister I told you about – the one who did a runner. She babysits for us sometimes. I can't think what she wants. She certainly doesn't have an appointment.'

Janice returned with Lizzie and stood surveying the scene.

Mike came out of his office and shook Lizzie by the hand. 'Hello, Lizzie! What are you doing in London? Is this about your father? Because there is not much I can do about that, unless your mother's having problems with benefits and I would really need to speak to her about that.'

Lizzie looked at Janice and said, 'Er, it's confidential.'

'All right, then. Come into my office and you can tell me what it's all about.'

Janice noticed that Lizzie walked just a little too close to Mike for a casual acquaintance. She would wait and see if there was any correspondence ensuing from this conversation.

Probably not, she thought. She turned her attention to the last of the day's mail. There was another Letraset offering from Mr Hall, about Jewish infiltration of rural sub post offices. He seemed to have copied it to about six other people. She wondered if he photocopied the original or if his whole life was taken up with creating a handmade masterpiece for every recipient. She was not even going to acknowledge it. She filed it in the shredder.

'What the hell are you doing turning up here? We agreed last night we were not going to see each other. You should be somewhere north of York watching the scenery rush past you at a hundred miles an hour.'

'I don't have enough money to get home.'

'What do you mean, you don't have enough money? You came here yesterday on a plane. How did you pay for that? You have a bank card, don't you?'

'I tried to get money out of the machine, but it says I have insufficient funds. I had to get a British Airways flight yesterday. Paying for the ticket must have put me over my overdraft limit.'

'You didn't have to get any flight, actually.'

Mike looked in his wallet. He had twenty pounds. He escorted her from his office and took her through several corridors till they reached a cashpoint. He took a hundred pounds from the machine and handed it to her.

'There, take that and get on the next train. You will be back in Edinburgh by this evening. Just go to lectures and keep away from the press.' He then walked with her to the exit which led into Westminster station. 'Go and get the Tube to King's Cross. Goodbye, Lizzie.'

As Mike had been handing over the money, Janice had walked past taking letters to the postroom. On her return to the office, she met her friend Cathy in the corridor.

'I still think I'm right about that researcher, but their babysitter from home has just been in to see him and I swear there's something going on.'

At five o'clock, Cathy came down in the lift with the twenty-three-year-old secretary to the Labour MP, the one who provided favours for Drew, the political correspondent, whom she was about to meet for a drink. By six thirty, Colin had the confirmation he needed about Lizzie, but he still wasn't sure about the researcher.

Gill had spent most of Wednesday trying to clean her house. A two-year-old, a crawling baby and six puppies made it a lost cause. The previous evening, as the manse was a no-go zone, she had to host the mother-and-toddler meeting about the upcoming jumble sale and had been encouraged by large attendance, not realising that everyone was keen to see the layout of the house in order to get a picture of how Mike and Lizzie might have managed to do it in the bathroom while the children were asleep.

As she sprayed Dettox on to a rather unpleasant stain on the carpet, she considered the state of her own marriage. At least she knew Mike wasn't gay. Well, she thought she did. Having said that, it seemed to have come as a surprise to Ali. My antennae are well enough tuned to know if something is wrong, she thought smugly.

She was now able to think beyond the next opportunity to sleep. A meal out together at the weekend would be good. It was a pity Chez Marguerite was closed, but the Indian or the Chinese would be fine. Then they could come home and watch a DVD and have another glass of wine. Perhaps Ruth would babysit. It was unlikely she would be going somewhere else.

Chapter Twenty-One

When the phone rang on Thursday morning, Gill was in a sea of chaos. Puppies, children and toys were competing for floor space as she tried to mix puppy feed and prepare bowls of cereal. She lifted the receiver, tucking it under her chin. It was her mother.

'What on earth is this about Mike and some teenager? It's in the paper.'

'What are you talking about, Mum?'

'Your Aunt Christine phoned me at seven o'clock this morning. She had just stopped to buy a paper on her way home from night duty. She reads that awful tabloid – you know the one. I made your father get up and go to the Pakistani shop. It says that Mike is having an affair with some eighteen-year-old whose father is a gay minister. What is all this about?'

'What? Where on earth did this come from? He's not having an affair. He was just giving her a comforting hug after her father ran away.'

'Her father ran away? Where? You know this gay minister?'

'Yes, Mum. You know, my friend Ali's husband.' Gill just could not resist adding, 'He was the one who was going to christen Kate.'

There was silence for a moment.

'Just as well he's gone, then.'

'You must have heard about it. It's been all over the papers the last few days. It was even in the *Scotsman*.'

'That is just further confirmation that the *Scotsman* is a tabloid masquerading as a quality paper nowadays. Your father and I have been getting the *Telegraph* the last few months.'

'Well, that explains why you are ignorant of anything taking place north of the Home Counties.'

'Perhaps you should stop making snide remarks about our choice of newspaper and look at the one that I have in my hand at the moment. More than a comforting hug, if you ask me. There are photos of them making silly faces in one of those photo booths, and the girl's flatmate says she disappears off to London during the week and sees him in Edinburgh on Fridays.'

'This must be some sort of mistaken identity. It can't be Mike, though nothing Lizzie could get up to would surprise me.'

'The picture in the paper is of Michael and a girl. Do you think I don't know my own son-in-law?'

Gill stopped stirring the puppy feed. A horrible creeping doubt was entering her being: those Friday nights with Gavin in Edinburgh; Lizzie's sudden departure after she heard them on the day of the party; the prolonged visit to her house on Sunday afternoon. Oh, surely he wouldn't?

'Are you still there? Do you want your father and me to come and see you?'

'No! No! Stay where you are. I'm going to phone Mike and sort this out. I'll speak to you later.'

She phoned Mike's mobile. It was switched off, so she left a message. She tried the landline at the flat. No answer. Then she phoned his office at Westminster and got Janice's dulcet tones inviting her, if she wished, to leave a message for Mike Andrews and to speak after the tone. She tried his pager. A lady who sounded as if she had a problem with her adenoids intoned, 'Mike Andrews's paging service. What is your message?'

'Phone home now. End of message.'

Gill had no option but to become engrossed in the breakfast routine. While the children both had their cereal, she made a cup of coffee and looked at the clock. Fifteen minutes since she had paged him and silence.

'Bastard! Bastard! Bastard!' she shouted inside her head.

Kate was smearing oat and apple gloop over both herself and the highchair, while Ian, having realised that his mother was distracted, had dispensed with his spoon and was eating with his fingers. Gill ignored the globs of milky cereal that were spreading outwards from her children like a tsunami and decided she would give Mike five more minutes.

Then the phone rang. She jumped to her feet, ready to interrogate, but it was not Mike. It was an aggrieved Ali.

'What has your husband been doing to Lizzie? She's young enough to be his daughter. According to my mother, it's all over the paper. As if having a gay husband wasn't enough, I now seem to have a daughter who is being portrayed as if she was some sort of Lolita. What's it about? You must have known what was going on under your nose.'

'Hang on a minute! Don't blame me. I have no idea what has been going on. Like you, my mother has just told me what is in the paper.'

'You must have had some idea. You're not stupid.'

'Well, you're not stupid and you had no idea about Tom, did you? I do not know if he is having an affair with Lizzie. Believe me, it is the number-one question I wish answered at the moment, but I would assume he had more taste and discretion than that. If this is true, which I'm sure it isn't, then it will more than likely have been her idea. She's not the innocent you think she is, you know!'

'That's right! Put the blame on Lizzie. She's only eighteen! He's thirty-six! It's tantamount to child abuse.'

'Oh, get a grip, will you. It's common knowledge she has been putting herself about since she was fourteen. Everyone but you seems to know that she was Darren Connerty's moll while she was at school.'

'Darren Connerty? Don't be ridiculous! What would she have in common with him?'

'Shagging!' said Gill, and put the phone down.

She was shaking now. Why was she defending the man? He was probably guilty. She phoned Mike's pager again. This operator seemed to have left his glasses at home.

'Mick Andre's— No, wait a minute . . . Mike Andrews's paging service. What is your message?'

'Phone me now. The longer you leave it, the worse it will be. End of message.'

She needed to know what was in the paper. She couldn't bear to phone her mother to ask her, and she couldn't walk to the newsagent while she was waiting for Mike to call. Then she remembered it was *Corrachan Times* day too. Was it in that as well? It suddenly occurred to her that she should be able to see the papers online, so she started to make her way upstairs to the computer. The doorbell rang.

She opened the door. Cameras flashed and there seemed to be crowds of people on her front path asking for a comment about her husband. She slammed the door and locked it. Then the bell rang again and someone shouted through the letterbox, 'What do you feel about your husband having an affair with your babysitter? Why don't you give us your side of the story?'

She backed into the kitchen and nearly died of fright when she saw a young woman standing there holding a mewling puppy and speaking to the children.

'Who the hell are you and what are you doing in my house? Get out!'

Michelle ignored Gill's hostility and smiled at her in a friendly way. 'The back door was open, so I thought you might like to give me an exclusive. These puppies are really sweet.' She held the puppy up close to her face and crooned at it.

Penny, who should have been protecting both her puppies and her human family, ignored everyone while she licked up the milky detritus left by the children.

'We'll give you a good fee. I bet you're really pissed off! Stuck here with small children while he's shagging the babysitter.'

'This is our business, not anyone else's. Now get out of my house.'

'Why don't you let us have your side of the story, Gill? Like I said, we can offer you an exclusive interview, for a fee of course.'

'I have already asked you to leave. If you don't go immediately, I'm calling the police.'

'It's a matter of public concern if our elected politicians are committing adultery – especially if he's cheating on a lovely wife and children. Here's my card with my number. I'm on your side, Gill. I think he's treated you very badly.'

Gill picked up the phone.

Michelle tapped the card on the table. 'OK, I'm going, but remember, anytime you want to give your side of the story, just phone.'

She went out the back door and Gill locked it. Michelle knocked on the kitchen window as she passed and mouthed something. Realising that the press pack could peer in the windows at her, Gill picked up both children and ran upstairs.

Phyllis was watching the gathering on the Andrewses' front path with great interest. She had ordered all the tabloids to be delivered in case she missed something about the Graham scandal and, having already sifted through this morning's delivery, felt the expense of six daily papers was justified. Jack had refused to discuss the scandal and disappeared off to his office, almost running over some of the press corps loitering at the end of his driveway. Phyllis wondered if she ought to go and tell these reporters all she knew. She thought she would get dressed and apply her make-up before asking them if they would like a cup of tea or to use her lavatory. She hoped they might ask her opinion of her neighbours. They could use the downstairs cloakroom. She didn't want dirty footprints all over her lovely bathroom.

When she considered herself ready to face the world, she phoned Joyce.

'Have you seen the papers this morning? I was right. I knew I was! Mike Andrews has been playing around with the Graham girl.'

'Really? I've just got the paper now, but I haven't read it. This is an unexpected boost. If there's been a scandal, he'll have trouble holding the seat and so will Annie Cochrane at the Scottish elections. We'll have to adopt a good candidate soon, so they can get to work.'

'Never mind elections! That's not for ages, Joyce. This is much more exciting. The *Daily Scot* says that it's been going on for months. Just a minute while I find the bit I want.' She turned the pages till she found Colin's article. 'Here it is. Are you there?'

'Yes, Phyllis, I'm here.'

'"Lib Dem MP Mike Andrews, thirty-six—" Is he only thirty-six? I would have thought he was nearer forty.'

'Get on with it, Phyllis!'

'"Lib Dem MP Mike Andrews, thirty-six, has been having a tempestuous affair for months with feisty eighteen-year-old babysitter Lizzie Graham." Hear that? Months! And "feisty", that's an interesting word to use.'

'It's a euphemism for a tart!' said Joyce.

'Well, she's certainly that! Where was I . . . ? Oh, yes, here we are: "Lizzie is the daughter of Rev. Tom Graham, Corrachan's gay minister, who came out to his congregation before leaving to live with his lover, chartered accountant Mark Stevens, in Edinburgh."'

'Oh, it's someone called Mark! We were wrong about Frank, then,' said Joyce. 'The Heriot Row flat wasn't the Hamilton-Sinclairs' pay-off. Good thing I hadn't said anything to anyone about that.'

Phyllis was trying to think how many people she had mentioned it to. There was Moira at Jack's office, the receptionist at the health centre, several people at the golf club dinner dance, the hairdresser and the plumber who had been to fix the dripping tap. Well, she was sure they would see the paper and realise it wasn't correct.

'Well!' continued Joyce. 'If he's got in tow with a chartered accountant, he'll be all right. It won't matter if he hasn't got a job.'

Phyllis continued, '"There were nights of passion in London and in an Edinburgh love nest, while Mike's wife, Gill, and two children, Iain (three) and baby Katy, were at home in Corrachan." They've made a mistake with the names again. But "nights of passion" in a "love nest"? There's a bit about her flatmate, then listen to this: "One of his constituents, who wished to remain anonymous, said, 'We always thought he was a devoted family man. I'm disgusted that he should have an affair with such a young girl. He's taken advantage of his position as a friend of the family.'" Who do you think said that? It wasn't you, was it?'

'It certainly was not! It could have been anyone.'

In fact, it was no one, as Colin had made it up to pad out the article.

'All right. Don't get offended. Now there's a bit about your Mrs McCafferty's Leanne: "One of Lizzie Graham's school friends, Leanne McCafferty, nineteen, said she wasn't surprised as Lizzie always had to be the centre of attention where men were concerned." Centre of attention? That's a new way of putting it! What's wrong with the word "promiscuous" I'd like to know.'

'Any more?'

'No, that's about it.' Phyllis glanced out of the window. 'It's very busy next door, you know. The Andrewses' house is surrounded by reporters and photographers. I was going to ask them if they wanted some tea and to use my loo. Listen, why don't you come over for a coffee and we can watch the goings-on? I was going to phone Helen too. She won't want to miss this.'

'I'm sure she'll want to tell us Richard's latest opinion!' said Joyce cattily. 'Have you seen Gill this morning?'

'Well, she opened the door and shut it again. She was in her dressing gown! It didn't even look clean. You would have thought that she would have made sure she was dressed before she opened the door.'

'Perhaps she wasn't expecting them, Phyllis. I will come round later, though I might go and see Gill too. But now, if I want a quiet life, I had better go and sort Bill's breakfast. Bye.'

'Bye,' said Phyllis to the silent phone.

She put the kettle on and laid out her second-best mugs. She decided against using the silver teaspoons and eventually found some stainless-steel ones at the back of the cutlery drawer. She popped two Earl Grey teabags into the pot and filled it with hot water. While it was brewing, she considered the packet of handmade ginger biscuits from Marks and Spencer but decided that Jack's Rich Tea would be sufficient. She filled the mugs, carried the tray with the Prince of Wales crest, which she had bought in the Holyrood Palace shop, to the dividing wall and rested it on top.

'Would any of you good people like a cup of tea?' she inquired.

Reporters walked over the lawn, trampling snowdrops and emerging crocuses underfoot. Mugs were taken from the tray and the biscuits vanished from the plate. Colin put his hands round the Queen and Prince Philip and took a large mouthful from his Silver Jubilee mug, then spat it out.

'Christ Almighty! That's not tea, it's creosote!'

'It's Earl Grey, you ignorant sod. Don't you know class when you drink it?' said another reporter.

Phyllis hated bad language. She changed the subject. 'If any of you need to wash your hands, feel free to use my cloakroom.'

'What did she say?' asked someone.

'She says if you need to take a leak or have a crap, you can use her downstairs toilet,' said someone else.

They were so coarse. She collected up the mugs and checked that the teaspoons were back on the tray. As Colin handed his half-full mug to her, he remembered from Sunday that she was not short of an opinion.

'Thanks, Mrs Caldwell. What do you think about your neighbour and little Miss Graham, then?'

Phyllis was in a quandary. She knew more about this than anyone else, but Colin had upset her with his rude remarks about the tea. She decided she wouldn't say anything at the moment. She told him she did not wish to comment and went inside.

Gill stood several feet back from her bedroom window. She could just see Phyllis handing out the tea. She just loves this, doesn't she? she thought.

'Wan to watch *Thomas Tank*,' whined Ian. 'Do downtairs.'

'Not at the moment, Ian. Just watch the TV here. We're staying upstairs for a bit.'

'Not here! *Thomas Tank* downtairs!' The whiny voice was more insistent.

'Ian, could you stop whining! Not this morning, please!' She turned on the bedside portable. 'Look – it's *Balamory*!'

'No wan *Balamory*.' He stamped his foot. 'Wan *Thomas* downtairs now!'

'No, Ian, we are not going downstairs at the moment!'

'Go down now! Now! No wan *Balamory*! *Thomas Tank*!' He was screaming and stamping his feet.

Her usual coping mechanisms departed. She lost control.

'Ian! Will you shut up! I can't take this, not this morning. Just sit down and watch bloody *Balamory* and give me some peace to think!'

'*Thomas Tank*! Now!'

'Shut up! Shut up!' She picked him up and threw him down on the unmade bed. He bounced several times. There was a moment of silence before he began to scream. A horrified Gill realised what she had done. She picked him up, cuddled him and stroked his hair. 'Sorry, sorry, sorry. Mummy's upset. Please just sit here and watch *Balamory*.' She put him down on the bed, gently this time.

'Bloody *Balamory*!' said Ian, his sobs subsiding. He settled back on the pillows and inquired, 'Shit?'

She handed him his sheet. Then he put his thumb in his mouth and leaned back, concentrating on the TV.

She looked at her watch. Still no word from Mike! The papers are saying he's shagging the babysitter and then he won't even call back. She paged him again.

'Mike Andrews's paging service,' said a bored male voice that sounded as if it was coming down a tube from somewhere on the Indian subcontinent.

'Your children and I are imprisoned in the house by a horde of reporters. Phone me now!'

The bored voice woke up and asked her to repeat the message. He then broke all the rules and asked her if she was all right.

'Not really, but thanks for asking.'

Mike was with the chief whip. He had been summoned to the hastily arranged early-morning meeting, convened when it was realised that it was not just the Scottish papers running the story but the national tabloids also. Seated on the sofa, Mike was six inches lower than the chief whip and the press officer, who were on office chairs. After congratulating Mike on his ability to pull an eighteen-year-old, the chief whip had gone on to ridicule him for being so naïve as to think no one would find out.

'If you want to have extramarital rumpy-pumpy, for God's sake choose someone who understands the rules and is discreet – do not choose your eighteen-year-old babysitter!'

All through this interview, Mike's pager was vibrating. He had glanced at the messages and had seen they were from his wife.

'We will sort this out first. You've got the rest of your life to try and sort things out with your wife.'

When the final message came through, he told the chief whip that his house was besieged by the press.

'Well, I suppose you had better go and speak to her, then. Get her to phone the police if they are being a nuisance.'

Mike went out into the members' lobby, which, except for the duty police officer, was deserted at this time of the morning, and turned on his phone. It received six text messages and then it rang to tell him that he had four new messages on his answer service. The texts were from Lizzie. She too was besieged by the press. They had used her photos. They had got into her room on false pretences. What was she to do? Why didn't he phone her? The messages were from Gill, his mother wanting to know what this was all about, and Annie Cochrane saying that she sincerely hoped that the Edinburgh love nest referred to was not her flat. Before he could phone Gill, it rang again. He looked at the display and answered it.

'Gavin.'

'Jeez, mate. What the hell have you been up to?'

'It's a long story, but it's all your fault.'

'My fault? How can it be my fault?'

'That Friday in November when we were going to meet up and then you had to work late with . . . what was her name? Kelly? That was when it all started.'

'Blame not accepted, pal.'

'Anyway, I've finished with her. Look, I can't talk now. I must speak to Gill.'

'Good luck with that! Anything I can do?'

'Not at the moment, thanks, but I'll call you in a few days when things quieten down.' He cut the call and dialled home.

Gill was tearful, frightened and demanding explanations. He told her to phone the police and he said he was sorry but he couldn't discuss it now, as he was standing where people could hear him and he would phone her again as soon as they had worked out how to deal with things. He rang off and glanced at the policeman, who gave no indication that he had heard anything. He went back to the whip's office to ask for advice about Lizzie. The Scottish press officer was given the task of phoning her.

'Now, Mike, we need to draft a statement. You said the affair is finished?'

Mike nodded.

'Your wife will take you back?'

'I don't know.'

'The best way to kill the story is to admit it. Say you're sorry and then have a family photocall. You'll then be seen as a repentant male. Women like that. Your wife'll be seen as a noble, forgiving soul who has been badly done to. Women like that too. Men will see you as the lucky bastard who got the eighteen-year-old.'

'And what about Lizzie? What do we do about her?' asked Mike.

'Will she go quietly?'

'With Lizzie, it's difficult to tell.'

'Was she a virgin? Were you the "wicked paedophile" who deflowered her?'

'I was not the first to be there and will certainly not be the last.'

'Well, that's something. We can use the fact she was promiscuous if she gets difficult. You are a fairly junior MP, Mike, and if this girl's father hadn't been involved in a scandal, no one but your wife would have been interested. The wider world will have forgotten this in a fortnight, but you might have a bit more bother in the constituency, because a double scandal is exponential and will take longer to go away.'

'What should I say to her?'

'Nothing till we have a statement drafted. Then you tell the mistress what's in it and have nothing more to do with her.'

It did not take long to agree the wording. Mike was told to phone Gill, and as he left the outer office, he stopped to let the attractive researcher through the door ahead of him. She smiled sympathetically and walked in the direction of the library, where a striking Indian lady called Seeta was at the desk. The researcher requested the article she had been sent to collect.

Seeta handed it to her and brushed her fingers. 'Same time tonight?'

The researcher nodded. Phyllis's friend Evelyn glanced up from her desk and smiled. She liked to see the younger ones enjoying themselves.

About nine fifteen, after toying with a coffee and a croissant, Mike could put off the phone call to Gill no longer. He told her he had a statement drafted.

'Shall I read it to you? "I had a short extramarital affair with Elizabeth Graham, which finished several weeks ago by mutual consent. I accept that this was very foolish and I deeply regret the hurt and distress caused to my wife and family. I ask that the media will leave us in peace to resolve our differences and rebuild our marriage."'

There was silence on the other end of the line.

'Gill? Are you there?'

'Oh, yes, I'm here!'

'What do you think?'

'Where shall I begin? Let's start with Monday, shall we, when you told me you were just giving her a hug because she was upset. Then this morning, my mother tells me that the whole of Scotland, not to mention the rest of the UK, knows it was a good deal more than that. After many attempts to contact you, eventually you phone back to tell me how to get rid of the press, saying you'll call me later to discuss this. I don't think reading out a press statement that I expect has already been released is discussing it!'

'It won't be released until you OK it.'

'Well, that's good to know. This statement says you have been shagging that little bitch and you hope the press will leave you in peace to rebuild our marriage. Well, Michael, if you want to rebuild our marriage, you are going the wrong way about it.

You could start by not taking me or my reaction for granted and by coming back here and speaking to me face to face!'

'I'm sorry. I didn't mean to upset you even more. I've booked my flight. I'll be back in Corrachan by the middle of the afternoon. Is it OK to put that statement out?'

'I suppose so.'

Mike really ought to have known better, but he went on to voice the chief whip's suggestion. 'I suppose a family photo for the press is out of the question?'

'Fuck off! And you can tell the party machinery if it's thinking about majorities to do likewise. There's no way I'm going to demean myself and your children by leaning over a gate pretending I'm besotted with you. I'll see if someone will take care of the children this afternoon so we can talk about this. This might prove difficult. As you can imagine, Ali is not very keen on you, nor is she very keen on me, because she thinks I knew all about this. I don't expect she will want her other daughter coming to our house.' She slammed the phone down and burst into tears.

Chapter Twenty-Two

J oyce decided she would visit Gill briefly before going for coffee with Phyllis. Although this press revelation was not of her making, she was still trying to make amends for her earlier mistakes. As she walked along the road, she noticed the reporters on the pavement at the Andrewses' gate. A police car was parked a short way down the road with two slightly bored-looking officers drinking coffee out of Phyllis's Silver Jubilee mugs and eating superior ginger biscuits. Phyllis was hovering on the pavement with the Prince of Wales tray. Joyce waved and pointed at the Andrewses' path to indicate she was going there first. She pushed her way through the reporters and started to walk up the path. Colin recognised her and asked her for a comment. Joyce was in no mood to be cooperative.

'I think you had enough comments on Sunday. All, I may add, gained under false pretences. I have no intention of saying anything more to you. My husband is reporting you to the Press Complaints Commission.'

Colin looked at her. Time she fell off her high horse. 'Well, missus,' he drawled, 'I only said I was from Edinburgh. If you recall, I never said exactly where I was from. Perhaps you ought to ask some questions in future before you jump to conclusions about people.' The others laughed. Colin looked at the *Daily Scot* in her hand. 'Been buying the paper to get all the juicy details, then? Thought you wouldn't want to miss anything.'

The police constables paused mid-chew, watching what was going on. They were about to lay down their mugs and come to Joyce's aid when she continued up the path to the front door. She rang the bell and waited. Nobody answered. She could feel eyes drilling into her back. She rang again.

'Get the impression she doesn't want to speak to you,' laughed Colin.

Joyce felt like a swot being ambushed by bullies. Refusing to be intimidated, she made her way through the side gate to the back door and knocked loudly, but there was still no reply. She tried the door and found it locked. Now she wasn't sure what to do. If she came back round to the front of the house immediately, it would be obvious she hadn't been allowed in, but she couldn't stand in the back garden for twenty minutes in order to pretend that she had had a successful visit. She was trapped. There was no back gate and the stone wall at the end of the garden was too high to climb over. Her indecision did not last long. She knew she had no option but to go back round to the front of the house. As she passed the kitchen window, she saw Gill wiping the table with a damp cloth, so Joyce knocked on the window, giving Gill her second major fright of the morning, and pointed in the direction of the back door. Gill unlocked it and ushered Joyce in.

'Sorry – I didn't mean to frighten you to death. I thought I would come and see if you were all right.'

'Thanks, Joyce. It's been really scary with that lot outside.'

Gill looked at the papers Joyce was carrying. 'Is it in all the papers?'

'Most of them, I'm afraid. This one –' she held out a copy of Colin's paper – 'seems to be the most detailed.'

'I don't want to see, but I know I have to.' She took the paper and looked at the headline: 'Love Rat MP's Teenage Mistress.'

She put the paper on the table.

'I'll read it in a minute. Do you want a coffee, Joyce?'

'Thank you. Instant will be fine.'

'That's good because it's all I've got.' She switched on the kettle and took two mugs from the cupboard.

Ian appeared with a *Thomas the Tank Engine* book. He took hold of Gill's sleeve. 'Story, Mummy. Pease?'

'Not now, Ian. I'm talking to Mrs Macdonald.'

'Want Daddy! Daddy home today?'

Joyce looked at Gill and raised her eyebrows questioningly.

'Later, Ian.' She looked at Joyce. 'He's coming back sometime this afternoon. To say I wish to have a conversation with him is an understatement. Do you realise, the first I knew about this was when my mother phoned me this morning to tell me what was in the paper. Was it common knowledge? Were Ali and I the last to know?'

'Er, there were some rumours, but that was all. It's a bit difficult to say to someone you don't know very well that there are stories circulating about their husband. That's a best friend's department. And your best friend is Ali Graham and she was in the same position as you.'

'Not a best friend any more! She thinks I must have known all about it.'

After deciding that his mother was not in a story mood, Ian thought he would try the granny-person instead. He got hold of Joyce's skirt and tugged at it. 'Tank Engine!' He looked at Joyce through his long lashes and put the book into her hand. 'Read story, pease?'

Gill thought at least his speech had improved such that he hadn't said 'wank'.

Joyce took Ian by the hand. 'OK, then, let's go and sit in the

218

other room and I'll read you the story. I like Clarabelle best. Who do you like?'

'Dordon,' said Ian.

'I'll leave you to look at the paper, dear.'

Gill picked up the paper again. The front page had the picture from the photo booth. The quality wasn't wonderful, but there was no doubt that they were on more than friendly terms. She opened the paper and began to read the article. Beside it were pictures of Mike and herself, heavily pregnant, waving and smiling after the election result, and a picture of Mike addressing some conference on female circumcision with the unspoken implication that his interest in female genitalia was not confined to Africa.

Gill considered the extent of her humiliation. The rumours must have been circulating for weeks with everyone discussing her business and feeling sorry for her. If that wasn't bad enough, she had been willing to believe him when he had told her he couldn't spare the time to be with the children all weekend as he had so much work to do. Work he should have done during the week, when he was spending time with Lizzie.

She picked up the *Corrachan Times*. Gerry Martin had written the piece about Tom, and the letters page gave the self-important the chance to comment. There were several lengthy offerings on the Christian response to homosexuality, which varied from toleration to the equivalent of public stoning. There was also one from Mr Hall, which had been so severely edited to avoid litigation that it was completely incomprehensible. She was already dreading next week's paper, when her own scandal would be the fodder for the moralists and those of a different political persuasion.

She turned the pages in a half-hearted fashion until she came to the 'In Memoriam' section, which was considerably longer than usual. Along with poems to long-dead grandparents, there were nine under the name 'Hamilton-Sinclair'. The first was from Frank and unlike the others that followed, had been composed by him:

In memory of my life partner, Alistair:

I wasn't home when you left that day
I wasn't there when you passed away
We said no goodbyes
But you are with me always
Al, my all, my Al.

Keep a table for me in Heaven. I'll never forget you.
Frank

She scanned down the column and looked at the other entries under 'Hamilton–Sinclair'. These had obviously come from the book of rhymes in the newspaper office. There were many references to angels, heavenly plans and going before. There was one that stood out for its banality:

A bouquet of roses just for you
Sprinkled with tears instead of dew
And in the middle forget-me-nots
To show you, Alistair, we haven't forgot.

With treasured memories from all those at the Corrachan Gay, Lesbian and Transgender Helpline

Gill wondered if, with the reference to sprinkling, the rhyme had been penned by the author of Phyllis's bathroom motto.

Joyce came back into the kitchen with Kate on her hip and holding Ian by the hand.

'OK?'

Gill sighed. 'Yeah, I suppose so. I've just been looking at all the "In Memoriams".' She pointed to the paper. 'They seem to be a statement from the gay community.'

'And very successful, I suspect. I can't believe that Charles and Primmy are thrilled. "In Memoriam" rhymes are not quite the thing, you know.' Joyce paused. 'Look, Gill, I don't know you very well and we are from different sides of the political divide, but would it help if I took the children for the day? Wouldn't it be easier if you were on your own when Mike gets home? I've got all the things needed for small children at my house, as my daughter uses me as a babysitting service when she wants a weekend off.'

Gill hesitated, but only for a second. 'Joyce, for the second time you've come to my rescue. Thank you.'

'Glad to be of help.' She turned to Ian. 'I think you should come to my house and look at all the toys I've got. There's a Clarabelle and a Gordon and lots of storybooks.'

Ian went to the front door and came back with his coat – obviously easily tempted by the promise of exciting playthings.

Like father like son, thought Gill.

Chapter Twenty-Three

Joyce was correct. Sir Charles Hamilton-Sinclair was extremely displeased by the 'In Memoriam' rhymes. He had been in his study replying to the condolence letters and cards. He had always thought it lazy to send a card at a time of bereavement. One didn't have to say much, but surely it was an indication of a substandard education if one couldn't even string several sentences together. He quite accepted that the estate workers and some other people were not able to articulate their feelings, but he was surprised how much standards had slipped. He would have expected Bill and Joyce Macdonald to have written a letter, not to send a card with 'In deepest sympathy' on the front. It was casual and sloppy.

Primmy came in with a cup of coffee, a ginger-snap biscuit and a copy of the *Corrachan Times*.

'There are some "In Memoriams" in here from friends of Alistair's,' she said hesitantly. She didn't tell him that she had had a little weep when she had read the one from Frank.

'What are you talking about? Let me see!'

She passed him the paper and waited.

'Christ Almighty! This is an organised effort to make fools of us. It gives all the tittle-tattlers something to tittle-tattle about.' He read through the list of contributors and jabbed his finger at one rhyme. 'Here we are! Here's who is responsible! These two old lesbians from the pottery: "With fondest memories, Mags and Connie, the Wee Pottery Shoppe and Tearooms."'

Mags and Connie were two ladies, now in their seventies, who had lived together for many years. They were tenants of Sir Charles and they had been in dispute with him for a long time over the level of rent expected. He was correct in his assumption they were the instigators. The plot had been hatched at the wake, when Frank decided that by putting an announcement in the paper, he could pay his own tribute to Alistair, which would be both fitting and an irritation to Sir Charles. Then Connie, who had consumed at least half a bottle of a rare single malt, had an idea.

'I know how we can really piss off the old bugger. Lots of "In Memoriam" rhymes! He'll think they're common, and if we can make it obvious who they are from . . .' So, as well as the ones from Connie and Mags and from the helpline, there were rhymes from Derek and Tim at the Gay Bookshop and Mandy and Trace at the Women's Health and Awareness Centre. The rest were made up in the hope of raising Sir Charles's blood pressure to boiling point: the Gay Ex-Servicemen's Association, the Where to Stay If You're Gay Guide, In the Pink Interiors and the Out Now Café.

Sir Charles slammed the paper down on the table, causing his coffee to spill into the saucer. 'Damn, damn, damn them to Hell! This is not what Alistair would have wanted. Well, the old trouts have gone too far this time! They owe me nearly two years' rent. They'll have a notice to quit in the morning.'

Primmy decided that she had kept her mouth shut for too long. She was going to say what she thought for once. 'I think it would be better if you just ignored it. They've done it to annoy us, so we shouldn't let them know that we are upset.'

Sir Charles picked up his cup of coffee and soggy biscuit and sat down at his desk. 'Well, we'll see.'

He sifted through the pile of letters and cards and stopped at the one from Mr Hall telling him that Alistair had been a Mossad agent working to promote homosexuality and a consequent reduction in the birth rate and that his death was a contract killing ordered by Osama bin Laden.

'Letter here from that man Hall who writes to the paper. He's used some sort of toy printing set. Talking complete load of bollocks.' He ripped up the offending letter and tossed it into the fire.

While Joyce was with Gill, Michelle had taken up Phyllis's offer of the use of the cloakroom, which unlike the bathroom was not pink but a delicate shade of peach with matching accessories, including a notice in a shell-encrusted frame, which read, 'Would all gentlemen depositing gold in this bank take care not to leave change on the counter.' When she had finished, she wandered into the kitchen, where Phyllis, bedecked in her yellow Marigolds, was washing up mugs.

'That's better,' said Michelle. 'Thank you. Can I help you with the drying-up?'

She picked up a tea towel with a picture of the Queen Mother with a corgi on her knee and began to dry a mug, which had been issued to mark the marriage of HRH Prince Andrew and Miss Sarah Ferguson.

'They made a nice couple,' said Michelle, admiring the mug. 'Shame it didn't last.'

'People don't have the same moral values they once did. Marriage used to be for keeps,' replied Phyllis.

'Must have been a shock for you to find out what has been going on.'

Phyllis regarded Michelle and felt that in the interest of accuracy, she shouldn't tell an untruth. 'Well, not really, no.'

'Oh?'

Phyllis hesitated as if to indicate reluctance, and put some more mugs into the soapy water. 'Well, I've known for some time that something was going on. I saw them together in a restaurant in London, you know. That was a few weeks ago. They were all over each other. Then at the Andrewses' party, they were canoodling in the kitchen.' She paused and turned to look at Michelle. 'On Sunday, the day her father left, she was next door for a long time. Gill had gone to the manse and that little trollop took the first opportunity to come running round here to see him. Threw herself into his arms on the doorstep! He got her in the door fast enough.' Now she had started, there was no stopping her. 'They were together for over three hours till Gill came home. Disgusting! And with the children in the house too! There seem to be no standards of decency these days.'

'You think they were carrying on with the children in the house?'

'Well, I wouldn't know about that, but I do know that the children usually take a nap in the afternoon.'

The *Corrachan Times* had been delivered to the manse at breakfast time. It was now nearly three o'clock and Ali hadn't been able to bring herself to open it. It is one thing to be at the heart of a national tabloid scandal, but it is another when your friends and neighbours all have the forum of the local paper to express their opinions. She felt very lonely. Ruth was still refusing to go to school and now she didn't even have Gill to talk to. Perhaps she shouldn't have shouted at her this morning, but Gill hadn't been very pleasant to her; in fact, she had been particularly unpleasant and vindictive. She looked at the folded paper and decided she couldn't ignore it any longer. Perhaps it wouldn't be as bad as she feared. She took a deep breath and picked it up. It wasn't as bad as she feared; it was worse. Everyone was having their tuppence worth, name in print, opinion being passed off as fact. She thumbed through the pages of news, came to the 'Intimations' and laughed for the first time in days. How Tom would have enjoyed them. She wondered what he was doing. Had he realised what a dreadful series of events he had started? Probably not, she thought.

Wearily she trudged upstairs and looked out of the window and then went and sat on her bed. There were only a couple of reporters on the pavement hoping to glean some information from comings and goings, but they were very bored, as Ali had made no comment and hadn't gone out. The only visitor had been someone from the Board of Ministry, who had called on Monday and told her that she would be subject to four weeks' notice when they found a replacement, but could stay in the manse in the meantime.

Before she went to sleep last night, she had decided she would stop hiding and go out: go and find out about benefits, put her name on the housing list, talk to the headmaster about Ruth and go shopping. She would hold her head up high and deal with things. Then her mother had phoned her about Lizzie and Mike. All resolve had vanished and she was a cowering emotional wreck again. They would have to live on the contents of the freezer and the sprouting potatoes for another day. She was grateful her mother was quite frail and wouldn't be coming to help, but she did feel so alone. The members of the congregation seemed to be too embarrassed to call, the people she thought were her friends were nowhere to be seen, and Matt was being more than usually difficult. He sensed something was wrong, and although it had been explained to him that Tom had gone away to live in Edinburgh, he still kept asking, 'Where's Daddy?'

The doorbell rang, so she went and took up her now familiar stance behind the door and asked who was there. It was Donald Cumming, accompanied by Mrs Cumming, on a pastoral visit. Not what she needed at present, but she had no option but to let them in.

'Ali, another terrible trial for you. You're being sorely tested. This is my wife, Martha. I felt it might be good for you to talk to another woman about this.'

Ali nodded at Martha Cumming. Although they were about the same age, she had a suspicion they would have little else in common. Martha had a large sleeping baby of indeterminate sex dangling face-out in a sling.

She put a comforting hand on Ali's arm and said, 'With God's help you can get through this. I have looked out some readings for us to consider together and then pray about. Perhaps your daughter Ruth might like to join us. I'm sure she is hurting and would benefit from the healing power of the Spirit.'

'It's, er, very kind of you both to come round. Let me put the kettle on.'

'I can't stay at the moment,' said Donald. 'I'll go and collect the children from school and come back for Martha in an hour or so.' He nodded at both of them in turn and left.

Ali realised there was to be no escape for at least sixty minutes. She smiled weakly at Martha. 'Tea or coffee?'

'Do you have any herbal teas? I try to avoid caffeine. It's a powerful drug, you know.'

'No, I'm afraid I don't.'

'Well, a glass of water – Adam's wine – will be lovely.'

Ali filled a glass of water, made herself a coffee and invited Martha to come and sit down.

'What about Ruth? Will she join us?'

'Well, she is trying to work for her prelim exams at the moment, but I'll go and see.'

Ali climbed the stairs, knocked on Ruth's door and explained that Martha wanted her to join them for prayer and Bible study. Ruth didn't look up from her maths folder.

'No, I don't think so! I'm kind of off religious experiences at the moment. In case you hadn't noticed, everything my life has been based on has been rejected by my father. I think I'll stick with calculus.'

Ali felt she should stay and talk, but she knew this would take more than a few minutes. She was conscious of Martha and her bookmarked passages downstairs.

'Look, I'll get rid of her as soon as I can. Then we can have a talk.'

'Whatever.'

Matt, who had been in Ruth's room, decided that he wanted to be with Ali and trailed downstairs behind her with all his dinosaurs in a carrier bag. Martha had unstrapped the baby and laid it on the sofa. It continued to sleep. She had settled herself in the armchair and gestured Ali to the other one.

'Ruth's a bit busy at the moment.'

'One should never be too busy to praise the Lord and hear His word.'

Was this a remark that required a response? She decided not. She looked at the baby, thinking she ought to say something nice about it.

'What a good baby. How old is . . . ?' Ali trailed off, trying to decide if it was a he or a she.

'Malachi is six months now. We feel he might be the last, so we called him after the last book in the Old Testament.'

'You have other children, don't you?'

'We have six: Isaac, Esther, Naomi, Samuel, Nathaniel and Malachi.'

If they only *felt* Malachi might be the last, Ali reckoned that they had not worked out it might be something other than

God's will that was causing all these children. She remembered that Lizzie had told her the older children were known as the 'Orgasms' at school, and poor Isaac had been given the middle name of Malcolm. The initials I. M., combined with Cumming made him sound like Phyllis or one of her friends in the throes of sexual climax. Despite calling himself Zak and smoking cannabis in the swing park, he found life at school quite difficult.

Ali sat down in the armchair and Martha began, 'Let's start with a few words of prayer.'

Ali shut her eyes and waited.

'Lord, we ask You to be with us today and to give Alison the strength she needs to overcome this trial. Amen.'

Ali opened her eyes and Martha opened her Bible.

'I thought we should start by considering what God's word says about the sins of your husband and your daughter. In Leviticus, it says, "Thou shalt not lie with mankind, as with womankind: it is abomination." And in First Corinthians, the apostle Paul says, "Know ye not that the unrighteous shall not inherit the kingdom of God? Be not deceived: neither fornicators, nor idolaters, nor adulterers, nor effeminate, nor abusers of themselves with mankind, nor thieves, nor covetous, nor drunkards, nor revilers, nor extortioners shall inherit the kingdom of God."' Martha paused and looked at Ali. Doing her best to be polite, Ali smiled weakly and Martha took this to be a sign that her words were having a comforting effect. She continued, 'In First Timothy, Chapter Five, there are words for Elizabeth: "But she that liveth in pleasure is dead while she liveth." And in Proverbs, Chapter Eleven, verse twenty-two, it says that "As a jewel of gold in a swine's snout, so is a fair woman which is without discretion." Pigs wallow in the mud and Elizabeth has been wallowing in the sin of sexual immorality. God's word tells us that the wicked are damned, but for those who live an upright life and for those who repent, the Kingdom of God is theirs. Hear what it says in the book of Isaiah: "Let the wicked forsake his way, and the unrighteous man his thoughts: and let him return unto the Lord, and He will have mercy upon Him; and to our God, for He will abundantly pardon."' Martha paused again and glanced up.

Ali took a deep breath. This woman either knew her Bible by heart or had spent all morning with a concordance searching for suitable texts. She suspected it was probably the former. She wasn't the sinner and this was more of a lecture than a comforting pastoral visit. How dare Martha compare Lizzie to a pig? She wished she could summon the energy to argue.

'I think we should have a few moments of silent prayer,' continued Martha. She slipped off the armchair on to her knees.

Ali was finding this session embarrassing enough without having to kneel on the living-room floor. As a gesture, in the way a nonconformist does in an Anglican service, she moved a little closer to the edge of her chair.

Up till this point, Matt had been sitting quietly in the corner. He had tipped all his dinosaurs out of the bag and was now arranging them, as usual, in order of size. Into the silence came the commentary from his dinosaur DVD, which he had learned by heart. He was even able to reproduce the dark-brown tones of the original commentator.

'Brachiosaurus. This dinosaur was from the Upper Jurassic period and lived about a hundred and fifty million years ago. It was up to thirty metres in length and was herbivorous. It was thought to live in Europe, North America and sub-Saharan Africa.'

There was a thud as the largest of his dinosaur collection was placed on the floor. Ali opened her eyes. Martha was still kneeling at the coffee table with her eyes shut and beyond her she could see Matt selecting the next dinosaur.

'Diplodocus. This dinosaur was also a herbivore from the Upper Jurassic period and lived about a hundred and fifty million years ago. It was up to twenty-six metres in length and was also found in North America.'

There was another thud as the diplodocus was placed next to the brachiosaurus.

Martha now decided that the silent prayer was over and that she ought to share her entreaties to the Almighty with Ali. 'Lord, we ask you to help Tom and Elizabeth realise the enormity of their sins and the extent to which Satan has entered their lives.'

'Tyrannosaurus rex,' said Matt. 'This dinosaur is from the Upper Cretaceous period and lived about sixty-five million years ago. It was up to twelve metres in length and was carnivorous. Fossils have been found in North America.'

'We know that You forgive all sinners who repent and we ask that You help Tom and Elizabeth to renounce the influence of the Evil One and to return to God's light,' intoned Martha.

'Triceratops. This dinosaur, like Tyrannosaurus rex, is from the Upper Cretaceous period and lived sixty-five million years ago. It was up to nine metres in length, herbivorous and was found in North America.'

'Comfort Alison, Ruth and Matthew in their distress and let them feel Your peace around them.'

'Stegosaurus. This dinosaur was from the Upper Jurassic period and was smaller than diplodocus, being only nine metres in length. It, too, was a herbivore and was found in North America. Velociraptor.' He paused to select the next in his size sequence and realised that the velociraptor was missing.

'Now we sit in silence to feel Your love and hear You speak to us,' intoned Martha.

'Velociraptor, velociraptor, velociraptor,' Matt chanted with rising anxiety as he searched for this dinosaur.

Ali opened one eye and looked at him again. He was starting to flap his hands with anxiety and hyperventilate.

'Not here! Not here! Not here!' he wailed. He then started to scream.

If this was God speaking, He was articulating just how Ali felt. She would rather be anywhere but here.

Chapter Twenty-Four

Minty Oliver had always believed in the power of the written word and with the advent of the computer, she had taken an evening class in computing and word-processing. Now, at the age of eighty-six, and several computers later, she was in possession of a state-of-the-art model complete with desktop publishing. When it came to computers, all her usual frugality disappeared and only the best would do.

She spent many hours in front of the screen, working on political leaflets, and that was what she had been doing for the past week. She had experimented with various layouts before discovering an interesting article on the Internet on the psychological effects of different fonts on various target audiences. This article had cited several others, which Minty had also accessed.

Armed with her newfound theories, she had then spent two days redrafting her leaflet and she felt it was much improved. She had been living on biscuits and cheese, packets of Cuppa Soup and glasses of vintage Burgundy from her wine cellar. Now in need of something more substantial to eat, she went into town to get supplies and decided that on her way home she would take a draft of the leaflet to Mike Andrews for his approval. She stopped at the newsagent to pick up the three copies of the *Guardian* as well as the *Economist*, which were waiting in her folder. The shop assistants seemed to be gossiping about a man who was having an affair with an eighteen-year-old, but she paid scant attention. She was not interested in the doings of others. That she considered was their business, and as she cared not a jot what others thought about her, she said and did exactly as she pleased.

The reporters on the pavement outside the Andrewses' house heard the orange Metro, which was in need of a new exhaust pipe, before they saw it. It came to a halt two feet away from the pavement and there Minty abandoned it, with the keys in the ignition, confident that no one would want or dare to steal it. She had no idea who these people were and she marched through them oblivious to requests for a comment, made her way up the path and vigorously pressed the doorbell. Gill, who had been expecting Mike to arrive at any moment, had seen her from the upstairs window. She went downstairs and let her in.

'My dear, how nice to see you. How are you? Must say you look a bit peaky. Children keeping you awake at night?' She looked around. 'What have you done with them? I brought them a present.' She rummaged in a battered plastic shopping bag with a picture of Burns Cottage on it – another find at the Liberal jumble sale – and produced a polythene bag with a great deal of condensation on the inside, making it quite difficult to discern what it contained.

'Chocolate cake! Left over from the last Liberal coffee morning. Took it home and put it in the freezer. Used to love chocolate cake when I was small. Thought Ian and Kate would like it.' Minty had a habit of speaking like a telegram.

Gill remembered the cake. Things usually disappeared quickly from the baking stall and anything that was left had to be very suspect. This one had been made by Mrs Collins, who had several years on Minty, was incontinent and in need of a double cataract operation. She was known to make cakes from stale ingredients kept in her mouse-infested cupboards, and there had not been a rush to buy her contribution. Minty, immune to this sort of knowledge, was unaware that it might be a hygiene risk.

'Thanks. That's kind of you,' said Gill.

'Now,' said Minty, peering into the Burns Cottage bag, 'I've got the proof of the latest focus leaflet here and I wanted Mike to see it. He has such a good eye for a layout and this is a new format I've discovered. The Democrats have been using it in Minnesota in their state elections with a great deal of success evidently.' She thrust the leaflet at Gill. 'Mike will be home tomorrow?' she asked.

'He'll be home anytime now, actually,' said Gill.

'Oh good. I'll just wait, then. Give me something to do for you while I wait. Your ironing, or I'll read to the children. Where are they, by the way?'

'Joyce Macdonald has taken them for the day.'

'Joyce? Nice woman, shame she's a Tory.'

'Minty, in view of all that's happened, I don't think that this is a very good time to speak to Mike. I need to talk to him as soon as he gets home, and as you can imagine, leaflets do not come high on our list of topics of conversation at the moment.'

Minty was puzzled. There was something going on here that she didn't understand. 'I'm sorry, my dear, I'm a bit confused. Has something happened?'

'Mike has been having an affair with our babysitter Lizzie Graham. The press have found out and it's all over the papers. That's why there are reporters outside.'

'That explains the gaggle of people at your gate! Lizzie Graham? You mean the minister's daughter? I thought she was about ten.'

'Time flies, Minty. She is now a very attractive eighteen-year-old. She was the waitress at our party.'

'Ah, the vamp! My dear, how difficult for you. Difficult for her father too, in his position. It's always very embarrassing for the clergy when their children go astray, and a lot of them do, you know: something about not wanting to be seen as a goody-goody. There was a girl at school with me whose father was a bishop and she was caught stark naked in the potting shed with the gardener's boy. It all had to be hushed up.'

'Haven't you heard about Tom Graham either?' asked Gill.

'No. What's happened to him?'

Minty listened while Gill explained, digesting the information with the same level of surprise had Gill told her he had gone to a retreat for the weekend.

'My, my, what a week for the gossips!' She paused and looked at Gill. 'So what are you going to do about your errant husband, then?'

'I wish I knew. I need to talk to him face to face. I only found out this morning – when it was in the papers. I heard about it from my mother. That's why Joyce has got the children – so we can talk when he gets home.'

'Well, my dear, I'm an old woman and I've been around a long time. I've seen and heard most things before. Nothing is new. It's just everyone has to know everyone's business nowadays. You aren't the first woman with small children who is too exhausted for sex. Mike isn't the first man who has looked elsewhere. In times past, the new father rogered the nursery-maid and no one commented on it. Nursery-maid, babysitter, same thing. Men view sex differently from us. They keep their sexual judgement in their testicles. We want all the cuddling and the commitment, but they have a hunger and if someone as attractive as your babysitting waitress is offering to supply a slice of cake, so to speak, then most men will say, "Thank you very much." Much more worrying if he'd fallen for someone his own age who wasn't attractive. That would be love. This sounds like lust. I'm going to say something that might sound obvious. Things cannot be undone. You have to adapt to circumstances and you have to be careful that you don't end up losing even more. Think carefully, my dear, before you throw him out. Do you want to be a single parent? Do you want to have to arrange access visits, fight over maintenance payments, start looking for someone else?'

'Oh, Minty, I don't know.'

'Well . . . one thing to remember, if you *do* take him back, is that you are one major indiscretion up. This means that at some later stage you are entitled to take a lover – purely for the sexual thrill, though, no commitment. You may not feel like it now, but perhaps in ten or twenty years' time you might enjoy an attractive young man – nothing like it to make a middle-aged woman feel better about herself. Believe me. I know.'

Gill looked at Minty with new eyes.

Minty continued, 'Expect Ali Graham is in a state too. Married gay men used to be able to find someone in a similar position and everyone turned a blind eye, or the wife took a lover and life continued as normal. Honesty's not always the best policy. Gay clergy aren't new either, especially in the High Church. All the vestments and embroidery, not to mention the incense and bells, are a great attraction. Church of Scotland is so repressive most of them probably go to their grave not realising why they found their married life so unsatisfactory.' Having come to the end of her summing-up of the gay Christian debate, Minty decided she had better go. 'Well, better be getting along. I'll leave the leaflet. If Mike has a moment, perhaps he can give it a glance.'

Gill escorted her to the door and, as she opened it, found

Mike on the doorstep fumbling for his key, while the press took photos and called for a comment. He shot through the door and closed it behind him.

'Jesus! It's like coming through a picket line.' He laid down his bag and saw Minty.

She raised an eyebrow at him and looked over the top of her specs. 'Hello, Mike. Home to face the music? Careless of you to get caught. It causes so much upset. I'm on my way now, but remember what I said, Gill – one in hand!'

With that she opened the door and swept down the path, stopping only when she reached the reporters. 'Why don't you lot go and report on the things that matter in life. Hypocrisy is hateful and I expect at least half of you here are having or have had sex with someone you shouldn't. Leave them be and go and bother those who destroy the environment, or give exorbitant loans to the poor, or start wars. These are the people who should be harassed, not that poor couple in there.' She got into her Metro and roared off in a cloud of black smoke.

Colin and Michelle had missed Minty's lecture about hypocrisy as an hour previously they had repaired to Colin's room at the Corrachan Hotel to discuss how to develop the story further. That discussion had taken about ten minutes. The horizontal discussion had taken somewhat longer. Michelle, whose attitude to men and casual sex was not unlike Lizzie's, liked working with Colin as he was always amenable if the chance presented itself. A story like this which provided a hotel room allowed for greater comfort and privacy, and certainly more space than Michelle's Ford Ka. It was also much more interesting than standing on the pavement outside the Andrewses' house.

Chapter Twenty-Five

A li eventually got rid of the Cummings. By the time she had dealt with Matt's screaming fit, which had woken the baby, Martha was sitting on the sofa with one breast exposed feeding the 'Last Prophet'.

Matt looked at Martha, then at Ali and announced, 'It's very rude to show breasts. Tell the lady to put it away.'

It was encouraging to hear him use some functional language, but perhaps this wasn't the best moment to start.

Donald had arrived then with an elderly minibus full of Orgasms of various sizes and they had all returned to Invercraig. The velociraptor had been found under a chair and Matt had returned to his commentary. Ali lay down on the sofa, shut her eyes and thought how surreal the afternoon had been.

The doorbell went again. Having been ignored for days, this was obviously her afternoon for visitors. This time she discovered it was Tom's brother, Peter. With a sigh she opened the door.

'Hello, Peter. Come in.'

'Hello, Ali. I have come to see how you are.'

'Well, we're still alive, but death might be preferable!'

Peter looked alarmed and Ali remembered he didn't under-stand irony. 'I hope you are not considering suicide,' said Peter.

'No, no. I was joking.'

'I never know when people are joking. It's very difficult to tell.' He paused and thought carefully about what he was going to say next. In fact, he had been thinking for several days about what he ought to say and he had decided he had to do three things. He had to find out how they were. Well, he'd done that. He had to say he was sorry about what had happened, and he had to see if there was anything he could do. He found it very difficult to talk about emotional things and he had been practising phrases.

'I'm sorry Tom has left you. It is very difficult for everyone.'

'It sure is,' replied Ali.

Peter had been researching on the Internet and he continued, 'It is believed by many that homosexuality is an innate condition, and despite trying to deny it, many people eventually reach a crisis. In order to find their true self, they have to admit to what they are.'

'Fair enough,' said Ali, 'but I think finding one's true self in the middle of the morning service was lacking in judgement, to say the least.'

He detected an implied criticism here. 'Yes, it was a surprise to everyone, but I expect he thought it was best. It was a good way of letting everyone know.'

'You can say that again.'

Peter thought she was telling him she hadn't heard, so he repeated himself. 'I said, it was a good way of letting everyone know.'

Peter decided that having covered two of his three topics, he now needed to offer help. This was more practical and therefore much easier. 'Can I do anything to help?'

'Well, you are a councillor, so you can tell me how likely we are to get a council house. Apparently, we can have a few weeks here and then we will have to move. I have no savings and three dependent children.'

This was easy! It was like being at one of his council surgeries. He gave a long and complicated explanation of the qualifications for emergency housing and the likelihood of getting a council house or something from the Housing Association. He then started on the rules for the number of bedrooms one was entitled to, depending on the age and sex of one's children, and the criteria for Housing Benefit.

Ali managed to interrupt. 'Hang on a minute, let's summarise. What you are saying is that we would get one of the emergency flats in the town centre owned by Jack Caldwell, and if these are full, we would get put in a bed and breakfast until a long-term let became available.'

Peter considered very carefully whether there would be any possible exceptions to this summary and decided that there weren't. 'I think that is the case.'

There was silence for a moment. Peter realised he hadn't said anything about Lizzie. He had also done some Internet research about men who have sex with younger women. His search on Google had produced a large quantity of pornography, but he had found some more factual articles. He thought Ali might find it helpful if he shared his findings with her.

'I think Mike Andrews might have been trying to recapture his youth. The fear of growing older makes men seek out younger partners, and younger girls are often pleased to discover that the older man is better at lovemaking than someone their own age. Perhaps Lizzie was looking for a more proficient lover than Darren Connerty. I understand that lovemaking is a skill that can be perfected. Young women are also attracted to power and Mike is seen to be a powerful person because he is an MP.'

'Just a minute,' said Ali. 'What did you say about Darren Connerty?'

'I said that perhaps Lizzie was looking for someone who was better at lovemaking than Darren Connerty.'

'You knew about Darren Connerty?'

'Yes. Everyone knew about Darren Connerty.'

'Well, I didn't!'

There was silence again.

Peter now felt that he had said all he wanted to say. 'Well, I think I should be going. I have to read the minutes of the meeting of the last Economic Development Committee before tomorrow's meeting of the full council, as I want to question how some of the funding has been allocated. I think that there has been an error in the calculations and that all is not as it should be. It is important to get these things right, because small mistakes often add up to make a large error and then it is difficult to correct. We, as councillors, are there to make sure officials carry out our wishes to the letter, not interpret them in their own way. There was an article in *Liberal Democrat News* about a council down south that had an ombudsman's ruling against them and there were a lot of officials who had to resign.'

Ali decided that she had had enough of this. 'Well, thanks for coming round, Peter. Have you heard from Tom?'

'No. He hasn't called me.'

'Me neither.'

It was nearly five o'clock when she came back into the kitchen after showing Peter out. She saw the bottle of brandy that had been sitting untouched since Sunday – that seemed about a million years ago. She poured herself a generous measure and sat down at the kitchen table. She fingered her mobile, wondering if she ought to try to phone Tom. She thought he might have phoned her, in view of Lizzie's behaviour.

The doorbell went again. Wearily she went to the front door with her glass still in her hand. It was Bill Macdonald, who had finally plucked up the courage to come and apologise for his indiscretion with the press and to see if he could do anything to help.

Mike and Gill sat at the kitchen table with untouched cups of tea in front of them.

'Why?' said Gill.

'I don't know why it happened,' said Mike. 'It's all over now, anyway.'

'You'll have to do better than that. It may be over but you still did it, that's what matters. I'll ask you again. Why?'

'Oh, I don't know. Perhaps I just needed some fun in my life. When I come home, you're so wrapped up in the children. You're not interested in what I've been doing or how I feel.'

'Oh! So it's my fault now? Well, I'm really sorry that I forced you to sleep with our eighteen-year-old babysitter who happens to be the daughter of the one and only friend I had in this town where you have dumped me, while you go off and pursue an exciting life in London. I'm sorry, too, that looking after your children does not leave me dressed in a suspender belt, gagging for it. My every waking moment is taken up being responsible for them.' She got up and walked over to the window, then turned to face him again. 'You don't understand, do you? There is no time off. Even when they are asleep, I have to be listening. I give emotionally all week and then you come home and want me to pat you on the head and be a wow in bed. By that stage, sleep, in the knowledge that there is another responsible adult present, is all I want. It would be nice to be able to take emotionally for a change, but taking seems to be your department.'

'That's not fair! I try to be supportive to you, but I do work four hundred miles away and I can't be home at six o'clock every night. You knew that when we agreed I could go for the nomination as candidate.'

'You are expecting me to apologise for misunderstanding what life would be like. I don't think being humiliated was part of the original package. You obviously saw me as a boring drudge and went looking for excitement.'

'She made all the advances towards me. I didn't chase her.'

'And that is an excuse? You are twice her age. All you had to say was, "Thanks but no, thanks."'

'I was lonely. My job is very stressful too. And when it comes to supporting each other, it works both ways. You weren't much help over the visa debacle, were you? You were either asleep or worrying whether Ian's spots were about to do something new.'

'And I was supposed to ignore a sick child and go over, yet again, what you should or should not do?'

'I don't think you had any conception how stressful it all was. You know how small my majority is. I can't afford to get things wrong.'

'And you think having an affair is going to increase your vote at the next election?'

Mike ran his hands through his hair. 'This isn't getting us anywhere. You have to admit we've become disconnected. We don't laugh any more. We don't have fun. It's all work and children. I've said I'm sorry. I don't know what else to do.'

Gill looked at him and walked back to the table. She picked up her cup of cold tea and poured it down the sink. She put the cup in the dishwasher and then forcefully began to fold washing from the laundry basket, daring it to become unfolded as she put it on the pile.

Mike watched her for a while until his patience snapped. 'Will you please stop doing that and come and sit down?'

'I don't know what to say to you.' She continued folding baby vests.

'Well, at least let's try to talk.'

She stopped folding and sat down again. 'Well, talk, then.'

'Can we sort this? I don't want to lose you and the children. It is over with Lizzie. It has been since the day of our party.'

'I don't know if we can. As I said, you have humiliated me. It's obvious the children and I are quite far down your list when it comes to attention and consideration. Perhaps you could try looking at things from my point of view for a change. When you are away and nearly all the time when you are home, I do not do anything – and that includes going for a pee – without thinking where the children are and what they are doing. Has Ian managed to get into the kitchen cupboard and drink a bottle of Domestos, or has Kate stuck her fingers in an electric socket? When you are going somewhere, you pick up your car keys and go out. I have to put on everyone's coats and shoes, pack all the necessary paraphernalia and then endure battles as I attempt to strap them into the car. And to go where? An exciting meeting regarding the transport networks in this country or the problems of ethnic diversity? Oh, no, I go to mother-and-toddler group or Tesco. You will jump through hoops to make things hunky-dory for your constituents so they will vote for you next time, but when you get home, you want peace and quiet and to be waited on. The trouble is, you don't think what I do is difficult. You give lip service to how important it is to give children a stable, loving home, but you think your job is more important than mine and therefore you don't see why you should help when you come home. You, after all, have had a trying week. Well, so have I! A mind-numbingly trying week!'

'Look, I've said I'm sorry and I am. I don't know what more I can do. I'll try to spend more time with you and the children. I'll try to help you more. Do you want to get a job? Will we get an au pair? What do you want to do? Tell me! Please!'

'I don't know. I don't know anything any more. I went to bed last night thinking our marriage was OK and that we should try to spend more time together alone, and I woke up this morning to learn that you had been having an affair and the whole town knew about it. I need some space to think. Just leave me alone for a while.'

Gill left the kitchen, climbed the stairs, lay down on her unmade bed and closed her eyes. The tears seeped through her closed eyelids and ran down her cheeks, making a large damp patch on the pillowcase.

Mike sat at the kitchen table for a few moments, then got up and made himself another cup of tea. He didn't know what to do next. It wasn't just the affair, Gill had obviously been unhappy for a while. That had been quite a tirade. Could she have postnatal depression, or was Kate too old for that? Then he turned his mind to Lizzie. He would have to speak to her sometime to make sure she understood it really was over. He put milk in his tea and then he noticed the now defrosted chocolate cake in its bag on the table. He found a plate and took it out of the bag, cut himself a large slice and took a bite. He reached over and picked up Minty's leaflet. It really was an interesting layout.

It was after seven o'clock, having delivered the children back to a house bristling with tension, when Joyce finally went to see Phyllis. She accepted the offer of a drink and listened to Phyllis list the day's excitements.

'He had trouble getting in the door. Minty Oliver was there and she let him in. She must have been sent by the Liberals to find out what's going on. I wonder if they'll deselect him.'

'Well, Gill told me that she knew nothing about it till this morning. He must have known the story was going to break. Imagine not telling her. Her mother saw it in the paper and phoned her up to find out what was going on. I wouldn't have thought her mother read that kind of paper. She looks much more like a *Scotsman* or *Herald* sort of person to me.'

'Is she going to throw him out?'

'Well, he's still there at the moment, but talk about atmosphere. You could cut it with a knife. Oh! She's fallen out with Ali, who thinks Gill knew about what was going on. Talking of Ali, Bill went round to see her this afternoon and she came to the door with a huge glass of brandy in her hand. I don't think she can have been sober since Sunday.'

Phyllis pulled aside the net curtains and glanced out of the window. 'Reporters all seem to have gone now. They had to get the police, you know – two of them in a panda car. I took them some coffee and biscuits; most appreciative they were. More than could be said for that Colin. You know, the one who came to your house.'

Joyce wrinkled her nose in disgust.

Phyllis continued, 'There was an extremely pleasant young girl who came to use the facilities and she helped me with the washing-up. Very interested in the Royal Family she was. That's unusual nowadays in young people. I told her that I had known for ages about this and all about Lizzie being there for hours on Sunday. It's important that the full story comes out, don't you think? Especially as he's supposed to be a pillar of society.'

After Joyce had left the children, Gill suggested Mike might like to have some quality time with them before finding himself some accommodation for the night.

'Can't I stay here? I'll sleep in the spare room.'

'No. I need some space and privacy. You can go to the Travel Lodge on the far side of town.'

'I can't go there! It will be obvious that you've thrown me out!'

'Oh dear! What a shame!'

'I suppose I could go to Minty's and risk electrocution in the damp bed with elderly electric blanket.'

'You can do whatever you like. You've been doing that for months, so why change now?'

After the children had been bathed and put to bed, Mike came downstairs to find Gill toying with a bowl of soup and a piece of bread.

'There's some soup in the pot if you want it.'

'Don't think I will. I'm feeling a bit sick, actually. I've got a terrible pain in my stomach.'

'Wonder what caused that,' said Gill, glancing at the pedal bin in which rested the chocolate cake with a slice out of it.

Mike had no intention of going to the Travel Lodge, so he tried to phone Minty, but she was out and didn't believe in answering machines. He sat in the study and tried to sort papers to fill in time until Minty came home. He was feeling very queasy and the stomach pains were getting worse. Half an hour later, when Gill came upstairs to find out why he was still in the house, he was in the bathroom and it was obvious he was going nowhere for a while. She fetched a bucket and a drink of water, then made up the bed in the spare room before retreating to what she now considered to be her room.

The Mike and Lizzie story might have petered out after everyone had voiced their opinions, had it not been for Mrs Collins's bacteria-laden baking. If he hadn't been ill, Mike would have phoned Lizzie and discussed the situation with her, in which case she might not have been so scared and angry when Michelle knocked on the door of her Edinburgh flat. Perhaps she might have turned down the offer of what seemed to her an extremely large fee for an exclusive interview with the *Daily Scot*.

★ ★ ★

After their discussions in the Corrachan Hotel, it had been decided that Michelle would go in search of Lizzie and try to negotiate a deal. Colin would return to the Edinburgh office to draft an outline for the article. He looked forward to her return and debriefing her – he had always liked puns – in the walk-in cupboard they had discovered on the top floor of the newspaper's offices.

Michelle knocked on the door of Lizzie's flat and Zoe opened the door just wide enough to see who it was.

'God! You've got a cheek coming back here after all the lies you told me. Now bugger off. No one wants to talk to you.' Zoe tried to shut the door with considerable force, but Michelle had employed the age-old trick of putting her foot in the door-jamb. The pain in her foot was excruciating, but she managed to continue and raised her voice in the hope that Lizzie could hear her.

'Just wanted to speak to Lizzie and apologise for the way we got the information. I think Andrews is a shit to treat her like that.' She paused, but there was no reply, so she changed tack. 'I've got a business proposition.' There was still no response from behind the door. 'Does she know what he's said in his statement? It's a bit dismissive, isn't it! Lizzie, can you hear me? Let me quote it: "I had a short extramarital affair with Elizabeth Graham, which finished several weeks ago by mutual consent." Was it mutual or did he ditch you? What's the next bit? "I accept that this was very foolish." He thinks you were a foolish mistake, Lizzie. How does that make you feel? "And I deeply regret the hurt and distress caused to my wife and family." No mention of you, is there? You're out of the loop, Lizzie! "I ask that the media will leave us in peace to resolve our differences and rebuild our marriage." Does he deserve to be left in peace?' She could sense some movement behind the door, so she pounced. 'Lizzie, I am authorised to offer you seven thousand pounds to tell us about your affair and three thousand to tell us what it feels like when your father comes out. That's ten grand. Lizzie, can you hear me?'

The door opened. Lizzie was standing there beside Zoe.

'You'd better come in.'

'Lizzie, are you mad? Don't speak to her!' said Zoe.

'Why not? You did. Just go and mind your own business, Zoe.'

Zoe shrugged her shoulders and picked up her bag. 'Suit yourself, then!' she said as she went out on to the stairs.

Michelle came into the flat and they made their way to Lizzie's room. 'Thanks for speaking to me, Lizzie. You must be very upset by all this.'

She was. She was upset, hurt and abandoned, just as her mother was. The only person to have been in contact was a Liberal Democrat press officer, who advised her to phone the police if the press were a nuisance. He had phoned again two hours later to say he would email the statement to her and that Mike would call her later. Then her mobile had begun to ring unceasingly. Some member of the press had been clever enough to approach Darren Connerty and offer him fifty pounds, which he had talked up to seventy-five. Lizzie turned her mobile off, switching it back on every half an hour for a fruitless check for messages from Mike. By the time Michelle arrived at eight thirty, Lizzie was ready to get her own back. Ten thousand pounds seemed to her a great deal of money, especially as she now had an unemployed father.

'What do you want for the money?' asked Lizzie.

'An exclusive. That means you tell us all about your affair – how it started, where you met, how you kept it secret, how you feel now he's ditched you, that sort of thing. We'd also like something about your father and how you feel about that. You'll get a photoshoot too. You are a good-looking girl – you might even get some modelling work from it. That would help with your living costs, wouldn't it?'

'When do I get the money?'

'I've got an agreement here for you to sign. It says you won't talk to anyone else. I'll give you a cheque for two thousand now, and if you have kept to your side of the agreement, you will get the balance on Saturday evening. It will be in our sister paper, the *Saltire,* on Sunday. We'll do a photoshoot and the interview tomorrow.'

'What are we waiting for? You sign the cheque, I'll sign the agreement!'

They arranged to meet the next morning. As Lizzie closed the door and kissed the cheque, an exultant Michelle walked back to the office, where Colin congratulated her on a job well done and suggested that they might celebrate by visiting the top floor.

There was plenty to celebrate. It is not for nothing that people are advised to use a solicitor or some other trained negotiator when selling a kiss-and-tell story, someone who knows a first offer is never the best offer. Michelle had authorisation to offer up to £20,000 for the combined exposé.

Chapter Twenty-Six

By Thursday, Tom Graham was sliding back into depression. Immediately following his walkout, he felt liberated and happy for the first time in years. On Monday, he unplugged the phone, disconnected the doorbell and spent most of the day asleep. Now the weight had been removed from him, he managed to sleep soundly for the first time in months.

Tuesday saw some reporters still remaining outside, so he stayed in again, this time watching property shows on daytime TV and wondering how Ali was getting on in Corrachan. He considered phoning her but didn't know what to say or how he would deal with her despair. The sense of freedom was just beginning to diminish, and was being replaced with a feeling that this might not have been the best way to deal with things. They had hoped to eat out, but Mark had been hassled as he tried to get in the front door, so they phoned for a Chinese takeaway to be delivered. As they ate, there was an underlying tension that had never been there on their illicit meetings. Mark was having a difficult time at work. It had been no secret that he was gay, but his employers had not been happy with the press interest and there had been requests from some clients that someone other than Mark handle their business.

On Wednesday, Tom had cooked dinner and a very edgy Mark criticised the grilled fish and salad, and suggested it was time Tom thought about getting a job. Tom had been thinking about nothing else for most of the day but had not reached any conclusions. His degrees in philosophy and divinity, followed by twenty years as a parish minister qualified him for nothing else. He had skills relating to public speaking and pastoral care, but he could think of no gainful employment there. He had no idea what he wanted to do. His and Ali's savings had been minimal: £15,000 put by for the down payment on a small house for their old age. That would have to be divided now.

He had first thought he wanted to be a minister when he was twelve, a feeling that grew in certainty throughout his teenage years. At twenty-one, he had been accepted for the ministry and now, more than twenty years on, he was trained only for a job he could no longer do. He relied on Mark for everything and he was aware that the clandestine nature of the relationship had given it an excitement that now seemed to be evaporating. They were beginning to annoy each other.

On Thursday morning, the press were back, wanting comment about Lizzie. The flat was again besieged, so he couldn't fulfil his promise to Mark to go to the Job Centre. He knew he ought to call Ali and got as far as punching in the number but couldn't bring himself to press the call button. The feelings of despair and indecision that he thought he had left behind in Corrachan were enveloping him again. Paternal concern made him call Lizzie's number, but he was not strong enough to leave a message. He felt useless. He looked at Mark's array of rare malts, selected a bottle of twenty-five-year-old Highland Park and one of the Edinburgh Crystal glasses and settled down to watch *Countdown*. Never what could have been described as a drinker, he was asleep on the sofa with Channel Four news blaring when Mark came home from work. Mark removed his crystal glass from the sleeping hand, put the empty bottle in the recycling box and went out. When he came home at eleven, Tom had not moved, so he put a rug over the unconscious form and went to bed.

Minty Oliver was spending Friday in Edinburgh. The Metro was making a strange noise over and above the usual cacophony, so not wanting to risk a breakdown, she had taken advantage of her free bus pass and chatted at length in French to a tourist from Marseilles who was sitting next to her. When she was fifteen, she had spent a summer in Chamonix at an establishment for young ladies, and spoke French filled with slang from the thirties. This had sounded strange to the French student, especially as the discussion was about the merits of the European monetary system.

Preferring to keep her affairs private, Minty avoided the Corrachan lawyers. She had had an appointment with her solicitor in Hill Street at ten o'clock, and now, an hour and a half later, she was striding along George Street, making for her next port of call. The meeting with the lawyer had been successful. They had discussed the family trust and Minty had added some legacies and removed others. She did this frequently as one good cause overtook another. At eighty-six, one never knew the moment when one might not wake up, or worse still, when one might wake up incapacitated. She had her affairs in order – a power of attorney drawn up in favour of her niece, and instructions as to the nursing home in which she wished to spend her last days. Those who mattered knew what was to be said and sung at her funeral.

She crossed Charlotte Square and stopped outside a café at the top of Queensferry Street to retie her shoelace. As she stood up, she looked at the tables set up outside in hope, rather than expectation, that someone might sit there. Despite the cold, there was one pale, unshaven man huddled in an anorak, staring straight ahead over the top of a cold cup of coffee. It was Tom.

'Tom Graham!' said Minty. 'Hello there!'

Tom made no move to acknowledge her, or give any indication that he had heard. She took a step closer and looked carefully, because it wouldn't have been the first time she had greeted a total stranger as a long-lost friend. It was definitely Tom Graham.

She approached and touched his arm. 'Tom? Are you all right?'

Tom jumped and looked up. 'Mrs Oliver! Hello. Sorry – I was miles away.'

'Minty, please. Are you feeling all right? You look very pale.'

'Hangover. Had a bit too much whisky last night.'

'Celebrating your newfound freedom?'

'Not really. Escapism, if you must know.'

Minty took in the look and the tone of despair. 'Listen, I'm gasping for a cup of coffee, but it's a bit chilly out here. Come inside and keep me company while I have mine and you can tell me what you are going to do with your new life.'

Tom stood up wearily and followed her into the café. They settled at a table near the window and a waitress from the southern hemisphere appeared.

'Yes, what can I get you?'

'Two coffees, please! I hope your coffee is fair trade. I don't like exploiting workers in the Third World.'

The waitress had no idea, but if this woman wanted fair-trade coffee, that was what she would get. 'Yes, all our coffee is fair trade. What kind of coffee?' The girl pointed to the menu on the table.

Ignoring the menu, Minty asked Tom if he wanted black or white. He said black. 'One black, one white.'

The waitress sighed in exasperation. 'What sort of black coffee? Espresso, double espresso, Americano?'

Minty looked confused. Coffee was coffee. She had a faint memory of something very strong from her tour of Italy after the summer in Chamonix. 'Espresso is about a thimbleful, isn't it? Fine for after dinner but not quite elevenses, is it?'

'Americano,' said Tom.

'Large or regular?' said the waitress.

'Regular.'

'And what about you?' asked the waitress.

'White, please, dear.'

'Cappuccino, latte, skinny latte, flat white, Americano with milk . . . ?' She really wished that old biddies like this would go to Jenners, where she had heard that they employed someone to explain to the fur-coat brigade what all the coffees were. Minty looked around. The couple at the next table had cappuccinos.

'I'll have the frothy one with the cocoa on top. And regular, whatever that means. Sounds like it's some kind of laxative to me. What is wrong with small or medium?'

The waitress took that to be a rhetorical question and, glad to have finished interpreting, disappeared behind the counter.

They sat in silence for a moment or two.

'Not as good as you thought it might be?' ventured Minty.

'No.'

Minty waited to see if he was going to say anything else.

He started, 'I don't . . .'

'You don't what?'

'I don't know what to do.'

'About what? Your sexuality? Your wife? Your wayward daughter? Your job? Your lover?'

'Yes . . . all of that.'

'Wish you were still in the closet and minister in Corrachan?'

'No! That was hell!'

The waitress arrived with the coffees. She couldn't work out the relationship between the posh but rather shabby elderly lady with her cardigan buttoned up the wrong way and the depressed man who had been sitting outside for most of the morning. She took up her stance behind the counter and, because she had nothing else to do, watched them with interest.

'Well, that's something. At least you are glad to be "out" and to have left your job.'

'Yes, but I've managed to create more problems than I have solved.'

'Go on.'

'I have a wife who has not worked for years, a daughter at university, a daughter going to university next year, a son with autism and I have no job. I don't have skills that are transferable. Who is going to employ a gay ex-minister in his mid-forties? And . . .' He paused. 'I don't think I will have accommodation for much longer.'

'Ah! The reality doesn't match the expectation? Life tends to be like that, especially when you've wanted something for a long time. Is he going to put you out on the street?'

'No, he won't do that, but put it this way, we appear to have less in common than we thought.'

'What are you going to do with your new life, then?'

'Don't know. Like I said, not many openings for gay atheist ministers.'

'What would you like to do?'

Tom rubbed his hands over his stubbly cheeks and thought. 'I would love to travel. I've not seen much of the world, but that costs money. It doesn't support an ex-wife and family.'

'Hmm,' said Minty, 'you do have a bit of a problem. Your daughter has been something of a worry too.'

'I know.'

'Have you spoken to her?'

'No. I tried yesterday, but her phone was switched off.'

'Don't you think you ought to try again? What age is she? Eighteen? We all thought we knew everything at eighteen . . .'

Tom remembered himself at eighteen, in a university residence, scared of the big bad world. The Christian Union was the extent of his social life in his first year. Pity Lizzie hadn't spent her time there instead of jetting to London.

Minty continued with her reminiscences. 'Life was waiting, full of parties and men and excitement. It was the war then, of course, so we were all doing what we shouldn't with unsuitable people. And it's fine till something goes wrong; eighteen, or nineteen, or twenty is very young to cope when everything goes pear-shaped.'

Tom took out his mobile and dialled Lizzie. It went straight to her voicemail. This time he left a message. 'It's Dad. Are you OK? Give me a phone. Love you.'

Minty drained her cup and stood up. 'I've been thinking! Come with me.' She went to the counter and paid for the coffees. 'What was the one with the cocoa called again?'

'Cappuccino,' replied the waitress.

'Cappuccino! I'll remember that for next time. Good morning to you.' She dropped ten pence into the bowl on the counter. Minty still thought of it as two shillings and considered it a generous tip.

With Tom in her wake, she began to walk briskly towards Haymarket. Tom, nearly forty years her junior, was out of breath trying to keep up and even without a hangover, he would have been struggling.

'Where are we going, Minty. What is this about?'

'Patience is a virtue, as my nanny used to say.'

She strode on. Opposite Haymarket Station, she made a sharp right-hand turn, walked up the path to the front door of a terraced house and went inside. Tom was not only gasping for breath but feeling very nauseous with the combination of coffee, hangover and what amounted to a half-mile run. He followed Minty into the office and found her asking the lady on reception if she could see the person who dealt with motions. The lady, who had obviously encountered Minty before, told her that motions were dealt with by the committee, which was meeting next Tuesday. Did she want them to consider something?

'No! No! No! I don't want a committee to consider anything! I want to speak to the person who runs the committee. All committees have a sheepdog and lots of sheep. I need to speak to the sheepdog. It's no use giving motions to the sheep: they end up mangled beyond recognition. In fact, I'm sure that's what's happened. I sent in a motion and what has come back bears no resemblance to the original.'

Tom couldn't follow this. Was it some sort of gastroenterology lab that examined stool samples? Was it something to do with that woman on the TV who was always raking about in Tupperware containers and making disdainful comments about people's diets? The waves of nausea were sweeping over him and the thought of motions being examined by a committee was making it worse. He took several deep breaths and with no evidence of a toilet, he knew he had to go outside. He put his hand over his mouth and made for the door.

The occupants of the number twenty-six bus, which had stopped at the traffic lights, were surprised to see a slightly dishevelled man burst out of the Scottish Liberal Democrat headquarters and vomit all over the path.

'Ach, politics! Wid make anyone want tae puke,' remarked an elderly gentleman on the top deck to his neighbour.

The lady on reception glanced out of the window and suggested to Minty that her friend was not feeling very well. Minty stepped outside. Tom was now sitting on the doorstep wiping his mouth. She came back inside.

'Better out than in! Can you get me a bucket of water and I'll wash down the path?'

The traffic lights changed to green and then to red again, and the occupants of the next bus were treated to the sight of an elderly lady throwing a bucket of water at the path.

'Did you see that?' said a middle-aged lady to her companion. 'You'd have thought they would have given that old soul a retirement package by now. Imagine her having to be a cleaner at that age. That's political parties for you. They should be giving the job to school leavers. They're all talk, but when it comes to getting young folk into jobs, they do nothing about it. Disgusting.'

When the path had been sluiced to Minty's satisfaction, she spoke to Tom. 'Feeling better?'

He looked at her and nodded sheepishly.

'Right! Off we go, then!'

'You mean this isn't where you were taking me?'

'No! No! This was on the way. I was wanting to sort conference motions. Your brother and I submitted one about Third World debt. It was very clear and well drafted, but they have combined it with one about conservation of the rainforest. A worthy cause, no doubt, but not the same thing. Just assume it's abroad and can be lumped together. A sign of falling standards. Come on, then, let's get moving.'

'Where are we going?'

'Marchmont!'

'Marchmont?' echoed Tom. Only a taxi driver on the make would have gone to Marchmont via Haymarket, and it was obvious that Minty had no intention of taking a taxi – they were going walkabout again.

Risking death by ignoring the Red Man, they crossed Morrison Street, making for Tollcross. The brisk pace was doing nothing for Tom's insides and they had to take one enforced stop. By the time they were crossing the Meadows, however, he was feeling better. Minty refused to say where they were going and why. Halfway up Marchmont Road, she made another sudden right turn and this time walked up to the door of some tenement flats. Tom expected her to press one of the buzzers on the entryphone system, but she delved into the Burns Cottage bag and produced an enormous bunch of keys. Having located the one she wanted, she opened the door. They walked along the tiled entrance hall and up the stone stairs to the second floor, where Minty again produced the bunch of keys, opened the locks and went inside. It was a bright, roomy flat with a large living room and bedroom to the front and two bedrooms, a kitchen and bathroom to the rear. It was equipped with rather elderly but otherwise functional furniture, though there was no sign of personal belongings.

'At least they've left it clean,' said Minty, going from room to room. She finished inspecting the bathroom and turned to Tom. 'Well, what do you think?'

'It's a nice bright flat.' He didn't quite know what she expected him to say.

'Do you think it will do?'

'Do for what?'

'For you, you silly man. Do you want to live here?'

'I couldn't afford to live here. Is it for sale or something?'

'It belongs to me. I need a new tenant.'

'It would be lovely, Minty, but as I said, I couldn't afford the rent for this place. It must be eight hundred a month at least.'

'I wasn't going to charge you rent. I actually own all the

flats in this close. They're rented out and I need a factor to look after them. Lot of students live here and things get damaged and broken, so someone has to sort things out. Find a plumber when there's a flood and so on.'

'But this is a three-bedroomed flat, Minty. You can't let it just to me.'

'Aren't you going to have your children to stay? You can't exist in a bedsit. You won't get visiting rights. And anyway, I have other flats round here that need to be factored too.'

'Other flats? How many?'

'Oh, about ten.'

Tom did a quick calculation. These flats were worth at least £250,000. Sixteen of them amounted to over £4 million! He knew she was supposed to be wealthy but this was something else and presumably just a small part of the empire.

Minty interrupted his thoughts. 'Wouldn't be a full-time job – only occasional work – plenty of time to do something else.'

Tom didn't know what to say. Had he still been a believer, this would have been an answer to his prayers – a place of his own, a place to think about his future.

'Yes, Minty! Thank you. That would be wonderful.' He went over to her and gave her a hug.

She detached the keys to the flat from her large bundle and handed them to him. 'Here you are. Move in whenever you like. I'll have a tenancy agreement sent to you. Don't want me evicting you for no good reason.'

Tom took the keys, sat down on the elderly sofa and looked around him. This would be just fine to start with. He could look for a job and not have to think about accommodation costs.

They made their way down the stairs again and on to the street. Minty set off down the road towards the Meadows, pointing out her flats as she went. 'There's one in there . . . and 'two in there . . . and one in there.' She glanced up at a top flat to which she had admitted ownership, and thought it looked as if there was a crack in one of the windows. She stepped off the pavement to get a better look and was inches away from being knocked down by a bus.

'My God, Minty, that was close! Are you OK?' said Tom, taking her by the arm.

'Fine, fine. Now I know what you should do!' She pointed to the back of the speeding bus and at the advert for bus drivers. 'Learn to be a bus driver!'

Tom looked at her as if she was mad. It was not a suggestion that appealed to him. 'I really don't think I want to be a bus driver in Edinburgh.'

'No, no. Not Lothian Transport! Take a PSV licence and take an HGV licence. Then you can be a freelance driver. Travel the Continent and get paid for it. There's your answer.'

It was a novel idea and it certainly had its attractions, but it also had its drawbacks.

'Sounds interesting, but I don't think I could afford the lessons. I'll bear it in mind, though.'

'There is the Barswick Educational Trust, set up by my grandfather. Has lots of money sloshing around in it. One of its functions is the education and retraining of those from the Sheffield factory and the town of Corrachan. I'm sure you're eligible. Think about it.'

'If I become a long-distance lorry driver, I can't be your factor.'

'If you become a long-distance lorry driver, someone else can be my factor. Tenants change all the time.'

'So have there been other lame ducks before me?'

'One or two. I prefer not to think of them as lame ducks – temporarily displaced fish is better. A bowl and a little water and most of them start swimming again.'

Some weeks later, Tom went to a flat to check that a repair had been carried out satisfactorily. The door was opened by Frank — another of Minty's fish in his new bowl of water.

Chapter Twenty-Seven

Phyllis was up early on Friday morning in order not to miss the comings and goings next door. She had stayed up till nearly midnight in the hope of seeing Mike leave the house and she was sure she hadn't missed him. Jack was in London at a Volvo-dealership conference, so she had been able to sit in her darkened bedroom and watch without being told to mind her own business. Although she had nodded off at one stage, Mike's car was still outside when she woke and it was still outside now.

Well, well, she thought. She must have taken him back. You would have thought she would have had more pride. She wondered about phoning Joyce, but thought a call at seven thirty might not be welcome. Bill, like most men, wasn't that interested in gossip, especially if it disturbed his breakfast. The curtains of the main bedroom were still shut. She wondered about their spare room, which faced the back, so she put on her dressing gown and slippers, and defying all her own standards of decency, went downstairs and out into her back garden. The curtains were open.

They were open because they had never been closed. Gill had made up the bed but done nothing else. When Mike eventually went to sleep about five o'clock, pulling the curtains had not occurred to him. He just wanted to get underneath the duvet and die.

Gill had not slept well. She had gone over the events of the day, considering all her options, including Minty's suggestion of a chance to sin in later life. Her thoughts had been accompanied by the sound of groaning, retching and toilet-flushing. At 3 a.m., she wondered if he was in need of a doctor. At three thirty, she hadn't heard him leave the bathroom and there had been silence for fifteen minutes. She wondered if he had passed out. Worrying that Ian might find him dead on the floor in the morning, she got out of bed and as far as the door before the retching started again. Satisfied he was still alive, she got back into bed and reconsidered her options.

She could throw him out. If she did that, she could either stay here in Corrachan or go back to Edinburgh. Edinburgh would be preferable. Small towns are not a good place in which to hide.

She could take him back and they could try again. That would mean staying here with everyone watching to see how they got on, but they would still be a family unit. There were a few weeks till Easter recess, so she would only have to see him at weekends. On the whole, she thought that staying together might be better. He was certainly contrite, and if he remained in the spare room for a while, it might work.

She had slept fitfully until the children had woken at six. At about half past seven, she opened the spare-room door. Mike was lying on the bed in his shirt and boxer shorts with the bucket beside him. He looked dreadful. His skin had a grey-green pallor and his eyes were sunk into their sockets.

'How are you feeling?'

'Awful! I think the runs have stopped, but I can't stop being sick even though there's nothing to bring up.' He sat up and gingerly took a sip of water. 'Ooh, the room spins when I sit up.' He lay down again, then sat up suddenly and got out of bed. 'I take back what I said about the runs – I need to get to the loo.' The room swam and he blacked out, hitting his head on the bed-end as he fell. Head wounds are notorious for producing a lot of blood, and although Mike opened his eyes quite quickly, he was incoherent and unable to get up. Confusion and severe bleeding were reasons enough for Gill to phone for an ambulance.

Having come back inside, Phyllis made herself a cup of tea, then went to the front of the house to open her living-room curtains. She parted the olive-green velour to see an ambulance with a blue flashing light in the Andrewses' driveway. The paramedics were manoeuvring a stretcher, carrying someone with a pad of gauze on their head, down the front steps.

Gill followed the stretcher with a very frightened Ian in her arms, who was shouting, 'Daddy, bloody Daddy!'

Ian was only making a statement of fact. Daddy was very bloody indeed.

That child never opens his mouth without swearing, thought Phyllis. That must be Mike on the stretcher. Gracious, has she assaulted him? He seems to have a head wound. What had she hit him with? She watched the paramedics load the stretcher into the ambulance, close the doors and drive off. Gill was left standing at the front door with the children. Phyllis thought this callous in the extreme, to pack him off in an ambulance on his own. The practicalities of ending up at the Infirmary twenty miles away with no car and two small children did not occur to her.

It had occurred to Gill. However reluctant, she knew she ought to follow him to the hospital as soon as possible, but she didn't want to take the children. She considered asking Phyllis to babysit. She had the advantage of being nearby, but apologising for broken royal memorabilia was not what Gill needed today. Perhaps child-friendly Joyce would oblige again. Gill dialled her number but found it to be engaged. Phyllis had rung Joyce as soon as the ambulance had disappeared out of sight, disseminating conjecture that, with one or two retellings, would become fact.

'She must have hit him. He was bleeding a lot – you could see the blood coming through the bandage. He looked unconscious. I expect she threw something at him.'

'How did she look? Upset? Angry?'

'Difficult to tell. She watched the ambulance drive away. Then she went inside and I came to phone you.'

When the line was no longer engaged, Gill managed to speak to Joyce, who agreed to babysit. As Gill brought the children and their paraphernalia into her house, Joyce, keen for details, inquired as to what had happened.

'I feel awful. It's my fault really. If I had been thinking properly, I would never have left Minty's present on the table. Then he wouldn't have been struck down.'

'Minty's present?'

'A frozen cake,' said Gill.

'A frozen cake?' said Joyce doubtfully.

'Yes, a frozen cake. I should have moved it out of harm's way. When I first realised what had happened, I thought, Serve you right. Then when he was on the floor and couldn't get up and he was bleeding, it was dreadful. That's when I called the ambulance.'

'Well, you'd better go to the Infirmary and find out what's happening. The children will be fine here till you get back.'

'Thanks, Joyce. I'll try not to be too long.'

When Joyce's cleaning lady, Mrs McCafferty, arrived at nine o'clock, she found Joyce sitting watching a DVD with a child on either side of her.

'Are they the Andrews children? Why are you minding them?'

'Well,' said Joyce, 'you'll never guess what's happened! She's thrown a frozen cake at him and knocked him out and he's been carted off in an ambulance. Very contrite she is now and she's gone to the Infirmary. I can understand her being angry, but hurling frozen cakes about is domestic violence. It wouldn't surprise me if the police get involved.'

'Bloody, bloody Daddy,' said Ian in a conversational tone. He picked up his bit of sheet and saw the ladies looking at him. 'Shit,' he said in an informative fashion. He held it up to his face and returned his attention to the TV.

'Did you hear that?' whispered Mrs McCafferty.

By the time Gill had got to the Infirmary, Mike was still lying on a trolley but had steri-strips over the wound in his fore-head and a drip in his arm. He was a better colour already and was able to tell her he was being admitted for observation of his head injury and rehydration.

He smiled weakly at her. 'Seem to be causing you no end of trouble, don't I? Did you bring any of my stuff?'

Gill held up a small bag into which she had jammed a pair of pyjamas, his shaving kit and some other toiletries. 'Here you are.'

The house officer came up to them. 'Mrs Andrews? Your husband should be feeling a bit better soon. He was danger-ously dehydrated, but the drip should sort that. We need to discover the source of the food poisoning, so samples have been sent to the lab. Have any other members of the household had stomach pains, diarrhoea or vomiting?'

'No,' said Gill.

'Was there anything that your husband ate which no one else had?'

She hesitated, then decided on honesty. 'He had a slice of cake.'

'What sort of cake? A homemade one? A bought one?'

'A homemade one. It had been on a baking stall. Someone gave it to me as a present.'

After that admission, it was out of her hands. The remains of the cake had to be extracted from the pedal bin, where it had had twelve hours to allow the bacteria to multiply further, and were sent for analysis.

On Friday evening, Darren Connerty was in the public bar of the Corrachan Hotel with most of the other eighteen- to twenty-five-year-old residents of Corrachan, before they went on to the one and only club in town. His girlfriend, Sharlene, was at home with their baby. As Sharlene was still only sixteen, the hotel's strict policy on underage drinking meant she was not able to accompany Darren on a night out.

'Seventy-five pounds for Lizzie's mobile number. Talk about easy money. I'll have a pint of Special and a vodka chaser, Angie baby.'

Leanne appeared at Darren's elbow. 'Hear you're in the money, Darren. Going to buy me a drink, then?'

'What's in it for me, Leanne? Don't buy drinks without expecting something in return.'

'Well, buy me one and you might find out.'

Darren did not usually enter into any expense unless guaranteed a return, but he was feeling generous. 'OK, then, what do you want?'

'Watermelon Breezer, thanks.' She turned to Angela. 'Do you know? Mike Andrews's wife didn't know about Lizzie and then she sees it in the paper. She was so angry she hit him with a frozen leg of lamb and knocked him out. Now he's in the Infirmary.'

'How do you know that?'

'My mum cleans for Mrs Macdonald – you know, her that's married to the lawyer. Well, Mrs Macdonald had to babysit the

Andrews kids while Mrs A went to the Infirmary. Mum says that Mrs Macdonald says that the police are going round to arrest her for domestic violence. Can't say I blame her, but I wouldn't have thrown meat at him – I'd have gone at him with a pair of blunt scissors.'

'Remind me not to offend you, then, Leanne,' said Darren.

Leanne ignored him and continued, 'My mum says that the wee boy was swearing all the time, swearing about his father and saying "shit" when he got upset and he said he wanted to watch "bloody *Balamory*". It's no wonder the woman lost it – a swearing kid and a shagging husband!'

Angela decided to tease Darren. 'So was it worth Mike Andrews's while to risk his marriage and his job for Lizzie? C'mon, Darren, tell us.'

'Well, she was quite energetic and willing to try anything.'

'Meaning?'

'Meaning *anything*!'

'And there's her famous for her sexual adventures, and here's you, Darren, her instructor in the art of shagging, totally forgotten.'

'I could be famous too! I could tell the press all about it. If I got seventy-five pounds for a phone number, what d'you think they'd give me for an exposé? "My Nights of Love with Lizzie, the MP's slag." How much do you think I'd get for that?'

'Thousands, I bet,' said Leanne. 'You could treat us all to a party.'

'Dream on, Leanne. If I get money, I'm not wasting it on you lot.'

Having hatched the idea of selling his story, Darren wasn't sure what to do next. He had no idea who had given him the money for the phone number or what paper they were from. He turned to Angela for help.

'It was one of the ones who were staying here,' he said. 'It was a woman about thirty with dyed blond hair, nice tits but a bit of a big arse! Come on, Angela, you work here. You were serving them. What was her name? What paper was she from?'

Angela could picture who he was talking about, but couldn't remember her name. She disappeared from behind the bar, returning with the hotel register. 'It'll be in here. Let me have a look . . . Here we are, Lynn McKechnie, *Sunday Clarion*, Glasgow.'

'Right, I'll just go and phone her up.'

Lynn was more than happy to meet him the following morning. Darren, who had long been disposing of stolen goods, knew that the first, second and often the third offer were not all that is available. For the promise of a detailed story featuring his nocturnal visits to the manse, Lizzie's sexual preferences, her occasional drug use and the deception of her parents, Darren emerged with the promise of £25,000.

Mike remained in hospital overnight but was released back to the spare room on Saturday afternoon, when the doctors were satisfied he was no longer a bacterial health risk or likely to die of a cerebral haemorrhage. After the children were in bed, he raised the subject of their marriage again. Gill stood looking out of the spare-room window because she still couldn't bear to look at him properly. He addressed her back.

'Please can we try again?'

'I couldn't stand you near me at the moment. I would smell her. I would think you were comparing everything with her.'

'I'll stay here in the spare room for as long as you want.'

She was silent.

Mike lumbered on, 'I'll do whatever you want. I love you and the children. Lizzie was just sex.'

She continued to look out of the window, considering the options again. Then she turned to face him. 'I need to be sure that you have told me everything. Never again do I intend to find out what you have been up to by reading it in the paper. Is there anything else you haven't told me?'

'No. I told you everything. It started in November and I finished it the day of our party. We met in London and Edinburgh. Nothing ever happened here.'

'I have to think about this. I'm not promising anything.'

Sunday was a good day for Darren. He was £25,000 better off and he was featuring in the Scottish *Sunday Clarion*. There was a picture of him sitting with Sharlene and baby Krystal as well as an old photo he had found of Lizzie, aged fourteen, sitting on his knee. There was also a photo of the manse. On account of his limited schooling, Darren was almost illiterate, so he asked Sharlene, who had intended to go to college to do business studies before motherhood intervened, to read it out to him.

She handed him a grizzling Krystal and picked up the paper. '"Under-Age Sex and Drugs in Gay Minister's Manse."'

'I can read that bit! Tell me what the rest says!'

'"MP's mistress Lizzie Graham was only fourteen when she started allowing Darren Connerty through her bedroom window for nights of passion in St Andrew's Manse, Corrachan. Every night, while minister Tom Graham, who last Sunday shocked his congregation by telling them he was gay, and his wife, Ali slept, Lizzie and Connerty would drink vodka, take drugs and make love."' Sharlene, who had just left primary school when all this had been going on, had not been totally aware of the extent of her fiancé's previous sexual adventures. 'Did you really go there every night?'

'Most nights I did. Go on, read some more!'

'"Darren, twenty, an unemployed builder, said, 'Sometimes we smoked joints, and sometimes we popped something to help us relax. It made the sex much better. We did it four or five

273

times a night. She couldn't get enough of me. As soon as we finished, she would want to start again. She was like a nympho-maniac.'" Ugh, Darren! Too much detail!'

'No, it isn't. Makes it much more interesting for the reader and much more money for us, so stop complaining and get on with it.'

'OK. "On Sunday mornings, when the rest of her family were at church, we used to do it in different rooms in the manse. She liked the shower, but I liked doing it in the minister's study or on the kitchen table." That's gross, Darren! Is it true?'

'Sort of . . . Keep reading. Don't keep stopping all the time.'

'Where was I? Oh, yes . . . "Darren now lives with his fiancée, Sharlene McPhee, sixteen, and their baby daughter, three-month-old Kristin." They've got her name wrong! I told them what her name was and I spelt it out for them.'

'Get on with it, woman.'

'All right, keep your hair on. "'Now that I am in love with Sharlene, I know my relationship with Lizzie was just sex.' Brainbox Lizzie, now a first-year medical student at Edinburgh University, was the secret mistress of the MP Mike Andrews, but he dumped her last week, saying the affair had been a stupid mistake." You know Mrs Caldwell saw them in London? They were snogging on a street corner.'

'Not what I heard,' said Darren with a leer.

'What did you hear, then?' asked Sharlene.

'Angie says her mum heard that Mrs Caldwell's friend who works at the Houses of Parliament caught them doing it in his office.'

'She caught them at it?'

'So Angie says! Go on, read us the rest.'

'"Andrews, who was admitted to the Strathperry Infirmary on Friday with a mysterious head wound, was unavailable for comment."'

'It was a frozen chicken that she hit him with. It's lucky she didn't kill him. Leanne says the police have been round and arrested her for assault. Read the next bit.'

'That's it!'

'Is that all?'

'What else were you expecting?'

'I talked to that Lynn for ages. I thought there would be more. Makes me sound like a sexual athlete, doesn't it?'

'Ha, so what happened, then?'

'Piss off! Mind your mouth or I'll mind it for you!' He passed the now crying Krystal back to Sharlene. 'I'm off to the pub to talk to people who appreciate me. Text me when my dinner's ready.'

As he walked down the road, paper under his arm, he thought he would enjoy being famous for having the sexual prowess of a stallion. He hadn't realised that he had admitted to a criminal offence – having sex with an underage girl. He was surprised therefore, on Monday morning, to receive a visit from the local constabulary with a warrant for his arrest for offences under the Sexual Offences Scotland Act 1976, and for offences under the Proceeds of Crime Act 1995 for benefiting from his crime.

Since the paperboy had made the Junior Sunday League football team, the Corrachan newsagent had not offered a Sunday delivery. Jack usually took the early-morning stroll to the shop, so it was a novelty for Phyllis to walk to the town centre to collect her large pile of papers. She stood in the queue behind Helen Cooper, who was trying to hide the *Saltire* and the *Clarion* under the *Sunday Times*.

Phyllis tapped her on the shoulder. 'Extra reading matter today?'

'Richard says it's important to know what's going on in the town. For his pastoral work, I mean.'

'Mmm, I'm sure,' said Phyllis, who couldn't wait to get to church to tell Joyce that Richard had spoken yet again. That would make a tally of 108 'Richard says . . .' since the committee meeting in October, when Helen had deposed Joyce from the cake stall.

Back at home, Phyllis read the *Saltire* and the *Clarion* with her breakfast. Then she found a pair of scissors, cut out each article, folded them carefully and put them in her handbag. She knew Joyce never got her papers till after church and there might be a chance to show her between choir practice and the service.

The practice was shorter than usual, as last week's unsung hymns and the anthem had been transposed to this week. Phyllis practised her solo, not realising that with age her vocal range was diminishing. In the fifteen minutes to spare before the service, Phyllis took Joyce by the arm and steered her towards the Ladies'.

'Come in here and I'll show you what's in the paper.' Joyce was handed the *Clarion* cutting and she started to read.

After a few sentences, she looked up. 'There were rumours she was on drugs. Heroin, wasn't it? You remember, Phyllis, she disappeared for a whole summer about two years ago.'

'They invented some story that she had gone to France.'

'Well, the clinic was in Lyons, wasn't it?' Joyce read on. 'I knew he used to visit the manse in the evening sometimes, but on a Sunday morning! It's very explicit, this article. Children might read it. There really ought to be some sort of control over what they are allowed to print.'

Phyllis dipped into her handbag and produced the cutting from the *Saltire*. 'Look at this one. It's Lizzie's version. How much money do you suppose she would get for that?'

'These papers have unlimited funds, you know. Fifty thousand?'

'Oh, at least.'

Joyce took the article. There was a photo of Lizzie posing rather suggestively in the entrance to Annie Cochrane's flat below the headline, which read, 'My Lover Dumped Me and My Dad's Gay – Lizzie, Mistress of Love-Rat MP, Tells All.'

Phyllis was trying to read the article over Joyce's shoulder.

'Look, Phyllis, will I just read it out? Then you won't have to peer over my shoulder.'

Phyllis stepped back. 'Sorry! Yes, read it out.'

'"Attractive medical student Lizzie Graham, eighteen, has the week from hell." I'm sure her mother's week hasn't been heaven! "Last Sunday, her father, a Church of Scotland minister, shocked his family and congregation with the news he was gay and quit his small-town life in Corrachan." Small town? That's rather derogatory.' She looked at the byline and saw it was written by Colin. 'Look, it's written by that man. No wonder it's snide. Where had I got to . . . ? "On Thursday came our exposé that Lizzie had been having an affair with Lib Dem MP Mike Andrews, thirty-six, who immediately dumped her and issued a statement he was going back to his wife and children." Is he still there or has she thrown him out?'

'Well, she brought him back from the hospital yesterday afternoon and I haven't seen either of them come or go since.'

'Would you take Jack back if he did something like that? I don't think I could take Bill back if I knew he'd been carrying on.'

'Jack and Bill are both past that sort of thing, don't you think?'

'Let's hope so!' Joyce picked up the article again. '"Lizzie met Andrews when she babysat for his children, aged two and six months. She told our reporter, 'I met him by chance in Edinburgh. He plied me with vodka. Then he took me to someone's flat and we made love.'" Chance? That'll be right.

"'After that first time, we used to meet whenever we could. I was infatuated. Sometimes he asked me go to London so I would miss lectures. Now I'm behind with all my assignments. When he came to Edinburgh, we met at his friend's flat.'" Do you think he paid her fares? It's expensive going up and down to London.'

'You don't have to tell me. My trip cost nearly two hundred and fifty pounds, what with the plane and the taxis,' offered Phyllis.

Joyce continued, 'Then it says, "'He was much more experienced.'" Only a little bit, I would have thought! "'And I was impressed that an older and important man like Mike would be interested in me.' Asked when she last saw him, a tearful Lizzie confessed, 'He was comforting me last Sunday after my dad left.'" Comforting! That's a new word for it. "'And I saw him in London on Tuesday. We spent the night in his flat and he gave me a hundred pounds, but I haven't seen or heard from him since.'" Well! She's been in London this week. And he's given her money! The enthusiastic amateur becomes a professional girl!'

'Is that what they charge?' asked Phyllis.

'Is that what who charge?'

'Prostitutes!'

'Oh for goodness' sake, Phyllis! I don't know! I suppose it depends on what they are offering. Let's see what the rest of this says. "The Edinburgh love nest is believed to be the flat rented by Annie Cochrane, MSP, who receives a parliamentary allowance for her accommodation. (See editorial comment.)" That's excellent! If Ms Cochrane is implicated, then she'll be vulnerable at the next Scottish election. It's under two years away now, so we'll have to get our candidate selected pronto to give him time to get a profile. Don't you think so?'

Phyllis was still considering Joyce's last remark. 'What do you mean by "what they are offering"? I thought they just had sex. Do they do other things?'

'Yes, Phyllis, they do, but the church toilets are not the place for this discussion. I'll tell you later over a large gin.' She continued reading, '"Lizzie explained, 'No one in the family suspected Dad was gay.'"' Well, neither did we, but surely Ali must have had an inkling. Things can't have been, well, you know . . .'

'Can't have been what?' asked Phyllis.

'Can't have been . . . Oh, Phyllis, use your imagination!' Phyllis looked at her blankly.

'Can't have been very satisfactory!' Joyce paused. 'That might be why she took to drink! Now what else is the girl saying? "When he came to Edinburgh for his church meetings, he would take me for a pizza but he was always in a hurry. I know now he was going to meet his gay friends. My mum is trying to find us somewhere to live. My little brother has got autism and my sister is sitting her Highers, so we need to be settled somewhere,' explained Lizzie."'

'That's the one I'm sorry for,' said Phyllis. 'Poor girl, she's a well-mannered, pleasant young lady, not like her sister at all.'

Joyce continued reading. '"A heartbroken Lizzie said, 'No one from the Church seems to care what happens to us. All they want is a new minister.'"' That is a lie! Bill's been most concerned. It's kept him awake at night, and don't I know it. "The Rev. Donald Cumming denied the Church had been uncaring. He said he and his wife had visited on several occasions to offer spiritual support." That must have been all the poor woman needed. That man is so godly he makes me hope I'm off to Hell. I'm sure the company would be much better.'

Lizzie woke early on Sunday, and after venturing out to buy a copy of the paper, she climbed back into bed to read the article.

She had banked the advance, and the cheque for the full amount was ready to pay in to her account. On Friday, she had spent two hours with Michelle discussing her affair and then she was photographed in various locations, including in the doorway of Annie Cochrane's flat. She hoped these might result in some modelling work, as Michelle had hinted.

She read through the article with satisfaction. That would teach him to ignore her. Seeing the reference to editorial comment, she turned over the pages and skimmed through the predictable sentences:

We ask whether the taxpayer should be expected to pay for the premises where Ms Cochrane's Lib Dem colleagues can commit adultery. Why should the public subsidise this immoral behaviour? We expect our elected representatives to spend their time working for their constituents, not making love to them. Those in public life have to accept that they have to set an example . . .

Blah de blah, she thought. She couldn't be bothered to read any more. She spent the rest of the morning catching up on sleep.

At lunchtime, Zoe knocked on her door. They had not spoken since Lizzie had told her to mind her own business.

'Did you used to go out with someone called Darren?' she asked, poking her head round the door.

'That's my business, Zoe.'

Zoe shrugged. 'Not just your business any more. Darren seems to have been telling everyone about it.' She waved the paper at Lizzie and disappeared towards the kitchen.

Lizzie followed her and grabbed the paper. 'Let me see!'

'Careful,' said Zoe, 'you'll rip it.'

Lizzie read the article with increasing anger. It made her out to be a drug-crazed nymphomaniac. She was only doing the same as half her year at school. The lying bastard, he could never manage it more than once, and on only one occasion had he come round on a Sunday morning when they had stayed in her room. He usually had such a hangover that he never got up before lunchtime. Then she came to the bit about Mike and his head injury. Gill must have thumped him. Serve him right.

Zoe had been watching her as she read. 'What do you think about that, then?'

'It's all lies and exaggeration. He must have got money for that, the bastard.'

'Sauce for the goose,' said Zoe. 'Have a nice afternoon.' She picked up her mug of coffee and went to her room.

Chapter Twenty-Eight

By Sunday morning, Ali Graham was feeling better both about herself and her predicament. She had tried prayer, but found it hard not to include God in the list of those responsible for her present situation, so she decided on direct action instead. On Friday, she had coaxed Ruth to school to sit her prelim maths exam, and taking Matt with her, she had gone to the Benefit Office, the council and the Housing Association. The people she had dealt with had been brisk in order to cover their embarrassment, and several members of the congregation had crossed the road as she approached. The headmaster had been sympathetic, but he, too, had trouble looking her in the eye. It had been agreed that Ruth could sit the prelims she had missed during the following week.

Because it was lunchtime, there were pupils everywhere when they left the headmaster's office. With Matt clinging to her, she hurried out of the teeming building and walked towards home. As she approached the primary school, she could see a crowd of children near the railings shouting something at two academy pupils who were walking past. As she got nearer, she realised that the older pupils were Ruth and a weedy-looking boy and that Ruth was being taunted as she walked along.

'Ruthie, Ruthie, come and play. Your sister's a slag and your daddy's gay.'

All Ali's suppressed anger erupted. She ran and caught up with Ruth, putting Matt's hand into hers.

'Take him home! I'll sort this.'

'Mum! No! Just leave it!'

'Take Matt home!' There was something about her tone that made Ruth do as she was told.

The taunters, sensing trouble, had melted away from the railings. It was unfortunate for some of these girls that their parents were churchgoers, because these were the ones Ali recognised.

'Gina! Jade! Cara! You little cows! Come back here now!'

Ali went through the gate into the playground. The teaching assistant on duty realised she was in the middle of an 'incident' involving a ranting woman intent on chasing some of the Primary Six girls. She sent a child to fetch the headmistress and then went after Ali and caught hold of her arm.

'Excuse me, what do you think you are you doing?'

Ali stopped and looked at her. 'Gina Lauder, Jade Thompson, Cara Craig and some of their poisonous little friends were shouting things at my daughter about her sister and her father. Don't they think we have enough to deal with without people making fun of us? None of this is our fault. We are doing the best we can and no one is helping us.'

The headmistress arrived and indicated she would deal with the situation. Taking the now weeping Ali into her office, she made her a cup of tea and waited until the sobs subsided into sniffs.

'You must've had a very difficult week. I'm sorry about the girls. Tell me who they were and I will speak to them. Then they will apologise to you and Ruth.'

Now that the anger had left her, Ali was appalled at what she had done. All she wanted to do was to go home without any more fuss. A discussion at assembly on considering other people's feelings was promised and Ali was able to leave.

Back at home, she told Ruth she had sorted it out.

'Sorted? I don't think so! You'll just have made it a million times worse! You don't know the half of it. That was nothing to what I've had to listen to all morning. Just leave it alone, Mum. Please!'

'Who was the boy with you?'

'Zak Cumming. We both know what it's like to be humiliated by our parents and ridiculed by the whole school.' She walked out of the room, slamming the door behind her.

Saturday had brought phone calls. The first was from the Cummings, inviting her to attend their church tomorrow. She had thanked them for thinking of her but said that she didn't feel she wanted to go out quite yet. Donald promised to call round on Sunday afternoon. The second was a stilted call from Tom. Things were not working out with Mark. She was very short with him.

'Why are you telling me this? I hope you are not expecting me to sort this out for you. You can solve your own problems now.'

'I'll work something out, I suppose,' had been the slightly pathetic reply.

'Don't you dare suggest you want to come back! After all the mayhem you've caused, it's too late for that!'

'No. I can't come back and I know I've got to sort things out by myself. I just have to go forward somehow.' He had told her he was moving into a flat on his own. He gave her the address. Were they OK? He was thinking about becoming a bus driver.

'A bus driver?'

'Yes. It will be something completely different.'

'It sure will.' Ali had decided he had definitely lost the plot.

'Can Ruth and Matt come and see me for the weekend sometime? I need to speak to Ruth properly about this.'

'I'll ask her, but you are not her favourite person! As she's sixteen, you can't force her to see you. Matt would be too distressed to come on his own.'

He had just said he would do what they wanted and had rung off. He sounded depressed again. She hoped he could get some professional help before he reached the bottom again. How had he got a flat in Marchmont? How could he afford it? Then she had a thought. He must have been at their joint savings account. There wasn't much in it, but it certainly wasn't all his. She would have to go to the bank on Monday and she had better go and see Bill Macdonald about her legal rights.

Ali had passed Sunday morning sorting Tom's possessions. She had to start sometime and it wasn't as bad as she thought it would be. In fact, it was quite cathartic. Ruth had gone round to Sacha's but had come back in tears at lunchtime.

'What's up now?' Ali had asked.

Ruth put the *Sunday Clarion* and the *Sunday Saltire* on the table. 'That's what's the matter! Why can't she leave things alone? She never thinks about anyone else.'

Ali read the *Saltire* first. What was Lizzie thinking of? Here it was, all raked up again for everyone to read. The fact that money might have changed hands did not occur to her. She picked up the *Clarion* and read Darren's article. This couldn't be true! Surely he couldn't have been in the house every night without them realising, and if Lizzie was on drugs, she would have noticed. Then she got to the bit about the kitchen table. She lifted her elbows off it and went to get a bottle of anti-bacterial spray and wiped it down. She then got a tablecloth and covered it up. She wondered where else they had been. Her bed? Oh, no, surely not.

She went upstairs to find Ruth, who had retreated to her room.

'Is this true?'

'Some of it.'

'Which bits?'

'Darren used to come into her room after you and Dad had gone to bed.'

'And the drink and drugs?'

'Vodka sometimes. Don't know about the rest.'

'And Sundays?'

'Don't know, do I? I was at church with you, remember.'

'Why didn't you tell us?'

'It is bad enough having Lizzie for a sister without having her after me for telling tales.'

'Who knew about this?'

'Everyone at school, so I expect most people's parents knew as well.'

'Look after Matt, please. I have to get out of here for a while.'

She went downstairs, put on her coat and climbed into the car. Then she drove north out of town.

Gill had spent Sunday morning trying to do the ironing. Mike was back and home, still confined to the spare bed, but he had been able to deal with the tea and toast she had taken him. As she ironed, she felt more positive. She had decided she would give it a go as long as she was allowed to do things in her own time. The phone rang as she was folding the shirt that Mike had bled all over. She let the answering machine kick in and listened to see if anyone would leave a message.

'Gill? Are you there? Pick up the phone, please. I need to speak to you.'

'Yes, Mum. What is it?'

'Well, if you are asking that, you don't know.'

'Don't know what?' she said slowly. It did not sound like her mother was about to impart something good.

'There are two bits in the papers. Your father went to collect the *Sunday Telegraph* and the man in the newsagent told him Mike was in the news again. He felt he should buy these dreadful rags to see . . .'

'What's in them, Mother?'

'Well, do you want the good news or the bad news?'

This was definitely not good. 'Bad first.'

'Well, Miss Graham is telling the world about how and when. I thought you told me the affair finished a while ago. She says she was in London with him on Tuesday.'

'Tuesday? Last week?'

'So she says.'

'And what's the good news?'

'Well, her ex-boyfriend is saying that she was having sex with him when she was fourteen and that she took drugs. It makes her appear a proper little tart.'

'What papers are these in, Mother?'

'The boyfriend is in the *Clarion* and she is in the *Saltire*.'

Gill held on to the edge of the work surface in an effort to keep calm. 'Thank you for letting me know. I'm going to get a copy of each. Then I need to speak to Mike.'

'Are you all right, dear? Are the children all right?'

There was no reply because Gill was already on her way to the newsagent. Church had just finished and there was a queue waiting to pay for their papers. She walked in and picked up a copy of each. The queue, which included Joyce, parted like the Red Sea and she found herself at the counter. She drove back home, parked in the driveway and opened the *Saltire*. Then she read the *Clarion*. When she had finished, she got out of the car, took the papers inside and climbed the stairs. She opened the door to the spare room. Mike was reading a novel.

'How are you feeling now?' she asked.

'Bit better. I might get up later.'

'Oh good. By the way, when did you say that you finished the affair?'

'The day of our party.'

'The day of our party! I thought that was what you had said. How come Miss Graham says she was in your bed on Tuesday night and that you paid her?'

'What are you talking about?'

'This!' said Gill, and threw the paper on the bed. 'Go on, read it.'

Mike picked up the paper.

'Well?' said Gill.

'I did finish it on the day of our party. Then she heard that people were talking about us and she turned up in London, out of the blue, at my flat, at midnight. What was I supposed to do? Have a public argument and leave her with no money in Central London? The money was for her train fare home.'

'It must have been first class at that price.'

'I slept on the couch, I promise you. She tried to jump on me in the middle of the night but I fought her off. I'll sue her, the lying bitch!'

Gill picked up the *Saltire* and found the article. 'It says, "We spent the night in his flat and he gave me a hundred pounds." That seems quite plain to me. I'm glad you are feeling better because you can get up and take care of the children this afternoon. I am going out. I don't know when I will be back, but it will probably be to collect my things. You blew it, Mike. I told you that I never wanted to find out what you had been up to by reading it in the papers. By the way, the children have not had lunch.'

She went downstairs, oblivious to his protestations of innocence, grabbed her coat and went out to the car. She backed out of the drive and drove west out of town, ignoring the thirty-mile-an-hour speed limit.

Phyllis had walked back from church and was halfway up her front path as Gill drove away. After watching the car disappear, she went inside, poured her Sunday sherry and made some biscuits and cheese. These she took to the conservatory, which afforded a good view of the Andrewses' driveway. She sipped her amontillado and took a bite of her royal oatcake with Brie and Duchy Originals pickle and settled down to watch. It was actually quite dull, as nothing was happening next door, only a couple of children on bikes on the road outside. The sight of the two girls reminded her of Joyce's gem of gossip: Ali had been raving at some children at the primary school, called them 'little cows'. She must have been drunk again. It was quite disappointing Jack wasn't home to discuss it further, so she rang Helen Cooper.

'Oh, I heard that!' said Helen. 'Richard says that she was swearing at these little girls who were just playing a game of hopscotch. He heard from Mrs Eadie, who was on play-ground duty, that she ran into the playground raving and was totally incoherent and Mrs Ramsay had to send her home in a taxi. Richard says that family must have been on the verge of falling apart for years and he doesn't know how Tom had the brass neck to pretend otherwise. The level of hypocrisy is so unchristian.'

'Oh, I quite agree,' said Phyllis. 'As members of his congre-gation, Jack and I are just horrified at the level of deceit.'

Ali had driven out of town towards Invercraig. She parked in a layby for a long time, before turning round and driving back towards home. She saw the tourist sign to Loch Corrachan, turned off the main road and drove into the car park. There was a path round the loch, which, in times past, had been an attractive and quite adventurous walk, but it had recently been resurfaced and equipped with litter bins and picnic areas and called the Loch Corrachan Millennium Nature Trail. Despite the fact that it was no longer the challenge it used to be, it was still a popular Sunday walk, but by the time Ali got there, it was nearly four o'clock and the light was beginning to fade. The few remaining walkers were preparing to go home. The circuit was about two miles long and she reckoned that by walking briskly she could complete it before it got fully dark. She really needed to clear her head, so she zipped up her jacket, put on her gloves and set off.

Gill had driven out of town on the Strathperry road, but unlike Ali, had continued to drive through Strathperry and beyond. Eventually, she had turned round and started to drive back towards Corrachan, still undecided about what she should do. She ended up in the car park on the far side of the loch, and like Ali, reckoned she could walk the circuit before it got dark. Had they chosen to walk in the same direction, they would not have met, but Ali had started to walk clockwise and Gill anticlockwise.

Ali had stopped to rest and was sitting on a bench staring at the water when she heard someone approaching. The light was fading fast, so she stood up in case she had to make an escape. The approaching figure hadn't noticed her and was walking quickly with head down and hands in pockets. She realised it was Gill and they would have to pass each other. Ali started to walk towards her and Gill, hearing footsteps, looked up. The path was narrow and one person would have to move aside to let the other pass. Ali stepped off the path and Gill passed with a curt 'hello'. Ali walked after her and touched her shoulder.

'Gill? This is silly. I'm sorry I shouted at you. I know it's not your fault.'

Gill stopped. She looked at Ali and sighed. 'I'm not sorry I said Lizzie put herself about.'

'Well, it was true and everyone knows now.' Ali gestured to the bench. 'Let's sit down for a moment.'

They sat in the dusk and looked at the ripples on the water.

'This has been the most God-awful week of my life,' said Ali. 'Eight days ago, I didn't know any of this.'

'I've only had a dreadful four days – that's bad enough.'

'Have you seen today's papers?'

'Oh, yes! That's why I've walked out. He swore blind to me last night that he finished the affair the day we had our party and then I read that he's been with her this week and he gave her money! I thought we might be able to salvage things, but not now.'

'You obviously knew all about Darren. I didn't believe you the other day, but there it all was today for the world to read.'

'Some of the people at toddlers had mentioned it, but I didn't know all the details.'

'Well, you do now. I feel such a fool, not realising what was going on.'

Gill touched her arm. 'I've missed your company.'

'I've missed you too. I so needed someone to talk to who wasn't my mother.'

'Truce?'

'Truce.'

Gill picked up a handful of gravel and started throwing stones into the water.

'I have no idea what to do. I can't stay with him at the moment, but I don't know where to go. Back to Edinburgh, I expect. I came out here to think.'

'I came out to think too. I can't stand the mixture of pity and sympathy from all these people who've known for years about Lizzie. I've put my name on the housing list because

291

we'll have to stay here till Ruth's finished school, but I really want to be somewhere else.'

'I don't think I can face walking down the High Street ever again.'

'I did that yesterday and everyone crossed the road. Do you want to know another bit of news? I expect by tomorrow there will be a distorted version doing the rounds. Tom seems to have left Mark – the shortest cohabitation in history! Not only that, he has found a flat in Marchmont. Bloody man always falls on his feet. He walks out and leaves us and we're the ones who end up homeless.'

'We're the innocent parties and we're the ones in a heap of shit. Mike will end up continuing much as usual. He'll just have to factor in access to the children, but as he's been stopping regularly in Edinburgh on Fridays anyway, I'm sure he won't find that too difficult. It's me who has to start again. I'll get a job supply teaching, but I'll have to sort childcare. God! Why am I in this mess?' She threw some more stones into the water. 'You know the bastard ended up in the Infirmary? Minty brought us a frozen cake made by Mrs Collins and Mike ate a piece. He got terrible food poisoning, passed out and banged his head. Boy, did it bleed!'

'I heard from Ruth, who heard from Sacha, whose mother had spoken to God knows who, that you hit him on the head with a frozen turkey.'

'Wish I had,' said Gill. 'That's much more interesting. Think we could let that rumour run.'

'Oh, and you have been arrested for domestic violence.'

'Really? He's lucky it wasn't murder.'

Ali looked around. 'It's getting really dark. I think we had better move from here while we can still see a little.'

They decided to stay together and make for Ali's car, which they reckoned was the nearer. They were in a wooded area, which meant it was really difficult to see the path, so they linked arms and started to walk. It was raining now, which made it even darker. Gill put her foot in a large puddle and got a shoe full of water. Suddenly, there was a crashing in the undergrowth and an animal appeared out of the bushes and brushed past their legs. They screamed.

'What was that? Was it a fox?' asked Gill.

'Don't know!'

Then it appeared out of the blackness again and jumped up at Ali, who screamed again before she realised it was a dog – a rather elderly, out-of-breath spaniel.

'Hello. Where did you come from?' She bent down and patted it.

The answer to that soon became obvious. They heard someone calling and a torch beam could be seen further along the lochside between the trees. An apparition wearing an elderly raincoat, galoshes and a sou'wester loomed out of the darkness. It was Minty. She shone her torch at Ali and Gill, showing no surprise at finding the two most talked-about people in the area together in the dark halfway round Loch Corrachan.

'I see you've found the dog, then. Well done, you. Left the side gate open and he was off rabbiting, but he's getting doited now and he forgets the way home. Don't you, Paddy? He's called after Paddy Ashdown. We've always called our dogs after Liberal leaders. Had a Jeremy before this, and it was a Jo before that. Though Paddy Ashdown's real name is Jeremy, so I suppose he should have been Jeremy the Second. Seem to have missed out a David. Jeremy was quite an age when he went.'

She took an antique plaited leather lead from her pocket and clipped it on to the dog's collar. 'Right, Paddy, time to take you home.' She looked at Ali and Gill. 'Do you two often go walking together in the pitch-dark?'

'We were talking and it got dark. It's a bit difficult to see now,' said Ali.

'Well, you had better follow me.' She set off, shining the torch on the path and towing the breathless Paddy behind her.

Ali and Gill followed. They reached the car park and found Ali's solitary car.

'Right, then,' said Minty, 'you can give us a lift down the road. This old fellow's about done in.'

She opened the rear door, heaved the dog on to the back seat and got in beside him. The dog was wet, had halitosis, canker in its ears and sent noxious fumes in huge waves towards Ali and Gill. Minty didn't seem to notice. Luckily, it was only a short drive to Minty's house where she manhandled the ancient dog out of the back seat. Ali rolled down her window, ostensibly to say goodbye, but also to allow some fresh air into the car.

Minty bent down to speak to Ali, then hesitated and looked over at Gill in the passenger seat. 'My dears, are you two friends again?'

Ali and Gill exchanged glances.

'I think so,' said Gill.

'Well, I've been thinking a lot about you both over the past few days. Will you come inside for a minute? I'd like to talk to you both.'

They went into the back porch, which was filled with perished Wellington boots and coats even older than the one Minty was wearing. She took off her galoshes, hung up her coat and hat, then found a towel so full of holes as to be useless and attempted to dry the dog, who decided it was easier to shake himself and this he did, covering everyone in filthy droplets.

'Horrible dog! Go to your basket,' said Minty.

The dog waddled off into the kitchen beyond and had a

huge slobbery drink from his bowl before collapsing into his basket, on top of what looked like a black tail suit.

Minty caught Gill looking at it. 'My father's morning coat. It was a bit moth-eaten, but it makes an excellent dog blanket.'

She ushered them into the kitchen, which had last been updated in the thirties. There was a cream-coloured coal-fired Aga and large, dark-stained wooden cupboards lining one wall. In the middle of the room was a marble-topped table littered with piles of correspondence and surrounded by a selection of mismatched rickety chairs.

'Sit down, sit down. Warmer in here as the fire's gone out in the sitting room. One of these days I'll get some radiators, but my father always believed that central heating gave you colds. Might be something in that. Now, a drink? Gin? Sherry? Whisky?'

'Sherry, thanks, but just a small one. I'm driving,' said Ali.

'I'll have a small gin and tonic. I'm driving too. My car's on the other side of the loch. I'll have to go and rescue it.'

By lifting several copies of the *Guardian*, Minty unearthed a silver tray on which were placed crystal glasses of various sizes. She then opened a cupboard and from among what looked like shoe-cleaning materials, she produced a bottle of sherry and a bottle of gin. She gave Ali her sherry. Then she poured a generous measure of gin and looked around for tonic. She opened several cupboard doors and moved various piles of paper but couldn't find any.

'There was a bottle of tonic I opened when my niece was here about six weeks ago. Can't think where it's gone.'

Gill was relieved she couldn't find it, but after Minty had poured a generous slug of neat Rose's Lime Juice into the gin and handed it to her, she thought flat tonic would have been preferable.

'Used to drink gin and lime all the time. Then got very

squiffy on it one night. Nineteen forty-two, I think it was. Haven't been able to face gin since.' Minty poured herself a large measure of Glenmorangie and sat down opposite them. 'Well, Gill, you first. Have you decided what you are going to do?'

Gill took a sip of her gin. 'I was going to give him another chance until I saw today's paper. He swore he had told me everything, but he hadn't. I don't think I can bear to be near him at the moment.'

'Hmm,' said Minty. 'Stupid, stupid man. If you are caught, own up to everything.' She turned to Ali. 'And you, Ali, what are you going to do?'

'I don't know. I can stay in the manse at the moment but we will have to get out sometime. Ruth is still at school, so it's difficult to move away, but I would really love to get away from this place. After today's papers, I know that everyone has been laughing at me for years because I didn't know what my daughter was up to and now it's worse – they're sorry for me too. I would love to be able to walk down the street without everyone knowing who I am.'

'Well, I agree you two need to get away from here for a while. You both need time to think. How would you like a summer in Rosshire?'

Minty explained that when her brother had sold Corrachan House, he had bought a smaller estate with a grouse moor and two salmon-fishing beats on the River Conon. His son had now inherited, but he spent only three weeks there in August. The rest of the time the house and its sporting opportunities were let, mainly to rich Americans and German industrialists.

'My nephew needs someone to run the house. It's quite small – only ten bedrooms. He needs a cook and a housekeeper. You could do that between you, couldn't you? There's the staff accommodation in the old stables. All you need to do is cook, clean and make beds. Isn't that what you do all the time?'

Before they could point out the flaws in this arrangement, Minty continued, 'Starts in the beginning of April and runs to the end of September. You provide breakfast, picnic lunch for the guests to take to the fishing hut or the moor and a three-course dinner. George is going to advertise next week, so you have about five days to think about it.'

Gill spoke first. 'What a lovely idea, Minty, but I have two small children, a dog and six puppies to consider, and I fear I'm a bit old to be a chalet girl.'

'This isn't Klosters, and George doesn't want gals, as there is precious little social life. I would assume you're still at the wound-licking stage and not wishing to go galavanting. The children you can take with you. Between the two of you, you can take care of the children and work. Now, the dog! Are you fond of the dog?'

'Not really,' said Gill. 'Mike brought her home one day to keep me company, but it's just like having to mind someone else's teenager, and a promiscuous one at that.' Realising what she had said, she glanced at Ali, but the remark appeared to have gone unnoticed.

'Have you found homes for all these puppies?'

'Not yet. They are only three weeks old, so they can't go for another month or so.'

'It's John Cowie's dog, isn't it?'

'Yes, I think so. Some old man who had to go into sheltered housing.'

'That's him. I'd told him I would take his dog, but he was so forgetful. He must have gone and asked Mike.'

Gill thought of the hassle this dog had caused and she hadn't even been about to be homeless in the first place. Great!

Minty continued, 'I'll take the dog off you. Paddy's getting on and I'm too old to train a puppy again. Would have to get her spayed.' She pointed to the basket in the corner. 'He may be twelve now, but he can smell a bitch on heat three miles away. Excitement of one under his nose would probably kill him.' She paused. 'Five more weeks till the puppies go. That takes us to the middle of April. Easter is at the end of March, so Mike will be on holiday first fortnight in April. Problem solved. He can take over the last two weeks. Advertise now . . . free to good homes, and when Parliament ends, you can go north.'

'Sounds good, Minty, but I would have to think about it. And we both need to be able to go as we would have to share the childminding. Ali has commitments here.'

'I do. I'll have to stay around, at least till exam time. Ruth has taken all this very badly. I can't farm her out just because it suits me. I would lose my priority place on the housing list too.'

'I was going to say that she could come and stay with me,' said Minty.

Ali looked around her and thought that the stress of living in an unheated, old-fashioned house five miles out of town with an eccentric old lady and a very smelly dog was not what Ruth needed at the moment.

'That's very generous of you, Minty, but I think she needs my support right now. The idea of several months away is lovely, but unfortunately it's not on for me at the moment.'

After finishing their drinks, they thanked Minty and left. On the drive to the other side of the loch, they discussed the offer again and agreed it needed both of them to be workable.

'Pity,' said Gill. 'It might have been fun. I'll just have to make Mike spend his Easter holidays puppy-sitting while the children and I go to stay with Mum and Dad.' It was only a minor piece of revenge, but it was satisfying nonetheless. 'I'll tell him when I get home. I suppose that's where I'll have to go now.'

'Leave it a bit longer and come to the manse. I'll make

something to eat. I braved Tesco on Friday. It was easier than I thought. Everyone just looked the other way, so I didn't have to talk to anyone.'

Back at the manse, Gill opened a bottle of wine, while Ali made macaroni cheese. Ruth came into the kitchen with Matt behind her. She sat down at the table and picked up her knife and fork.

'Oh! The Reverend and Mrs Orgasm and the two littlest Orgasms came round, about three o'clock.'

'I forgot about them! Just as well I was out. Did you have to pray?'

'No. I didn't let them in. Said you were out and I was busy.'

'I hope you weren't rude.'

Ruth sighed. 'No, I wasn't rude.'

'Zak not with them?'

'No.' She continued toying with her macaroni. 'Auntie Jen phoned too. I said you would call her later.'

'That's my sister in France,' said Ali.

They ate in silence for a moment. Then Ruth announced, 'I'm not going back to school.'

Ali paused with a forkful of macaroni halfway to her mouth. 'Oh, yes, you are! You can't leave now. This is the most important year in your school life.' Ruth said nothing, so Ali continued, 'It's only a few months till the exams. Then perhaps we can talk about whether you should do sixth year. You can't run away from things.'

'Why not? Dad did. He seems to be doing OK.'

'This is slightly different. You need your exams if you want to do physio.'

'I don't want to do that any more. I'm going to leave now and get a job.'

Please don't make things any more difficult, thought Ali. I don't have the strength for this at the moment.

'Even if you don't go to university, you'll need Highers if you want a decent job,' ventured Gill.

'You are both so elitist. You don't need Highers to work in Tesco or be a waitress. I'll learn far more out working than I will doing a degree, which will probably only qualify me to be a waitress anyway. And besides, we need the money.'

Ali turned to Gill with a look that said, Help me, please.

Gill chose her words carefully. 'It's good you want to help out financially, but I think you should at least sit your exams and then you can discuss with your mum whether you want to leave school after that.'

'Mum, I can't go back to school. You thought what the primary kids were saying was bad. That was nothing to what happened at the academy. I'm not going back. I mean it. I don't have to take all the shit caused by my father and sister. It's not my scandal.'

'I'll go back and speak to your pastoral care teacher and see if we can sort something out – stop the bullying.'

'No!'

'Please?'

'No!'

'Can you not work out some sort of compromise?' asked Gill.

Ruth looked up, then looked down again and started moving the now congealed pasta round her plate.

Ali folded her arms and sat back in her chair. 'Well, Gill, what do you suggest?'

'I think you two have to work this out without me.'

Still with her head down, Ruth said quietly, 'There is perhaps a way. Auntie Jen said I could go to France.'

'Well, you could go for July and half of August if you want.'

'No, she said I could go now.'

'Now?' Ali sighed. 'No. We've just been through all this. You have to sit your exams.'

'You said we should compromise.'

'Yes . . .'

'How about I sit the prelim exams on Monday and Tuesday. Then I'll speak to the teachers, get textbooks and all the hand-outs and do my revision in France. I'll come home to sit the exams. Then I'll go back for the rest of the summer.'

'Would the school allow that?' asked Gill doubtfully.

'Perhaps, but I don't know if you will be able to manage all the work on your own,' replied Ali.

'There's email . . . I'm sure the teachers would answer any questions I might have.' Ali still looked doubtful, so Ruth kept going. 'I've looked on the Internet and I can get a return flight next Thursday from Prestwick for eighty-five pounds. I've got two hundred and eighty in my savings account, so it won't cost you.'

'You've had this worked out all the time, haven't you?'

Ruth had the grace to look slightly sheepish. 'Only the running-away bit, not the exams.'

'I don't know about this. Are you sure Jen wants you for so long? You'll have to do something to help. You can't just sit around and expect her to feed you.'

Ruth was defensive. 'It's this way or it's no Highers. And I'll help with the children and the gîtes. I'm not Lizzie, you know. You could put everything in storage and come out too – Auntie Jen wouldn't mind.'

'OK,' said Ali. 'I'll go and speak to the headmaster tomorrow and see if it would be possible.'

Gill looked at Ali. 'Why don't you tell her about our offer?'

'I suppose I could come back here for a few weeks in May for Ruth's exams. Could you cope?' she asked Gill.

'We could work something out, I'm sure.'

'Mum, what are you talking about?'

They told her.

'But that's brill! We can all get out of here. And I can stay at Sacha's when I come back. Her mum won't mind. Go for it, Mum. Please!'

Now all three of them saw a way out, it turned into quite a jolly meal. They were all mildly drunk, Ruth included, on wine and hysteria when they heard the doorbell. Ali went to answer it and found Donald and Martha, mercifully minus the small Orgasms, on the doorstep.

'Alison, your trials continue. We came to see how you are.'

'Donald! Martha! Thank you for coming round. Come in! Come in!' Ali ushered them into the kitchen. 'We're all fine, actually. We are having a victim-support meeting. Sit down, have a drink, and we'll tell you what the Lord, in the shape of Minty Oliver and my sister, have done to rescue us from the Slough of Despond!'

It was half past nine before Phyllis saw Gill come back. This was half an hour after she had phoned Joyce to say that Gill had gone and that she had left Mike with the children. Gill returned on foot on account of the gin and lime and the wine, and Phyllis would have missed her, had she not been upstairs in her bedroom with the light out looking through the window. She considered continuing her vigil to see if there were any further developments, but she had so much housework to do in the morning before Jack returned. Reluctantly, she closed the curtains and got ready for bed.

Chapter Twenty-Nine

The next morning, Phyllis was up and dressed by seven thirty. She hoovered, dusted, changed the bedlinen and put a fresh blue-flush tablet in the bathroom lavatory. She paused between each task to check if anything was happening next door, but there was nothing to see. After she had a pot of lentil soup simmering, she put a shepherd's pie in the oven and set the table. Then she went upstairs to change from her house-work clothes into something smarter. She looked out of the windows, both front and back. There was still nothing happening at the front, and the back garden contained only the horrid puppies.

Jack had said he would be home about one o'clock, and although he used to be punctual, his time-keeping had been erratic lately, adding to the tally of early dementia symptoms. At one thirty, when there was still no sign of him, she phoned the car showroom. It kicked into the answer-phone message immediately, suggesting Angela's mother, Moira, who had been secretary there for many years, must be at lunch. At two o'clock, the trainee car salesman, having returned from his lunch break, told her Moira had taken a day off and he was the only person at the showroom. At three o'clock, there was still no sign of

Jack and by now Phyllis was seriously concerned. Perhaps his forgetfulness had escalated and he couldn't remember who he was or where he lived, or worse still, perhaps he had suffered a fatal stroke or a heart attack. At five o'clock, just after Joyce had suggested she think about phoning the police, two detectives and a uniformed policewoman arrived at her door. She saw them come up the path and she was certain her worries of the afternoon were about to be realised.

Had Jack been found dead in his hotel room, Phyllis would have received universal sympathy and slipped into a comfortable widowhood, but it transpired that, as far as the police were aware, Jack was neither dead nor confused. They, too, were interested in his whereabouts and those of Moira because they had a warrant and were keen to talk to them both about certain irregularities. Phyllis told them that Jack had been in London and should have been home at lunchtime and that she assumed Moira was at her house on Invercraig Road.

Moira had in fact taken more than the day off. She was sitting on the terrace of a new luxury villa near Kyrenia, in Northern Cyprus, with a jug of brandy sour on the table in front of her. Her daughters, Angela and Kayleigh, her son, Kevin, and Angela's boyfriend, Davie, were still in the swimming pool. Beside her sat a relaxed Jack Caldwell with his grandson, Allan, playing at his feet and his other grandson, Kieran, on his knee. He was enjoying family life. He shouted to the Sri Lankan maid to bring him another beer.

Phyllis took a long time to believe that Jack had gone for good. When she discovered the allegations of fraud and false accounting, when she discovered that the businesses were bankrupt, when she discovered that the bank accounts were empty, she still believed it was all a horrible mix-up. Only when she was about to become homeless, after the bank told her the house was to be repossessed, did she accept that Jack was not coming back.

It was Joyce who had to tell her that Moira and her family had all left Corrachan and were thought to be abroad somewhere. It was Joyce who had to tell her that Moira's fatherless children were not fatherless at all. Phyllis had never been a tall woman, but she seemed to shrink and age visibly before Joyce's eyes.

The Macdonalds had been horrified to discover about Jack's secret family and his shady business deals. What they thought had been a mutual friendship had been debased, and they found it very difficult to know what they could say or do to help Phyllis. Joyce was the only one of Phyllis's friends who came to see her in the week before she had to move out. Helen Cooper had sent a 'Good Luck in Your New Home' card with a handwritten message: 'Richard says that in adversity we find ourselves.' It had been sent with good intentions, but had only served to underline the extent of her reduced circumstances. As a 'vulnerable older person', she had been offered a place in one of the council's emergency flats – one they had bought from Jack's repossessed empire. Her wider circle of friends, who seemed to find plenty of time to talk about her behind her back, were too busy to call round and talk to her face to face.

When the doorbell rang, Phyllis was wrapping china and packing it into cardboard boxes. Most of the furniture had already gone to the saleroom. She placed a Coronation plate in the box and went to answer the door.

'Joyce! Hello. Please come in.'

'I came to see how you were, and if you needed any help.'

'It's a bit untidy, I'm afraid.' She opened the door to allow Joyce into the bare hall. 'That's very kind of you, but I think I'm all sorted. I'm moving the day after tomorrow. The council

have found me a temporary flat till I find somewhere permanent. I'm forgetting my manners. Would you like a cup of tea?
The best china is all wrapped, but I have two cups left.'

'Well, if you are making one, that would be nice.'

They moved to the echoing kitchen and Phyllis switched
on the kettle and put teabags into teacups without saucers.

'No biscuits, I'm afraid.'

'Tea's just fine.' Joyce looked round the kitchen. Then she
looked at her friend. Phyllis had always lacked confidence and
deferred to Jack, so it was upsetting to see her like this – alone
and having to deal with the mess and shame he had left behind.

When the teabags had been removed from the cups, Joyce
hesitantly got round to the purpose of her visit. 'Er . . . Bill and
I were wondering if you wanted to stay with us for a while. I
don't like to think of you in that poky little flat. You could
have our spare room until you find somewhere decent.'

Phyllis had been dreading the move to the dark flat, with its
well-used, shabby furniture, complete with the stains of previous
tenants, but she knew immediately that Joyce's offer, kind though
it was, was not going to be the answer. She could not be their
long-term guest with all the reminders of what had been and
everyone watching what they said. Now she had been offered
an alternative, she knew she would stick to her plans. She had no
money, no living relatives and fewer friends than she had thought,
but perhaps this was another chance. She had never taken a
risk in her life. Under the guise of sheltering her from difficult decisions, Jack had controlled her. He had had the final
word on everything from adopting children to the Christmas-
card list and she had known better than to argue. Perhaps
Richard was right – it was time to take control, to create something that was hers alone.

'No, Joyce. I won't do that. It's a very kind offer, but I'm
going to live in that flat. It will only be temporary and I'll no

306

doubt get a council house up on the estate or even one in the sheltered housing where Jack's mother was. I'm over sixty now so I'm eligible. They've got a warden and all the buzzers and things. It'll take a bit of getting used to, but I was getting too set in my ways. I'll have my independence and perhaps that's just what I need. Don't you worry about me – I'll be fine.'

Joyce had protested, but not too much. She knew Bill would be relieved. Phyllis watched her walk down the drive past the carefully tended rockery and the daffodils, which were just coming into bud, and she found she no longer cared that it would soon be someone else's garden, She closed the front door and continued packing the china, a slightly taller woman than she was half an hour ago.

At the end of March, Ali and Gill loaded their belongings into their respective cars and drove north. As they left Corrachan, each woman felt her spirits rise, just as Tom's had done on his forays to Edinburgh. For Ali, the feelings of escape were permanent. She knew she would never go back, so her only option was to look forward, and as the distance from Corrachan increased, the feelings of hopelessness that had so overwhelmed her decreased. It was only a temporary job, but with all that had happened to her, the jump into the unknown was not too difficult. Her main worry now was Lizzie, who had dropped out of university and found herself a job as a tour rep in Crete. All Ali had been able to do was to ensure her university place was held open for a year, but she had a feeling that Lizzie's flirtation with the medical profession was over.

As Gill drove down the hill towards Inverness with two sleeping children and the CD of banal nursery rhymes silent at last, she knew she was running away. So many issues still needed to be resolved. Mike had continued to protest his innocence over the night of Lizzie's visit to London, and deep down she had a suspicion he might be telling the truth, but she was not ready to forgive. She needed to try being a single parent before making decisions about the rest of her life.

As Mike watched his family disappear for what was, at best, five or six months, and at worst for good, he felt an overwhelming sense of loss. Although he had been away so much in the last year, he had known they would be there when he came home. He went back into the silent house. Sitting on the kitchen table was one of Ian's pieces of sheet. He held it up to his face and sat down. The dog came and laid her head on his knee and looked at him sympathetically.

'Shit,' he said very quietly.